LOUEY LEVY'S
HEADING
HOME

GENIE ABRAMS

outskirts
press

Outskirts Press, Inc.
http://www.outskirtspress.com

ISBN: 978-1-9772-4665-3

This book is dedicated to everyone who has ever spent a miserable and gloriously happy time newspapering.

Part 1:
NEWSPAPER DAYS

She was old.

Louey Levy had had her life, and now she was old. How cool was that?

She was retired, which meant she could look back over her seventy odd years and try to make something out of them. But what, she wondered?

She didn't see patterns or even any paths that made any sense or led anywhere, so she decided to try to remember it all.

She had started working just a few months after she got her master's degree, and she had got her master's just 14 months after graduating from college.

That degree was—right in line with the pattern of her whole, entire life, she felt—kind of absurd. It was called a "Master's of Science in Mental Health Journalism."

Don't ask.

Or, Reader, go ahead and ask, but it won't do you any good, because she herself never exactly knew what it meant.

No one else ever understood it, either. It was just a few days after she landed her first job, as a reporter on a daily paper near her old hometown of Newburgh, that The Publisher of the Record, whom she had previously neither met nor seen, strode into the newsroom and loudly demanded of Tim Clay, the Slot man, "Where's Louey Levy?" Without looking up from his work, Tim, who by virtue of being Slot was in charge of the copy desk and perpetually overwhelmed, pointed his pencil toward his newest reporter.

The Publisher was a tall, distinguished-looking fellow with a skein of white hair and a pair of red suspenders. To Louey, he was the picture of the word, "WASP-y."

"Right here," Louey piped up, more curious than terrified. She raised her hand, as if she were still in college answering a question from a professor. Clay had assigned her to a spot not far from his "slot" position in the middle of the U-shaped copy desk, as though to make it easier to keep an eye on her. Or to hit her with balled-up wads of copy paper to get her attention, when the general mayhem in the newsroom was too loud for his voice to be heard.

For the previous hour, she had been making fruitless calls to the area's police departments to see if anything exciting had happened that day. But it seemed that nothing exciting happened before her shift began at 3 p.m.

The Publisher loomed over Louey's not-quite-cowering form. He looked down, shook her hand and said, "Jim Osterhout. What the hell is Mental Health Journalism?"

Oh, so the two guys who'd interviewed her had told him about that. At Syracuse University, she had volunteered in a psychiatric hospital for academic credits and written a paper about that work, and she had also agreed to ghost-write a book for a professor about adolescent psychology, which she had never taken a course in and knew nothing about. But, boom: The book turned out pretty well, and 14 months later, she had a "Master's of Science in Mental Health Journalism."

Well, congratulations to me, she thought with an ironic little smile when a certificate sporting those words caught up with her in the mail. It was the main event in a fat, fake-leather folder that you opened like a large, horizontally oriented book. The words, "Suos Cultores Scientia Coronat," were imprinted in gold foil on the dark-blue cover.

Syracuse's motto. "Knowledge Crowns Those Who Seek Her."

But Louey, with both a bachelor's and master's degree from SU, was still waiting for her crown. Maybe she wasn't seeking hard enough. Maybe she didn't have enough Knowledge. Maybe she didn't care that much about Knowledge. Maybe she cared more about friendship and doing some good in the world and giving people a few laughs and figuring out what she was here for. She wasn't sure she'd learned anything. She tossed the diploma into a box in her parents' basement and never saw it again 'til it was literally moldering. But meanwhile, she'd applied for and won the job reporting for the Record.

When The Publisher asked her what the hell Mental Health Journalism was, she blathered for a few moments about how Governor Rockefeller had asked several universities to start master's programs to develop writers who could "interpret for the public" his recent efforts to get thousands of patients out of New York State's decrepit mental hospitals and "back into their communities." In other words, Rocky wanted writers who could understand what a grand idea that was and sell the people of New York State on what a grand idea it was, too.

Louey described it with a cheerful, slightly ironic demeanor, hoping to convey, "So you see, the program made perfect sense, despite its amusing name." And she must have succeeded, because The Publisher replied, "Oh, OK. I was just curious about what the hell that was." And then, with no handshake, no word of farewell, no nothin', he stalked out of the newsroom as fast as he'd entered it, rarely to be seen there again 'til he himself was pretty much moldering.

For this he drove in from Campbell Hall? Louey thought. *Odd duck. Oh, well.*

She had been hired at the Record to be a general-assignment reporter, driving to accident scenes, fires, school board, city council, town board and zoning board meetings, taking notes and also taking photos with her Rollei twin-lens reflex camera that she had rented-to-buy for her college photography classes. You loaded into it a roll of two-and-a-quarter by two-and-a-quarter-inch film, and when you stumbled upon a cool scene or needed to photograph some politician, you held it against your stomach and looked straight down into the viewfinder, took your shot and cranked the handle around to move the next negative into position (and if you forgot, you'd get a double-exposure, ruining your first shot. You would then tell the Darkroom that you'd done that on purpose, to be artistic.) The Record's friendly team of four photographers would give reporters all the rolls of film they wanted; they always had a good supply of both the two-and-a-quarter kind and the 35-millimeter kind, though by the time Louey joined the paper it had already been determined that no more two-and-a-quarter film would be purchased after the current batch ran out. It was those professional in-house photographers who, 99% of the time, took the Page One photo, but reporters were encouraged to take one of the paper's new, 35-millimeter cameras with them on all assignments, "just in case" a shot was needed and the real photographers were all tied up. Sometimes, a reporter got lucky and took a good photo, and then his name would appear triumphantly on Page One of the tabloid.

The Darkroom guys liked it that Louey used her old camera; its large format resulted in printed photos that had hardly any grain, no matter how much they were enlarged. The photographers themselves were using the lighter, 35-millimeter cameras almost exclusively now. Paul, the photography editor, had quickly taken a shine to Louey because of her Rollei. He occasionally strolled into the newsroom to slip her rolls of two-and-a-quarter film in a surreptitious manner, as though they were bags of marijuana. She went along with it, dropping them into her shoulder bag like a shoplifter, humming a little tune and idly gazing at various parts of the ceiling as though searching for *le mot juste* for a story she was writing.

After getting her peculiar graduate degree, Louey had lived with her old college pal Roz in New Mexico for a few months before looking for a job. She had truly had enough of school and had decided to reward herself with a break. Roz had determined to take some time off before starting grad school at MIT and had managed to find a place with rent that was right in her price range (zero). It was an abandoned adobe hut at the edge of an Indian reservation on the western slope of the Sangre de Cristo mountains in Taos County. It had no electricity, but they got heat from their wood stove and the previous tenants had left behind two nice hurricane lanterns and a can of oil for them, too. Sticks for the stove lay all over the ground around their place, even though the only trees in that high-desert area were three small piñon pines scattered about like a 2-8-10 split in a very large bowling lane. Their otherwise barren "yard" also sported an outhouse, a well and a pump from which they got fine water for drinking, cooking and washing. Not only that, but a Bookmobile stopped on the road nearby every week. In other words, they had everything two young women could possibly ever need or want in 1971.

They felt as if they were in Heaven, and at their altitude in New Mexico, they were pretty close. Louey wrote poems, jotted down thoughts in her diary, and began sketching the birds she saw on their hikes. Roz played music on her harmonica and her jug. When the mood struck them, they hitchhiked the 30 miles to Taos to buy milk and flour and vegetables with the food stamps they had received from the county Social Services office. When those stamps didn't last the month, they got more from the Social Services office in Rio Arriba County next door, and then they had enough.

Rozzie, unlike most squatters on food stamps in adobe huts, had won a temporary job starting in mid-February in Boulder as, literally, a rocket scientist. So the roommates knew from the start that their New Mexican idyll wouldn't last long. And then one January day, Louey got a letter from her sister, Clare, saying her brother Danny and his wife had had a baby girl. Danny was working in the Corporation Counsel's office in the Levys' old hometown of Newburgh, and Louey got to thinking that maybe now was the time to go back home and get a job herself. And so she did.

It had broken Louey's heart to find that there were no jobs available on the Newburgh News, her mother's old paper. Ruth Levy had reported for the News in the 1940s, starting right after the war and continuing through her three pregnancies and right up until she got sick in the late 50s. But since then, the News had become an afternoon paper, and few people subscribed anymore. People were watching the news on TV when they got home from work, and the News was all but out of business by the time Louey finished grad school. She moved in with Danny and his wife, Sue, while she scanned the classified ads in the papers for jobs. It wasn't long before she found an ad for a reporter at the Record, the daily in the city of Middletown, 20 miles west of Newburgh. She sent in her résumé and cover letter. A few days later, she got the call.

The two men who had interviewed her were the executive editor and the managing editor. The exec, Al Rome, unlike The Publisher, was at the Record every day. He approved Page One and the positioning of the stories in the news hole—the first ten pages—before the paper was printed each night. He also wrote the editorials, which were terrific. They also had color comics on Sunday, and a great sports section covering all the local high-school teams, and, because of their brand-new photo-offset presses, the best photos in any paper anywhere. She really hoped this job would pay what she had carefully figured out she'd need for rent, food, gas and oil and utilities. She'd given it a lot of thought: $140 a week. She wouldn't take a penny less. She had standards.

The other person interviewing her was Ted Daley, the managing editor. He remained standing for the entire interview. Louey thought that maybe his butt hurt, but then she noticed that all the other chairs in Rome's office, except the ones that she and Rome were sitting in, were piled so high with newspapers—way higher than the armrests—that there was literally no place for Daley to park himself.

Rome's big, wooden desk practically groaned with huge, precariously leaning towers of various newspapers, broadsheets and tabloids together; a typewriter; and one opened ream and several unopened reams of copy paper. Scattered on a side-table were old issues of both the Record and The New York Times.

As he questioned Louey and listened to her answers, glancing from time to time at her résumé, Rome continually tore off bits from the right edge of Page One of that day's Late Final. He rolled the torn-off pieces into little spit-balls and chewed them thoughtfully, mouth closed.

Is he swallowing them? Yes: He must be. I'm watching a man eat his own newspaper, Louey thought. *Maybe he's on some kind of a diet. Maybe he has that disease where people eat weird stuff like dog poop, or cigarette butts. Some of the patients at Syracuse Psychiatric did that. There was a word for it. Or maybe he likes the smell of it? They say nine-tenths of flavor is actually scent.* Louey always loved the smell of newsprint, but not in a way that made her hungry.

He's hungry for information! He's starving for culture! OK, ignore it. Focus. Keep a straight face.

But I'm not going to forget this.

Rome asked about what kinds of things she'd like to cover. She wanted to say Newburgh, of course, but the ad was for a general-assignment reporter to work out of Middletown. So she said, "Anything: politics, fires, courts, features; anything." He asked if she were a fast and accurate typist, and she confidently said yes.

"More fast? Or more accurate?" he said, eyebrows dancing.

"Both," she said. She was hoping he would make her take a typing test, because she'd kill it.

Instead, he moved on. His head moved up and down as he scanned her résumé.

"You say you're a good speller."

"Yes," she said. "I am." She hoped she wasn't starting to sound too conceited.

Rome jumped, shoving his chair backwards with the backs of his knees. He bent over his desk and narrowed his eyes, thrusting his head forward 'til his nose was almost touching hers.

"Diarrhea!" he growled slowly, while looking her up and down, as though she had just insulted him.

Louey's immediately thought was that "diarrhea" must be Rome's eccentric way of saying, "Bullshit." Like on M*A*S*H, the way Colonel Potter always said, "Horse-hockey." But there now was nothing to do but stick up for herself. She looked him right in the eye.

"No! Really! I *am* a good speller!" she protested.

Daley, standing off to the side of Rome's desk, chuckled loudly, shook his head and took his eyes off her miniskirt long enough to interpret. "No. He means, spell 'diarrhea,' if you're such a good speller," he said.

"Oh. D-I-A-R-R-H-E-A." Diarrhea, apparently, was the ultimate test for Record reporters, and Louey had passed it.

Daley joined Rome in throwing her a few other hard ones: complement, when it means an addition that improves something; omitted; recommend; ukulele; defense; pharaoh; and tendinitis came sailing at her from various angles. Louey hit them all out of the park. By the end of this impromptu quiz, Rome and Daley were both smiling and nodding at each other. Now she knew she had them. But for good measure, after nailing deterrence and superintendent, she added, sincerely: "But if there were something that I was unsure of, I would just open my dictionary or my Associated Press Stylebook and very quickly look it up; I wouldn't be ashamed to do that."

They told her starting pay was $143 a week and asked her if that was about right.

Why, yes. Yes, it was.

They asked her when she could start.

The next morning, she found herself a dirt-cheap apartment in a strange place called Scotchtown, a few miles outside of Middletown.

It was listed in the Record's classifieds.

"Lovely, quiet spot in the woods near Middletown," it said. "$120/month, heat and hot water incl."

Perfect. She could write her poems and stories in peace

there, and be close to work.

Scotchtown was more a campground than a hamlet. A curving gravel road that might have been a driveway led to her building through a heavily wooded area. You parked anywhere you wanted on the pine needles among the towering evergreens. When you got out of the car, it smelled great, like those little "balsam pillows" that are sold along the tourist roads in Maine.

Her building was a small, rustic, wooden structure, the kind of place where the nurse might live at a sleepover camp. It was two stories tall, and the only other tenants were a young couple on the ground floor. Her three-room place, which you reached via a set of rickety wooden steps from the outside, was unfurnished, but that was perfect. Other than her camera and watch, Louey owned just clothing, books, notebooks, stereo/radio, speakers, albums and five posters, so it was easy to move in. She would buy a mattress and box-spring and sheets and a blanket and two pillows, and she would sleep on the floor. The place had a refrigerator and stove and a shower, four electric outlets in the bedroom and two in the kitchen plus one more in the bathroom, so what else could she ever need? She could use planks and cinder-blocks as a bookcase, and get someone to help her drag a wooden utility-cable spool up to her kitchen to use as a table. Spools like that could be found rather commonly around the shoulders of roads in those days. Then after her first pay-check, she would buy a couple of lamps and four cheap folding chairs, or borrow some from Danny and Sue. And now with a steady income, she'd have enough soon for a TV set, in addition to kitchen supplies. Plus, she was close enough to Danny and Sue's house in Newburgh that she'd be able to visit them often. She would have some good meals that way, as well as the pleasure of their company. Whoa! Louey Levy could easily be mistaken for a grownup.

Ted Daley stalked slowly among the reporters' desks and glowered and twirled his handlebar mustache like Snidely Whiplash. He even did the Whiplash evil chuckle whenever he caught a reporter in an error, whether it involved grammar, spelling, substance, or any violation of the Associated Press Stylebook.

"Nyah-hah-hah?" you could hear him chuckle as hovered over the black, manual Underwood of some harried striver. Nearly all the reporters were young, because the Record paid less if you had no experience. So they tended to hire recent college grads, like Louey.

Every once in a while, when a female reporter had turned in a story and had a minute to breathe, Daley would concoct a reason to call her into his office. It had a big plate-glass window onto the newsroom, but the curtains inside it were nearly always pulled closed. The reporters he called in would emerge several minutes later silent and red-faced, avoiding eye contact with anyone. He never summoned the men. Louey hoped it would be years before she'd ever be called in there.

Daley seemed to take special pride in knowing stuff about Middletown that no one else knew. And he did know Middletown really well—you had to give him that. He had grown up there, gone to high school there, and then immediately started working at the paper, back in the Forevers.

Louey learned all this during her first tête-à-tête in his office, about a month after she joined the paper. That meeting was mostly all about him. He complimented a story she'd written that involved an interview with a state trooper, and then proceeded to his personal history. He told her that, as a kid, he'd wanted to be a state trooper, and had passed all the exams for it, but was rejected because he didn't have good teeth. This information startled her.

"You have to bite people to be a state trooper?"

"No!" he chuckled; "It's just that if you have bad teeth you end up having to take a lot of time off for dentists' appointments, getting your teeth pulled, and getting prescriptions filled for painkillers and stuff like that. But growing up, no one in my family ever went to the dentist. We couldn't afford it. My father, my mom, my brothers—we all have false teeth."

What am I supposed to do with that information? Louey thought. *Am I supposed to feel sorry for him? Why would God designate me to be the recipient of the knowledge that Ted Daley has false teeth? Am I supposed to go and think about them now? I will never be able to concentrate on my work again. I wonder if he's looking for pity-sex because of his bad teeth. I wonder if they're wooden. I wonder if it makes him feel like George Washington. I wonder if this information will someday end up in a story.*

After failing to become a trooper, Daley said, he had applied for a copyboy position on the paper and worked his way up over the decades to the esteemed position of managing editor. It didn't seem a likely career trajectory for a toothless kid who never went to college, but in Olden Times, reporters and editors did indeed rise from jobs like delivery-boy and copyboy, with almost no formal education at all. And he had wisely latched onto a mentor: Al Rome. Rome, a Jew from Chicago with a master's degree in political science, had inexplicably taken a shine to him, and promoted him to various positions, all of which he apparently had worked very hard at and, under Rome's guidance, succeeded at. He did know Middletown better than almost anyone; he knew the mayor and the mayor's family; all the aldermen and their families; and the chiefs of the fire and police departments and most of their men. He had gone to school with them. He had their numbers in his Rolodex. Reporters sometimes slunk into Daley's office when their efforts to reach a city official came up dry; he had an uncanny ability to know when such people would be at the movies or when they were babysitting their grandchildren in Arizona, or when they were on vacation, and he often knew when they'd be back and how to reach them in the meantime.

Rome could depend on Daley to know what local news was and where to find it. Consequently, the ten-page news hole at the front of the paper was always filled with good stuff, and both men were justifiably proud of the Record. Maybe the one other thing they had in common, Louey thought, was their excellence at and respect for good spelling. Because otherwise Rome and Daley were like—well, not apples and oranges, she thought; more like kumquats and chainsaws.

On arriving at the Record for her first day at work, Louey was happy to see that she could grab her "lucky spot," where she'd parked for her successful interview. It wasn't until a couple of days later that she found out that reporters were generally prohibited from parking there. Unless they were racing in to type up a story with an immediate deadline, re-porters were supposed to park at the side of the building, or around back. The "front" parking lot, on Mulberry Street, was reserved for management, public-relations shills and an-gry or breathless readers who came to demand retractions or propose stories about their own or their children's amazing achievements.

Louey was a few minutes early. As she was about to make a right turn into the lot, a semi tractor-trailer, approaching from the opposite direction, pulled up nearly even with her. Louey figured it had probably been at the loading dock, dropping off a roll of the newsprint that the paper need-ed tons of to thread around the rollers of their famous web press. She didn't need to stop; there was plenty of room on the one-block-long street for both the truck and her bright red 1963 Plymouth Fury that she called "Fury," with its 318 V8 engine and black rag top.

But then she noticed the driver leaning out of his win-dow on that ice-cold February afternoon, and she watched as he leaned out. At first she thought he was speaking to her, so she rolled down her own window.

"Hey, Legs! I got something you can wrap 'em around!"

Louey looked to her right. Striding up the sidewalk, very fast, was a tall, slender young woman with long, straight brown hair cascading from beneath a knit ski-cap. She wore a winter coat that fell nearly to the hem of her miniskirt. A shoulder bag hung down to one hip, and a camera dangled against her chest. Instantly and without breaking stride, she glared at the driver and gave him the finger. She continued looking straight at him, arm raised high, finger in the air, for the five seconds or so it took her to get to the front door, which she opened by turning around and pushing it inward with her butt so as to continue glaring and holding her gesture until she disappeared inside.

As the truck moved off, Louey applauded and laughed and cheered inside her car. *Oh my God, it's Mary Tyler Moore!"* she thought; *Mary Tyler Moore works here! I'm going to love this job.* And then it was Louey's turn to go through that door.

The woman she had seen was standing in a second doorway—the one that led to the newsroom—and had turned to wave goodbye to the receptionist, whom she'd apparently been chatting with. She held that second door for Louey.

"Are you looking for the newsroom?" she said.

"Yes. It's my first day, and I'm supposed to find Al Rome."

"Oh, you're the new reporter! Welcome! Come on in. I'll show you where he is. I'm Charlotte Farley."

Louey had seen Charlotte's byline on many Record stories, and she had seen her in action with the trucker, and now she was going to be her colleague. This was a great day already.

The newsroom immediately sang to her. It drew her in with its old metal desks and older Underwood typewriters; the reporters hunched over them, smoking; reporters and editors alike answering their phones with a curt, "Newsroom!" followed by just their last name: "Newsroom! Plummer!" "Newsroom! Miller!" "Newsroom! Jackson!"

Everything was immediate and clipped. Reporters stopped typing on their heavy Underwoods just long enough to grab a notebook and pen, put their cigarette down (or not), stash the phone between their ear and shoulder, and start scribbling. Everyone was talking, a thousand conversations at once: "When? Did you hear him say that yourself? And what's your name, again? Sorry, could you spell that? Tell me your number. Where did this happen? Is it still on fire? How do you know? Who told you that? Do you have her number? Where can I reach him? Is the coroner there yet? Who'd you hear that from? Spell it again, please."

And then, the soundtrack: the police and fire monitor's intermittent squawk that could be definitively translated only by the wire editor, Ed "Flash" Hannigan.

Louey loved that they called each fully typed-up page a "take," not a "page"; she loved the paste-pot that they all shared, to stick their takes together like a kite-tail to avoid the rips and jams of stapling; she loved the fragrant fog of cigar smoke near the desk of Plummer, the guy she sat across from; she loved the jadedness of the old reporters and the earnestness of the young ones; she loved all of it.

Very quickly, she found out that Charlotte covered the courts and that everyone on the paper called her "Charlie." *Charlie Farley! God, if I had a great name like that,* Louey thought, *I'd use that as my byline on every single story I ever wrote.* And yet, mysteriously, Charlie always used "Charlotte."

One day, Daley sneaked up like a weasel behind Charlie. Peering over her shoulder as she banged out a two-take story on an accident involving the superintendent of schools, he loudly said, "Who told you how to spell Crumblach? I've known Jake Crumblach for years. I went to high school with Jake and his sister Cathy. They lived two doors from us on Moroney Street. That's not how you spell Crumblach. Didn't you ask him how to spell his name? Jeez Louise, you interviewed him for 20 minutes at his house and you didn't ask him to spell his name?" Ted invariably said, "Jeez Louise," instead of "Jesus," because he was Catholic. (Ted, not Jesus.)

"I know how to spell Crumblach," Charlie replied with a sigh, backspacing. "I just hit an 'e' instead of an 'h.' And you don't have to sneak up on me like that. You scared the crap out of me." She bent down to retrieve a pencil that she'd knocked off her desk when he'd started speaking.

You hit an 'e' instead of an 'h'? How in the heck do you do that? The 'e' is nowhere near the 'h'! Jeez Louise!"

Another evil twirl, and off he went to torture another reporter.

Louey immediately wondered if poor Crumblach's friends in grade school had called him "Crummy," as she surely would have. She and Charlie exchanged eyerolls, head-shakes and open-mouthed jaw-juts: a sign of true Sisters-in-Journalism.

The first payday after Louey joined the staff, Charlie invited her to join some reporters at the Dugout for beers after work. A dark dive near the Record with good burgers and fries, it was the only place in Middletown open after midnight. First to arrive after Charlie and Louey was the raven-haired Annie McDowell, a very good writer and a bulldog of a reporter who never let politicians on her beat—city government in Middletown, and the Middletown School District—get away with non-answers to her tough questions. She was, like Charlie, a devout Roman Catholic with a delightful sense of humor.

They settled in at what apparently was the reporters'

regular table. Next to burst through the door were Mike, the "late man" from Sports; and Jake Rosen, the Newburgh bureau chief, whom Louey had determined not to be jealous of just because he was covering Newburgh while she was stuck in Middletown. Finally, in came Bill, chief of the Sullivan County bureau. He'd had to drive down from Monticello for this gathering.

After they'd ordered a pitcher of Miller High Life, Louey turned to Charlie with an expression of deep seriousness. She looked as though she were going to take notes.

"Charlie," she said, "Charlie Farley is just the greatest name ever. Why don't you use it for your bylines?"

"I like 'Charlotte.' My mother named me for Charlotte Brontë because she loved *Jane Eyre*. It was her favorite book. She must have read it to me and my sisters at least five times."

"Thank God she didn't like *Moby-Dick*," Jake said. "She would have named you Herman."

Mike from Sports chimed in, grinning and reaching across their round table for the bowl of pretzels. "Or, Vladimir Nabokov! She would have named you Lolita! Lolita: That would have been worse, right?"

A grin, raised eyebrows and vigorous nods on Mike's part sought validation all around the table, but in vain. After a moment of puzzled silence, the gang did a collective forehead-slap. Bill broke the news.

"Mike. Mike. She named her after the *author*, not the *book*."

"Is there an 'Emily' among your sisters, for *Wuthering Heights*?" Louey asked.

"No. I don't even know if my mother ever read *Wuthering Heights*. She stopped with the authors' names after me;

otherwise, we might have been Charlotte, Margaret (for *Goodnight, Moon*) and, let's see, maybe … what else did she read to us? Oh, *Charlotte's Web!*' My youngest sister would have been … uh … what was E.B. White's real first name?"

Louey knew that one as well as she knew her own. *Charlotte's Web* was still her favorite book, and she still cried whenever she read, on the last page: "It is not often that someone comes along who is a true friend and a good writer. Charlotte was both." It always reminded her of her mother, who was a very good writer and her own true friend, for the whole nine years that they knew each other.

"Elwyn," Louey said. "Elwyn Brooks White was his real name, but everyone called him Andy, for the stupidest reason: He went to Cornell, and they had this tradition there that every male student whose last name was White got called "Andy" in honor of the first president of Cornell, Andrew White. And so for the rest of his life, all his friends called E.B. White 'Andy.'"

"How the hell did you know that weird factoid?" Mike from Sports asked. And that must have been what they all were thinking, because everyone stopped chewing and leaned toward Louey, smiling and frowning and slowly shaking their heads.

"It was in 'The Years with Ross,' by James Thurber, about his time working at the *New Yorker*. It had a lot about E.B. White, who was, you know, one of Thurber's colleagues there, and I guess, one of his best friends. But can you imagine anyone wanting to be called Elwyn? I'd call myself Andy, too, if I were an Elwyn."

At least "Charlie" was a reasonable nickname for

"Charlotte." Louey herself was born Louisa May Levy, because her mom had loved Louisa May Alcott's *Little Women.* That was an oddity that she and Charlie had in common and that they both got a kick out of. Louey, who had taken umpteen college credits in 19th Century British Literature, was a *Jane Eyre* fan herself. You had to get into it, though. You had to decide that you were going to enjoy every old-fashioned sentence that depicted so well those old-fashioned times and attitudes and clothes and ways of speaking. And then, you *would* enjoy it; otherwise, not so much. For Louey, the best part of *Jane Eyre* was when Charlotte Brontë addressed the reader directly now and then, especially that part near the end, where she wrote—and set off as a separate paragraph— "Reader, I married him."

As though Brontë were writing for a newspaper.

That was so cool. That was startling and strong, after all those long, periodic sentences in those interminable paragraphs written in that florid, 19th-century style.

So, in the end, Charlie had a good reason—Louey knew she would—for using "Charlotte" for her byline, and for introducing herself to strangers that way. And she was glad that Charlie's mom, unlike her own, had lived to see her daughter grow up and choose her own damned byline.

Among friends, though, Farley was fine with everyone calling her Charlie.

Dear Diary,
It's too bad no one could ever use a line like, "Reader, I

married him" again—unless they were trying to be funny. Or even a variation of it. I mean, you could do it, for sure, but you'd have to be careful not to use it too much. Just a little bit, or else it would get tiresome.

One night just after deadline, as Charlie and Louey were putting on their coats and getting ready to go to the Dugout for a beer, Ted Daley called them in to his office. Since he wanted both of them together, they weren't worried and just looked at each other as if to say, "Oh, brother: What did we do now?" But in kind of a humorous way. It turned out he was assigning them—together—to do a Big Story about the Housing Situation in Orange County.

They would have to "crisscross the county," he said, talking to sources like real estate agents and homebuyers, mostly from the Bronx. Orange County was getting flooded with people from New York City who, lured by the cheaper cost of living and the relative peace and quiet, were looking to buy homes upstate.

For the first few weeks that they were on the story, Louey wasn't sure of what the word "mortgage" meant. She wasn't even too sure that it was a loan. *I mean,* she thought, *if it's a loan, why don't they just call it a "loan," or at least a "housing loan," instead of a "mortgage?"* Neither she nor Charlie had ever owned a house nor dreamed of owning one, and they knew no more than the newcomers about mortgages. Charlie did most of the real work on the series, interviewing new homebuyers or property buyers. Almost all of those properties and houses were in the farm area known as Wallkill, just outside Middletown, which was rapidly being bought up by developers and chopped into half-acre lots. The houses were style-free, cookie-cutter, 2- or 3-bedroom abodes with yards cleared of all the trees, meadows, bushes and wildflowers those places had previously supported. The lots were bare, muddy and silent. To Louey's eyes, the gently rolling farmland was becoming depressing and ugly, like a half-built industrial site. Still, many of the newcomers could imagine themselves raising their families there in peace and quiet, and the mortgage payments seemed no higher than their monthly rents in the Bronx or Queens. Wallkill was very attractive to these blue-collar white and Latino folks, and they were starting to move into the area in droves.

The reporters hashed it out and decided that Charlie would talk to people and provide the info, statistics and quotes, while Louey would take photos and do the rewrite. She thought that one particularly sad shot of a bare, muddy lot in the rain, with a half-built house in the background and a huge mound of dirt off to one side of it like the high piles of snow looming over shopping-mall parking lots in the winter, would suffice to let everyone know how these innocents were being ripped off and would soon own cheaply constructed homes in these barren lots. They'd have flooded basements needing expensive repairs, for sure. Charlie had already gotten several good anecdotes about families with nonstandard electrical and plumbing hookups, wells that didn't work, and other problems. Some of the new home-owners, in fact, were already suing the developers over various deficiencies in their houses. Lawyers in Orange County were fully employed. Despite never having owned either a home or any land in her life, Louey nevertheless decided to take a "sophisticated-reporter-warns-the-naïve-newcomers" tone with the whole series.

In her innocence, Louey was stunned to learn how much a young couple would end up spending on their 30-year mortgage after it was paid off, with all the interest: "Eighty-nine thousand dollars," she wrote as her lead. "For a $40,000 home." As if that were an attention-grabbing scandal. Luckily, Marv, the copy-editor who was reading that installment of the series, stood up and called loudly to her.

"Louey!"

"What!"

"Guess how much the sticker-price was on my house! And then guess how much I'll end up paying after 30 years! Go ahead, guess! We've got three bedrooms!"

He then looked around the desk for backup. The other copy-editors nodded and called out what the original price was on their own homes and how much they would end up shelling out after their own 30-year mortgages were paid.

"That's standard! That's what a mortgage is! Don't you know that?" Marv asked in amazement.

They made Louey change not only the lead, but also the focus.

"That's not a story: That's the way it's always been!" they yelled over to her. "You always pay more in interest than you do for the house! That's how mortgages work!" She was lucky they didn't tell Al Rome what a dope she was. They just had her rewrite it.

After the series had been nominated for a New York State Newspaper Editors Association award for Best In-Depth

Reporting—but didn't win—Louey became known as the paper's "feature" reporter, a polite way of saying they didn't want her writing stories that required financial insight, high-school math, or much common sense. She was assigned to interview a local teacher who'd invented a remote-control car-starter; a woman who'd had triplets one year and then again two years later; a one-armed high-school pole-vaulter; the music teacher who brought a group of elementary-school kids to sing the National Anthem at a Mets game; a 72-year-old retiree who'd been on a cruise ship that caught fire in the Atlantic and had had to drop 15 feet down into a rescue boat; and a poetry-writing police chief. Readers started calling and asking for her when they had an idea for some offbeat story that had no hard news value.

One day, her phone rang just as she was walking in.

"Newsroom! Levy!" she sang out as she scooted her chair under her desk.

Oh, she loved saying that. The smile in her voice reflected the one on her face.

It was a farmer, Stanley ("Stosh") Polaski, whose plow had turned up some huge, weird bones. He called the Record's main number and asked for Louey because her byline was on some oddball story that he liked.

At first he didn't know what they were, he said, but he thought they might be something interesting. He'd put in a call to the State University at New Paltz Archaeology Department, and based on his description of how large the bones were and the size of its skull and its teeth, they called the New York State Education Department in Albany, which ran the State Museum. The Museum's experts came down and proclaimed them to be a complete set of mastodon bones from a creature that had lived 12,000 years ago and had sunk into the rich, black dirt of Orange County's farmland, the second-largest onion-producing region in the U.S. They put them on the only nearby dark, flat place big enough to hold them: the hard-dirt floor of Stosh's barn. There they laid the critter's bones like pieces of a jigsaw puzzle, with its skull and gigantic tusks and teeth at the front, and its whole long backbone and ribs following, and its long legs underneath, as though it had fallen asleep on its side. They'd left with a warning, Stosh said: "Don't touch them." They asked him to keep them in the barn 'til they could send a climate-controlled truck, a week later, to take them up to the Museum, where they would be glued and screwed together and stood upright.

"And keep them wet," they'd told him. "Whatever you do, don't let them dry out."

He had taken good care of the bones. He hadn't said a word about them to anyone, and he'd kept them wet with his hundred-foot garden hose. But now he wanted everyone to take photos and write stories about his find, before they got hauled off to Albany.

When Louey told Paul about it, his immediate and only question was, "Does it have teeth?"

"Yup; a full set, he said."

"OK then, I'm there!"

Louey wasn't the only one Stosh called; the Education Department had let radio and TV stations statewide know about the find, and when and where Stosh would be "showing" the bones. When Louey arrived at the farm, he said he couldn't say anything 'til the Ed Department's PR man and the AP reporter showed up. He had promised the Ed Department that. They said he could answer everyone's questions at once that way, and hand out the one-page information sheets about mastodons they'd sent him, and then he could get back to his tractor. It was planting time. Still, he ended up giving Louey a few good quotes that no one else got, because she was the first one on the scene by several minutes. He told her, for example, that he turned his hose on the bones faithfully three times a day: before breakfast, before lunch, and before turning in for the night.

Paul arrived shortly after Louey, in his own car. They were soon joined by a flock of reporters with microphones, tape recorders, video recorders and lights, and by Polaski's six-year-old daughter, Emily, who was far more fascinated by all the visitors and their equipment than she was by the bones, which she'd seen already.

Inside the dark, good-smelling barn, there it was on the dirt floor. Clearly, a huge thing had died. Everyone started taking flash photos. *The flashes can't possibly be good for these ancient bones*, Louey thought. Funny that Mr. Polaski hadn't told them, "No flashes, please." But he hadn't. The Albany people must have told him only, "Don't let anyone touch it," not, "Don't let anyone take photos of it."

Oddly, Paul wasn't taking any photos at all. He was idly looking around the barn, standing against a wall and gazing up at the rafters. His Nikon with its built-in flash hung around his neck, but he wasn't using it. Louey knew he had something up his sleeve.

No more than ten minutes later, the wire reporters and

TV and radio people were done. Stosh had answered all their questions ("How do they know it's not a mammoth? Do you know its sex? Have you given it a nickname?"). He had not named the bones, and his response to many of the other questions was simply, "Call the State Ed Department."

When all the other reporters and photographers had driven down the dusty road, Paul swung into action. He went to the trunk of his car and pulled out a five-foot-long plastic "toothbrush" that he had bought God knows where. The bristles on it were about six inches long. He asked little Emily to kneel at the animal's skull and pretend to be brushing its teeth. She was delighted to do that and bent to the task with enthusiasm, giggling all the while.

Of course that would be the Page One photo the next day, but Louey now had a dilemma. For the caption, she didn't know whether to say Emily was "brushing" the animal's teeth, or "pretending" to brush them. Record photographers were not supposed to set anything up that wasn't there naturally—they could get in a lot of trouble for that. They could get fired. But this was such an over-the-top, obvious gag, that no one would mind … would they? In the end, she decided to go with a caption saying that the kid was "brushing" the thing's teeth.

And she certainly had her lead: "Three times a day, Stanley Polaski goes out to water his mastodon."

Nobody got in trouble.

Louey was also the go-to reporter for weather and holiday stories. On Valentines Day she went to the Dugout at dinnertime and started conversations with a couple of women who, like her, were sitting at the bar alone. On the first warm day of spring, she stopped at local ice-cream stands and interviewed the owners and workers about sales and asked sticky-faced kids about their favorite flavors; she stopped at automotive garages and asked if people were getting their heavy-duty windshield wipers and snow tires removed. And on the first day of school, she interviewed a school-bus driver about what "First Day" was like for him. She was sick of photos of tearful moms taking pictures of their kindergartners and stories about how hard it is to say goodbye on that day. *Why is that hard?* she asked herself. *It's not like they're going off to their deaths: They'll be home at 3 o'clock, for Chrissake!* They just struck her as so trite, those stories.

One afternoon the news editor, Ben Jackson, came to Louey with an unusual assignment. The local chapter of Alcoholics Anonymous was celebrating its 35th anniversary. Contrary to its very charter, the members had decided to allow a reporter, just this once, to interview one of its members about how great AA was and what important work it was doing and how new members were welcome and how to go about joining, as long as that reporter promised to keep that person's name and face out of the story. The chapter thought they could drum up more members with that publicity, which actually was a good idea. A guy from AA would be calling her shortly, Jackson said.

"So expect the call. He won't be giving you his real name, and if you do happen to find out his real name, don't use it, OK?"

"OK, sure." This would be a fun one.

"I'll bet money that Jackson is a member of that chapter," Louey told Annie that night. "What d'ya bet?"

"I wouldn't be surprised," Annie said, drawing in some cigarette smoke. "I mean, Plummer told me he keeps a hip flask of scotch in his desk drawer for 'emergencies.' But did you ever see him have a belt of it?"

"Not yet."

Louey solemnly promised Jackson she'd ensure the fellow's anonymity by photographing him only from behind, by not describing his appearance or naming his job or his employer, and of course by referring to him only by a fake name. She thought it sounded like a fun, easy story and was happy that Jackson had given it to her. She took the guy's name and number and called him right away.

At that point in her life, Louey would have bet money that she had never met a real alcoholic—because it would just be obvious if someone were an alcoholic, wouldn't it? She had no alcoholic family members that she knew of. Her college friends included no drinkers to speak of, though they weren't teetotalers, either. Her Record friends, when they went to the Dugout, chipped in and bought a pitcher of beer, which they all shared and which lasted for the hour and a half they spent talking and wolfing down the free popcorn from the latticed, waxed-paper-lined plastic bowl the waitresses kept refilling at their table. And no one she knew of— except Jackson himself—kept a flask in his desk. Of course, very few women were alcoholics—none that she knew of, anyway—and she had never known anyone who had ever got sick from drinking. Except—now that she thought about it—she herself, that one time in college when she drank that whole 12-ounce water glass of port wine someone gave her at a party and passed out where her friends had laid her on her back in her bed and she threw up while unconscious and could have died. But that was another story.

The AA guy called her at her desk just a few days later.

"Newsroom! Levy!" In a minute, they had the interview set up.

When she arrived at the address he gave, he seemed to be no alcoholic at all. He didn't smell of booze, and neither did his house or his clothes. He didn't stagger or talk funny, and he wasn't unemployed.

She was confused and disappointed; she could have used a lot of juicy details like that. His house, in fact, was a really nice, middle-class, Leave-It-to-Beaver one, complete with a white picket fence, and he himself, you'd swear, was a completely normal, middle-aged guy, whose only outstanding feature was that he was very tall. Six-five, easily—maybe six-six.

To amuse herself, Louey decided to refer to him in her story as "Mr. Tallman (not his real name)." Editing it, Jackson asked her if she was sure she wanted to use a "cheesy inside joke," and added that his friends might recognize him from the "tallness" she was implying. So, in the paper, it ran as "Mr. Newman (not his real name)."

The AA guy asked her if she wanted coffee. She had learned long ago that the correct answer to that question is always yes, even though she abhorred coffee and had to concentrate on not making a face as she drank it. Drinking coffee with someone gives you a longer time to be with him, and accepting always seems friendlier, somehow, than saying no thanks.

He talked about AA like a PR guy. He disabused Louey of a lot of notions that she'd held all her life. He said you're always an alcoholic; you don't get over it. He told a joke: "You can always tell who the alcoholics are at the Christmas party: We're the only ones who aren't drinking." He went on about how many members their local chapter currently had (to her surprise, you never officially "drop out," because they always take you back; as a result, that number had remained relatively stable over the decades), and how most of the members are working folks, including professionals—but yes, there are unemployed people too, and how women and men are equally welcome, although it was true—it was the one preconception Louey had that turned out to be true—that there were very few women in their AA chapter.

"That doesn't mean there are fewer women alcoholics, though. It's probably just because there's more stigma attached to women alcoholics than to men," he said. "People are harder on them for drinking."

People are harder on us for everything, Louey thought.

She couldn't help asking him about his own problems that might have led to his alcoholism. She was hoping for some gripping stories of violence, being fired, auto accidents, wife-beatings, suicide attempts or other horrible disasters illustrating "how bad it had gotten" before he joined AA. She could start her story with a dramatic incident from his past, and go from there. It turned out, however, that this AA guy was never a falling-down, rolling-in-the-gutter, driving-while-drunk drunk. It was just that alcohol always made him "sick and mean," he said, and his wife finally had taken the kids and left him.

And how did he manage to not-drink now? Just by going to AA meetings and hearing other people's stories?

Yup.

He told her about the AA adage that you have to take sobriety "one day at a time," and how that's the only thing you really have to remember and try to succeed at—just that one day—and then you'll be OK. To her it sounded banal and obvious to the point of meaninglessness, and it would be stupid to put that in a story. "Mr. Newman," however, had adopted it like it was the Golden Rule. He even had a framed needlepoint over his couch: "One Day at a Time."

"Just get through today," he said softly, nodding and staring into the middle distance. He folded both hands into fists in his lap and continued as if he were giving himself a pep talk. He squeezed his eyes tightly shut and added, "Just concentrate and put all your effort into getting through today. Give it everything you've got."

Then she asked him a question whose answer made her reflect again, as she drove the few blocks back to the Record, on how little and unimportant the crap was that she'd learned in college:

"So, how long has it been since you've had a drink?"

He brightened a bit and raised his eyebrows, smiled shyly and leaned forward a little as he answered.

"You know, it's funny you ask me that, because on Saturday—day after tomorrow—it'll be exactly 30 years!" And then after he'd fully exhaled, his face grew solemn.

"If I make it," he added.

Well, this story just wrote itself, Louey thought. Also, she thought: *Wow, I finally learned something: People who look like the most ordinary shlubs in the world can be leading these terrifically brave, strong, good lives, right under your nose.*

She did learn a couple of other things in her rookie year: *Shut up* was a good one, especially when interviewing people; and, *When you're done, stop.* But in her diary that night, she took several pages writing about her AA story, an assignment she was sure she'd never forget.

Louey also learned something else during her tenure at the Record: She learned that they were never going to assign her to the Newburgh bureau, because Rosen and His Crew of Two (as the editors called Jake and his pair of fulltime reporters) were so good, and they were never going to leave. They had the best beat—Newburgh—and they knew it. Louey would be the general-assignment, holiday, weather- and weirdo-story reporter until she died.

Charlie, one early June day, suggested they take a canoe trip with Sandy, Mike from Sports, Annie and Jake down the rocky, roaring Delaware River. What better way to celebrate spring—and the impending Revolution? For it was clear that the Revolution was coming: The President's two top aides, Haldeman and Erlichmann, had resigned, along with his Attorney General, and then his lawyer was fired, too. The whole house of cards was tumbling, and pretty soon the White House War Monger was going to be impeached.

"Just watch!" Jake said. "Woodward and Bernstein aren't gonna let this drop. They've got too much on him now. All the evidence is pointing to Nixon being indicted." Louey believed it with all her heart, as did many of the other reporters. Oh, he would be indicted, for sure. It was getting exciting now. The Record's wire editor, Flash Hanigan, hovered over the wire-service machines that were constantly clacking away with stories being filed in "real time." He ripped off long streamers of yellow paper at the first set of perforations after the "-30-" symbol, announcing the headlines and running with them in both hands across the noisy, smoke-filled newsroom to the Desk like a child holding the tails of multiple kites. Tim was under orders to bring any damning Watergate Hotel burglary-related stories to Al Rome, who was staying late every night now. He spent his time reading and chewing his way through the papers in his office, just in case, based on the latest information, he had to change his editorial. Reporters also stopped banging out their own stories momentarily, just long enough to make cynical or hopeful comments before returning to their typing.

Jackson assigned Sandy and several other reporters to get reactions from local politicians—both Democrats and Republicans—and let Louey do the "man on the street" roundups of how random local residents were feeling about the momentous news out of Washington. This was one of her favorite things to do, these roundups. She began spending most hours of her shift at the shopping mall or at car-repair shops or the Dugout and other bars, or in parking lots, diners, beauty parlors and playgrounds, talking to working men, moms, students, grandparents, waitresses, and any other adult who had an opinion about Nixon and didn't mind sharing it.

And now, from her interviews, it seemed as if most people were beginning to believe that the President was a liar and the head of an especially incompetent burglary ring that he'd hired as part of his effort to get re-elected.

Oh, this was delicious. This was the best time ever to be a reporter.

Anyway, in response to Charlie's idea about a canoe trip: The Revolution hadn't quite come yet, but the reporters were determined to celebrate anyway. Saturday was a regular day off for Louey. The snowmelt-laden Delaware flowed not far west of Middletown, within sight of the Port Jervis bureau. The Port Jervis reporters, having covered more than enough drownings of adventurers, begged off and recommended they wait 'til some time when the river was running lower and slower.

But Jake said he'd call in sick to join them. He loved canoeing; learned paddling as a 6-year-old, since his family had a lake house; hadn't had a chance to swim since last summer; still had his lifeguard certification; couldn't wait. Charlie was up for anything involving rivers. She and her father had kayaked every summer in a long, two-seater kayak on the little rivers in the Adirondacks. And Mike from Sports, a former swimmer for his high school, said he'd been looking for a way to work on his "paddling biceps" since he got to the Record two years ago, but just hadn't had a chance, so they could count him in. He didn't start work 'til 4, so he could easily join them on a three-hour canoe trip that started in the morning; and Sandy Miller, from the Sullivan County bureau, said yes without hesitating.

Sandy had been born, literally, *on* Lake Michigan. Her parents, older and wealthier than they should have been, owned a sailboat that they kept at the marina near their home in Traverse City. Such expert and enthusiastic mariners were they that the couple had engaged a babysitter for their four kids and nonchalantly set sail one summer day while Mrs. Miller was eight and a half months pregnant. Five miles from shore, Mrs. Miller went into the world's briefest labor, and Sandy, presumably bored in the solitude of the dark little pool she'd been swimming in, decided to join the fun on the big, bright blue lake. Out she slithered. Mrs. Miller, the story went, laughed through the whole thing, referring to it as "a hoot" even as her fifth child was being born.

Meanwhile, Sandy's dad calmly sailed back to shore by himself, raising the beams and hoisting the giblets or whatever sailors do, all by himself, while his wife cut her own umbilical cord with a serrated fishing knife that her husband had thoughtfully wiped on his pants. The knife was meant for "cleaning" fish—that is, chopping off their heads and slitting them stem to stern so you can stick your fingers into them and rip their slimy red guts out. And so Sandy Miller was washed in the briny water of Lake Michigan as soon as she had taken her first breath. Now, as an adult, she would rather swim than walk, and in fact could do so rather better. Yet as a reporter for the Record, she had not had a chance to go swimming even once in the year and a half since graduating from UM, where she had captained both the women's swimming and diving teams.

As for Louey, she decided it might be best not to mention to her pals that she couldn't swim. She knew never to stand up in a boat; what else was there to know? Canoe-rental places surely supplied all their customers with life vests. Besides, her friends would be there with her. What could go wrong?

She brought her precious Rolleiflex with her, to document the fun day. They'd start off at 9 a.m. (Annie had reserved three canoes), and they'd have plenty of time at some point, no doubt, to enjoy the sandwiches, apples and Cokes they'd bring in their backpacks. They gathered in a supermarket parking lot in Middletown, where the editors wouldn't see them, and piled into Fury. She had bought it for $220 from a used-car dealer in Syracuse, who himself had bought it for his own daughter. The daughter had intended to go to college in Massachusetts, but then decided to sell the car and live at home and attend Onondaga Community College, instead. Meanwhile, she'd work part-time and save all the money she'd otherwise have to spend on gas, license and registration fees and insurance. And that's how Louey, who must have reminded the dealer of his own daughter, got the cool car.

They all gabbed and listened to the radio, which was pre-set to WWKE, the local rock station, as Louey put the top down.

"A long, long time ago," Don McLean sang, "I can still remember how that music used to make me smile. ..." The music really did used to make Louey smile: the music of Buddy Holly, Elvis, the Shirelles, and then the music of the Beatles, Phil Ochs, Dylan, Joni Mitchell—all of them.

By God, this was the best time ever to be young.

They arrived a few minutes before their reserved time: 9 a.m.

The Delaware Outfitters, the company that rented the canoes, was housed in a little shack that smelled of insect repellent and Coppertone in the mosquito-filled woods at the edge of the river. The blades of a box-fan on the floor were turning slowly and resentfully, and somehow not moving any air. Outside, a dozen or so canoes were tipped onto their sides against the trees. The inside of the shop comprised two rooms: the room where you sign the papers and the Gift Shop. You had to "Exit through the Gift Shop," as the sign said, and over the open doorway between the two rooms, an arrow helpfully pointed the way, as though you could get lost. The Gift Shop's walls were lined with shelves holding key chains with miniature wooden canoes attached; tiny boxes of adhesive bandages; suntan lotion; candy bars; tins of lip balm with pictures of bears on the lid; camouflage hunting caps; maps of Orange, Sullivan and Pike counties and northern New Jersey; field guides of the wildlife and plants native to that area; jokey metal signs about bears; and several pairs of thick, wool socks in men's sizes. Louey tried to think of a way to get to the river without Exiting through the Gift Shop, but she couldn't.

Each of the six had to sign a contract saying they not only could swim, but also knew how to rescue a drowning adult and revive him, plus right a canoe, bail it out and get it floating again if it capsized. They also had to sign, at the very bottom, a clause saying neither they nor their families would ever sue the Outfitters, even if they turned into a vegetable from lack of oxygen or died, and neither would their "assignees or heirs, forever." Louey had no trouble signing this amusing, four-page agreement four seconds after it was handed to her, as soon as she found the signature line—and when the guy looked at her suspiciously and asked if she'd really read it, she looked him straight in the eye and had no trouble nodding and quietly saying, "Yes. It gives you a lot to think about, doesn't it?"

What she did have trouble with was putting on her life vest. First, she put her arms through the straps, instead of the arm-holes, which wasn't her fault as there were two of them and they were already buckled, so that they could look quite a bit like armholes to anyone who had never worn such a contraption. Then she saw her mistake, unbuckled the straps and put the thing on backwards. She had started putting it on upside down when the Outfitters guy, who'd been watching her the whole time as though she were the only one there, finally yanked the life vest from her, sighing, and held it up behind her like a gentleman holding a mink coat for a lady. She backed into it, and he cinched it up tight and buckled it for her.

There. Done.

Everybody took off their socks and left them in a pile outside the Outfitters' front door and shoved their bare feet into their sneaks to wear in the boats. Jake and Charlie slid away in the first canoe, and Mike and Sandy in the second. The four of them took off awfully fast, Louey thought, standing on the shore, listening to them whoop and watching as the Delaware whipped them around a bend and already out of sight. With her camera around her neck and her car keys in her cut-off jeans pocket, Louey threw her backpack into the boat and climbed into the front seat of the third canoe. It was half in the river and half on the tiny, sandy Delaware Outfitters beach. Annie climbed into the back seat while the guy steadied them, handed them their paddles and pushed their canoe into the water, getting his legs wet up to his calves.

It was nice and quiet for a minute, and Louey liked that feeling of the canoe gently rocking and the water slapping against it as she and Annie discussed which side each would paddle on. It was odd and fun to talk to someone who was sitting five feet behind you, when you couldn't turn around. Also, it was hard to hear the other person. Anyway, off they went.

The river quickly became much faster-moving, and while Louey easily figured out how to paddle—it was common sense, really—she didn't know how to slow down. She figured you just paddled backwards, but that succeeded only in turning the canoe broadside to the current. Which is what you don't want.

Rocks poked up here and there, with white froth splashing all around them. Well, she'd just stick her paddle out and fend them off, that's all. They'd get past them real quick that way.

"You know how to swim, right, Annie?" she called over her shoulder, trying to sound nonchalant.

"No," Annie said. "I never learned."

In other words, four strong swimmers—trained, experienced racers and lifeguards—were crammed into the first two canoes, and the two who couldn't swim shared the other one. Whose idea was this?

Less than a minute later, Annie and Louey were not only far behind, but also out of voice-range of the others. Still, for that minute, it was fun. Louey couldn't deny that. She giggled nervously, and the bouncy pop song, "Rock the Boat," by the Hues Corporation, written by Wally Holmes, floated into her head. She began bopping her upper body in time to the music: "So I'd like to know where / You got the notion / Yes, I'd like to know where / You got the notion / To rock the boat / Don't rock the boat, baby! / Don't rock the boat; / Don't tip the boat over …" It was a big hit that year.

Reader, she rocked the boat; she tipped the boat over.

Her first thought, as she went under the water, was that she was now going to be the cause of the death of Annie McDowell, a good writer and a good friend. Annie, like her, had lost her mother at a young age. Who would have to tell Annie's elderly, widowed father about her drowning? Her second thought was that she had now water-logged her beloved Rollei, which was hanging, twice as heavy as before, around her neck. Nineteen-sixties-era twin-lens Rolleiflexes did not survive getting wet, much less getting drowned. And immediately after the Annie's-father thought and the camera-drowning thought had splashed over her brain, another thought swam up to it: Her keys surely had fallen out of her pocket and sunk to the bottom. But wait: Her keys were on a ring that was attached to a small, round, colorful plastic thingy that was supposed to look like a tiny hot-air balloon, so maybe they'd float! But wait: That was worse. If that were true, then they were being swept along, bouncing their way to Philadelphia already, if not Morocco. So even if she and all her friends lived, they'd have no way to get home. Louey couldn't hold her breath any longer, and her camera was weighing her down. Panic rose in her throat like a tide.

Then, somehow, her head was above water, and her lungs were furiously filling with air, and Louey Levy had instantly developed a new top priority: learning to swim. She had seen people swimming a million times. It looked so effortless!

One arm forward; other arm forward; kick! Kick for all you're worth! That's how you propel yourself. Kick! Kick! And, son of a gun, she felt herself making a little progress. But where was Annie? She hadn't heard a sound from Annie in a long, long time. Had it been fifteen minutes? Twenty minutes? If she could only keep her head above water and gather enough breath, she could yell, "Annie! Annie! Where are you?!"

The hard truth is that the difficulty of finding Annie was compounded by the fact that Louey had not yet opened her eyes. In her entire life, Louey had never been able to open her eyes underwater. In a pool, she couldn't bear the sting of the chlorine, and here, she was afraid she'd be blinded by stinking, eely, prickly things: the nettlefish, crawlybugs, riverworms, slimeworts, seaweed and leeches that she was trying so, so hard not to breathe into her lungs. But by now— how long had it been since their canoe overturned?—Annie might be drowning in the brown, awful water. She called out in a squeaky voice to her friend but could hear no reply over the roar of the river. Or was her own heart pounding so loudly that it was deafening her?

To make things worse, she couldn't figure out how to turn in any direction, with the current so strong and nothing to push off of. It was hard enough just to keep moving her arms and kicking. But this was serious. She had to find Annie and save her; she had to open her eyes, even if only to see, as her last sight on earth, the rock that was about to crush her head.

As had happened before to Louey Levy when she really, really needed to do something, she found that she could do it. She summoned her courage and opened her eyes. There was Annie, beside her and just a few feet away, making childlike swimming motions with her arms and legs but, like Louey, swiftly being carried downstream. And the two of them were still near the middle of the river, but a bit more toward the Pennsylvania side.

"You OK?" Louey called urgently. Not that she could do anything if the answer were no.

"Yeah, I'm OK!" Annie panted. "Let's get to shore!"

So, for what felt to Louey like hours, they did a version of swimming. Louey kept a bit ahead 'til her shoulders hurt so bad from fruitlessly flailing her arms and fruitlessly kicking her legs that she couldn't go on. She would have to give up and be carried off, and her head would be banged against the rocks, and she'd be knocked out and her lungs would fill with water, and her body would be found—if at all—somewhere in the Delaware Bay, probably, off of New Jersey. She arched her neck backwards to keep her face from going under. It was while she was in that position, looking at the sky with her heart beating in her eyes, that the Phil Ochs song, "Pleasures of the Harbor" floated into her consciousness: "Soon your sailin' will be over; / Come and take the pleasures of the harbor ..." In her head, it played slowly, an almost eerie sound, with strings and flutes.

This is a good song to die to, Louey thought; *very comforting and gentle and welcome-to-the-next-world. If I live through this, I'll have to write that down somewhere where Dad or Clare or Danny can find it: "For my funeral, please play 'Pleasures of the Harbor,' by Phil Ochs, so that I can hear it as I swim away to Heaven (or wherever the Hell I'm going to.)"* But then she thought, *No, I've never been a swimmer; that wouldn't make sense for me. What would be a good death-bed song for me? Let's see. ...*

She was mentally running through a list of songs she hoped would be played at her funeral when she noticed something: She was drifting closer to the Pennsylvania side of the river. It was only, like, 25 feet away! It would be crazy to die now, so close to shore! With a lurch, Louey grabbed a jagged rock that was protruding from the water and let her body stretch out flat to the downstream side of it, grateful for the rest and for the feel of the water flowing fast under her bruised legs.

"Grab on!" she yelled, reaching a hand to Annie, who wordlessly grabbed it before getting a hold on the rock herself. Now they were stretched out side-by-side in the rushing river, like two kids learning to swim by holding onto the edge of a pool, or perhaps two particularly incompetent salmon headed upstream. They needed to catch their breath, they both knew, and regain strength for one last mighty swim to a place they hoped would be shallow enough for them to stand without getting knocked down by the current.

They were too winded to speak, but after a minute or so Louey's eagerness to get to land, plus all the adrenaline coursing through her, prompted her to say, "You ready?"

Annie grimly nodded.

"OK; let's go!"

She didn't care about the mosquitoes that were biting her face, ears and shoulders. She didn't care about her precious, useless camera that was still hanging from her neck. She didn't care about the lost canoe, the lost paddles, and the lost backpacks with their food and drinks in them. She was focused solely on survival. The "Dueling Banjos" theme from the movie "Deliverance" began playing in her head. To that tune, she launched herself towards Pennsylvania, an impenetrable wall of prickle-bushes that was the one and only goal of her heart.

At her second great kick, her knee hit something. Then her fingers jammed on something. Sand. Sand and muck and rocks cushioned by long, stringy green crap. She stood up straight, the dictionary-picture of the word "bedraggled" in her soaking T-shirt and cutoffs, and was surprised and grateful to find that the river was about 14 inches deep.

How could she have known? She thought the mighty Delaware was a real river, two hundred feet deep or so, like rivers were supposed to be! Like the Hudson! But anyway: Who cared? They would live! She looked back and saw Annie just a few feet behind and off to one side of her, also vertical and staggering toward shore, zombie-like, panting, not looking at her.

A few seconds later they threw themselves onto the muddy riverbank. They did nothing at first but swat at mosquitoes and say, "Thank God," and "Oh my God I thought we were gonna die," and "The others must be calling the cops by now," and statements of that nature.

She peeled her right pocket open. Her car keys were still there! Some of her panic faded as she said out loud: "Baruch haShem, baruch haShem!"

Annie, still standing, raised a salient point.

"Where's our canoe?"

Louey thought she'd read somewhere that canoes always float, even filled with water. Why hadn't she grabbed onto it when it flipped? As it was, the canoe, the paddles, the backpacks—all had gone bouncing down the Delaware. Louey didn't care. They were alive! Her Rollei was, of course, ruined, but maybe she could get the Record to pay for it? Since she sometimes used it for them?

Hahahahaha.

But now they had to think, and that was something Annie was good at. Their friends must have seen their empty canoe whipping along, Annie reasoned, because without them in it, it would be light as a cork. And if they had seen it, they would have been terribly alarmed, and leapt into action. They were probably right now paddling hard against the current, over the rocks and rapids, trying to find them, yelling for them as loud as they could, one canoe near the Pennsylvania side and one nearer the New York, and scanning the river for their bodies. Who knew how many miles downstream they had been swept? They themselves had no idea. They could hear no traffic—only rapids tumbling and birds chirping and mosquitoes buzzing.

"So, look; let's just keep walking south," Annie said. "The whole trip is only five miles, the contract said. It's got to be only a mile or so farther, to where the Outfitters bus is supposed to meet us to pick us up at noon, remember? The contract said there's a 'short, wide' path from the riverbank there up to a road, and there's a big red sign there that you can see easily from the river. That's exactly what the contract said. We should be able to find it easily. And, listen: We might see the others, coming back to look for us, before we even get to that spot."

Louey hadn't read that part of the contract. Or any other part. But she was happy to hear about this, and to go along with Annie's plan.

So off they walked along the steep bank, pocked with the holes of fiddler crabs. They were now so covered with bites that mosquitoes had no place to land that wasn't already taken.

"Do mosquitoes bite right through other mosquitoes' bites, or avoid them, on the theory that all the best blood has already been sucked out of there?" Louey mused aloud.

"What time is it, do you think?" Annie replied.

"I don't know; noon? I bet it's close to noon, though. It's hot enough to be noon." Louey had left her watch in the car with her wallet, so they wouldn't get wet.

They trudged in silence for what Louey guessed was three or four miles, breathing hard on the steeply slanted shore, the mud sucking their sneakers off their feet now and then with a juicy, yucky sound as though it were trying to eat them. Louey wondered if it were quicksand, but said nothing about that. Finally, as they scraped past the dense river's-edge prickles and brambles, they heard, then saw: humans! Adults! On a flat rock that rose a foot or so above the middle of the river. Just a few yards farther, and they could make out that it was their friends!

"They must be calling for help, or trying to signal for help using a mirror," Louey said. She was surprised, however, that none of them was yelling, "Help! Help!" Oddly, it sounded as if they were just laughing and chatting. She must be hallucinating; this group of carefree revelers couldn't be them, could it? She started running, stumbling every few steps but somehow staying upright, panting, cupping her hands on both sides of her mouth and calling loudly and slowly, "We're-O-K! We're-O-K!" Like a chant at a football game.

Sandy, now clearly visible standing in the middle of the rock, pointed toward Louey. She and the others stopped frolicking and gathered silently, staring as their two companions, canoe-less and paddle-less in Pennsylvania, drew nearer. Sandy shook her head with a confused frown, cupped her hands around her mouth and called back, loudly and slowly, as though mocking Louey's tone, "Why ... wouldn't ... you ... be ... O-K!"

Jake chipped in with the obvious question: "Where's your canoe?"

This is what had happened to the four strong swimmers: They had pulled up in their two canoes at a flat-topped rock, some 15 feet wide, whose gently sloping sides protruded just a foot or two above the water. They had dragged their canoes and equipment up there and peeled off their clothes, so that they were all in just their swimsuits, and had begun some kind of body-surfing festival, sliding down a slippery part of their perch into the river, laughing and having just a jolly old time and never thinking once of Louey and Annie. It was clear after each splash, as they waded back to the rock, that the water was quite shallow here.

"What time is it?" Louey called out urgently. She and Annie had arrived at a spot on the shore that was even with the others, and now didn't even have to yell; that's how close they were. She was afraid the Outfitters' bus would have given up waiting for them, or its driver would have seen the overturned canoe and paddles crashing past the meetup place, and had already called for a rescue. She scanned the sky for a helicopter.

Jake took his watch from his backpack and replied

through cupped hands: "Nine-twenty. Why? You in a hurry? What are you doing over there?" And then he repeated, "Where's your canoe?"

Louey saw that there would be a long story to tell.

"You tell it," Annie muttered, without looking at her.

So the bedraggled adventurers waded through the shallow water, which never became more than waist deep, out to the rock, and there Louey told it.

They made her tell it again and then once again, because it didn't make sense. When it flipped over, why didn't they just grab onto their canoe and get back in? Why didn't they just swim with it a bit, if they really were in a spot that was over their heads (which Mike seriously doubted)? Why didn't they just drag it to shore and empty it of water there, and shove off again?

"We can't swim. We can't swim," Louey said.

Jake, Charlie and Sandy, too, couldn't believe that the water was deep enough anywhere in that area of the river that day, that they'd have needed to swim. They looked at each other quizzically, but said nothing.

What Charlie couldn't believe was that they had let go of their paddles.

"Don't you know that paddles always float?"

"The paddles were halfway to Philadelphia already. You see how fast the river is flowing today! Oh, man: I guess you just had to be there," Louey said, and that, mercifully, put the inquisition on hold.

Neither Louey nor Annie minded about the food they'd lost, especially since the others very generously shared their own snacks with them. Jake offered not only half of his chips and Coke, but also his bug-spray and sunblock to Louey.

After 10 minutes of telling her tale and eating and scratching and answering the questions of her companions, Louey climbed into the middle of Jake and Charlie's canoe, and Annie got into Sandy and Mike's, and off they went. Now Louey did notice, as Jake stood in the river and steadied their canoe for this embarkation, that the water was not even hip deep on him.

Now the paddlers kept their canoes close together, so they could all continue to ask questions of Annie and Louey and hear the answers.

"Why were you trying to *swim*? The river's only a few feet deep around here!" Mike said.

"You mean you walked all the way on the bank?" Charlie said. "How did you do that? There's no path over there!"

"What would you have done if we hadn't stopped to body-surf—would you have walked all the way to the red sign?" Sandy said. "And where are your backpacks?"

At this point Louey was answering rather automatically. In her head she was far away, wondering how it could possibly be only 9:20 in the morning—the very same morning they had started out. She had almost asked Jake, "Nine-twenty a.m., or nine-twenty p.m.?" She and Annie had just survived a harrowing—it felt like—10 hours or so in a river and then a bug-infested jungle. Their canoe had flipped over! They had almost drowned! They had been swept away and battered by rocks—their elbows and knees and legs were wonderfully bruised already; their companions had noticed that—and had swallowed stinky, murky Delaware River water while swimming for their lives 'til their muscles were cramping.

She was starving, sunburned, and covered in the bites of, no doubt, malaria-riddled mosquitoes; it must be nearly dinnertime, and they hadn't had lunch, while all these pampered lifeguards and super-swimmers—their so-called "friends," who hadn't spent one minute looking for them—hadn't given them a single thought, in fact, even when they hadn't seen nor heard from them in hours—were having a lovely time for themselves, sliding and swimming around and splashing and laughing and being gay as Youth itself. It could not possibly be that just twenty minutes had passed since they'd all slid into the river at the Outfitters.

And yet, it was. Huh. And now here she was, safe in the company of her best friends, who really did care about her, soon to be safe in her dry, wonderful car whose key was, miraculously, still safely jammed into the pocket of her cutoffs. Huh.

Mike and Sandy, especially, remained amazed that anyone could fall out of a canoe, much less fear drowning while wearing life vests. They kept pestering Louey and Annie about how that possibly could have happened, and why in the world they had not hung onto their canoe and paddles, and how they could have thought they were in danger in four feet of water, and why they'd tried to swim anyway, when they could have just stood up and slogged their way to either shore.

For her part, Louey was amazed that no one had seen Louey and Annie's empty canoe, or their paddles.

"Well, we weren't looking for them! Why would we be looking for them?" Sandy asked with her now more or less perpetual confused-looking smile.

"Well, I'd think a goddamned canoe bobbing along upside down, and two paddles with bright yellow blades on them, might catch your attention," Louey said, all annoyed.

"It wouldn't be upside down," Mike pointed out. "Canoes don't float along rivers upside down. They'd be kind of on their sides, if they hadn't righted themselves."

Well, look at this, Louey thought. *Here I am with Esther Williams and Johnny fucking Weissmuller, who literally can't imagine any trouble arising on a raging river.* But she couldn't stay mad at her friends for long. Relief and gratitude buoyed her as if she were riding one of those air-filled tubes that kids use in swimming pools, and she felt light and safe now, on top of the water. Everything was beautiful and interesting.

A belted kingfisher posed on a bare limb overhanging the New York side. Down he plunged into the water, wings folded upon his back 'til he was thin as a pencil. Straight and fast he dove, and disappeared, and up with a fish he came! It looked as if it weighed as much as he did, yet he flew with it easily, smacked it around on his branch a few times, flipped it above his head and gulped it down whole, catching it in his wide-open bill as a boy would toss a piece of popcorn and catch it in his mouth.

"Whoa! Did you see that?" she said.

"What?" Jake and Charlie asked.

But they were already past it, and she didn't want anyone twisting around in a boat to see anything. Ever again.

"Just a pretty bird," she said mildly, with no energy in her voice. They paddled on in silence. But she never forgot the bird, master of the river.

They saw the sign for "Outfitters Pull-In" a couple of

hours later, and the paddlers pulled hard for the little beach on the Pennsylvania side. There they had their lunches at a fine picnic table, where Mike, Sandy, Charlie and Jake offered to share their sandwiches and water with their two hapless pals. Louey didn't want to take any more of anyone's food, and besides, she wasn't hungry. She was too full of peace and happiness to eat. She was content to watch her friends jabbering away, laughing and enjoying themselves. She had a feeling that she would sleep that night, though sleeping was never her strong suit. And she was eager to get home and write about this. Annie, now rested and well-fed, had regained her usual conviviality and also seemed close to seeing the humor in the day.

The Outfitters bus driver, a college-age kid, arrived as scheduled and cheerfully asked how everything had gone. Then, looking about, he quickly added, "Wait. Where's your third canoe and the other paddles?"

Jake said, "Well, we've got good news, and we've got bad news." But in the end, it was just about all good news. It seemed that this was not the first time that something like this had happened on the Delaware. The company was insured for the loss of its canoe and paddles, all of which would probably still turn up somewhere in a snag in the river anyway. All the equipment was emblazoned with the Outfitters name and phone number. The bus driver thought the whole thing was kind of funny, and he was correct in his prediction of what would happen when they got back: All Louey and Annie had to do was sign something, and they could be on their way. Jim Outfitter, or whatever his last name was, seemed OK with everything that happened on the river short of drownings.

Annie signed the paper and Louey signed it before she even read it, and none of them ever heard from the Delaware Outfitters again.

The Rolleiflex, against all odds, was not irreparably damaged. She sent it off to the factory and they were able to fix it, at hideous expense—more than it would have cost to buy a new, 35-millimeter. When she got it back, she kissed it, and it worked OK, but she could feel ever after a slight reluctance—a resentful hesitation—on the part of the shutter, to operate when she pressed the button. Also, the shutter's click was softer and lower-pitched than before, and the resulting photos all had a thin, hazy halo at their edges.

Never get a camera wet, she wrote as "No. 1" on the list in her diary, under the heading, "What I Learned from My Experience on the River." She had recently become interested in trying to figure out if she had learned anything at all in her life, or anything important, anyway, and had begun writing down things she thought she might have learned. *That's the worst thing that can happen to any camera. Also: Don't go swimming in the Delaware River while your wonderful camera, which helped get you through college and has been your faithful friend for your whole life ever since then, is hanging around your neck. For it will just bang against your stomach and collect sand and mud and chunks of river-crap for hours and hours and hours and hours. Or 10 seconds. Or whatever it was. It will go from trusty to rusty, in a heartbeat! And then you'll really be sunk.*

And she also added into her diary something else she was thinking: *We're all just like the leaves that drop into a river as it flows to the ocean. We are borne along taking the sunshine and the rain as they come, with no control over any of it, and* we get scratched and dragged under and dinged and mashed and ripped along the way, but that only makes us more interesting. The old ones are more colorful, of course, but our beauty is not in our own color, but in the crazy-quilt we make as we get tossed around, a kaleidoscope of all the leaves that are being swept along with us. New leaves drop into the stream all the time, and you get to meet them and comfort them if they're scared, and tell them stories about your older friends—the ones that have been sailing along with you for a long time, and also the absent ones. We get blown around and lifted up into the air or sloshed against a rock, growing ever softer as we age, turning into a piece of the most diaphanous lace or spider-web filigree, more air than veins as we slowly dissolve. And then finally, you yourself leave. You hit a snag or get caught in an eddy off to one side and stick there, swirling and spinning round and round while the others—the ones who've loved you and whom you've loved or hated and fought with—those who've played the role of the villains and heroes in your story—continue along past the calm places and the falls and rapids, meeting new people on their way. And if you're lucky, you get a chance to wave goodbye.

G-d must be very pleased with the river bubbling and lapping, because to G-d it must sound like people laughing and working together, all "busy" doing stuff and trying to make sense of it all and to figure out why we're here at all and, at the end, what it all meant. And then finally, She tells you. And that's wonderful! And it would be wonderful even if all it meant was: You were supposed to enjoy the ride.

And Louey Levy did get old and did love getting old, but along the way, there was this other thing that happened at the Record.

Months after the river trip with her pals, on the bitterest winter day ever in the history of Middletown, N.Y.,—seriously, you could look it up—she started smelling smoke just as she arrived at the paper. Not the soft, musky cigar-fog that she loved so well as it wrapped around Plummer's neck and head like a balaclava; not the cigarette smoke from Charlie's ashtray or Annie's; just acrid, bitter, yucky smoke that said something awful was burning. Something like plastic.

"Holy crap, what's that smell?" she said, frowning and sniffing before she even took her coat off or pulled her chair out from the table. Plummer paused from banging on his typewriter and looked around the floor as though he had lost his cat, but he said he didn't smell anything. No wonder, with that big, fat cigar in his mouth all day.

The smell was coming from the very top of the steep street that ran down to the Record. Jackson took a 35-millimeter camera from a desk drawer and held it out to her like a quarterback handing off the ball to a runner, but she waved her refurbished Rollei in reply and hustled back outside with pen and notebook in her mittened hand. The smell was now very strong. She could see a huge, funnel-like cloud of thick, black smoke at the top of Mulberry Street. How had she not noticed that, coming in to work? WWKE, the radio station she listened to all the time, that played all the great Top-40 songs and now some that they called "hard rock" as well, was up there. She ran all five blocks from the Record, holding her camera against her chest so it wouldn't bounce.

At first, Louey thought it wasn't so bad; there'd be a tremendous financial loss, but everyone must have gotten out safely; there were no people yelling or leaning from the windows crying for help, thank God. But she'd have to ask a firefighter, as soon as one was free: Was anyone still in there? Surely not "Marcus in the Morning," her favorite morning guy with all the"oldies" quizzes you could call in and answer? No, he must be gone by now. Surely not "Drivetime Davey," who played oldies as well as the new songs? She felt nervous and a little sick.

A crowd had gathered, despite the weather. WWKE was on the top floor of this four-story building, and surely WWKE was insured, and would recover, better than ever. She would miss her rock and roll meanwhile, though, if they didn't have any backup facilities. But they must. They were a business. That was a question she'd now have to find the station manager to ask: What were they going to do meanwhile? Go off the air? For how long? Were all their records ruined? And of course, was anyone hurt? That would be the first thing. But it didn't seem as if anyone was hurt.

The smell of large stacks of vinyl burning is not pleasant, however. As she approached, she was becoming alarmed that the acrid black smoke felt like it was coating her lungs, as well as leaving oily, sticky soot all over her camera, which indeed been "refurbished" at the Rollei factory after its dunking in the river the previous spring.

Then she heard something ugly. Two ugly somethings. She turned to see what it was, and then she tried to take a photo of it, but her focus-glass was all fogged over from the cold, and then she couldn't turn the film-advance crank; it seemed to be frozen; it broke off the camera. Then she fainted.

She woke up on her back in a stationary ambulance right

there at the top of the hill with a blood-pressure cuff around her upper left arm and a very calm woman sitting next to her.

"There you are," the woman smiled, patting her hand. "Feeling a little better?"

"Yes. Yes, I'm OK. What did I do, faint?"

"Yes. Did you eat breakfast today?" As though there were no other reason why anyone would faint today. Just a regular day, featuring two naked, black, crisp bodies like the bits on the edges of a macaroni and cheese casserole.

She sat up—way too fast for the nice lady, who tried to push her back down—and thanked her, and said she was fine, and leapt off the back of the ambulance. She walked back down the hill staring at nothing, thinking of nothing, feeling nothing, to bang out her story, but when she'd finished it ("Fire officials could not say immediately what caused the blaze. Station managers were unavailable for comment yesterday."), she told Jackson she had to go home sick. He looked at her and said, "Sure, go; take care of yourself. It's very upsetting to see that kind of thing."

At her apartment, she got right into her bed and tried to sleep, but sleep wouldn't come. She sat on her mattress on the floor, with her back against the wall, and wrote in her diary.

Dear Diary,

I wonder what the DJs thought as they jumped, all burning up. They say your life flashes before you; I hope that's true. I hope G-d sends you, as you're dying, pictures of the good parts—the good things you did and said to make people feel better, or the kind things you wanted to say and the merciful, joyful scenes you wanted to create but just couldn't because you didn't have the guts or the money or the time. Maybe G–d sends those scenes to you, as a kind of parting gift! Maybe we really do all Exit through the Gift Shop.

The rest of the night she spent writing a poem. And then in the morning, for the first time in a long, long time, she fell asleep.

Two Dead in Blaze at WWKE

Disc jockeys die queerly
as the radio station burns in winter.
They thud to the hard rock walk four flights below,
absurd, flaming snowflakes. But it's too cold to snow.
The reporter only knows she wants to go.
"Christ," someone says, and someone else says, "Twenty–below."

On impact, the DJs shatter.
The weather has them brittle as a platter.
Splintered glass glitters in the beds of their charred, bare skin,
and shards of their joints and their battered bones point
across the knobs of spines to the reporter.

Her breath fogs the focus–glass: She can't remember why she is there.
The film–advance lever snaps in her mittened hand.
"This is not being recorded," she thinks, and long ago, she'd care,
but not while she stands in the razor–wind,
her face cut by gusts of twenty–below air.

The busted boys are black and naked. The reporter wants to know
why disc jockeys would be naked in the winter,
in the red and ruined snow.
And now the firemen come, while from inside somewhere,
still the demented jingle, the Number-One single blare.

They try to pry them from the ice. No luck.
They stick, like the water is stuck in the hoses,
and reporters in poses they don't understand,
while stars and cops' bubble-lights
freeze moments the reporter too clearly sees
silently piercing her life
like pricks from the tips of invisible picks
so fine that, for the longest time,
you feel nothing—nothing at all.

She needed a change. Louey needed to shed the sleezy politicians and their reps and the reps of companies and organizations who would stroll into the newsroom with pre-written stories about themselves or their companies or organizations (sometimes with photos) and expect that those stories would just magically appear in the paper the next day exactly as they'd written them. And then when they didn't just appear that way—when Louey needed to get more information, or a quote from someone else, or the other side of the story, or more likely when the "story" they'd given her was not a story at all, but just a self-serving promotional piece for themselves, so it never ran at all—they would call her and bawl her out for being biased against them. Everybody else—Charlie, Annie, all of them—had their own beats, which kept them out of the office for 90 percent of their day; they just came running back late in the afternoon or in the middle of the evening to make phone calls and type up their stories. Louey, as the "general assignment" reporter, had to hang out in the newsroom all day, sifting through the promotional crap that PR people had dropped into the basket on the copy desk, rewriting the halfway decent ones, calling the several local police departments to see if anything had happened before her shift, and waiting for all-too-rare feature assignments. After about a year or so, it already was getting tiresome.

She was also tired of getting dressed in her miniskirts and good blouses every day, and pulling on those damned pantyhose, which very often developed runs from her rather raggedy fingernails or from some unknown object that she would inevitably brush against. On the other hand, she did love working the 4-to-midnight, Sunday-through-Thursday shift. Sunday through Thursday was a coveted schedule, since it felt to its lucky owners almost as if they had a 3-day weekend every week. It gave you one weekday off—Friday—to go to the bank or your dentist ("or your accountant," was the example Tim Clay always used) without having to take a vacation day. Plus, nothing much happened on Sundays, and the reporters could go out for dinner ("lunch," they always called it) instead of brown-bagging it, and often several of them could go together, which was great fun. The Sunday-through-Thursday schedule also rocked because that meant that Saturdays were always somebody else's problem. Saturday was the hardest day due to all the sports stories and the many, many pages those poor bastards had to fill for Sunday's huge paper, which routinely exceeded 80 pages in length, even in the slowest months.

Finally, the time came: One of the copy-editors left, and there was a vacancy on the Desk. Louey jumped at it, still hoping to keep the Sunday-through-Thursday shift. No such luck. She got the job but was moved to Tuesdays-through-Saturdays. Ah, dammit. Still, she'd have one weekday off per week. Not bad.

She did expect a bigger increase in pay for being an editor rather than a reporter but was disappointed: The raise was so small as to be almost unnoticeable. Still, she settled into her new gig pretty quickly. She took to wearing comfy, men's shirts to work that were so large and splotched with colors that they looked like painters' smocks, and indeed that's pretty much what they had been when she acquired them back in her college days, when she had done some silk-screening, painting and other artwork. She wore them hanging outside her jeans—and jeans were something no reporter could ever wear to work. The men on the desk had always dressed like slobs, but for Louey the copy-editors' relaxed dress code was liberating and relaxing. All she needed was a palette, a paintbrush and a beret, and she'd look just like an art major who'd got lost on her way to class. And yet, with all that, she wasn't much worse dressed than any of the other copy-editors, who, like her, never had to leave the office and whom no reader or PR guy ever came to see.

Headline-writing was a word-puzzle Louey enjoyed and was good at: Fit words describing the story into the space allotted to you, and sometimes, the less space you had, the more fun it was. Going with "eyes" instead of "considers," "hike" instead of "raise," "panel" instead of "committee" was second nature to her.

On the Record copy desk, you got extra pats on the back—though no extra money, of course—for any alliteration, light-hearted turns of phrase, good puns or intriguing angles you could work into your headlines, and since that type of snappy "headline-speak" came so easily to Louey, she got lots of praise. Which is to say, her work gave her nothing except the great pleasures of making her friends and colleagues laugh, and knowing she was appreciated.

Correcting their spelling and making sure nothing crucial was left out of their stories were two things the reporters appreciated and routinely thanked Louey for, and they often tried to ensure, via whispers and quick phone calls, that she, not anyone else, was the one who grabbed their copy out of the big basket on the desk.

She did her job fast and well and often drew Tim's praise. He sometimes read her heads out loud, drawing the other editors' laughter and applause. Louey was usually the first one to yell out a usable answer when, sweating, snapping his fingers and punching himself in the head with 30 seconds to go before deadline, another copy-editor would rise and call out, "What's a longer word for 'deny'?" or "What's a shorter word for 'increase'?" or "Do we capitalize District on second reference in a story about the school district?" or "Is it biannual or biennial? He means twice a year!"

She loved the immediacy of it. Every question needed an answer right now, and everything was in the present tense. It was "3 die," not "Three died." It was "Council votes," not

"Council voted." It was insider, tabloid-headline-writer's language, with words no human ever spoke, though everyone knew what they meant: "Smith mulls try for Dem nod."

Also, as in all tabloids, the honorifics were discarded, in headlines as well as throughout the stories. It was "Jones," not "Mr. Jones" or "Dr. Jones" or "Mayor Jones." "Jones denies he's ill." "Jones misses 5th straight meeting." "Jones says he's ready to return." "Jones dies." Cut to the chase: What they were writing was too important to waste ink on "Mr.," "Mrs.," "Miss" or even the new one, "Ms." Get to the point. Cut the crap. Drop the niceties and the articles, definite or indefinite. Just tell people what happened and tell them fast. Hurry: Backshop is waiting for that page. Go. Go. Go!

This paper should be called the Middletown Miracle, Louey thought proudly. *We make every damned deadline every damned night! We make deadline for the Sullivan County edition! The Pike County edition! The Newburgh edition! Late Final! Somehow, we make them all. Sometimes by just a few seconds, but we make them.*

The Record quickly hired a new general-assignment reporter to replace her, and now Louey Levy wasn't the newest kid on the paper anymore. She was an old-timer—a 23-year-old who somehow, practically overnight, had become a veteran reporter and editor. Her replacement, a fellow right out of college, might have thought that Louey had been there for 18 years, if it weren't for the fact that she still looked about 18 years old.

Louey was bemused and surprised to find herself feeling a bit comfortable. Is that what that feeling was? Comfortable? It also felt a bit ominous. She was a grownup, no question, with her own car, apartment and job. Was this it, though? Would she be doing this for the rest of her life? She certainly could see herself being OK with doing her copy-editing well, being respected for her expertise at solving the little head-line-puzzles, winning Tim's "Headline of the Night" award regularly (prize: getting a pencil thrown at her) and having a few good friends, which was all she'd ever wanted or needed. But that Peggy Lee song, "Is That All There Is?" by the Great Jewish Composers Jerry Leiber and Mike Stoller, kept playing in her head. She'd hear it most often at night, when she was supposed to be sleeping but instead used all that empty time to try to figure out what else there was.

One copy-editor, Doug Hohn, was older than the others. He was really incredibly old; he looked as old as Louey's father. He was approaching retirement age, for sure. But unlike Abe Levy, Doug Hohn was drawn and haggard. Too many years on the Desk, perhaps. And too many slugs from the flask in his coat pocket. Louey saw him every day. She was assigned, in fact, to the same copy-desk seat he used, since he was the Dayside guy and was always leaving around 3, just when she arrived. They usually had time to exchange only pleasant "Hello"s and "Have a good night, now"s and "Take your time; I'm in no hurry"s. Doug always seemed in a hurry, though, to get the heck out of there, just like the reporters at the end of their shifts. Nobody hung around the Record long.

As the Dayside copy-editor, Doug had an entirely different portfolio from everyone else. He assembled the colored Sunday comics pages, the advice and puzzle pages, the stock-market pages—all the back-of-the-book pages that were filled with syndicate- and AP-provided material, in other words—and he almost never had occasion to interact with the local reporters at all. He was an odd duck: a soft-spoken, reserved, elegant person with an almost British affect, who always wore a fedora atop his thinning, grey hair.

Then one evening a couple of months after Louey started working on the Desk, Doug stopped still on his way out and gazed at her.

"Tell me your name again," he said. Louey told.

"Levy?" he said. "As in, Abe Levy, who used to be the City Manager in Newburgh?"

"Yes."

A few seconds passed before he spoke again.

"So, you're Ruth Abrams's daughter, then?"

"Yes!"

Whoa. There was somebody here who knew her mother? Louey herself had hardly known her mother!

Doug Hohn grabbed the back of his chair as if he were going to faint, and he did actually go a shade paler.

"My God! You look just like her."

Louey looked nothing like her mother. Her mother was a beautiful, tall blonde who wore makeup and jewelry and always dressed impeccably. Louey was … not. But maybe Doug was talking about her nose, or her eyes, or her smile. Those she had.

"I loved your mother," he continued softly. "She was a lovely person. She was very caring and friendly. And funny! We loved her. We all loved her."

Louey said, "I know," as Doug continued, speaking over her: "She was a very good reporter, too—and fast! She could get hold of sources and get great quotes from them and write a story in ten minutes that would take anyone else two days. I heard you're good, too. And are you very fast, as well?"

Louey said, "I hope so." But obviously, she wasn't a reporter anymore; she was a copy-editor. Didn't he know that? She really wanted to get him to talk more about her mom. Ruth Levy had died so goddamned young.

Doug seemed to have revived a bit. "Well, I know you've got to get to work, but we have to have a cup of coffee someday, OK? When's your next day off? Sunday?" He sounded almost as excited as Louey was.

"Yes. Sunday."

"Well, that's too long to wait. How about meeting me for a late lunch at the Colonial Diner at 2 o'clock Saturday? I can leave at 2 if I don't take a lunch hour."

It was now Thursday; Louey could wait that long. She could wait 'til Saturday. Hell, she had waited her whole life to find someone who'd known her mother. The Colonial was just a few blocks from the Record. They could have a few laughs, and she could get lots of good stories about her mom from this sweet old newspaper guy, who'd worked with Ruth Levy, and still get to work on time. How great would that be? That would give her something to look forward to before starting her hard day. Plus, he probably would buy: He was older, and a man, and he might have five bucks saved up, despite working for the Record.

"Oh yeah, sure!" she said, with a big smile. "I'd be delighted to do that."

"Good! It's a date, then."

He tipped his hat to her—nobody even wore hats anymore, so that gesture was exceedingly charming and eccentric—and sauntered off. Louey called after him, "Great! So if I don't see you before then, I'll see you Saturday!"

Louey started while at work, and then continued when she got home after midnight, to make a list of all the things she would ask Doug Hohn. Tell me all your stories about her, she would say. Tell me everything you knew about her. Tell me the stories she told you. Tell me what she said about me, and about my brother and sister, and my dad. Tell me everything she said, wrote, wore, liked and drank. Did she really wear earrings to work—and high heels? I have a photo of her in a dotted Swiss navy dress with a matching navy-blue purse. Tell me what she laughed at; tell me things she said that made you laugh.

Oh, she had a whole list. She couldn't wait for Saturday afternoon.

The next day, just as he was leaving work, Doug Hohn died.

Louey breezed in to find him laid out stiff and grey on the copy desk. Ted Daley and Paul from Photography and the copy-editors were standing, silent, heads bowed, as if in prayer. Doug's eyes and mouth were open, as if he had died while trying to say something. He didn't look as if he were in pain, but it pained Louey—and Ted and Tim, too, it seemed—to look at him. Someone had put Doug's hat over his face and folded his dead arms over his stomach. Tim turned away and quickly walked over to Sports. As if he needed a change of scene, sort of. Louey followed him fast.

"Tim, what happened?"

"Nothing! He was just finishing his shift, and he stood up and dropped dead!"

"When?"

"Ten minutes ago! I had just gotten here. He never made a sound. He never groaned, or said he felt sick, or 'Oh God I'm having chest pains,' or anything! He just fell across the Desk. I called the ambulance; they're on their way. Paul tried to revive him, but he had no pulse. We didn't know what to do with him, so we put him on the desk." Louey looked back at the desk. Doug's ass was exactly where Louey would be editing stories that night.

Tim hadn't finished speaking when two EMTs wheeled a gurney up to the copy desk. Louey turned around to watch them take the stupid hat off Doug's face and feel his neck and his wrist and put a blood-pressure cuff on him and listen fruitlessly with a stethoscope for a heartbeat and bang fruitlessly on his chest and breathe into him for about two minutes before they, thank God, gently pressed his eyelids down over his opaque, dead eyes. As soon as they did that, both of Doug's arms slowly lifted straight up as in a zombie movie, and the EMT's wordlessly and gently pressed them back down to his sides. They then asked Ted a bunch of questions about Doug's personal life (name; age; address; divorced; two grown kids and their names and addresses. Ted had it all). Then they fished in Doug's pockets for his wallet and keys, which they gave to Ted, and Ted went with them to the ambulance and returned in a moment to close his office door and make the horrible calls to tell Doug's family the news.

All Louey could think of was, *Who's going to write the obit? And when? With all the writers around here, you'd think somebody would be assigned to write, like, a "memorial" or something. But they'd have to notify the family first, and then wait until funeral arrangements had been made, so all of that could be in the story, too. Or, would that be in a separate, paid obit, like everyone else's? Do we make staff's families pay for their obits? OK, I don't want to think about this anymore.*

Doug's body was wheeled away, and Louey sat down in his chair as she always did. Wait: Was his bottle of Scotch still in … yes. Yes, it was. She sat very still for a while as the other editors took their own seats in silence, and then she took out the bottle and drank a mouthful of booze from it. *Here's to you, Doug, my new friend, my mother's old friend. May you be at peace in Heaven, with all your deadlines gone.*

She took another quick swig and brought her chin down to her chest, staring at the desk where Doug had lain. Could she touch it? Could she put someone's story on it—three takes, four takes, five takes, pasted together into a long kite-tail—and take her red pen and read it and mark it up and send it to the "done" basket as though nothing had happened, without a prayer, without a … ?

An outstretched hand appeared next to the bottle. It was Jackson's. He gently took the bottle from her and had himself a long swallow before returning it to her. She swung her chair around to look at him.

"You know what the difference is between a drunk and an alcoholic?" he said.

No, what.

"We drunks don't have to go to all those damn meetings."

She somehow knew that that was an old joke, even though she had never heard it before. She also knew that she would remember it for a long, long time. It was a weird night, but they got through it.

"OK; let's play newspa-puh!" Tim yelled, and they all hopped to it, albeit mostly like robots.

Things slowly returned to normal. On Saturday they ran the paid obit that the family had submitted, and whoever wasn't working went to the funeral. Al Rome himself came in on Friday night and wrote a touching column about Doug, and his career, and what a good friend he'd been, and how he'd died doing what he loved. (*He did?* Louey thought. *He loved editing the huge fucking Sunday paper and the back-of-the-book pages in the weekend editions? He loved assembling the comics and the puzzles and the advice columns and the stocks? He loved not being a reporter for the Newburgh News anymore?*) Rome had left many details out of his column, such as Doug's divorce and, of course, his famous drinking. Instead, the Record played it as they would the death of a local celebrity or politician, with quotes from Ted and other colleagues who'd worked with him for many years.

At the Record, the guy with the five-foot-long toothbrush in his trunk wasn't the most eccentric photographer. That title went to Francis ("Frankie") P. LeFranc. Word in the newsroom was that Frankie kept in the trunk of his brown Renault, which was always breaking down, a wagon wheel. An actual wooden wagon wheel that he had lifted from an actual wooden wagon, apparently. It was for "slow news days," or days when the news had no "art" to go with it. He needed to pad his portfolio so he could be hired by *National Geographic* or *Paris Match*, or some other fancy publication. When he couldn't get some unusual angle or some odd, extremely closeup shot of a local politician or criminal, he would drive off to the nearest bucolic area—Otisville or the Black Dirt or Minisink or somewhere that had a rustic wooden fence, preferably with a horse munching hay in a field behind it. There he would take the wagon wheel out of the trunk (which was in the front of his car) and, despite all the rules against "faking" a photo, lay it in what he considered an especially artistic angle against the fence and shoot it, sometimes with the horse in focus and the wheel all fuzzy; sometimes with the wheel in focus and the horse and field all fuzzy. Then he needed a caption, and he couldn't write.

Well, technically, he could write; that is, he could type, albeit very slowly, but he considered that skill far beneath him, and he vastly preferred to give a copy of his art to Louey, right from the start of her employment as the general-assignment reporter. She did so well describing in one or two lines (whichever the Desk needed) the beauty of Orange County's sunsets or sunrises or rain dimpling a puddle on a city sidewalk or his favorite subject, old farm implements like rusted hay rakes, lying forlornly in some field, that she became his go-to girl for "bullshit captions." And word quickly spread among the other photographers. Whenever anyone needed a "bullshit caption" for an artistic shot of a tree or a hill or a snow-covered something-or-other, they came to good old Louey.

"Hey Louey, could you write some bullshit caption for this?" they'd say, laying a nice picture down in front of her.

"Sure," she'd say, turning it this way and that. "What is it?"

"It's a girl on a swing, taken from underneath the swing. I got her name."

"What park was she in?"

"No, no; it was right in her own backyard. I got the street name."

"Hey Louey, could you write some bullshit caption for this? It's shadows of a picket fence on the snow near Otisville."

"Hey Louey, could you write some bullshit caption for this? It's storm clouds over the river."

"What river?" The Wallkill, the Delaware and the Hudson all flowed through the Record's coverage area.

"What difference does it make? I don't know; I took it a week ago, during those four days of rain! The Hudson, I think! Say the Hudson!"

The Hudson it was. "Bullshit-Caption Queen" was a title Louey proudly bore. In addition to her own stories, she spent a great deal of time writing bullshit captions quite beautifully—and very fast.

As Louey Levy was the Queen of the Bullshit Captions, Frankie LeFrank was King of the Bullshit Photos. He was a world traveler, well-known in Paris, where he had been not only an acclaimed photographer with one-man shows all over Europe, but also a producer of dirty movies. What he was doing in Middletown no one knew. He had retained his highly imitable accent and his imperious, French way of speaking that annoyed Louey no end.

One dark, wet evening, coming back from her "lunch hour" at the Colonial, Louey found Frankie in the Record parking lot. His legs were outside his Renault, getting soaked, and he was leaning back into the car while trying to button his coat around his camera. Louey, carefree, was wearing a hooded raincoat and holding an umbrella over her head, as well.

"Frankie! Here! Use my umbrella! I've got a hood!" she called.

"No, but that is very kind of you," he said, taking the umbrella. "The worst thing you can ever do to a camera is get it wet."

"Oh, don't I know it."

As he locked the car, she noticed in the miniscule back seat an open box holding one woman's high-heeled shoe and one man's black dress shoe.

"Frankie, how come there are two different shoes in there?" she asked, highly amused.

"They're for art," he said. "To achieve great art, you have to evoke in the viewer two things: passion and drama. You can't just illustrate an accident story with a shot of a wrecked car being towed away. That's banal. But a shoe, a single shoe, in the middle of a rain-slicked road: That's passion. That's art."

Not twenty minutes later, Louey was writing a Bullshit Caption for Frankie. It was a closeup of a woman's high-heeled shoe, the one from his car, lying in the middle of a rainy highway. It was taken from a very low angle: Clearly, to get the shot, Frankie had had to lie down flat in the right lane of Route 17 North, where someone had driven drunk off the road where it twists up Wurtsboro Mountain in Sullivan County. Both the driver and his wife had died. In the photo, the lights of the emergency vehicles lit the raindrops on the shoe and the rain on the road.

Well, cheers to him for driving up there and getting that shot of the double fatal, Louey thought as she gazed at the photo.

He probably had to get his clothes and his stupid goatee soaking wet and lay the camera right on the asphalt, in this storm and everything, but what the hell can I write? She decided to go understated and not mention the shoe at all. The story wasn't about the damned shoe. She just took the bare facts from the story by Sandy and wrote: "Not much debris was left on the highway after the crash on Route 17 last night that killed two Monticello residents …"

Frankie sounded as if he believed that he had all the answers to everyone's problems, and that his special expertise was in the areas of love and sex. Louey had lately read about some problems that might be caused by birth-control pills, so she'd stopped taking them ("I'm never going to need them, anyway," she told Charlie with a resigned sigh), and that worked out fine, except that her old plague of intense menstrual cramps fired up again immediately. One night when she shouldn't have come in to work in the first place, because she was in so much pain, she was sitting bent over the copy desk, red-faced, sweating, with her head on her arms like a little kid who was being punished for talking too much in school. Along came Know-It-All LeFranc, who was approaching the Desk after dropping off film in the darkroom.

"What's the matter, Louey—boyfriend trouble?"

She quickly looked up and nodded without looking at him. She'd be damned if she would tell Frankie LeFranc that she was having her period.

"No, but listen to me. It's very simple. Either he was worth it, and you'll move on and find someone else, or he wasn't worth it, so you're better off without him."

There. There you had it. He swiped his hands together as

if to say, Problem solved. Problem solved by Frankie LeFranc, artiste, pornographer and therapist. Louey nodded and offered Frankie what she hoped was a French-looking, raised-eyebrow, wry smile and a sadder-but-wiser chuckle, and momentarily sat up a bit straighter. And Monsieur LeFranc sashayed off, satisfied in the certainty that he had fixed this pathetic copy-editor, poor misérable, in two seconds, hardly breaking stride.

After swallowing a few Midols from Annie's top drawer and two more from Charlie's, she started feeling better. Loopy, but better. At the Dugout that night, Louey's friends were seated at their usual table, a pitcher of beer for décor. She grabbed the liquid centerpiece with one hand and pulled up a seat for herself with the other. The waitress had thoughtfully set out a glass for her on a paper napkin. Still agitated about Frankie, she started right in.

"If two Americans are having a disagreement," she declaimed, "at one point, one of them always says, '*Yeah*, but ... .' LeFranc, on the other hand, always says, '*No*, but ... .' In fact—did you ever notice this?—he starts nearly every single sentence—not just in an argument, but in every discussion— with the word, 'No.' Someone could say, 'Gee, it's beautiful today,' and he'll say, 'No, but it's going to rain tomorrow.'"

"That's very European," Bill from Sullivan noted. "The Germans do that, too. It shows how culture affects language, and vice-versa. By starting every sentence with 'No,' it encourages the other speaker to continue talking to you, if only to defend his first proposition. Then *that* speaker says, 'No, but ... ,' and they have a nice, animated conversation at a sidewalk café all night long that way, until someone comes along and starts playing a guitar."

Bill was older than the rest of them, and he had been around. He was a World War II vet, and he was married. He rarely came to the Dugout, but they were all glad when he did.

Well, now I've learned something, Louey said to herself. She had been almost nowhere, and she was itching to travel around the world and learn a few things. Which was something she'd never done, despite going to college and grad school for five years. She started thinking about the places she'd most like to go to. Israel, for sure. Africa, for sure. Europe, absolutely. She wondered if she could get along in France with her high-school and college French courses and the total absence she'd had so far in her life of anyone to speak French to. Asia? Somehow, Asia was leaving her cold. She wanted to see Israel and Africa, though, for sure.

Louey was itching to ask Bill, as a veteran, what he thought of the war in Vietnam, but she didn't get a chance to that night. The other reporters had already started him talking about Hunter Thompson, who had worked at the Record with Bill and got fired for putting his foot through the candy machine there exactly one decade earlier.

"Kind of a nut," Bill said. "Nice guy, though."

"What did he do when he got fired?" Charlie asked. "Where did he go from the Record?"

"I think he went to Puerto Rico and worked for some papers there. He must be a quick study, because I'm pretty sure he didn't know a word of Spanish when he was here. The Black Dirt was getting to be a story, with how badly the farmers treat the Mexican migrant workers, and the working conditions on the farms, y'know, but Thompson never wrote anything about that. We missed out on a lot of stories because of not having any Spanish-speaking reporters back then."

"Or now," Louey interjected. "Do we have any Spanish-speakers? I don't think so."

No. No, they didn't. A few reporters claimed they could speak a few words of Spanish. Well, so could Louey, and she could also read a little. But she could not for the life of her understand what real Spanish-speakers were saying when she heard them talking with one another in the bodegas that were springing up around Middletown and Sullivan County. She had taken one Spanish class in high school, and that was it.

Finally, Jake walked in, and now the real purpose of their gathering could begin: It was a union meeting. Negotiations for their new Newspaper Guild contract were going to start soon.

"Why don't we make management hire a few Spanish-speakers? Why don't we make that a demand during negotiations?" Louey asked.

Mike from Sports sighed, "Yeah, like that'll ever happen."

"Well, we could try, and at least that way we'd be on record as to where we stand about it. Maybe we could give up something else to get a Hispanic reporter," Louey said.

"Yeah, like one of our non-existent Black reporters," Jake said.

"Seriously, aren't negotiations coming up this fall?"

"They're going on right now. The contract actually expired last December, and we've been in negotiations for almost a year. And they're not going well. We're not getting anywhere."

"Wait. So we're working without a contract right now?"

"Check out the contract!" Annie said. "It's on the inside back cover."

Louey had her contract on her. She always carried the little booklet in her shoulder bag.

"Oh yeah! I never noticed that. Or it never sank in, anyway."

"That's OK. The terms and conditions all stay the same until a new contract is signed," Charlie said. "That's standard language."

They sat in silence for a while, draining their beers.

"Hey, Joe Hill," Charlie said, pointing her chin at Louey and blowing a plume of smoke straight upwards, "why don't you join the bargaining team?"

"Yeah! We need you on it. We're not getting anywhere," Annie said.

"Yeah! New blood! Management will cave when they see the Angry New Copy Editor sitting across that table," Mike said.

"You know, it couldn't hurt. We could always use another voice," Jake said.

"Who's on our bargaining team now?"

"Just me, Annie and the lawyer the Guild assigned to us, Joe Louis. Not the boxer, though he spells it the same way. Nice guy. Not terribly effective."

Annie chipped in with some further description: "Yeah, he's this perfectly lovely, disheveled-looking guy who drives up from Long Island for every session. He's disorganized as hell, but he's passionate about the labor movement. He's a very nice guy, but … we're just not getting anywhere. We'd love to have you join the team, Louey. We really would."

"Other members have sat in from time to time," Jake said. "I mean, anybody can sit in with us. I think everybody at this table has sat in for a few sessions, haven't they?"

General nods. "But nobody has the time to devote to this. They just have too many other things to do, so that's why we've only had a couple fulltime members."

People have things to do? What do they do? Louey thought. *Why am I the only one without a life?*

The gang started chiming in: "Do it! Yeah, Louey, do it!" They seemed perfectly sincere.

God knew Louey had nothing else to do. And besides, it might be fun. Yelling at management? Yeah!

"Don't I have to be elected, or something?" she asked.

"All in favor of Louey joining the bargaining team?" Jake replied. He smiled without even looking up as he poured himself another glass of beer.

Unanimous.

"There. You're in. A toast to our newest negotiator!" Jake proclaimed. And they did toast.

"To Louey!"

"Yay, me!" Louey said, crossing her eyes and taking a sip of her beer.

Annie asked her what she thought her top priorities would be. Louey went back to what they'd been talking about: Force management to hire at least one Spanish-speaking reporter, for God's sake, and at least two Black reporters to cover Newburgh.

"Hey, I'd be happy with two more reporters of *any* color in Newburgh," Jake said. "It's so stupid to have just three of us in a city like that. It's just like New York in so many ways, they call it 'The Sixth Borough.' But we'll have to give up something to get them. What do you guys want to give up?" He looked around the table. He was always so goddamned realistic.

"A little salary?" Annie suggested. "If we all gave up, like, one or two percent, that might help pay for some new blood."

"Or we could give up the health insurance," Charlie said. "Does anybody here ever use their health insurance?"

"I sure as hell do, and my wife uses it, because I cover her, too," Bill said.

"Uh, if I may add," Jake said, "we fought long and hard for health insurance last time. This contract is the first one the Record has ever had that included health insurance, and it would be a terrible idea to give it up. The Guild negotiator has statistics on how much it's worth, and it's a lot. It's like, one-third more, on top of your salary. That's one of those things that you always think you don't need, until you need it." But the great majority of the Record's reporters were young and had yet to need it. Nobody but Bill, according to the results of a survey they'd sent around, had yet to go to a doctor without being driven there by their parents. So it wouldn't have been a priority at all, except that they loved Bill so much.

Louey then proposed that they let the Backshop people join the union. She couldn't understand why they weren't included in the Guild. They all worked for the same employer, right? And that would be more dues money coming into the Guild, right?

Jake regretfully reported that the Guild had rules about who could join, and that all members right now had to be on the Editorial side. No Backshop, no advertising people. He'd double-check with the Guild's lawyer, but he wasn't hopeful.

"I mean, Louey's right. It would be great to add ten new people to the ranks, for sure. Strength in numbers, right?" he said.

"Strength in numbers!" Louey offered, raising her glass. And they all repeated their new mantra, and clinked, but Jake was right: No one but reporters at that time was allowed to join the Newspaper Guild.

Four times a night, John, the press manager, would walk through Backshop yelling at everyone: once before the Sullivan County edition was due to go to press; once just before the Pike edition; again just before the Newburgh edition was due; and once more just before Late Final. He would see what the goddamned trouble was, and there was always goddamned trouble. The phototypesetters who were copying the edited stories were typing too slowly, and when they ran those copies through the rollers to coat the backs of the finished strips of stories with warm beeswax, they were waxing too slowly; the people who had to slice those stories apart with their single-edged razor blades were slicing too slowly; and always, Tim Clay was sending stories out to Backshop too slowly. Tim also would spend, when the two-page "flats" had been pasted up, way, way too much time reading every goddamned word of every goddamned story and headline before he would put his initials on the flat. Often, he would send a story back to the phototypesetters to re-do a headline which he himself had written but which was too long or too short for the space allotted for it.

Just when blood was about to burst through John's eyeballs each night, he would poke his head into the newsroom, careful not to take a step past the time-clock that divided Backshop from News, and yell to Tim to come back and see how many goddamned stories had been sent out too long or too short for the space assigned to them. He resented how incompetent Tim was in calculating how many inches of type would be needed for stories of how many words, one column wide at 11 points per line with one point of ledding, as they called and pronounced and spelled it, even though the Record hadn't used hot lead in 18 years. In the early years of newspapers, typesetters would slide paper-thin sticks of lead below each line of type so the letters' ascenders and descenders wouldn't touch one another. But that, as 60-something-year-old John knew better than anyone, was a long time ago.

Tim was, in fact, a little carefree about the space the stories needed. He usually just eyeballed the number of takes the reporters gave him and took a guess as to how much space would be needed for them. Earlier in the day, Jackson would estimate with his reporters roughly how many inches long each story would be. At the Page One meetings in mid-afternoon, Tim developed a rough idea of what stories should go where. Often, sadly, that idea was a bit too rough.

It was not uncommon that some planned-for stories didn't pan out at all. A source would get cold feet; a reporter would get sick; a promised good story would dissolve for any of a dozen reasons.

Then Tim had to "drop back and punt," as he would

loudly put it. He seemed to enjoy the challenge of those situations. He would stand up in the slot and yell, "OK; let's play newspay-puh!" He'd fill that suddenly empty space with an "anytime" story that had been sitting in the basket; or choose a story or photo from the Associated Press, if it was to run on an "inside" page (behind Page 10); or maybe he'd just ask the darkroom to make a photo on that page (the "art") a little bigger.

John was old-school. He refused to edit copy in any way. Several times each night, he would poke his head into the newsroom and call out, "Checkout, please!" And he'd say how many taped-together, two-page flats needed to be approved and initialed by someone from the newsroom before he could make an aluminum sheet out of them and put them on the press.

John not only wouldn't change an obvious mistake in a headline, but he also wouldn't call anyone's attention to it, either. The "checkout" function, including spelling, was Editorial's job. If the typed-up story slid out of the machine 10 inches too long for the space allotted for it, he had Backshop workers paste it onto the flat and crease it just above the headline for the story immediately beneath it. As a result, there would be several flaps, grocery-store-receipt sized, attached to nearly every page. But it was Tim who had to come back from Editorial and tell the grunts—that's what they proudly called themselves—where to slice the stories. While Tim went through all the flats at a maddeningly slow pace, hesitant to put his initials on any page until he'd read every word, John stood beside him munching Tums and running each OK'd flat up to the press. Up and down, up and down John went, growing more visibly annoyed throughout the night. Some nights, he would peek around the corner from Backshop and call out, "We're missing Page 14!" or, "There's no art for Page 3!" or some other brief description of any of dozens of disasters, and Tim would look up at the clock and yell back, "We've got nearly two minutes yet! Hang on, will ya?"

Tim came back muttering after each of his nightly ventures into Backshop. They didn't recognize a spelling error in a 42-point headline; they waited for him to come out and see it and send it back to the typists to re-do. They couldn't figure out where to slice a story; they waited for him to come out and do it. They didn't know that you couldn't just end a story with a comma. He couldn't believe how stupid those guys were.

Louey Levy, on the other hand, knew for a fact that the Backshop people weren't stupid. She had gotten to know some of the grunts over the first few months she was on the Desk, as Tim started asking her to go to the time clock that guarded the archway between Backshop and Editorial and slam a page or two into it so as to be time-stamped. Sometimes she peeked in to see what those guys were doing, and exchanged small talk with them for a minute or two. She found one tall, young guy, Gus Johnson, to be especially friendly. When she was a reporter, she'd never had any reason to meet the Backshop people. But hell, they seemed perfectly nice, and as smart as anyone else at the paper.

Louey started inviting Gus and the other Backshop workers to join the reporters at the Dugout after work, and Gus and a few others sometimes did come. On those rather rare occasions, Louey would join them at their table or buy them a pitcher of beer. She learned that their lives and their jobs were completely separate, and that, unlike the reporters, they never talked about the latter. They were all young and single. It was the first job for all of them, and they were contented with it. They were all from Middletown. None had gone to college, but some of them, including Gus, did have a GED. They didn't seem to read anything other than the paper and some motorcycle magazines, but they were kind, generous and good-natured.

The grunts worked bent over at waist-high, slightly upward-slanting, three-foot-square light-tables—slabs of glass lighted from below by long, fluorescent bulbs. Built into the glass were rows of light-blue, horizontal lines, precisely a quarter-inch apart. They used three-foot-long metal T-squares, marked in both inches and picas, to place the strips of stories perfectly straight in the columns of the two-page-wide flats. They smoothed the stories and headlines onto the flats where Tim indicated they should go, using the "roughs" he sent out as their blueprint. They bent leftover copy upward, creasing it into a shameful flap like a shirt-tail hanging out, for each story. They used the "safe" edge of the blades—the reinforced, thicker, rounded edge—to make minute adjustments to the angle of the waxed strips, shoving them a hair this way or that to ensure the stories were perfectly straight on the flats before they went to press. They took pride in their work, as the reporters did in their own.

Thousands of new blades, tightly wrapped in thin, tan cardboard, were available in old coffee cans on all the light-tables, like M&Ms in a candy dish. Blades that were used but

not too sticky or dull to use again were laid against the metal
"lips" at the bottom of the light-tables; those no longer sharp
enough to cut through the shiny strips of prose that spewed
all night from the warm beeswaxer were just tossed into the
large garbage can at the end of the two rows of light-tables.

One of the grunts' favorite games while awaiting stories
to paste up was to fling the single-edged blades into the six-
inch-high wooden "backboards" at the top of the light-tables.
Over the years the backboards, originally plywood, had taken
on a punky, cork-like texture, and the blades made a cool,
dangerous sound when they hit the backboards just right.
One sharp corner could stick into the wood maybe a quarter-inch deep, leaving the rest of the blade vibrating with a
lovely, cork-dulled *whang*. The rules were: You took turns, but
you could keep going if you hit the bullseye. If you weren't
lucky, a reinforced corner instead of a sharp one would meet
the backboard, or maybe the dull edge would meet the backboard flat-on. Then the blade would just bounce down onto
the light-table, and you'd lose your turn.

Gus had made up this game and come up with its rules,
so everyone went by them. He'd stuck pieces of masking tape
to the floor four feet from the light-tables to be the "serving line"; measurement was simple, since the T-squares were
also yardsticks. He even had a "long-line," six feet back, from
which you got double the points if your blade stuck.

The crew whipped the blades Frisbee-style, trying to hit
bullseyes Gus had drawn on the backboards with a marker.
Bullseye was five points. If you buried the corner of your
blade in one of the four concentric circles around it, your
score dropped by one, according to how far away from the

bullseye you'd landed: 4-3-2-1. Penny a game went to who-ever had high score. Gus won most of the time.

"It's all in the wrist," he said proudly.

If there was one thing Louey had learned in Journalism School—and there may not have been, but if there was—it was that Backshop was supposed to ... (*drumroll*) ... "Follow the Copy Out the Window." Typographers, grunts and all other pressroom workers lived by that motto. They were never to assume that they knew better than Editorial about anything—grammar, spelling, common sense, current events—even if they really did know better, and in fact they could get fired for making such a bold assumption. If Editorial sends out the headline, "Jones Marks 1,000th Win," and you coached Little League with Jones for five years, and there's no way he could have 1,000 wins because they play just ten games a season in Little League, and he's only been coaching for ten years, so you know damned well they meant "100th," you still have to let that headline stand, because you're not supposed to read the copy—neither the stories nor the heads—and also it could very possibly turn out that Jones says somewhere in the story that every game he coached was so exhausting that it felt like ten games, so the head was supposed to be funny and why the hell, Tim would ask, did you call me back here?

"OK, hold your horses, I'm coming!" Tim yelled back to John multiple times each night. And then he would complain to Louey as he pushed his chair back and trudged away, "Goddammit, I have to fight those stupid bastards all night long, when I'm trying to put out a paper! I can't get anything done out here, and you see why? Do you see why I can't get anything done? Do you? Seriously. Do you?"

Louey didn't see why. One night she had an idea.

"Tim, why don't you send me to Backshop just before Sullivan Edition goes to press, and I'll do checkout? That way, you can be starting on Pike Edition while I'm checking out the flats and rewriting heads and stuff. I'll sign off on everything and then come back and help edit Pike edition, then go back out there and do checkout for Pike, and the same thing for Newburgh and Late Final!"

There. Done. At that very moment, Louey Levy had invented a job with no title but that she, and subsequently everyone else on the Record, called "Checkout Princess." Louey was the Record's Checkout Princess. Until then, there was an unwritten rule that no one from News was allowed into Backshop unless summoned by John, but John hated Tim so much that he quickly OK'd the idea. Louey was authorized to touch the light-tables—the first person from News-side ever to be able to do that. She would grab a single-edged blade and align the copy on some of the flats herself, taking a load off the grunts. Unlike them, however, she actually read the copy, so she could also make sure that the headlines were pasted above the stories they went with and that everything was spelled right; rewrite heads to fit properly and paste up the new heads herself; and, amazingly, initial the flats, taking responsibility for all of it.

Best of all, she got to hang out with her new pals, the grunts. She quickly learned to whip her single-edged blades into the backboards above the light-tables like an expert, rivaling Gus's accuracy even from the long-line.

It went well. She was the liaison between the two

departments—something they hadn't known they needed—and a cheerful one, at that. Basketball teams would have called her their "Sixth Man."

The Checkout Princess made everyone's job easier. From that moment on, there were far fewer errors in the paper, and none in the headlines, subheads or captions. If a story said, "Continued on P. 14," it really did continue on Page 14, not on Page 47 or 98 or 104. If a headline or a jump-head or subhead was sent out to the typesetters too long or too short, or with a misspelling, Louey quickly spotted and rewrote it, scribbling the new one and its size and font on a scrap of paper and handing it to a typesetter herself. Nobody had to run and get Tim. And after the new version slid out of a typesetting machine a minute later and went through the beeswaxer, she would paste it up herself, as well, lining it up on a lighttable using a big metal T-square and smoothing it down with the broad side of a blade. With Tim not going back there anymore, John's consumption of Tums was reduced from half a bottle per night to less than one bottle a week.

Sullivan edition made its 10 p.m. deadline with 10 or 15 minutes to go: Boom. John would carry the last flat for it up to the press with a smile. Pike edition, 10:25: Boom. Newburgh edition, 11:30: Boom. Late Final, 11:50: Boom. Nobody had to flip out, or yell or swear at anyone, or anything.

Just before Christmas, the paper ran 144 pages long, a Record record. But that paper, like all the others, got out on time. With blazing speed, Louey could slice a wire story in the middle of a sentence, amputate a dependent clause, or use a blade to cut the period out of the cut-off part of a story and paste it down after the newly-final word. The Record never came anywhere near having to put Backshop or the pressmen on overtime.

Then came a time when Louey decided to take a week off. She'd earned it. She would snuggle inside her apartment and read and write in her diary, which she'd been neglecting lately. Plus, she could visit her father and stepmother, Ree, for a few days. They had moved to a nice house in Slingerlands, just outside Albany. They would take her out to dinner, and she could regale them with stories of her Record adventures, and they could celebrate Chanukah together.

And all of that happened, and she came back relaxed and happy and eager to see her friends again.

When she returned, Tim Clay was very, very relieved to see her. He positively lit up when she walked into the newsroom.

Backshop was glad to see her, too.

"Boy, the place fell apart without you," Gus said, winging razor blades into a backstop.

"Yeah," John added. "It was hell back here."

"Really? Why?"

"Oh man, you're the only one from News-side who knows how to do anything. They don't know their ass from their elbow. We were late almost every night."

"Late? You mean, we missed deadline? You don't mean Late Final deadline, do you? Osterhout must have had a fit."

They'd have to put the whole pressroom on overtime if they missed Late Final deadline. That had never happened during Louey's tenure as Checkout Princess. She would have been fired, wouldn't she? Well, if it had happened more than once, she was certain she would have been. Osterhout would rather stab himself in the nuts than put 20 pressmen and delivery-truck drivers on overtime.

But John nodded. Yep, they'd missed deadline. Almost every night.

"Well, I'm glad to be back. I mean, I'm glad to see all you guys again!" she said. She had an inkling about how hard it must have been for them. The first two weeks of December, while she was there, the paper had exceeded 100 pages every single day, because of all the ads. She didn't want to think about what that meant to Tim. Maybe someone else came back to help him do checkout? But who would that have been? No one else knew how to do it.

Just after Sullivan Edition went to bed on her first night back, James Osterhout strode in. Everyone stopped playing Razor-blade Archery and stared. The Publisher walked up to Louey at her light-table, and peered down at her, past a stack of the six or eight Newburgh Edition flats she'd have to look at, fix and sign off on.

"Are you Louey Levy?" he asked.

Louey was nervous seeing Osterhout in Backshop. She figured she was being fired.

"Yes."

"I'm Jim Osterhout, The Publisher," he said, as if they had never met before. Well, she couldn't blame him. It had just been that one time, on her first day, that they had ever laid eyes on each other.

"Hello," she said. He shook her hand.

"Your stock is very high right now," he said.

Louey didn't know what that meant, but she knew it was

good. Was she going to get a raise?

"Oh, good!" she said smiling, and turned back to her work. "Oh good" sounded so lame, but she didn't know what else to say. She really didn't want to know what had happened while she was gone. She just wanted to do her job and go home.

Weirdly, that was all he said. He never explained *why* her stock was high. He simply turned and left, his white hair waving above his white suit, silent as a ghost, through the big archway. But she had an idea: He had had to put the pressroom on overtime while she was off, because nobody could do checkout as fast as she could. That had to be it. To that cheap bastard, putting the pressroom on OT was the worst tragedy the Record could ever suffer.

One night, a photo by Frankie came out to Backshop that needed a bullshit caption. It was beautiful, a classic LeFranc, and Tim had decided to run it large, in color, over four columns on Page 5. To Louey, it resembled a Matisse painting, with scattered pale yellow and bright gold blobs, some pointed, some rounded. She had no idea what it was. She took it to Frankie and asked him.

"No, but don't you see? You aren't using your eyes! Look at it!"

"I'm looking, but I can't figure it out. I really can't. That's why I'm asking you," she sighed. She was getting a little tired of him. "So I can write a caption for it."

"No, but don't you see the leaves? What do you think the thin lines are, running all through them? Those are the veins of leaves!" LeFranc said impatiently.

"What kind of tree is it?"

"No, but it doesn't make any difference what kind of tree it is! It's beautiful; that's all that matters! How the sun hits the leaves, and what happens to the light; how it becomes nourishment for the tree and then for all of creation; that's what's important!"

"Where was this tree?"

"No, but it was somewhere by the side of a road! It doesn't matter where it was! It only matters how the leaves filter the sunlight! You must use your eyes! You look, Louey, but you don't see! That is your problem."

She didn't know she had a problem, other than having to deal with that arrogant French artiste. She was going to ask what time of day the photo was taken, but instead she just walked away, nodding sagely. She could see that there was no sense talking to him anymore. He'd just say, "No, but it doesn't make any difference what time it was!"

She found the nearest typewriter that wasn't being used and slid a piece of copy paper into it.

"The sun paints abstract patterns on the leaves of a birch tree on a crisp early morning in Sullivan County," she wrote. "Residents and leaf-peeping tourists alike have been enjoying the striking Catskill Mountain scenery this fall."

She kind of liked it. She thought it was a perfect bullshit caption for that beautiful, abstract photo. She sent it to Backshop to be typed and pasted up.

The next day, LeFranc was pacing in front of the copy desk, holding the paper, when she came in.

"Who put this photo in the paper?" he demanded, waving Page 5 at her. He knew damned well who did.

"I did."

"No, but who pasted it into the paper this way?"

"I did."

"Don't you know the difference between right-side up and upside down?"

"What do you mean?"

"This photo is upside down! You do not put photos in the paper upside down! You can be fired for that! What do you think this is: a joke?"

"No!"

"Were you drinking?"

Now she felt as if she were going to cry.

"No! I'm sorry! I didn't know it was upside down!" Drinking? She didn't drink, except for a beer of two after work now and then.

"No, but that is because you don't know how to use your eyes! You don't know how to see! You only look at things, but you do not see anything! Now, tell me: Where are the shadows in this photo?"

Oh God: Now she was back in kindergarten.

Louey pointed to several darker areas: "Here, and here, and here, and here," she said. She was shaking like a birch leaf in November.

"No, but where do you think I was standing when I took this shot? Did you even think about that? Did you think I was flying in an airplane, and shot downward at the tree?"

"No."

"No, because we don't do that, do we! Well, where was I, then?"

"On the ground?"

"Of *course*, on the ground! So these are the bottoms of the leaves, not the tops! I was shooting upwards at them!"

"Oh," she said in a little voice. Louey felt like a little kid being scolded, and she was trying not to cry. "OK."

"No, but it's not OK. Where are the shadows of leaves?" he demanded, poking a thin finger at her. "Do they fall on the top of the leaves, or on the bottom?" Now he was stamping his foot as he spoke. She had never seen anyone literally stamp his foot before; she had only heard that expression.

Reader, at that moment, Louey Levy had no idea where the shadows of leaves fall. He might as well have asked where Vanuatu falls in the South Pacific. And she would have cared more about the latter question, because she had drifted off in a much more interesting direction, wondering how many Record readers realized that, *bien sûr*, leaves cast shadows on other leaves. And of those who did, how many knew or cared where they fall, and of *that* number, how many had noticed that Frankie LeFranc's photo was upside down. How many people had called in anyway, and were they upset, or were they just delighted to show off by pointing out the goof? Was she getting yelled at because people were threatening to organize a mob to run through the streets of Middletown with lit torches, calling for a correction?

Eventually she came back to Frankie and noticed that words still seemed to be coming out of his mouth, and that, in fact he seemed to be waiting for a reply. *Let's see*, she thought. *If higher-up leaves cast shadows, then the lower-down leaves would have shadows on their top sides. But if the sun shone between the upper leaves, then the tops of the lower leaves would be in sunlight, wouldn't they? And the bottoms of upper leaves are always darker than the tops, aren't they? And what if some of the lower leaves are growing straight up, so that they don't really have a "top" part and a "bottom" part?* Wait. She was beginning to think that maybe she had a case. Maybe she would be acquitted in the Court of Al Rome.

LeFranc was now staring at her in an uncomfortable way, and his face was much too close to hers. He had asked something like, where on leaves would the darker areas be. She decided to just take a guess, in order to end the inquisition.

"On the bottom?"

"Of *course*, on the bottom! Now look at this photo!" he continued, rattling the page at her. "Where are the shadows! Tell me!"

"Oh, those are *shadows*?" she said. The situation had now entered the realm of absurdity. She was trying to look serious, but she feared her shoulders and stomach were visibly shaking and her nose was going to start making that little giggle-stifling noise, giving her away.

"No but of *course* they're shadows! You knew that, because you *wrote* that they're shadows! And why did you write that it was early morning? Who told you it was early morning? Who told you that? This photo couldn't have been taken in early morning! Look at it! The sun is directly overhead, making shadows on the leaves! In early morning, the light couldn't be shining straight down, could it! Your caption has now ruined this photo!"

As usual, Louey couldn't think of a reply when she needed to. But luckily, in an instant, she didn't need to, because LeFranc stormed off toward Rome's office, no doubt to get her fired. She ran to her phone to call Charlie and Sandy and

Annie to ask them to meet her at the Dugout after work. There she told her tale of woe, spreading out the page in question on their little table. Annie and Charlie bent over the paper and loudly proclaimed that her bullshit caption was the best ever. They referred to captions, in the journalist's way, as "cutlines."

"I give you a lot of credit, Louey," Charlie said seriously. "I could never think of anything to write about photos like these. How do you come up with that stuff? I mean, what can you say? They should run them with just a label, or a title, like in a museum: 'Leaves.' They don't need a whole cutline."

"Yeah, or how about just, 'Bullshit Cutline,'" Sandy said. "I guess he just couldn't find anything to photograph yesterday. I'm surprised he didn't get the wagon wheel out again."

Louey thought her friends, God bless them, were just trying to make her feel better. But then Jake Rosen showed up with the paper in his hand.

"Great cutline, Louey!" he said, throwing the paper onto their table, Page-5 up. "You did write that, didn't you?"

Charlie, Sandy and Annie laughed and sat back in their seats and nodded and applauded.

"See? See?" Charlie said. "I told you it was a great cutline."

"Yeah; that is so Louey. That is classic Louey," Annie said.

"I was just telling about the trouble I got into for it," Louey said.

"Trouble? Why?"

"Tell him! Yeah, tell him about it! Listen to this, Jake! You won't believe this! Tell him, Louey!" Charlie said, grinning and patting her buddy on the arm. So Louey told it again.

Everybody always asked Louey to tell about things that had happened, even when they knew what had happened as well as she did.

"No, you tell it," they would say. "You tell it better."

Jake, like everyone else in the world, apparently, except Frankie LeFranc, had no idea that the photo they were all admiring was upside down. As they all stood leaning over the table to peer at the page, Jake vehemently insisted that it looked better upside down than right-side up. They all agreed and vowed to go out on strike if she got fired for that.

Dear Diary, Louey wrote that night. *What good friends I have. I'll never have better friends than these. I'll love them forever.*

She didn't get fired. LeFranc apparently forgot about it, or he told Daley and Daley forgot about it, or Jackson and Jackson didn't give a rat's ass, or Rome and Rome forgot about it, in the press of things. In the newsroom, there was always a crisis that was brewing right now, a source who had to be interviewed this instant, a photo that had to be taken and developed on deadline. Nobody cared about yesterday's mistakes. "Yesterday's paper wraps tomorrow's fish," was the totally-true saying. If a reader called in to complain about an error, that was one thing. But who was going to complain in this case—the tree?

Nixon was re-elected that year, despite the McGovern buttons that Louey wore on her shirts and on her pocketbook strap every day, and despite the stickers she'd put on both her front and rear bumpers. The election made her very disappointed in her fellow Americans, and in herself, for not doing more for old George. She should have written letters. She should have gone door-to-door. She did none of that.

Ted Daley had told her, from the moment she started wearing those buttons to work, that it was very unprofessional for any newspaper employee on News-side to wear political buttons. He was going to make sure that, in their next contract with the Newspaper Guild, that would be spelled out.

"Those things totally undermine the profession and make it look like we're biased in the stories we publish," he said. "It's completely amateurish to wear them, as well as unprofessional."

Louey pointed out that she was no longer a reporter; that she no longer had sources, of either party; and that no one from the public ever saw or talked to her. "And anyway," she added, "the contract won't expire for another four years, when Nixon will have been deposed, so you won't even have to worry about it."

Daley didn't like that.

"If you're photographed taking part in any protests, you'll have to be fired," he said, twirling his mustache. His eyes looked a hundred times bigger behind his thick glasses. "And you can tell that to the rest of your little friends out there, too."

By glancing quickly at the newsroom, he made sure she knew whom he meant by her "little friends out there."

The reporters reconnoitered at the Dugout that night.

"'Little friends'!" Mike from Sports said. He was about

6-foot-2. "I love that!"

"'Little cabal,' he should have said," Annie added.

Charlie shook her head. "How could we re-elect a guy who sticks to this failed policy of sending our men off to die in a war just to bring capitalism to people who don't want it? How many American soldiers have been killed over there already? It's close to 40,000, I think."

"I know!" Jake said. "Nixon just wants to turn Vietnam into a colony of the U.S., so we can exploit their cheap labor!"

Mike from Sports wasn't so sure he agreed.

"Well, but like in poker, you want to cover your investment. We need to cover our investment over there. Otherwise our soldiers won't have enough backup, and we really will lose. It'll be a self-fulfilling prophesy, and it really will all have been for nothing! That's what I worry about."

"Yeah, but this is not a poker game," Jake said. "That's the difference. He's not gambling with chips; he's gambling with people's lives! He's throwing more Americans over there for … for what? To stop communism? Maybe Asian people *want* communism! Maybe it'll be good for them, compared to being ruled by a dictator!"

Louey rather liked the idea of communism.

"From each according to his ability; to each according to his needs," she recited, quoting Marx. "What's wrong with that? That's just plain fairness, isn't it?"

"But then there's no reason to show any initiative. There would be no competition if everyone had to wear the same clothes and eat the same food and live in those same little houses! That would be awful!" Mike said.

"Well, let's let *them* decide," Charlie said. "Our men who

are being sent to Vietnam probably don't care about communism, socialism, or any other ism. They're the Blacks, the poor, the uneducated ... They're the only ones going over there. The rich guys can always get out of it, somehow."

"Well, I'm out, but I'm not rich," Mike said. He stuck his left leg out to the side a little. "Broke my ankle playing football in high school! Never healed. That's why I walk so funny."

Louey had never noticed that Mike walked funny, but from then on, she did. She didn't say anything about it, though; she was just glad he hadn't gone to Vietnam. Neither of her brothers had gone. Danny supported the war and wanted to join the Officer Candidate School, but was prevented from doing so by his girlfriend, who told him he could choose between the war or her. He then went on to draw the highest number possible in the lottery, so he would never have been drafted anyway. Marc (technically a stepbrother), a pure pacifist, had drawn the lowest number possible—what were the odds of that?—and had immediately decamped to Canada.

No one had replied to Mike. Instead, they turned to look at Jake.

"I was 4F, too," he said. "Heart murmur. Born with it. I'm not sure I would have gone if I'd been drafted, though. I'm totally against the war, but if I'd gone, that would be one less Black guy who would have had to go, you know? I'm really torn about it."

My heart could murmur for Jake any day, Louey thought. *Come over here and listen to this murmur, Rosen. God, he is so cool.*

"But anyway," Jake said, "Why don't we organize a bus to

Washington? There'll be thousands of protesters there. Each person won't have to pay much if we fill the bus, and I bet we could fill two of them to leave from Newburgh and one from Middletown."

Unanimous. Jake was elected to organize it. As his reward, he was given the last of the pretzel pieces and the dregs of beer from the pitcher.

One hitch: The inauguration ceremony was going to be held on a Saturday. That meant Louey would have to work, instead of going to Washington with her pals and thousands of others to protest the war and disrupt the President's victory party. Unless, of course, she was sick that day. She had taken precious few sick days in nearly two years.

"You gotta work that day, don't you?" Annie asked.

"Yeah, but sometimes ya just don't feel good, y'know?" Louey said. And then she nodded and repeated very slowly, "Sometimes ya just don't feel good."

So emboldened were the reporters, and so excited and happy about their planned trip, that they got sloppy. They all made sure to turn in their Sunday stories by Friday of Inauguration Week, and some didn't work Saturdays anyway, so they were fine. But Plummer, who was an older, married guy who never joined in the general newsroom criticisms of Nixon, overheard a couple of them talking about their plans, and "casually mentioned" it in front of Ted. Anyway, *someone* ratted on them, and Louey couldn't think of who else would do that. Maybe Ted himself heard them talking; he was always skulking around.

The week of Inauguration Day, he called Louey into his

office. He didn't even sit down, nor did he invite Louey to sit; he just stood behind his closed door and, leaning a forearm against it, looked down her big shirt and said, "I hear some of our staff are planning to protest at the President's inauguration."

"Really? Cool!" Jaw momentarily dropped; pleasant voice; eyes wide; surprised, mouth-open smile; eyebrows slightly up. She should have been an actress, she really should.

"No, it's not. It's not cool at all. And I'll tell you why: Anyone who gets arrested down there is gonna be fired immediately."

"For what?"

"For unprofessional conduct. It's in the contract."

She was sure he was bluffing. What would unprofessional conduct be, for a reporter? Plagiarism, for sure. Making stuff up, for sure. Coming in drunk, carrying a weapon, breaking the law, not knowing the AP Stylebook ... using vulgar language in front of a source? Or, *dressing* unprofessionally, maybe? But what did "unprofessional" clothing even mean, in the 1970s? The guys rarely wore ties anymore, and Daley didn't seem to mind even the shortest of miniskirts. What else? She couldn't think of anything. She had read her pocket-sized Guild contract thoroughly and couldn't remember any clause about "unprofessional conduct."

"You can't fire anyone for getting arrested! They have to be convicted before you can even *threaten* to fire them! And, who's getting arrested? Nobody's getting arrested: It's not against the law to carry a protest sign! They have every right to go down there! That's exercising their freedom of speech! Remember freedom of speech? It's in the Bill of Rights! And in this country, you're innocent until proven guilty!"

Twirling his mustache, Ted looked down through his big, thick glasses and said matter-of-factly, "I wouldn't say you were *guilty*; I'd just say you were *fired*. For unprofessional conduct. You might want to pass that along to anyone who's planning to go to Washington."

Louey Levy, in her whole life, could never think of a good response to things on the spur of the moment. Instead, she thought of them at night, when she should have been sleeping. So she just shrugged, rolled her eyes, sighed and said, "OK, fine," and let herself out of Ted's office.

And at 4 a.m. on January 20, she got up and called in sick.

The best thing about getting up that early was that she didn't have to actually speak to Ted, nor answer any questions. She just told his message machine that she felt awful and was sick to her stomach and couldn't come in that day. The second-best thing was that she had plenty of time to shower, dress, pack her lunch, make a poster to hold up as Nixon was driven down Pennsylvania Avenue. She lettered in fat, black marker, outlined in red, simply, "BOO! HISS!" on the theory that, this way, she could save her voice. Near the edges of her sign (it was on thick posterboard, so it wouldn't bend in the wind) she drew a nice border of three thin lines: two black ones on either side of a red one. She drove to the supermarket parking lot from where the buses would depart at 6 and got there, as usual, before anyone else. It was exciting as the buses started arriving; there was that wonderful smell of diesel exhaust, like the smell of the waiting area in the Port Authority whenever a door opens.

It was a clear day and not too cold: perfect. Stars were still poking through the black sky as the bus drivers parked and got out leaving their rigs running. They gathered and talked with one another, smoking. Now cars started pulling in. Groups of gabby protesters emerged with fun signs. Louey saw Jake's old heap and got out of her car and ran over to him. He was all smiles; she held his backpack while he bent into his back seat to retrieve his "End The War NOW" sign, each word on its own line. It was stapled to a long, flat stick. *Good sign, but he should have made the letters thicker so it could be seen easier,* she thought. *Also, the stick will make it stand out above the crowd, but you have to carry the damned thing the whole day.*

Louey Levy had given a lot of thought to poster-making back in her college days, and she had some experience with it. If there was one thing Louey knew—and there might not have been, but if there was—it was how to make a good poster.

Her own sign was horizontally oriented, as wide as she herself was, and had two holes punched in it and a nice twine "handle" so she could carry it around her neck, no-hands. She had it on as she approached Jake's car and as he looked at it, she imagined for a moment that he was sorry he'd have to carry his big, awkward one all day.

They looked around among the cars for the rest of the Record gang, and they all showed up with various hilarious signs. Charlie's read, "Welcome to the Coronation," which Louey admired most of all. Nixon did act like a king, unresponsive to the millions of Americans who were against the war, not seeming to care at all about the peons he was sending to Vietnam to get killed for … well, for nothing, really. Bill from Sullivan emerged from his car with his sign, a small piece of posterboard, already hanging from a length of twine around his neck. "ALL WAR STINKS," it said on one line. And underneath: "STOP THE KILLING."

He probably had driven all the way from Monticello with it hanging around his neck like that. *Maybe so he wouldn't forget it*, Louey figured. He was of that age when people often forget things. He was really quite old. He must have been, like, 50.

Jake and Louey sat together near the middle of the bus, he by the window, she on the aisle. Charlie and Annie sat-sat directly across from them. Mike from Sports and Sandy and other reporters were nearby, but farther back. There were plenty of "civilians" on the bus, too, from around Orange County. Jake soon fell asleep with his head on Louey's shoulder, and that already made this a perfect day. By the time the sun rose, they were in the middle of New Jersey, making good time, and soon everyone woke up.

A little bit later, Louey walked up the aisle to Bill's seat, nearer the front. She thought he was extremely cool, but she hardly ever got to talk to him, because he rarely cared to drive all the way to Middletown after his shift. He almost never joined the gang at the Dugout, except for union meetings. All she knew about him was what Charlie had told her: that he was a pacifist, and he'd never fought in World War II. And that he had won some awards for both his coverage and his photography of Woodstock a few years ago. She wanted to talk to him about that, and now she had a captive audience.

"Yeah, that was a crazy time," he said, looking up at her. "Did you go?"

"Kinda," she smiled. "I got within eight or 10 miles of it, and then got stuck in the traffic. My friends and I never got to hear the concert, but there was plenty of music out on 17B; you know what I mean?"

"I know," he said, nodding.

"How did you even get in to cover it? Did you go, like, days before, and just stay overnight there in, like, a tent?"

"The Record rented a private helicopter for all three days, so I was in and out. I got home every night. I took aerial shots so readers could see how many miles the goddamned thing spread out for. And then I got some good closeups, too, because I had the telephoto," he said. "Plus, we'd been covering it for months in advance. The town meetings in Woodstock and Wallkill … all of those routine, boring meetings were where the real action was. The goddamned thing almost never happened, y'know, because the town fathers were afraid of the traffic and the 'hippies' that would come."

"Weren't you afraid to go up in a helicopter in all that rain?"

"No; there was no danger. I learned to pilot a copter in World War II."

"Wait. I thought you were a pacifist!"

"I was a conscientious objector. I was assigned to put out forest fires instead of fighting. I was a flying firefighter, you might say. I spent the whole war flying around the Catskills looking for fires and dumping water on them, and calling in coordinates to fire departments, and stuff like that. Woodstock was a piece of cake, believe me. But at

Woodstock I was just a passenger. We'd hired a pilot from the Air National Guard, and all I had to do was take photos. We had our own landing area not far from the stage. My only problem was, between the music and the chopper, I was deaf for three days afterwards."

"Seriously?"

"Seriously. Totally, completely deaf."

"Holy crap. What about the rain? It rained for three days straight! Can helicopters even fly, if it's raining?"

"Sure they can! There was no fog, no wind, no lightning. Those are the only weather conditions you have to worry about. We were fine. It was a fun assignment. The Record paid a fortune to rent that helicopter, but it was totally worth it. We got some great stories and shots."

"How much did the paper pay to rent the helicopter?" she asked.

"Don't know. I never asked. Rome didn't seem to mind about the money, you know, with a story like that. Those were the days, man. The paper was rolling in dough back then, and they didn't mind spending it. Now they've all turned into a bunch of cheap bastards."

Louey grinned, "Hey, did you see me there? I was the kid in the T-shirt and the cutoffs and the backpack."

"Oh, that was you?" Bill smiled. "Yeah, you and half a million other kids out on the road."

"Wow. Jeez. Well, thanks, man. I always wanted to know how we covered that."

Louey walked, steadying herself by grabbing the seat-backs every few steps, to her place next to Jake. He was staring out the window. He'd taken down his backpack from the overhead rack, for some reason, while she was gone, and he smiled and used kind of a hook-shot to stow it back up there when she said, "Excuse me, sir; is this seat taken?"

The bus had grown quiet.

Simon and Garfunkel's song, "America," came to Louey: "'Kathy, I'm lost,' I said, though I knew she was sleeping; / 'I'm empty and aching and I don't know why.' / Countin' the cars on the New Jersey Turnpike; / they've all come to look for America." That's what *they* were doing. They were looking for the America they'd learned about in grade school—the one where everyone is treated equally and everyone gets a fair shake. The one that doesn't start any wars, but whose brave men jump in and finish them when evil dictators try to rule the world. The America her dad, Abe Levy, had grown up in and believed in and loved.

She started singing it in her little, off-key voice, and two women in the row ahead of her joined in, and they sang the whole damned song, which was made much better when the guy with the good, loud voice and the guitar joined in.

There was always a guy with a guitar in those days.

Then they sang other ones, too: "Me and Bobby McGee" went loudly, if not well. There were so many good songs. Time passed quickly that way.

Louey and her pals laughed and leaned over each other to talk and got up to stretch their legs a little or use the cramped bathroom during the long trip. Sometimes they knelt on their seats to talk to the people behind them.

Annie and Charlie discovered during the ride not only that they both had gone to Catholic schools and colleges for their entire academic careers, but also that they were both scholars and lovers of Latin. Louey listened in, fascinated, as they harmonized on some hymns.

"Christ the Lord is Risen Today," they sang. And also, "It Is Well with My Soul":

"My sin, oh, the bliss of this glorious thought! My sin, not in part but the whole, / Is nailed to the cross, and I bear it no more, / Praise the Lord, praise the Lord, O my soul!"

The great thing was, they both had lovely voices and they knew all the words. Louey enjoyed listening to them. She laughed and clapped as they finished each one, though some of the other riders just shook their heads and rolled their eyes.

"God, you Christians have all the good songs," Louey said.

"Do Jews sing hymns?" Charlie asked.

"Well, not 'hymns,' I don't think. I don't think we call them 'hymns.' Like, we don't have a hymnal in temple." She didn't really know, as she hadn't been to temple in years, except on the High Holy Days, when she went back to Albany to attend shul with her parents. As to the music at those times, they mostly listened to the cantor and a paid choir singing.

"Do you go to confession every week, and tell the priest all your sins, and everything?" Louey asked. As long as they were asking.

"Of course!"

"Why? Will that keep you from going to hell?"

"Exactly. I don't want to die in a state of sin." She said it with a smile, but you could tell she meant it. "Do Jews believe in heaven and hell?"

"Not to speak of. I mean, as my dad always says, 'Two

Jews; three opinions.' It's not important to us."

"Why be good, then?"

"Because we're all God's children, and so we have to treat one another like brothers and sisters."

"That's a good answer."

That wasn't it, though. That was too simple an answer. The question made Louey think, and she and Charlie sat in silence for a long time. Finally Louey added, "If hell's where you go for not going to confession, then my grandparents are already there, and my sister and brothers and I are all heading there, too—not to mention all my atheist friends—and I'd rather spend eternity burning in hell with them than spend it in heaven with anyone else."

Her grandparents could not possibly be in hell. The suggestion did not insult or anger her, because it was beyond insult or anger. If her feeling about it could have a physical expression, it would be a closed-lips, raised-eyebrows, amused smile. Her grampa, Sam, was the wisest and kindest man ever, an Orthodox Jew who had no formal education but who could speak, read and write several European languages and who had cemented Louey's very early feminist respect for Judaism. He pointed out to her that Jewish men like himself awoke each morning and, before anything else, thanked God that God had not made them female—that is, for leaving femaleness to the stronger ones, who could face all the work, trouble and pain of bearing, raising, feeding and educating their families and still find a way to be happy, and to go on. Jewish men knew they'd lucked out by being set on the easier, male path, and they thanked God for it first thing every day! That's exactly what she would do if she were a man. Their job was just to lift things and learn how to love, protect and respect women, and to shut up. Her grampa said almost nothing, ever; he was like a monk with a vow of silence.

Orthodox Jewish women, meanwhile, started their day by thanking God for making them as God "saw fit." To Louey, nothing could be more sensible than that. What a practical and realistic religion, and how proud Louey was to be part of it! Her bubbe, Rachel, dedicated many years of her life to raising her three wild grandchildren, Danny, Louey and Clare, in Newburgh after their mother died. Until that time, Rachel had never been north of Harlem except for occasional summer vacations with Sam in the "kuch-aleins" of the Catskills. She never drove, and until the day she died, Rachel Levy described Newburgh's location as being "in the forest." "It's very nice up here in the forest. It's nice and cool in the summer," she said on the phone to her friends back in the City. She wasn't too sure where she was. But, bravely, she joined the Newburgh Hadassah, and raised her grandchildren, and made friends, and made herself happy there.

"That's the important thing," she always told Louey and her siblings; "to make yourself happy and to make your family happy." Anyway, Bubbe and Grampa being eternally agonized by flames was not a possibility. It was absurd, in fact. They were the two oldest people she knew, but also the two best. She spent a long, quiet part of the ride thinking about aging, and how she was enjoying it so far, and how she hoped to get even older. Maybe even as old, someday, as her grandparents were now.

As you grow older, you get heavier. You're heavy with all the wisdom and perspective and emotions and ideas that you can get only by going through life. Paradoxically, though, you also get lighter. You pare down the possessions that have held onto you as you free yourself up, like a butterfly leaving its chrysalis behind. Little by little, our possibilities get replaced by our memories, and the trail of memories just gets longer and longer as the list of our possibilities gets shorter and shorter. And it's all because of the choices we make: Who will be our friends? What will we learn? Who and what will we love? Which of God's and nature's creations will we appreciate and protect, and what broken things will we try to repair? Where will we go, and what will we do? With each choice you make, you chop off an infinite number of possibilities.

In Washington the Record gang piled out of the bus and joined thousands of other protesters lining the parade route. When Nixon's car finally came into view, they all booed at the top of their lungs. Jake, taller than most of the other protesters, held his sign with his right hand and gave Nixon the finger with his left. Then all of a sudden, just as the caravan drew even with their group, a suited, slender, evil-looking man with sunglasses, a dark mustache and an earpiece with a wire going down the inside of the back of his jacket appeared beside Jake and grabbed his sign and tore it from his hand. Jake went to grab it back but the guy ripped the sign right down the middle so that all that was left of it unhurt was the stick.

"Back off, you fascist bastard!" Jake yelled, but the guy replied, "Step back. Step back, or you're under arrest."

"For what? We're exercising our freedom of speech and assembly, asshole!"

"Not today, you're not," the guy said. He broke the slat over his knee and threw it on the ground. Then he ducked back under the yellow tape they'd gathered behind and caught up to Nixon's car. Louey figured that's where he'd been just before spotting Jake—jogging alongside Nixon's car and saying to himself, "Look how athletic I am, everybody!"

Louey was afraid Jake would be arrested, but this guy wasn't a cop: He was just a douche. Nonetheless, the sign was ruined, and now Jake's hands were free so he could give Nixon both middle fingers. Which he did, even though they were al now in the car's rear-view mirror. Louey was very relieved and proud that Jake didn't get into a fistfight with that dopey security guy.

Would she have gone with him to police headquarters, if he'd been arrested? Would she have tried to get bail money, somehow (she'd have to ask her dad for a loan), if Jake had been sent to jail? She was thinking these thoughts as she and Jake ran with the crowd, calling out moderately obscene slogans from the sidewalk while trailing the car, but there were just so many people there—women with baby carriages, old people, kids, people with crutches and wheelchairs—that they had to walk in stutter-steps more than run, and so fell farther and farther behind the President.

Still, it was an exciting and fun day, and they were exhausted and hungry when they got back to the bus in mid-afternoon. They'd memorized their bus number and location, and they were among the first to re-board. Louey retrieved from her backpack one of the two tuna-fish sandwiches she'd made the night before, and offered the other to Jake. She was glad she did, because it turned out he had brought only his water bottle and a Milky Way.

As each smiling person or group of two or three climbed into the bus, those already aboard yelled, "Yay!" eliciting big smiles as they pumped their signs up and down one last time. Louey made sure to tell what happened to Jake's sign and to describe the mustachioed shit-head who ripped up his poster.

That guy, despite Louey's prayers of petition to God, not only did not get run over by Nixon's car, but lived to, years later, have his own radio show. Louey heard it a couple of times.

"Louey, this sandwich is righteous," Jake said, munching away with an eyes-closed smile. He was leaning back and chewing slowly and shaking his head a little, as if he were the happiest person on earth.

"Thank you. My secret ingredient is sweet relish," she said.

There was also plenty of mayo and a lettuce leaf and a slice of tomato on it, for color, and she'd put in some salt and a bit of pepper. The bread was whole wheat, from the health-food store. Her grandmother was the first person she'd ever seen adding relish to tuna fish, and Louey now thought tuna-fish sandwiches were bland without it. She would never think of making tuna fish any other way. But her sandwiches had never been called "righteous" before.

Would she have gone to jail with Jake, though? Would she have stood her ground or at least sworn at that guy? Did she have any kind of courage at all? She didn't think so, but she hoped she did. She slept soundly for a long time on the ride home—she could always sleep in a car, bus or train, though never otherwise. She asked Jake if he'd mind if she leaned her head against his arm, and he said, "I'd be honored." She wondered if they'd be fired for going down to Washington. She didn't see how: None of them had been arrested, or interviewed, or anything that would upset Daley. Anyway, if they did get canned, the union would fight to get them reinstated, because they were just exercising their rights.

And if it couldn't, oh well. It would still be worth it. The great Donovan song came into her head: "Who's going to be the one / to say it was no good, what we done? / I dare a man to say I'm too young, / for I'm going to try for the sun."

Then the Phil Ochs song "When I'm Gone" supplanted the Donovan one: "There's no place in this world where I'll belong when I'm gone / and I won't know the right from the wrong when I'm gone / and you won't find me singin' on this song when I'm gone, / so I guess I'll have to do it while I'm here… / O my days won't be dances of delight when I'm gone / and the sands will be shiftin' from my sight when I'm gone; / can't add my name into the fight when I'm gone, / so I guess I'll have to do it while I'm here."

In the quiet bus, Louey got an idea: She would go to a gynecologist and get a prescription for birth-control pills again. Sure, there was no boyfriend in the picture, but she was sick of being practically disabled from cramps every month, and The Pill, as she knew so well, had that great side effect of eliminating cramps. Why hadn't she thought of that before? Anyway, she put that on her mental To-Do list. And then, of course, maybe the awesome Jake Rosen would fall in love with her, and she would need them. She fell asleep smiling.

Just two days after Nixon's inauguration, something

wonderful happened: The United States Supreme Court ruled that women throughout the whole country could have safe, legal abortions, like they could in New York. So Louey's hero Martin Luther King Jr. was right: "The arc of the moral universe is long, but it bends toward justice." And her father was vindicated in his confidence in America, his own private religion. He didn't go to temple much, except on the High Holy Days; didn't keep kosher the way his parents did; didn't speak any Hebrew and very little Yiddish—just a few punchlines and old sayings and swear-words. But he believed fervently that the country his father had chosen and risked his life to get to was going to be OK, because its people were OK and everyone—man and woman, Black and white—was going to be treated fairly and be able to learn and work and play and compete with one another and marry whomever they wanted—as he himself had married a Scots Presbyterian—and go wherever they wanted without fear, but rather with joy and love. He had gone into public service to help make that kind of justice happen, and now here was a perfect example of some of it really happening.

The day after that Supreme Court decision, Louey strode into the office snapping her fingers and singing the Helen Reddy hit from a couple of years earlier: "I am woman; hear me roar / In numbers too big to ignore / and I know too much to go back and pretend ..."

Tim couldn't help smiling as he said in a mock-kindergarten-teacher voice, "All right, all right, let's get to work, now."

But Louey was not just happy; she was gleeful; she was joyful. She was skipping. Skipping! Like a child! She skipped around the entire copy desk as she sang. She skipped and waved her arms in time to her song. The other copy-editors laughed as they turned and watched her. Even as she threw her coat over the back of her chair and sat down, spinning around in it, she continued: "Cause I've heard it all before / when I've been down there on the floor / and no one's ever gonna keep me down again. ... /"

Now Tim himself was talking through a big grin. He looked over from the slot and said, "OK, come on, we know you're all triumphant and everything, but discretion being the better part of valor, let's keep it down and try to concentrate, all right?"

She tried. She was excited to read and edit all the AP stories about the decision.

"Shouldn't we be doing local, Joe-Blow reaction stories, too?" she said. Those man-in-the-street stories had been her bread and butter. She knew that if she were still reporting, she would be assigned to—she would beg to—go out and do the "local reaction" piece. How she would have loved to call some Catholic priests and Right-to-Life members! Daley probably knew them all and would have their numbers in his Rolodex. And how she would love to then call some Women's Liberation group leaders and talk to them about it! She would take her camera and get photos of them all, which would run as thumbnails with the text wrapping around each interviewee, and ...

"Sandy Miller's on that, I think," Tim said. "And Jake's trying to reach a few OB/GYNs at Saint Luke's. So far, they're all saying they have to get permission from the hospital's flak before they can talk, though. And that frickin' story's due," he added, looking nervously at the clock, "in about an hour or an hour and a half. At the most."

Louey replied with a spin of her chair and a snap of her fingers and a snippet of song, not really under her breath. A little *above* her breath, actually, although quieter than before: "But I'm still an embryo / with a long, long way to go / Until I make my brothers understand. ..."

"OK, knock it off. Settle down, now," Tim said. "Try to contain yourself, for Chrissake." But he was grinning as he shook his head.

Ted Daley, on the other hand, was not amused. He stormed around the newsroom grumpier than ever, because they had to flag the story he was so sad about on Page One. Everybody tried to avoid him.

Tim handed her an updated wire story that included interviews with Justices Rehnquist and White, the two dissenters in the case. Instead of concentrating on a good headline for it, though, Louey Levy was thinking about skipping.

You can't skip if you're sad, she thought. *Every single person who's skipping has a big ol' smile on their face. Also: Grownups don't skip. Did you ever see a grownup skip? Never. What does that say about grownups? Nothing good. Only kids skip. I'm going to try skipping whenever I'm sad in the future, as an experiment. That way I'll figure out if happiness makes you skip, or if it's skipping that makes you happy.*

She was thinking about skipping because, despite the occasional cosmic victory like the abortion decision, Louey wasn't truly, deeply happy. Actually, she was lonely. She had no friends she could do stuff with on her days off. You can't play tennis by yourself, and none of her friends were athletes, anyway. And at the Record, everyone worked those weird hours and slept 'til late in the day or had boyfriends to do things with. A few, like Jackson, were very cool, and she'd like to get to know them better, but they were old and had families to spend their time off with. She'd like to volunteer in some way—maybe tutoring kids in writing?—where she could help people, but she also wanted to join some organization where she'd be able to, like, run around and play ball, or—teach kids how to play tennis?—or at least get some kind of exercise and learn new skills (in what, though?). She'd have to start giving that some serious thought.

The spectral Osterhout floated into the office later that year, his hair and ghost-white skin more or less matching his white belt and white shoes. He lacked only a sheet to complete the ensemble. His outfit was a pale blue-and-white seersucker suit with a blue shirt and a light-blue bow tie to match his eyes. Had he been playing golf? No; you don't wear a suit to play golf, and the shoes didn't have those little cleats that golfers wear. They were just regular, weird, white shoes, as though he'd just gotten off the plane from Florida. He went straight to Ted Daley's office and stayed there for a long time. Louey figured they were consulting about negotiations, but she was wrong. Shortly after Osterhout left, Ted appeared and posted on the union bulletin board—the only bulletin board in the office—a notice that he and Osterhout had cooked up.

"Help our YMCA!" it was headed. It seemed the Middletown Y had got itself into debt when it had built its 8-lane, 50-yard-long indoor Olympic pool. To raise money, it was having a "Middletown Y Olympics." You could sponsor someone to swim at so many cents per lap pledged, and then at the end of the event, the pledged funds would be collected and donated to the Y. Osterhout, as a board member of the Y, must have felt obligated to get Record staffers to volunteer for this silliness. At the next union meeting, convened around three shoved-together rectangular tables at the Dugout, Louey brought the flyer with her.

"Don't feel like you have to sponsor anyone, or swim in this thing, or anything," she said. "I mean, it might be fun, if anyone wants to do it. But it also might be fun to screw Osterhout by having nobody from his own company take part. And him on the board of directors, having rounded up zero people to participate! Wouldn't that be great? What do you think?"

Sandy Miller wanted to do it. She loved swimming more than she hated their cheap bastard publisher.

"I'd swim, if anybody would sponsor me," she said.

Oh, yeah: Sandy. Louey should have known she'd dive in. Who else was a good swimmer?

"Sorry; I love to swim, and I have nothing against the Y, but I don't want to help Osterhout," Jake said. "Negotiations are coming up, and I think it's better if we all collectively told him we can't afford to sponsor anyone, because, even if Sandy could swim 100 laps —5000 yards, more than three miles, right?—at let's say 10 cents a lap, we don't have 10 dollars apiece to spare for his little pet project. We hardly have enough for rent, food and utilities. Who has ten bucks left at the end of the month? I don't."

That drew nods of agreement all around, and Sandy

looked resigned, if a bit downcast, that her own friends and colleagues had thrown cold, chlorinated water on her offer.

Louey had an idea. "What if we tell him we have someone who has volunteered to swim—Sandy—if the Record itself would sponsor her? I mean, take the money from corporate funds or from Osterhout's and Daley's own pockets, if it's so important to them! Then he could tell the Y that his company did its share, and Sandy can swim her brains out, if she wants to!"

Unanimous. Louey was elected to relay that suggestion to Osterhout, via Ted Daley.

Daley didn't think it was a bad idea. It went up the ladder to Osterhout. Two days later, the publisher was in Daley's office, pulling apart the curtains a bit to spy on the newsroom. Louey figured Ted was telling him that Sandy was that chunky girl with big knockers. She didn't look like she could swim at all; she looked like she'd be winded after a few laps. Twenty, tops, for sure. The pool was 50 yards long, so, could she do 1000 yards, 20 laps? That's more than half a mile! That's halfway across the Hudson River! She could never do that many. So if they sponsored her at, like, $5 per lap: a hundred bucks. Osterhout had that kind of money in every pocket of his suit. And if he didn't, he could just sell one of his horses and get it. And then the Record would be listed in the Y's publicity as a "whale of an organization." Good deal!

That's what they're saying, Louey figured. *That's what they're thinking.*

She saw them laughing and nodding as they peered at their peon, before quickly letting the curtains fall together again.

Word got back to Louey the next week that the Record's board of directors (comprising Osterhout's very own family) wouldn't meet again 'til fall to vote on this, but that he himself, the grandest, most generous and community-minded philanthropist in Orange County, would sponsor Sandy at the magnanimous rate of $5 per lap.

When Louey related this information to Sandy, she smiled and frowned at the same time and went straight to her desk and got a pen and pad. She asked Louey to repeat the rate-per-laps again and said, "Are you sure? Did you get that in writing?" and spent a few seconds jotting. Then her frown went away, and her smile got bigger. With a giggle, she said, "OK; great."

The event started at 8 a.m. on a Saturday.

Before each "flight," the starter said into his bullhorn: "Remember, swimmers, this is not a race! Take your time, so you can swim as many laps as possible while swimming continuously! I repeat: This is not a race! Just do as many laps as *you* can; don't worry about the swimmer in the next lane!"

Three "flights" were scheduled. The first group of eight swimmers were told they had an 11 a.m. deadline, but all hauled themselves out of the pool, panting, long before then; the last one out lasted just over two and a half hours of continuous, slow swimming. The second group, diving in at 11:15 as scheduled, also drew eight swimmers—the maximum. These contestants all stayed in the water for less than two hours. The Y's managers huddled after that flight and congratulated one another. From the dollars-per-lap that had been pledged, it looked as if they had raised more than six hundred dollars, with still one flight to go!

Paul had arrived with his camera at about noon to shoot that second group and got a great, close-up, water-level shot of an elderly woman in a white, bubbly-rubber swimming cap with a too-tight-looking chin strap, mouth agape, miserable after six laps. That was the shot they'd run in the paper. He was still there when Louey arrived with Sandy. As Sandy walked off to the locker room, he whispered to Louey that he'd overheard Osterhout saying that the Y had made more than six hundred dollars on this thing already—if everybody paid what they'd pledged. So, Osterhout was practically giddy with success, and the fact that this final flight had only four participants didn't dampen the boss's spirits at all. He was sorry only that he'd had to stay all day.

"He's bored as hell," Paul said. The organizers didn't know how many laps people could swim, so they'd allotted six hours for the first two flights, when those swimmers were all done in four and a half. But Sandy's group was scheduled to start at 2, so that's when they all jumped in.

Not, however, before an ebullient Osterhout got on the microphone and announced that this last group, unlike the first two, would have no time limit. They could go as long as they could continuously make forward progress! They could go all night, haha!

Reader, Sandy Miller dove in and swam 150 laps before 3 o'clock. She was a blur. She might as well have been swimming in the real Olympics. Osterhout stood by the pool, growing paler with each lap. By 4 p.m., the other three swimmers had called it quits, and Sandy alone remained in that beautiful, new Olympic pool, in the clear, chlorine-smelling water. She was in Lane 1, crawling, backstroking, sidestroking, crawling.

Charlie and Louey made up lots of fun cheers from their seats on the four-row set of bleachers at the north side of the pool. "Swim to the left! Swim to the right! Crawl or backstroke; swim all night!" was one. "Sidestroke, backstroke, butterfly, crawl! Sandy Miller can do them all!" was a favorite. James Osterhout Sr., pacing on the opposite deck, did not seem to be enjoying the routine.

Charlie and Louey were delighted that Sandy could hear them; she rolled over onto her back, still kicking, and gave them the thumbs-up at the end of each new cheer. At other times her two fans just burst out clapping and yelling, "C'mon, Sandy!" as though it were the real Olympics and she was neck-and-neck with the Russians for first place, rather than all alone at the Y.

At 6 p.m., when Louey thought that Sandy was slowing down a bit, she hatched an idea that she thought was absolutely hilarious. She and Charlie went out and bought a turkey submarine sandwich and a can of Coke at Bruno's Deli on Highland Avenue. When they returned to the pool, Louey called out to Sandy, who seemed delighted. Louey knelt at the edge of the pool and held the sandwich out to her swimmer. Without stopping, Sandy flipped over and swam now on her back, very slowly, only kicking her feet a bit. She reached up with one hand for the sub, which Louey had thoughtfully had the proprietor of Bruno's cut into four smallish pieces. She also gave her friend a napkin—to be all dainty, and everything.

The photo of Sandy floating along with a turkey sandwich balanced on a napkin on her stomach would be the best photo ever, Louey thought. *Where's Paul when we need him?*

"Hey! No food in the pool! What are you doing? Get out of here!" the Y's director yelled. Louey said, "She was getting hungry; it's 6 o'clock, man! And she'll need something to wash it down with," she added, pointing to the Coke on the deck of the pool. The director scooped up the can immediately and trashed it, unopened. Charlie and Louey were escorted to the door by the official timekeeper, who was now the only official, other than the director, left in the building.

"You didn't say, 'No food in the pool,'" Louey complained.

"We didn't have to. It goes without saying," the snippy official said without looking at her. "There's a sign on the door. Everybody knows you don't take food into a pool."

Looking back from the doorway to the pool area, they could see the director holding Sandy's sandwich and heading for the same garbage can that was now housing the Coke.

"That is a person with no compunction about wasting food," Louey said to her accomplice.

Persons unknown alerted Osterhout to the swimming prowess of his employee. At 7:55 p.m., he was at the bar at a well-known, expensive Italian restaurant a few blocks away. He raced back to the Y, grabbed the mic and announced to the empty-but-for-Annie bleachers: "Ladies and gentlemen, this fundraiser will end at 8 p.m. Any swimmer still in the pool at that time will have to stop."

Sandy—who had been the sole swimmer for over an hour when Osterhout had made that announcement—painted the picture for the gang at the Dugout later, and they nearly vomited with laughter. What made it a bit frightening, Annie noted, was that Osterhout's complexion seemed to have gone from pure white to beet red while he was gone.

She was truly afraid that he would stroke out and she would have to revive him. She knew how to do it, but she would just not volunteer.

By the time Sandy Miller emerged from the pool, energized from her long swim and not even breathing hard, she had raised $2,100 for her local YMCA. And all of it had to come from the pockets of James Osterhout Sr., Publisher.

The next day, he stomped into the office, snarly as a stingray. He thrashed through the newsroom and into Daley's office while Charlie and Louey gave each other sidelong looks from across the room and tried to hide their secret snorting and closed-mouth, stomach-bouncing laughter. From behind Daley's closed curtains came the sound of Osterhout sputtering. They couldn't hear Daley's voice, but reveled in imagining it. It was a while before the Publisher emerged. Striding straight for the exit, he looked neither to the right nor to the left. Everybody on the Desk was silent.

As Louey made a foray through the big archway into Backshop to do checkout, she slipped a folded piece of copy paper next to Charlie's typewriter.

"So I guess this means we're not going to have an Awards Ceremony for Sandy, huh?" it said.

Charlie snorted once like a horse, and covered her face in her hand hoping it would look like she'd just coughed, not laughed.

It was a long time that night before anyone on the Desk spoke, and then it was softly, as if the newsroom might be bugged.

"I guess Osterhout wasn't too pleased with Esther

Williams over there," Tim said, as Sandy rushed past and flew to the nearest typewriter to file her stories for the day.

"I know. He's out over $2,000," Louey said.

Annie had to write the story about how the Record had generously topped all corporate donors to the Y's inaugural Swim-a-Thon. She had to get a quote from Osterhout by calling him at home. Oh, it was a glorious story, accompanied by a photo of the pool with Sandy splashing through it. In the photo, Louey thought she could detect a contented, unconcerned smile on Sandy's wet face.

Now it was spring, and Louey needed a vacation. She was getting tired of it all, already. She needed to travel—"to see something other than Mulberry Street," she told Charlie. And Charlie, in return, had a little surprise for Louey: She was applying to law schools.

"Don't tell anybody," she said. "I might not be accepted, so I don't want to blab it around, y'know?"

She'd applied to three: one in New York City, one in Boston and one in Buffalo. If she was accepted at any of them, she'd start in the fall.

Louey stood stunned, and stared.

"Wow, seriously? You want to be a lawyer? Where did *that* come from?"

"Why not? I interview lawyers all the time, and I always thought lawyers were, like, really smart? But these guys aren't smart at all! They're dumber than hell! What put me over the top was, I asked this one guy, who works in Goshen, how he was gonna plead his client. You know: if he was gonna plead him not guilty or go for a settlement, or what. And he got all flustered, and he looked like he was gonna cry, and he said, 'Do I have to tell you?'"

She snickered and shook her head as she added, "I mean, they say stupid stuff like that all the time, but that really got me thinking. I mean, if people like that can graduate from law school and make $50,000 a year, then I can, too. What am I doing at the Record, if I can help poor people directly, and do it better than these jerks, and make a lot of dough doing it?"

Louey admired Charlie for her decision, but she also hated it. How would she get along without Charlie? It wouldn't be any fun without Charlie! It wouldn't be the same paper. Surely Charlie would get into any law school she applied to; she was really smart, and she actually already knew a lot about the law and had a great batch of relevant clippings, just from covering the courts.

Dear Diary,

I hope Charlie gets into all those law schools: They'd be smart to take her, and she'll be top of her class wherever she goes. But I also hope she doesn't get into any of them, and stays with me forever.

Part 2:

UNIONS

In negotiations, Ted Daley was not just contemptuous, but also truly outraged by the reporters' demands.

"If you think you can dictate who we hire, you're out of your minds," he said. "Management always retains the right to hire and fire whoever we please. That's true everywhere."

The Guild team was supposed to let the Guild lawyer speak for them. Louey knew that. The rest of them were to just sit there and glare. But Joe Louis, unlike his namesake, was no fighter, so Louey decided to jump into the ring.

"Where is that written?" she said.

"It's right in your contract." He whipped open his copy of the pact (in headlines, contracts were always "pacts") and read aloud: "Notwithstanding any clauses in this contract to the contrary, management retains the right to hire and fire according to their own standards."

He peered through his thick, thick glasses, his watery eyes as large now as two egg yolks. If egg yolks were blue. She was sorry now that she'd asked that question, and given him the opening to drone on and on.

"You know perfectly well—or you should know, for Pete's sake—there's no newspaper contract in the country that gives the union the right to dictate hiring and firing decisions." Joe Louis said nothing. Daley had them on that one. All because Louey had opened her big mouth.

Jake was right: Management found laughable their proposal (their "demand," as the Guild called it) that they hire six Black reporters—three for Newburgh, and three to be assigned to the provinces.

John Jacobson, management's lawyer, repeated their tired refrain.

"Management retains the right to hire and fire, just like in every union contract in the world," the Record's lawyer said dismissively. "We're negotiating the terms and conditions of people who are already *on* staff. We're not going to sit here and have you tell us who we can and cannot hire and what race they have to be. So you can drop that item right now."

"You can't cover a city like Newburgh with no reporters from the minority community," Jake said. "You lose the trust of the people. We don't even have any native Spanish speakers on staff, and believe me, that's very short-sighted. We're going to need some Hispanics, too, in the next few years. You walk down Broadway now and half the people are speaking Spanish."

"Oh, so we should go into the Black Dirt fields and pick out a few Mexicans to be reporters?" Daley said.

Here the management team, led by the easily amused Jacobson, burst into derisive snickers.

"Well, I'm sorry to tell ya, but Jeez Louise, guys, that's just the way it is," Daley said when he'd stopped chuckling. "We're not hiring this many Mexicans and that many Black people until we've achieved your idea of a nicely-balanced newsroom. That's not our goal. That's not how you run a newspaper. We're looking for top-notch, experienced reporters."

Jake jumped in with agitated protestations that if the Record wanted "top-notch" people, they weren't going to attract any with the salaries they were paying. Also, they clearly weren't "looking for" anyone! They weren't advertising for any additional reporters and hadn't done so for … for how many years now? As he raved on, the Guild lawyer backed him up by passing around the table a list of the salaries of other newspapers in the state, which ranged from two to ten times higher than the Record's rates. It was a powerful moment for the reporters, but the managers snickered and pointed out that these were all much bigger papers—they'd even included the Wall Street Journal, for God's sake. The union came back by noting that those papers' unions all had contracts, while theirs had expired nearly a year ago.

Louey knew she was supposed to be paying attention, but she couldn't focus. She doodled artfully decorated song lyrics in her notepad as though she were taking notes on the proceedings, but really she wasn't even there. She had gone somewhere better. She was recalling a story her father had told her and her brother and sister a long, long time ago.

The whole family had been in the living room watching TV, and as soon as Ed Sullivan was over, Abe Levy had busted this one out. Abe's mother, Ray, had wandered off to her bedroom to write a letter to one of her cousins, and Sam, her husband, was already on his way to their room, to read his Talmud.

"OK, who wants to hear a Three Kid Detectives story?" Abe asked.

Unanimous.

The Three Kid Detectives Go to Israel

OK, well, I don't know if you knew this or not, but one night at the Levy house in Newburgh, President Kennedy was on the phone.

"Oh, c'mon, Dad: Make it at least a little realistic, would ya?" Danny whined.

"What d'you mean, realistic? This really happened! I wouldn't lie about a thing like that! President Kennedy really called the Levy house in Newburgh one evening. You could look it up! And in fact, Danny Levy—he was the oldest of the Three Kid Detectives, y'know— he was the one who answered the phone!"

"Yes, is, uh, Abe Levy there, please? This is the President speaking," Danny hears, as soon as he says hello.

"Dad?" Danny calls out. "It's Irving Green!" Irving Green was now the president of the Orange County Magistrates Association, and everybody was all proud of him, y'know.

So Danny's father—a very wise and handsome fellow he was—gets on the line, and he says, "Hey, Irv! How's Mildred?"

"No, it's uh, John Kennedy, the President of the United States."

"Oh, for Chrissake. I mean, I beg your pardon, Mr. President.

My son misled me."

"*That's all right,*" the President chuckles. "*I have two of my own, you know. But we have a problem here, and I'm afraid that, uh, only the Three Kid Detectives can solve it.*"

"*Oh, my God,*" the father says. "*What is it?*"

"*Well, there's an international diamond thief whom nobody can seem to catch. He flies all over the world with millions of dollars' worth of diamonds hidden in his coat, or his hat band, or his dog's collar, or somewhere.*"

"Dad!" Clare interrupted. "You can't get on a plane with a dog! That doesn't even make sense!"

"Hey! Who's telling this story, you or me?" Abe said. "I didn't say he had a dog; I just said he had a dog COLLAR. And besides, I know what Kennedy said: I was there! Now let me continue, will ya?" Not waiting for a reply—it wasn't really a question—Abe continued.

"*We can't seem to catch this guy,*" the President says. "*But let me say this about that: The CIA now knows that he, uh, stopped in Newburgh, New York just yesterday. That's where you are, correct?*"

"*Correct. What the heck was he doing here?*"

"*Well, apparently he found out that the bagels in Ettie's Delicatessen are the best in the world. You know Ettie's?*"

"*On William Street! Sure! We eat there all the time.*"

"*Well, the CIA believes he stole 144 bagels from Ettie's.*"

Here, Abe paused for the unison response from all three kids, which he knew was coming: "A hundred and forty-four?! Eww: That's gross!"

The Levys might not have been the smartest kids in Newburgh, but they knew their lines.

"… *and he intends to take them to Israel and sell them there,* *along with the diamonds. You know, they say that the folks in* *Israel love their, uh, bagels.*"

"What kind did he get?" Louey interjected.

"What kind? Who cares what kind?"

"I just want to know," Louey said.

Big sigh.

"OK, let's see, he got six dozen poppyseed … two dozen salt … two dozen pumpernickel … that's ten … and two dozen onion. That's 12 dozen, one-forty-four. Everybody happy now?"

"Yes," they all said.

Louey wasn't sorry she asked. She could picture them better now. You need to have details when you tell a story.

"So he's got them in a sack," she said, just to be clear. "A burlap sack, like burglars in cartoons always carry."

"Right," Abe said. "Sure."

Now Louey was really trying to picture it. "Because he can't be carrying a hundred forty-four bagels in Ettie's bags; they only hold a dozen. Twelve Ettie's bags filled with bagels would never fit in a suitcase. In fact, where is he putting them on these planes, if he's flying all over the world?"

"In the cargo hold! Jeez, can I continue now?"

"But that's so stupid!" Danny said. "How much money can you make selling bagels? What are they—a quarter apiece? How much is a hundred forty-four times 25 cents?"

"Thirty-six dollars," Clare piped up after a few moments. "Because four into fourteen goes three … "

"A diamond thief is gonna risk getting caught for a bunch of bagels that cost thirty-six bucks?"

"You get a discount for every dozen," Clare pointed out. Everyone ignored this.

"SO ANYWAY," Abe intoned, "now that we know the types and prices of bagels at Ettie's Delicatessen, which have nothing to do with this story, if no one else has any other interruptions to foist upon us, I shall now continue. Is that OK with you?"

It was.

"We have a plane standing by at Stewart Air Force Base," Kennedy says. *"Can you get the Three Kid Detectives packed and on that plane by 10 o'clock tonight? The crook is already on his way to Israel. The CIA says he got on an El Al flight out of Idlewild that left 15 minutes ago, but we think the jet out of Stewart can beat them to Lod Airport. That way they can be, uh, ready to catch the guy right when he lands in Tel Aviv."*

"Sure, I can get them to Stewart for you, Mr. President. The hard part will be getting them out of school this week! Danny has a math test tomorrow."

"I'll call their schools and ask if the kids can be excused," Kennedy says.

"OK, thanks, I'll get you their principals' numbers tomorrow," Abe says.

All three kids had run to the other phone and were listening in, and at that point, they all began silently jumping up and dancing and mouthing, "Yay! No school! Yay!"

Kennedy, who had very good hearing, apparently, says, "Well, thanks, and, uh, kids: Be careful when you get to Israel. He's armed and extremely dangerous."

"He's armed with bagels?" Danny asked.

"Sure! Bagels can be lethal! Didn't you know that? Now

shut up and let me tell this story, will ya?" Abe said.

At Stewart Air Force Base, they were met by a dapper, uniformed fellow who said, "Hi, I'm Frank, your pilot."

"Hello, Frank-Your-Pilot, I'm Louey, and this is Danny and Clare!" Louey said. She's always in a very buoyant mood when she's starting a new adventure, you know.

Anyway, Frank-Your-Pilot gave each of the kids a top-secret packet as they boarded the plane. It told everything the government knew about the crook. They could see it was going to be a tough case to crack. He had brown eyes, like every single other person in Israel. He was short but he sometimes wore boots with big, thick heels so he looked average-height, and he had black, straight hair but he sometimes wore wigs of various colors, and sometimes fake beards, too, and he spoke a million different languages, depending on where he was, but none of them very well. His skin was the same color as that of a lot of Mediterranean folks, like the Italians, or the Greeks, or maybe the Egyptians. Or the Israelis, for that matter! He went by various names, but his latest passport said Moishe Cohen.

"Well, how the heck are we supposed to find him, then? We don't even know his name or what he looks like," Danny said as he flipped through his packet on the plane, just before he fell asleep.

"We'll find him," Louey said. "We're the Three Kid Detectives!"

The flight from Stewart was very fast, just as Kennedy predicted. After all, they were the only ones aboard, except for Frank-Your-Pilot and his co-pilot, so their plane was about 100 times lighter than the plane the crook was on. Louey spent the entire flight studying a book called "Hebrew in 10 Hours." It was one of those books that magically appear in stories when they're needed and there's no other way to include them, because all the libraries

and bookstores are closed. You hear me, Louey?
"Yes."
Good. Anyway, it was right there on her seat when Louey strapped herself in.
Danny and Clare slept most of the way. The co-pilot was very nice to them and came back a few times during the flight to offer the kids water and snacks. But Louey was too busy to eat, and the other two-thirds of the passengers were asleep, so they were very poor customers.
Now, it was bright in Israel when they landed, and the sudden silence in the plane, after nine hours of engine noise, awakened Danny and Clare, who were seated side-by-side in the row ahead of Louey.
"Get up, you guys!" Louey yelled. "We're here!"
Frank-Your-Pilot led them through Customs at Lod Airport quick as a wink, because he had a letter from Kennedy that he flashed at everyone. The kids only had to show their passports and zoom, they waltzed right through.
"They hora'd right through," Louey interrupted.
Right. Right. They hora'd right through. Then Frank-Your-Pilot gave them each a hundred shekels, so they'd be able to buy stuff, and stay over in any hotels they needed to, and get around Israel by bus or train or cabs or whatever they needed, and then he gave them his number to call when they were done, and he said that as soon as they called, he'd meet them back at the airport.
Before he left, he asked, "How long do you think it'll take you to find this guy? A day or two?"
"Yeah, something like that," Danny said.
And then, right away, Danny started complaining that he was hungry.

"Hey, let's have breakfast first!" he says, but then Louey says, "I hate to tell you this, but it's 2 o'clock in the afternoon here. No one's serving breakfast now.

"Are you kidding?" Danny says. "I'm starving to death!"

"Danny," Louey says, "we're halfway around the world from Newburgh. There's these things called time zones. Trust me; it's 2 o'clock here." They all set their watches for 2 p.m., but Danny didn't stop moaning and grumbling about it. They have these great big breakfasts in Israel, with fish, and tomatoes, and fruit, and bagels, and egg salad, and orange juice and everything you can think of. That's how they eat, over there, and Danny knew it, too. He had actually learned something in school at one point, apparently. But they had no time to lose! They had to start looking for this diamond thief. And they decided to start with the airport, because the crook's plane was due to arrive within the next 15 minutes.

"Don't worry; we'll have a great, big, huge dinner tonight, after we catch this guy," Louey said.

"Ya mean, we gotta skip lunch?" Danny says. "We already skipped breakfast! I'm going on strike!"

Well, they looked all over the airport for this guy Moishe. There were hundreds of rabbis with their long, grey beards and long, black coats, jabbering away in Yiddish and German and Russian and Hebrew and everything else, and thousands of women trying to keep track of their kids and baby carriages and stuff, all backed up in long, raggedy lines all over the airport, and everybody complaining and fighting with one another and with the Customs officials, who weren't having a great time, either.

As the next few planes from New York landed, the kids looked closely at the faces and luggage and bags of every man who entered *the airport. No luck! They didn't see him anywhere.*

Then Louey sat down in a phone booth with her notebook and pen and opened the phone book that was chained there and started making a list of all the pawn shops in Tel Aviv, with their addresses and phone numbers. She was going to try to call them to say that this guy might be trying to pawn his stolen diamonds, and to be on the lookout. She really buckled down, and after just a few hours she had dozens of pawn shops' names copied down. She took a break only once, to gaze at a beautiful hoopoe bird that flew low right past her phone booth, coming in for a landing on the beach.

"Hoopoe? That's a stupid name. Is that a real kind of a bird?" Danny interrupted.

"Yeah; it's a beauty," Abe said. "I saw some of them when I went to Israel with the Jewish legislators. They're tan, with a long, downcurved bill and black-and-white wings and a black-and-white crest on its head, like … like an Indian headdress, kinda. 'Hoopoe' means, 'He is here' in Hebrew, you know."

"Hoo-poe! He is here! God is here! Get it? That is so cool!" Louey said.

Yeah, well, anyway: While Louey was copying pawn-shop names, Danny and Clare were looking around for the crook. Clare stopped in every deli and restaurant she could find, showing people the CIA photos that were in her packet. To her delight, everyone spoke English. To her dismay, no one had seen this guy. And even if they had, in the photos she had of him, he was always wearing big, dark glasses, which would have made it nearly impossible to say it was him anyway.

Danny wasn't having any luck either, but that may have

been because he was spending most of his time ogling the girls on Tel Aviv's beaches.

"WHAT was I doing to them?" Danny interrupted.

"This wasn't you; this was another kid named Danny Levy. You never caught a crook in your life," Abe reminded him.

"OK, what was Danny doing to these girls?" Danny said.

"Oh for God's sake: Don't you know what 'ogling' means?" Louey asked.

"No. Ogling? What the heck is that?"

"Looking at! And not in a polite way, either!" she responded.

"Excuse me; may I continue? Do you mind?" Abe said.

"Yes," they all said. But they meant, yes, he could continue.

Well, he was spending so much time looking at the girls swimming and surfing and playing volleyball on the beach, that he forgot to show them any of his photos or ask them any questions. But he was getting very hungry, so he went to a street vendor and bought himself two kosher hotdogs and a dozen falafel balls, which are these things they sell on every corner in Israel with something called tahini sauce on top, and it's delicious, and a Coke. Because they drink Coke in Israel, just like we do. And then he sat down right on the sand and had himself a wonderful lunch, and right after that he took a two-hour nap right on the beach, so he didn't even notice when his pages blew out of his packet, because he was asleep! And then he had to spend the rest of the daylight hours running around the beach gathering them up again. He didn't stop 'til he'd found them all, because he knew his sisters would kill him if he let those pages blow into the ocean.

Well, the kids didn't catch the guy that day. They finally gave up and had a huge dinner right in the restaurant of the hotel that the U.S. government had reserved for them.

"Did we all get separate rooms?" Danny interrupted the story to ask.

"Danny got his own room, because he's a boy," Abe said. "The girls shared."

"Oh thank God," Clare said. "Nobody wants to smell Danny's stinky socks!"

They all had a wonderful dinner of chicken soup followed by a nice brisket and chocolate cake for dessert, all paid for by U.S. taxpayers. Louey and Clare tried to take it easy, because they didn't want to spend so many shekels on their first night there, but Danny had two helpings of everything.

Anyway, the next three days were no better. By Thursday noon, Louey had visited all the pawn shops and jewelry stores in Tel Aviv, but no luck. Clare had visited almost all the delis and restaurants in the city, but no one had seen or even heard of this guy. And Danny had checked out the beaches, by very carefully looking at all the necklaces the girls were wearing, to see if there were any diamonds among them. He had bought himself a very powerful pair of binoculars to do this with. There weren't any diamonds to be seen, though.

Moishe must have slipped past them at the airport, amidst all those people, and taken off for some other place.

"Look," Clare says over lunch at the hotel, "we've been here three days now. He's probably miles away—maybe countries away! It doesn't seem like he stays anywhere very long."

"Hey! Maybe he's gone to Jerusalem," Louey said. "There's a lot of Jews there. They would have a lot of delis to buy up his bagels, and maybe a lot of jewelry stores, too, to buy his diamonds."

So that very afternoon, after a swim in the Mediterranean just for fun, they all got on a bus to Jerusalem. And half an hour later, there they were in the capital of Israel. That country is so small! It's smaller than New Jersey, the whole country!

Well, first they had to find a hotel and check in, and then they had to start all over again with asking everyone in sight if they'd seen this guy or if they'd bought any diamonds or bagels from a strange man recently. By the time they'd spent about three hours at that thankless task, they were dog-tired and ready to quit. And I don't mean just quit for the day: I mean they were ready to tell Frank-Your-Pilot they were going back to Tel Aviv for their flight home … and admit defeat for the first time in the careers of the Three Kid Detectives.

Here Abe paused for dramatic effect. His kids looked at one another with wide eyes and slapped their cheeks with both hands and squeaked in mock horror, "Oh, no!"

At dinner, they decided they needed to come up with another strategy.

"Well, now we're just the Three Kid Dejectives—get it? Because we're all dejected? —unless you guys can think of something, because I don't have any more ideas," Louey said. "I'm thinking that the trail has gone stale."

"I'm thinking that the bagels have gone stale," Danny said. "He must have sold them all by now, and we have no idea to who."

"To whom," Louey said. Everybody ignored her.

They were so sad, their faces hung down almost into their bowls of matzo-ball soup.

"Look, let's forget about the stupid bagels! He's got thousands of dollars' worth of diamonds he's hiding somewhere, President

Kennedy said! Let's forget about the stupid bagels, and look for the diamonds*! Let's give it one more try tomorrow, and then if we can't find him, we should just go home," Clare said. "We're wasting our time here." Sadly, they all agreed.*

Now, their rooms were up on the top floor of the hotel—the 20ᵗʰ floor—and on Friday morning, they all got a kick out of how fast the elevator zipped down to the lobby, where the hotel's breakfast buffet was being served. It was a brand-new hotel, and even the elevator was cool, with a mechanical voice calling out the floor numbers as they sped by, Twelve, Seven, Three, like a rocket ship getting ready to take off when everything is "A-OK."

Danny already knew all about the breakfast buffets at Israeli hotels. He piled tons of smoked fish on one bagel and egg salad on another. Then he piled hummus on top of a big triangular flat piece of bread they call a pita, and then he scooped a couple of spoonfuls of little cucumber cubes and parsley leaves into the pocket of another one and poured dressing into it 'til it was overflowing, and then after he was done eating all that he went back to the buffet table for seconds and grabbed some slabs of different kinds of cheeses, too, because the room price included an all-you-can-eat buffet at breakfast. Louey and Clare, meanwhile, had nice scrambled eggs and whole wheat toast for breakfast, because they had common sense, and they all had milk, and then they got down to business.

"OK, last day here. Let's give it our best shot, and then we can go home tomorrow and be able to say we did the best we could," said Louey. "So today, let's just make one really thorough sweep of Jerusalem. I'll try to hit all the pawn shops, like I did in Tel Aviv; you guys scout out the jewelry stores and restaurants. We'll meet back here for lunch around 2. Can you wait that long, Danny?"

"Yeah, I guess," he says.

"Good, because it'll take us that long to do a good job. And after lunch, I'll call Frank-Your-Pilot and we'll just pack up and leave."

Well. Nothing doing. There was not a single Kid Detective who came up with anyone who had ever seen or even heard of this Moishe Cohen the Crook. There were so many pawn shops, jewelry stores, restaurants and delis that they couldn't get to a tenth of them, and no one they did talk to had seen Moishe. So, after five full days in Israel, it looked like the end of the undefeated streak for the Three Kid Detectives. They had a sad, late lunch together and then went up to their rooms to pack their bags.

Now, it was already getting dark, and the girls had finished packing and were sitting on their beds watching TV when the phone in their room rang. Clare picked it up, expecting Danny to say he was ready to go.

"What?" she said. "He's where? How do you know? OK, OK!" She slammed the phone down and said, "Louey! Quick! We gotta go to Danny's room! He's got the guy in his sights!"

"What? Who. What sights?" Louey said, all confused, as they ran out of their room and into Danny's, next door.

Danny had opened his door for them already and had run back to his window with his binoculars.

"C'mere; c'mere!" he yells, waving one hand toward himself very fast.

He'd been watching the street below (well, he'd been watching the girls on the street below, to be exact) and he'd seen a guy carrying a big, lumpy gunny-sack that was bulging out in a bunch of funny directions. "There he is! Look!" he said. Louey grabbed the binoculars, saying, "Where? Where is he?" as Danny pointed down toward the street below.

Sure enough, a very short guy wearing what looked like red slippers was walking very fast along the sidewalk just past their hotel, toward the next corner, burdened by what looked like a very heavy bag that he'd slung over his shoulder.

Clare grabbed the binoculars from Louey. She brought him into focus. "But his hair is white!" she said.

"That's a disguise! Let's go!" Louey said. "Clare, keep the binoculars. Try to track him. When we get down to the street, signal to show us which way he turned."

Oddly, their blazing fast elevator took what seemed like forever to reach their floor. It must have been down in the lobby when they pushed the button. Danny was shifting from foot to foot like he had to pee, muttering, "C'mon, c'mon, c'mon, c'mon, c'mon," and Louey was just about to forget the darn thing and run down the stairs, when it finally arrived. Luckily, there was no one else in it. She pushed "L," for the lobby. The elevator went down to the 19th floor and stopped. The doors opened, but there was no one there. Danny and Louey couldn't believe it. They looked at each other in frustration. The doors slowly closed as Louey jabbed the L" about a dozen times. The elevator dropped for about two seconds, then stopped. The doors opened again as the "18" lit up. No one was there. The doors closed. Finally Louey got it.

"Oh, my God! This is the Shabbos elevator!" she yelled.

"The what?" Danny said.

"Come on!" she said as the elevator stopped at the 17th floor. "Get out!"

As soon as the doors opened just barely wide enough, Louey squeezed through and raced down the hall to the stairwell, with Danny in hot pursuit.

"The Shabbos elevator! It stops at every floor from Friday

sundown to Saturday sundown, so no one has to push any buttons on the Sabbath!" Louey yelled breathlessly, while running down the stairwell and leaping over the bannisters as she got halfway to each floor.

Out on the street, they looked up and saw Clare leaning out from Danny's window, waving frantically to them to take a right at the corner. But when they did ... he was gone. Moishe the Crook had disappeared. Could the Three Kid Detectives have let Moishe the Crook get away? Well, they weren't about to give up so easily. Not this time.

They ran more slowly, kind of jogging, like. They needed to catch their breath, even if they couldn't catch their crook. They peered into every store window ... but now the stores were all closed. He couldn't have ducked into any of them—not on Shabbos. He had to be out on the street somewhere. When they reached the next corner, though, Louey's heart sank. There were three ways he could have gone—straight ahead, left, or right—so even if they split up, they'd be able to cover only two of the possible routes. Just then, Danny yells, "He went this way! Come on!"

Louey ran just behind her brother for half a block, dying to know why he was so sure of himself, when he darted diagonally across the street and started sprinting up the block.

"There he is! Get him!" he called to Louey.

Sure enough, a little guy wearing slippers and carrying a big, lumpy gunny-sack was only half a block ahead of them. He turned briefly to peer back at them and then started running, head down. But he wasn't very fast, carrying that big bag.

Louey quickly passed Danny and took about six seconds to overtake the thief and tackle him like a cornerback on a wide receiver.

GENIE ABRAMS

"Stop, in the name of the United States government!" she cried as they fell, but he was already good and stopped. His white wig had fallen off, revealing jet-black hair, and his white beard was hanging off half of his face, too. His bag was open beside him.

Danny caught up and dumped the raggedy bag's contents onto the sidewalk. Even in the fading light, they could see dozens of sparkling diamonds among about 30 bagels, some of which were still slowly rolling away. The bagels, not the diamonds.

"Get up, Santa Claus, you're under arrest," Danny said, jerking the guy to his feet.

Within less than a minute, they were being swarmed by a group of six Israeli soldiers. The kids explained who they were and what had happened, and they all marched old Moishe to the Jerusalem police headquarters. It turned out that this guy was no Moishe: He was Wing Ka-Ching the Diamond Thief from China, and he was wanted all over Asia, South Africa and about five other countries, too.

Danny and Louey had to wait for a little while at police headquarters, until David Ben-Gurion was called at the President's residence and given the good news. He came right over to present them both with the Israeli Medal of Honor. They asked for one for Clare, too, because she had told them which way Ka-Ching had gone, and Ben-Gurion said he'd mail hers to her in Newburgh, because he had only brought two with him and he wanted to hurry up and get home for the nice Shabbos dinner his wife was holding for him.

"Man, when I saw all those soldiers running with their rifles, I couldn't believe they were there to help us: I thought they were after some Muslim fanatic," Danny said.

Ben-Gurion said, "Danny, we're not worried about Muslim

fanatics. We have enough problems with our own Jewish fanatics."

This struck Louey as funny.

"Jewish fanatics?" she said. "I didn't think we had any fanatics in our religion."

He said, "Louey, all fanatics have the same religion: Fanaticism."

As they walked back to their hotel, Louey said, "Danny, back at that second intersection, how the heck did you know which way he went?"

"I saw the trail of poppyseeds that were falling out of a rip in his bag," Danny said. "He must have had about 30 bagels left, y'know, and the seeds were easy to see on these white-stone sidewalks."

"Huh! You know, Danny, sometimes you're not as dumb as you look. I guess he was hiding the diamonds among all those bagels, thinking no one would ever suspect a poor old bagel-peddler of being an international jewel thief."

When they got back to the hotel, they found their little sister entertaining the guests in the lobby. They were gathered around her as she played the piano. She was singing the Jewish National Anthem, "Hatikvah," so Danny and Louey stood respectfully with everyone else. She had already played and sung a bunch of show tunes, and "Hatikvah" was the only sheet-music left in the piano seat. But then the audience began calling out their favorite songs, and she was so tied up trying to play and sing them that she could only smile and nod at Louey and Danny when they made their triumphant, sweaty entrance, giving her the thumbs-up to show they'd been successful.

"Well, friends, I have to get up early tomorrow, so I'll leave you now, but thanks for listening, and thanks for the nice reception,"

she said as she pushed back the piano bench.

Louey then quickly strode over to a spot right next to the piano and faced the room.

"Wait! Wait!" she said. "I have a great story to tell! You won't believe what just happened! My brother and I caught a diamond thief, just a few blocks from here! Just now! We really did!"

But after hearing Clare sing and play piano, nobody was interested anymore. They were all happy about the free concert they'd just had, and even as Louey spoke, they started wandering off in all directions, gabbing in little groups or heading for the slow, slow Shabbos elevators.

"So, let that be a lesson to ya, Louey," Abe concluded. "You try to tell a story, and then the slightest little thing happens, and right away you lose your audience.

"But then," he sighed, "that's what you gotta expect, when you're part of ... "

"The Three ... Kid ... Detectives!" his audience yelled in unison.

"Look. Bottom line," Daley was saying, back in the Real World. "We can't be spending time training folks with criminal records and no command of basic English; we have a newspaper to put out. We have a standard of quality to maintain, but you guys sound like you're more loyal to the union than you are to the paper! So I mean, if you don't like it, you can always leave."

Louey regained consciousness.

Adios, Bastards, she drew in bubble-style letters in her notebook. She spent the rest of the session filling in the letters with cross-hatching until, a droning lifetime later, it was time to go. At home that night, she added a big cross-hatched heart to that page, and she also wrote in her diary: *Guess what? I am not working for these prejudiced ignoramuses anymore. I really am not. I have quit in my heart. I'm still at the Record, but I have quit in my heart.*

She knew she couldn't quit the Record having put so little time in. She'd give it another year or so. Otherwise, it would look crappy on her résumé. Maybe Ted Daley would drop dead or retire or something in the meantime, and then she wouldn't even feel like leaving. Oh, she hated him. He was Pure Evil, a greedy, stupid, management pig. But she'd give it a while. Maybe things would get better.

At the end of each bargaining session, everyone took out their calendars to set a date for the next meeting. In a private huddle the union members once held in the hotel hallway, Louey asked the Guild lawyer why they even bothered with these stupid meetings. His answer was that walking out risked getting hit with a charge of "bargaining in bad faith." And so the reporters took out their calendars each time, and on they went.

It's like buying a Lottery ticket, Louey wrote in her journal. *You know you're not going to win, but it's something to do. It's a bad habit you can't kick, going to these sessions. Free soda, though, and at Christmas, cookies, too! Management is paying for that depressing, windowless Holiday Inn room and "refreshments," and I'm surprised they're not getting tired of that, but neither side wants to declare impasse. We're afraid we'd lose in arbitration because the paper's right about not having to hire Black reporters, and management is afraid to go to arbitration because then it would be in all the other papers ... and on the radio, and on TV, giving them a black eye. So nobody's declaring impasse, and we're just going on ... and on ... and on we go. Am I going to be doing this the rest of my life? Oh G-d, get me outta here.*

Charlie, to Louey's joy and pride and satisfaction and un-speakable sorrow, was accepted at the University of Buffalo Law School. She was going to be a graduate assistant to a prof as well, so her tuition was all paid, and she'd saved enough for the deposit and first month's rent on the little apartment near campus that the prof had told her about. His previous assistant had vacated it at the end of June to move to Illinois with her fiancé.

Helping her best friend pack was not Louey's idea of a good time, though she threw herself into the work on that gloomy afternoon.

I am precisely half envious and half sad, she thought. *The smart, talented people leave. They move on. They get something better. While I just stay here like a dope, climbing the Record's Ladder to Nowhere.*

They wrapped Charlie's few dishes, glasses and mugs in that week's newspapers. Annie and Sandy had gone to every liquor store in Middletown to get free boxes. Louey had plenty of colored markers with thick, chiseled tips, and used them to label and decorate every box before stuffing them into Charlie's car. Each item she packed seemed to weigh a ton, and they only got heavier as the day wore on: The de-flated blow-up mattress that she wouldn't need because the place was furnished; the manila bags of her clippings, sod-den with memories; the ominous, gun-shaped electric hair blower; the sad rubber-banded posters of Che Guevara and Bob Dylan. Finally they had somehow gotten into the car everything that could be moved, and there was nothing left but to say goodbye.

This could be awful, and Louey knew it. She had a plan, though: She would hang back from the others as Charlie stood by the door of her car, and then, as Sandy and Annie mobbed her, Louey would stand back a few feet. That way, when the others backed off and Charlie started to pull away from the curb, Louey would just wave jauntily and call out, "OK, take care, Charlie! Drive safe, OK?" With a big ol' smile. Easy-peasy.

It didn't go that way. Charlie did stand in front of the driver's-side door and say, "Well, guys ... "; and Annie and Sandy did do the smiling, group-hug thing with her, saying, "Yay!" and "Go get 'em, Charlie!" and "We'll miss you so much!" But then the two others parted so that Charlie was looking directly at Louey, and each smiled slowly and took two steps toward the other, and Louey, filled with both sentimentality and real sorrow, cried silently and shook and her face crumpled like a used tissue as she hugged her friend goodbye. And even as Charlie laughed and said "Goodbye," and "I'll miss you," the way the normal people do, Louey could only give a tight little closed-lip smile and nod a jillion little reverberating nods. She looked away from her friend. Her throat hurt too much to swallow, much less to speak.

Reader, Louey Levy didn't have to work for the Record much longer, and it was thanks to the Viet Cong. One fine day, the South Vietnamese people took their capital back from the invaders. U.S. troops were hastily—some would say frantically—being evacuated. At the Record, the telex started spewing long tails of yellow news, ceaselessly, all day. Louey closed her eyes and thanked haShem. Maybe now the killing would end. Maybe now her stepbrother Marc could come home from Canada without risking arrest. Maybe now the United States would do as Isaiah wrote, and not "learn war any more." Maybe this war would be the last.

Reading the first reports, Louey was pierced with joy. She covered her mouth, and tears spurted out from her. She couldn't wait to get home and call Peg Jansen, her college roommate who'd been a leader of the anti-war movement as well as of the feminist one. She'd also call her other pals from college who'd worked so hard for this day.

Flash Hanigan set some kind of distance-running record with his trips from the telex to the copy desk; the yellow pages, linked by untorn perforations at the bottom of each one, were a yards-long, happy flag of surrender that he held high above his head at one end and still trailed on the floor behind him. American troops and Vietnamese civilians alike were fleeing ("being evacuated," the story said)! Vietnam had won the war!

Al Rome had heard the news on the radio at home and rushed in to write a new editorial and opinion column and to supervise personally the production of the next day's paper.

Rome ran straight to the wire-service telex, already chewing on a wad of that morning's paper. He stood over the emerging yellow pages chewing and thinking, chewing and thinking. His bushy eyebrows rose and fell in time with his jaw. Hastily written opinion pieces from Republican and Democratic pundits were being processed, along with terrifying photos of packed U.S. helicopters taking off with human chains of soldiers and civilians dangling from their landing skids.

Rome called in The Publisher; that had not happened before in Louey's time at the Record. Together, Osterhout and Rome would review the wire stories and decide how late the Desk could accept new copy and photos. The Publisher ordered pizza for the whole newsroom; that had never happened before, either. Nobody was to leave. It was likely they would have to put the Pressroom on overtime.

Tim Clay, under the extreme pressure of deadline for first edition, jumped up, clapped twice and yelled to his copy-editors, "OK! Let's play newspa-puh!" As though they weren't already going as fast as they could.

Louey won the honor of writing the Page One banner headline.

"Hey, do me a favor and take a crack at Page One," Tim said to her. "Have Backshop run off one copy and show it to Rome before Checkout."

"Sure," she said. Well, this was exciting.

When she burst into Rome's office waving the mockup, she was surprised to see not Al Rome, but The Publisher standing there, alone.

"Excuse me; where's Al?" she asked. "I have to show this to him."

"Never mind; let me see it," The Publisher said. He stared at it a minute. Staring back at him were the words, in two decks in 46-point Futura Bold, centered: "Ho Chi Minh City Liberated."

"Who wrote this headline," he said. He didn't ask it; he said it. And he already knew the answer.

"I did."

"See me after First Edition goes to bed." Smashing the page into a wrinkly tennis-ball-sized piece of trash, he banged it into Rome's little garbage can and strode quickly into the newsroom.

She knew what was going to happen. Where was Al during this little exchange? Bathroom, maybe? She never found out. The next day's papers—all editions—sported the same 56-point, one-deck Page One headline: "Saigon Falls." But Louey didn't get a free copy, because The Publisher fired her after Late Final went to bed.

"What's your name, again?"

"Louey Levy."

"And how long have you been working here?"

"Too long."

"Well, your tenure just ended. You used abominable judgment in that headline—judgment that we cannot tolerate. It was un-American and completely unacceptable. Your last paycheck will be mailed to you. You may leave now. Good night."

Louey could only imagine what it was like putting the next three editions together, and how Tim Clay and Backshop would like doing that without her. She bought a copy of Late Final—the first she had ever paid for—at a gas station the next day, and it looked fine.

I bet they had a lot of overtime, though, she thought.

Four days later, they had a party for her at the Dugout,

during which her pals presented her with a copy of the Page 5 photo LeFranc took that she'd inserted upside down. They put it into a white mat and framed it with a shiny black wood frame and protected it with expensive, glare-resistant glass. The best part was, as no one had to point out, because she noticed it right away: It was one of those frames with four little "hanging triangles" affixed to the cardboard backing, one near each edge, so that it could be hung in any direction—right-side up (if anyone ever could tell which way was up) or upside down, horizontally or vertically. And on that backing, everyone had written good wishes and smart-aleck or touching farewells.

The next morning after the party, she decided to bite the bullet and make the awful phone call to her father and tell him the bad news. Would he be disappointed in her? Ashamed and disgusted that she'd written such a headline? Or maybe he, please, God, would laugh about it and tell her everything would be all right, and too bad for them, they'll be sorry, they lost the best copy-editor they ever had, and she could come up to Albany and bunk with him and Ree 'til she found a new job. That sounded like him, and she tried to hear his voice saying it.

She was still working on it, though, still pacing around her apartment thinking about it, when the mail came with a letter illustrative of the good luck she'd had all her life.

Her dad had seen an ad in the Albany Knickerbocker News two days earlier, and mailed it to her. The Civil Service Employees Union, the state's largest public-sector labor organization, was looking for a public relations person to cover the Hudson Valley. The position would be based in the union's Fishkill office, right across the river from Newburgh.

CSEU had a quarter-million members working for New York State and its cities; towns; counties; villages; the Thruway Authority; something called the Dormitory Authority, which Louey didn't know what that was; library systems; school districts; sewer districts and dozens of other types of public-sector entities. Most CSEU members, however, worked in low-paying jobs at the big mental hospitals for the emotionally disturbed and "state schools" for adults with developmental disabilities. These employees were the "therapy aides," who bathed and dressed the residents, planned their days and led games, crafts and art projects.

CSEU also represented the plumbers and electricians in those facilities, as well as janitors, food service employees and just about everyone else except the directors. Oddly, the union's members also included the doctors and psychiatrists who worked at those same hospitals, giving orders for the residents' treatment, as well as the bosses of all the other kinds of workers. In other words, uniquely in the world of labor unions, the supervisors were members of the same union as the people they supervised. Louey didn't get that, but otherwise felt she understood the job of a union's PR person very thoroughly. Also, she knew a few things about public psychiatric hospitals and schools for the developmentally disabled. She'd write press releases about the great work the union's members are doing, and what terrific volunteers they are in their communities, and how they deserve more money than they're making. Easy! She could do that in her sleep. And how she would love doing it! She was feeling excited and confident.

The hard part, she thought, would be figuring out whom to list as a reference. The ad said to enclose recommendations from two "supervisors" along with her application. Daley wouldn't do, certainly. But who else had been her "supervisor," really? Tim Clay? No: He would be angry that she was abandoning him to once again do checkout himself. He would never forgive her for that. He might "forget" to write her a recommendation right away, or he might even write her a mediocre one.

Ben Jackson! He would give her a great reference. And Jake, whose title of "Newburgh bureau chief" sounded impressive, would say he was her supervisor and knew her work was excellent, or some bullshit like that. He would lie for her in a heartbeat. She knew it.

Jackson not only instantly agreed, but went on to ask if she needed any money to tide her over 'til she got something. Her voice went squiggly with gratitude as she said no, but that was the kindest thing ever, and thank you, Jackson, thank you so, so, so much.

Her call to Jake resulted in a newsworthy surprise. He laughed and told her he'd certainly say she worked for him, and give her the best recommendation ever, but there was one slight problem: He himself was quitting. He had gotten a job with one of the best papers in the country, the Washington Post. As he tracked how the reporting of Bob Woodward and Carl Bernstein had brought down the Nixon presidency, Jake Rosen became convinced that he had to work for the Post. Nothing else would do. He had sent a blind résumé, enclosing a dozen of his best clips and saying he'd take any job there. He'd taken the train to Washington twice for interviews with various editors. They'd offered him a job at four times the pay he was making at the Record. He had given his month's notice three weeks before Louey was fired. So he'd have to write this recommendation within the next few days if she needed it on Record letterhead, he said, because Friday would be his last day.

No, plain paper would be fine. Louey didn't even know there was such a thing as Record letterhead, nor where any might be found. She'd never had occasion to see any, much less use it. Of *course* he could type her recommendation on plain white paper. But why hadn't he told anyone?

He didn't want anyone to make a fuss over him, he said, or to go to the expense of a party, or anything. Well, she understood that, and she surely wouldn't rat him out, but, boy, was the paper going to miss him! He had broken the story of Newburgh's cops looting the Sears on Broadway and planting drugs and stolen goods on Black men; he had written moving stories about the woman who had lost both sons in Vietnam and the big mutt that had been tossed from a moving car and rescued by a little girl smaller than he was. He'd written about city officials on the take and priests abusing children. Jake's wall in the Newburgh bureau was covered with wooden plaques and framed certificates and awards of all kinds from the New York State Association of Newspaper Editors. Boy, would they miss him!

Management probably didn't want anyone to know he was leaving because they knew what it would do to the staff's morale—what was left of staff, anyway. But meanwhile, he would write his recommendation for Louey and have it ready to mail off in a day or two.

She was offered an interview. It was in the Fishkill office with Tom Lupo, the director of CSEU Region 3, which included all the counties north of New York City on both sides of the river, as far north as Kingston. Lupo seemed polite but a bit distracted and didn't have many questions for her, even though he'd be her immediate supervisor. He was in charge of all the field representatives who negotiated the contracts for the dozens of locals in that region and filed the grievances for the members and represented them at hearings, and attended their meetings and gave them advice and answered all their questions. So, Lupo wasn't really concerned with public relations and didn't know much about it; he was concerned with the activities of his field reps. But he had a budget for a PR position and needed to fill it. The previous PR person had had a baby and decided not to return to work, and the position had been vacant for a month now.

Lupo smiled and walked her to the door and said he'd let her know if she would get a second interview—in Albany, with the union's statewide PR director. But he didn't say when, and Louey was too shy to ask.

A letter telling her to call to schedule the second interview arrived that very same week.

The PR director who interviewed her in Albany, Joe Arnier, immediately changed the opinion that she had formed of Frenchmen based on her experience with precisely one Frenchman—Frankie. Arnier, a tall, elderly, distinguished-looking man with salt-and-pepper hair and blue eyes, had been born in the U.S., but was of French heritage, and pronounced his name Arn-yay. He had the elegance of a European nobleman. He complimented not only the Record stories of hers that he'd read, but also the perfectly spelled, typo-free résumé she'd sent him. He asked her about the AA guy she'd interviewed—was he still sober, Joe wondered? Obviously he had done some homework on this job applicant. He was cheerful and seemed concerned with putting her at ease. He had a nice smile and a good sense of humor. During the interview she learned that the starting salary for this position was $22,000 a year—more than three times what she was making at the Record. Upon hearing that, Louey simply nodded, momentarily closed her eyes and replied, "That's fine; that's right in the range I was considering," while trying not to jump out of her seat and dance. Joe then mentioned that there was also a "mileage allowance" to pay her back for the miles she'd have to drive around the Hudson Valley visiting newspaper offices and interviewing union officials and attending meetings. In addition, there would be an "advance" each week of whatever amount she requested, in case she had to take people to lunch. She only had to send her receipts to headquarters in Albany. If she spent less than her advance, she could keep it and apply the extra toward her next week's advance. And if she documented that she'd spent more than her advance, they would reimburse her immediately upon getting those receipts. And then there were health and dental insurance and vacation—two weeks a year to start, then three weeks after your second year and four weeks' vacation after just three years on the job. At the Record, you were stuck with two weeks' vacation 'til you dropped dead on the Desk.

As a member of CSEU's PR Department, she'd be part

of the Headquarters Staff Union, and the contract listed all the benefits. She'd get a copy of the contract. He was trying to think of more of them ...

Louey, greatly amused, couldn't help interjecting, "You mean we have unions in our union?"

"Yeah. Oh, yeah. We could hardly refuse when our own employees wanted to organize. It would be pretty hypocritical."

"Yeah, I guess so."

Arnier went on. You also got paid sick days, personal days, bereavement days ... Oh, she'd get a lot of brochures laying everything out on her first day, which would be in Albany and for which she'd be paid for the whole day but which would consist of touring the building and meeting her future colleagues before going to the Human Resources office to fill out the paperwork.

Was she dreaming? Nope. It was real. This was how the Normal People lived, apparently. The non-newspaper people. The civilians.

Arnier said, "If you got the job, when could you start?"

She had thought about that on the drive up. She said Monday, August 3rd. To sound professional, she said that, of course, she'd have to give a few weeks' notice. This being July 7th, that would build in a nice little vacation for herself.

In reality, she would have been happy to start the next day.

Working for three years at the biggest newspaper in CSEU's Region 3 probably didn't hurt, and the copies she'd brought of stories she'd written about labor-related topics, including some quoting local CSEU shop stewards and presidents, probably didn't hurt. She was surprised that he didn't mention her famous master's in Mental Health Journalism; she was prepared to talk about that. But he didn't say a thing about it. She felt good about the interview, especially when Joe's assistant, Roger, walked her to her car afterwards, joking along the way about politics, which they totally agreed on.

All in all, that interview hadn't been like a job interview at all, she marveled on her drive home; it was more like a "welcome aboard" session.

When Joe called to give her the good news, she had the odd sensation of feeling, at the same time, both ecstatic and unsurprised. He told her to watch her mailbox for an important, one-page bureaucratic paper she'd need to sign—a "commitment to take the job." She got it two days later, signed it, and shipped it back to CSEU using Overnight Express.

There. Done.

Louey's first day at CSEU was spent going through Orientation in Albany. It began with Joe welcoming her and introducing her to the other public relations people (they had staff at headquarters as well as in each of their six regions).

"Louey, this is the 'bullpen,'" Joe said, waving in the general direction of the four people sitting in the large, open area outside his office. "They do basically the same thing you'll be doing in Fishkill, only they work on statewide stories, and they write for the major media, like *The New York Times*, and the *Public Sector*, our weekly newsletter. CSEU statewide officers and lawyers and staff come in here with ideas for stories, and whoever's free gets to do them. Sometimes the officers do what they're supposed to do, which is come to me first, and I dole out the stories to the writer who's most familiar with that topic, or who I think can handle it best, but most of the time they just waltz in here and start jabbering about their great story ideas to whoever hasn't dived under their desk. We're trying to break them of that habit. So far, we've had limited success."

Colleen Fishman was at the nearest desk to Louey, and she jumped up and reached over to shake hands and say hi.

Adele Jones remained seated as Joe and Louey stopped beside her chair. She had a pleasant smile and a nice, firm handshake.

Ralph Ward, seated near the back wall, was the staff cartoonist, producing pointed caricatures of anti-labor politicians and touching portraits of newly-deceased union leaders. He didn't have a desk, but a sort of high bar stool and a light-table, exactly like the ones in Backshop, only higher.

"Yes, I've heard a lot about you," he said with a smile.

"Oh-oh," Louey said with a fake grimace.

"No-no; all good stuff," he laughed.

"Oh; whew!" Louey said.

There was one more person to meet; he sat closest to Joe's door.

"Louey Levy, this is Roger Barr, our assistant director. He fills in for me when I'm out, and handles all the hard stuff."

Roger, already standing and smoking a cigarette, grinned and said, "Welcome! Look forward to working with you." And he accompanied Louey into Joe's office. He asked her if he could get her some coffee.

Louey Levy really, really did not like coffee, but this was a job interview, so she smiled and raised her eyebrows as if mildly delighted and said, "Oh, yes, please," because she knew that was the correct answer, as Joe had a cup on his desk. And when Roger then said, "Cream? Sugar? Both?" she said, "Just black, please," because she wanted to cause as little trouble as possible. Did she want Roger Barr to go looking around for cream and sugar at some office coffee-station? And a spoon or one of those little wooden sticks to stir with? She did not.

They then chatted about the union's priorities for the year, the first of which was to stop the emptying out of the mental hospitals and state schools.

"It sounds like a humane idea, to put people back in their homes, but the problem is, they have no homes to go to," Joe said. "Many of them have been institutionalized for decades. Their families don't want them, or they'd never have put them in these places to begin with. Most of the residents haven't had a family member visit them in years. In many cases, there are no family members still alive, or they can't be found. And they're not building new group homes for them—there's not a penny in the state budget for that. They came up with this big high-falutin' name for it—'deinstitutionalization'—but that doesn't make it any better.

"I mean, they might have thought they had a good idea, but good ideas are a dime a dozen. It's follow-through that's everything. And the state didn't think this through at all."

Roger chipped in.

"The thing is, they're not sending the staff out into the communities with their patients—they're just laying them off. That's why we're seeing a horrendous rise in homelessness in Utica, for example: People newly released from the mental hospital up there are just sitting around in the park all day, or walking the streets raving and hallucinating. A lot of people are afraid of them, and they're calling the cops on them. They don't know where to get their medications, or what their medications even are. They have no one to remind them to take it, no way to pay for it, nowhere to refrigerate it—it's a disaster. The state just thought that now that there's Lithium and Thorazine and all these other drugs you can take for schizophrenia, that the hospitals aren't needed anymore, and we can just open the doors and let everybody out, and save all that money on staff. But without staff to follow them, letting these folks out is just cruel.

"See what I mean?"

She did see.

Aug. 3, 1974

Dear Diary,

Reality turns out to be the exact opposite of everything I learned in school, and there's nobody I can sue.

Well, not the opposite, maybe, but way more complicated. Thank G-d they never asked me about my stupid master's during my interviews. Probably they never noticed that part. People don't care about a writer's degrees; they care about how creative and fast and accurate you are! PR executives care about how good you are at coming up with ideas to promote the thing that their company does, not where you went to college!

Her first day on the job, Louey had the feeling that Tom

Lupo was a bit cool to her, and that maybe that had something to do with office politics. She would be reporting to the Region 3 office every day, and Lupo would be assigning her to write the stories about the troubles and victories of various CSEU locals in the Hudson Valley, and yet Arnier would have final approval on everything she wrote. The setup was a little awkward. She decided to try to be especially nice and deferential to Lupo.

The two Fishkill secretaries, Judy and Alice, were friendly and helpful to her, and Louey could tell right away that she'd have friends in them and be able to trust them. When she finished her first week on the job, she gave them both low, ceramic vases with "desk plants" in them, and cards thanking them both for showing her the ropes and helping her feel comfortable working there.

Her first story for the *Sector* was one she was sure she could hit right out of the park. It was to be about how much better it would be for Orange County employees to vote to retain CSEU as their collective-bargaining agent, rather than to switch to PEU, the union that was challenging it for that right. The election was coming up in less than a month. Her story praised CSEU outlandishly, pointed out weaknesses in the contracts their rival had negotiated recently, and quoted a National Labor Relations Board decision that centered on PEU's somewhat shady tactics in another representation election it had lost. She did the research, quoted Lupo and the Orange County local's shop steward and president, and banged out the story in a day.

Excellent! she rated her work. *And, easy!*

It was the first piece she had ever written that didn't

present both sides of a conflict. So she added, almost gleeful-ly, the journalistic-sounding final sentence: "Representatives of PEU could not be reached for comment."

Thanks to the grace of God, she offered the story to Judy to get her opinion. She was quite sure Judy would like and admire it, but she was in for a surprise.

"You'd better leave out that last sentence. The Sector is our newsletter, not a daily paper. We never say things like that in the Sector. There's no reason to. It sounds weird in a PR publication."

Good point. Louey deleted the sentence.

"Whew! You're right. Thanks! You saved me. My head is still in the newspaper. I won't do that again. Sorry, sorry!" she said as she headed back to her office.

It's true, though, she told herself with a grin as she opened the bottle of Wite-Out; *they really* couldn't *be reached for com-ment. Because I didn't call them!"*

Louey moved in with Danny and Sue and their kids until she found, really quickly, her first-ever "real" apartment. It was a clean, unfurnished one that smelled freshly painted. It was right in Fishkill, just off Route 9 in a place called "The Garden Apartments." She paid the deposit and first month's rent, nearly draining her entire checking account to do it. Her indigence wouldn't last long, though: She could put everything on her credit card and pay it off with her first month's paycheck! She would buy a real bed and dresser and real bookshelves and a sofa-bed for the living room so she could have overnight company. She couldn't wait to have Danny and Sue and the kids over for dinner. She would be like a grownup!

As a "public relations assistant" in Fishkill, Louey's job was to try to get stories in the daily papers in Kingston, Middletown, Poughkeepsie, White Plains and Rockland County, and also in all the weeklies, showing what good people the Mental Health Therapy Aides were—how dedicated to their tough jobs they were, how they volunteered in various ways in their communities, and how they were general all-around heroes. And how underpaid they were.

One of her first assignments came from Joe, not Lupo, though Lupo agreed to it. It was to go around meeting the reporters and editors she didn't know. As a newspaper person herself, she hit it right off with them, and she excelled at the job. Papers in several counties began running features about CSEU's individual members and their interesting volunteer work, as well as about the union's very reasonable contracts and the grievances it won. Louey was doing quite well.

Still, something was missing: friends. Other than Judy and Alice, both of whom were older and married with teenagers, there was only one person in Fishkill whom Louey even liked—Luke Qualesworth. Everyone called him "Q."

Q was a tall, deep-voiced, handsome Harvard grad who'd majored in economics. He had started working for CSEU only a month before Louey did. Not yet 30, he was prematurely greying in a most attractive way. He was almost comically WASP-y and professorial looking, right down to his tweed jackets with the suede elbow patches. Unlike the other field reps, Q had a thorough knowledge of labor history and was passionately committed to achieving justice for working people. He eloquently argued CSEU's position in hard-won

mediation and grievance procedures and already had a reputation for never having lost a grievance.

He worked at being "one of the guys," laughing at their
jokes and trying to get them to laugh at his. Louey, Alice and
Judy agreed that it was an awkward effort. The other field
reps were vulgar, hard-drinking, cynical slobs whose game,
spoken openly and even bragged about when Lupo wasn't
within earshot, was to do as little as possible, while collecting
as much money in mileage and expense reimbursements as
possible. Louey often heard them discussing various ways of
milking their expense accounts. Judy told her that one even
went to the extent of buying pads of blank, yellow receipts,
writing any amounts he wanted on them, and attaching to
his expense sheets each week "explanatory notes" saying that
he had met at a diner with local union presidents or shop
stewards or committees, and had bought them all lunch.
Luke never did anything like that. He had too much respect
for the union's members.

Louey could barely stand them. But Q was different. Q
was pure. Q she loved.

Q was married.

To Louey's dismay, Q did not believe in the power of
public relations. He thought of publicity as merely a means
of self-promotion, and he disdained it.

One day when he was at his desk, she called his extension
and asked him to come into her office. To her delight and
surprise, he sauntered in a minute later.

Louey had done her research and had her arguments all
lined up.

"Luke, why didn't you tell me about the member who

died in the sludge pool at the Rockland sewage treatment plant? I only heard about it because Judy and Alice were talking about it when I came in today!"

"Don't worry; I've got it under control. I'm meeting with the unit president and the DPW supervisor tomorrow morning."

"Yeah, but now I hear it was in the papers in New City, and we had no comment?"

Luke seemed very unconcerned and even amused by the press's omission of the good guys' side of the story.

"Oh, it ran in the paper down there already? Well, we *don't* have a comment, but we'll have a grievance hearing on it next week, and if we don't win that, *then* you'll hear about it, I promise you that. I give you my word of honor. OK?"

"No! Publicity is a tool you have that you're not using!" Louey insisted. "You should let me help you. This is just about the most dramatic example ever, of management's abuse of the workforce. The public will be totally on our side if we come out guns blazing on this! I mean, this guy is dead because management didn't provide him with a safety rope, right? And he had a wife and how many kids? The power of public shame is amazing. I'm telling ya. It's a tool you're not using!"

"No, I totally agree with you about that, but the power of negotiating a stronger contract so that this won't happen again is even more amazing, and that's what I'm trying to do. Look, when we win this grievance and end up with a new clause in the contract about mandatory safety ropes, you can blast that out in *The New York Times*, if you want. But until then, we need a change in the safety procedures at that plant, not a PR campaign."

"OK, man, but don't forget I'm here if you need any PR."

"Deal," he said, smiling, and rose and shook her hand.

CSEU was winning representation elections up and down the Hudson Valley; it was winning more than 90 percent of the grievances its members filed; things were going well in Region Three.

Then, just a few months after Louey was hired, Tom Lupo went mad.

"Louey, come into my office, please," he said on the phone to her one day. "And bring your pen and notebook."

He told her he wanted her to write down everything that he was going to say. She dutifully sat with her pen poised over her lined notebook, like a college kid.

"Are you working for the Teamsters?"

"Pardon me?"

"Are you working for the Teamsters? Because I am accusing you of spying for the Teamsters Local 447, that wants to usurp our representation of Middletown city employees."

He was serious. She was speechless. Finally she said, "Why ... why are you saying that, Tom?"

"Yesterday I gave you a direct order to write a story blasting Local 447 for the Middletown *Record*, and I have the paper here before me and no such story is in it."

"Well, I haven't finished getting all the dope on them from the guys yet, and I'm still waiting for our shop steward there to return my call. I mean, I'm writing it, definitely ..."

He interrupted. "You were to have that story in today's paper. That was a direct order. I am now giving you another direct order to have that story in the paper tomorrow."

"OK, but the paper won't run a story without any specifics about what the Teamsters ..."

"You are not working for the Teamsters. You are working for CSEU Region Three. Do you understand that?"

"Well, sure, but I can't guarantee ..."

"You are now dismissed. By the end of the day today, I want to have your notes from this meeting, which I ordered you to take. That's all. You are dismissed." At first, she thought he meant she was fired. But then she realized he meant, he was dismissing her from his office, to shuffle back to her own in shame and type up her notes.

At 5, as she left the office, Louey dropped a typewritten, more or less word-for-word transcript of their meeting into his "In" box on Judy's desk. Lupo had already left the office and locked his door.

"Judy! Look at this!" she whispered. Judy read it for a minute and said, "Oh my God! Can I show this to Alice?"

"Yes!"

"Holy crap! He's really gone crazy, now! Send a copy to HSU!" Alice said. The PR specialists—nearly all women—in each of CSEU's six regions were members of the Headquarters Staff Union, despite being based in offices around the state. The field reps—nearly all men, and much higher paid—had their own union.

"I can't join HSU yet! I'm still on probation!" Louey said.

In the days that followed, Lupo stopped talking to Louey and giving her assignments. She didn't know whether to be relieved or nervous about that. He started giving the silent treatment also to Judy and Alice, which was bad because they never knew where he was nor when he'd be back when union members or officers called to talk to him. They just had to say that he was out, and that they'd be glad to take a message for him.

Lupo seemed not to believe anything the two secretaries told him, including the times and locations of his appointments. As a result, he began not showing up for his scheduled meetings, and local officers and rank-and-file members started complaining about it to the rest of the staff, including Louey. Judy, Louey and Alice decided to just tell everyone that they'd pass along their message or remind him about his missed meetings as soon as he came in, but he came in less and less frequently.

Through all of this oddness, Lupo's relationship with his male staff members never seemed to change, but that may have been because the field reps were usually out of the office most of the time themselves, so they didn't have to interact with him as much as the women did. They just laughed it off when Alice, Judy or Louey told them about it.

"Maybe he's having an affair!" they'd roar, and sometimes, standing with their coffee in groups or two or three, they'd suggest names of some of the least-likely CSEU members as Lupo's possible paramour: the 300-pounder; the one who looked like the Wicked Witch of the West; the one who was already married to two men simultaneously and was apparently looking for a third. They continued to brush it off whenever Louey asked some of them if they didn't think Lupo was getting a little paranoid. They said he was fine; just stressed out because of all the elections and negotiations and arbitrations that were going on, that's all. But they didn't have to deal with him as often as Louey and Judy and Alice did.

Lupo began berating them for failing to reply to memos he'd never given them; he yelled at them for coming in late, when it was he himself who had come in late; he demanded that they make reservations at meeting locations all over the region when the locals' own secretaries had always made those arrangements themselves.

One afternoon in mid-December Lupo insisted that Judy accompany him to an evening meeting at the Fort Montgomery Risin' Shine, a restaurant and meeting hall south of West Point on the west side of the river. He needed her to take minutes, he said. Judy didn't relish the thought of spending an evening this way. She'd have to call her husband, Dave, and tell him she'd be home late, and he'd have to make dinner for the kids. This was awfully short notice for that. Dave was working this year in a quarry even farther south than the Risin' Shine, and he usually got home late himself.

Alice, of course, sitting at her desk not 10 feet from Judy, heard the whole thing. The two secretaries quickly exchanged a silent look before Judy delicately pointed out to Lupo that the Fort Montgomery local had its own stenographer.

He loudly and slowly replied, with an impassive stare, "I am ordering you to accompany me to this meeting. We'll go together so we don't waste the union's money on two mileage reimbursements." Then he walked away. Judy and Alice looked at each other again. Louey, witnessing it all from her own open-doored office, couldn't think of anything to say. She was just grateful it wasn't she whom Lupo had ordered to accompany him.

It was to be a dinner meeting; Lupo and Judy would go straight from work. Unfortunately, it was already dark, and around 5 it started to rain. Or maybe that was sleet coming down; it was hard for Louey to tell, looking out on the office's steep driveway. To get to Fort Montgomery, Lupo had two options. He could take a two-lane, traffic-light-riddled road through Beacon and down to the Bear Mountain Bridge, whose western end was just a mile south of the restaurant; or he could go over the Newburgh-Beacon Bridge, whose eastern end was just a few miles from the Region Three driveway, and then take Route 9W south all the way, snaking up and over Storm King Mountain. The latter road was dicey even in good weather, with precipitous drop-offs on one side and imposing, near-vertical rock cliffs on the other. He chose 9W.

Judy didn't come back to work for two days. When she did, she told Louey what had happened.

They left way too late, and he sped like a madman the whole way in his new black Lincoln, though the rain had begun coming down harder. He didn't say a word during the whole ride. Judy tried several times to make conversation.

"It was like he had gone deaf," she said. "He was staring straight ahead, like a zombie. I was just thankful he had the wipers on. I was really worried that he was, like, having a stroke or something. Plus, you know how dangerous 9W is on a dry, sunny day. It's like one of the most dangerous roads in the state! And now it was icy as hell! It was totally icing over! Thank God there was nobody else crazy enough to be out driving.

"So we get about halfway down 9W—you know, just past the parking areas for the trailheads at the peak of Storm King? You know where I mean?"

Louey did know.

"And so we're starting on the downhill part, where all the sharp turns are and you're supposed to go 45 miles an hour when it's sunny and dry. You know that part?"

Louey knew it.

"So I'm focused on the speedometer the whole trip, and instead of slowing down, he speeds up to 60! So I start praying—even though I'm an atheist—for all I'm worth, and squeezing the hell out of the armrest, and all of a sudden, he swerves hard and we go into the ditch at the bottom of the rock cliff on the right! For a second there, we were headed straight for the rocks. I was sure I was dead. I was sure we were going to hit the rocks. And then, without slowing down *at all*, he cuts his wheels and swerves right back onto the road and he mutters"—here Judy imitated Lupo's weird, clenched-jaw speech—'Son of a bitch tried to cut me off!'

"Louey, you gotta believe me: There wasn't a single other car on the road. There wasn't a vehicle in sight, in either direction."

Louey dropped her palm from her mouth, where it had been for the entire last minute of Judy's story, and said, "Holy crap; you mean he was having, like, hallucinations?"

"Yup. I mean, I'm no doctor, but he *must* have been, right? And then he acted like nothing had happened! As soon as we got to the restaurant, I used the pay phone and called Dave to come and get me at about 8. I told Lupo Dave was working in Haverstraw and was going to stop by on his way home and pick me up. I tried to sound real casual."

"If Lupo had insisted on driving you back, would you have quit?"

"Oh, you bet! Are you kidding? It's not worth my life

LOUEY LEVY'S HEADING HOME

to please that nut-job. I would have quit right there. Dave said, 'Do not get back in that car. In fact, do not get into any car with him, ever again. If he fires you, OK; we'll file a wrongful-termination suit and see what happens. You can always get another job, but I can't get another wife. At least, not another one who'll put up with our kids,' he says."

After that, Louey tried to avoid Lupo as much as possible, which was quite easy, as he was spending less and less time in the office. She came up with story ideas herself, or got ideas from the field reps, and wrote them and sent them straight up to Joe in Albany. He didn't ask if they'd been approved by Lupo. It seemed to work well. Her stories ran full in the *Public Sector* and earned her many a nice note from Joe.

And then, for her six-month evaluation, Lupo wrote that her work was "unacceptable in every way."

Joe Arnier knew better. She had written many solid stories for the *Sector*, and he liked how fast she wrote them. Also, he had plenty of documentation of her work. Shop stewards and presidents of the locals around the Hudson Valley had called him to say how glad they were to have her, and what a good job she was doing for them. They'd sent him clippings, with nice notes attached, of the stories Louey had gotten into the papers for them. Joe had not only kept them, but also had mailed copies of them to Louey.

"For your treasure box," he always wrote on the envelope that was inside the big envelope.

Having failed her six-month probation, Louey was sure she'd be fired, but Joe was having none of it. He called her and said, "Look, I got a copy of your evaluation. I know how it is when there's a personality conflict. Sometimes a guy just won't admit he's wrong, and that the other person is doing a fine job. Why don't you come up here to headquarters, where you're appreciated? The job is exactly the same one you're doing down there, except it's more about doing statewide stories for the press and the *Sector* and interviewing statewide officers, rather than local ones. We'll all be glad to have you, and the other PR associates up here will be glad to show you the ropes if you need help with anything. Not that you will; you'll be a very welcome addition to the bullpen. Up here, you won't be getting mileage or an expense account, but to make up for that, the salary is a little higher. What do you say?"

Ever since Judy's adventure with Lupo in the car, Louey had been considering requesting a sit-down with either Joe or CSEU's statewide president, Bill Terwilliger. Bill, a semi-literate, cigar-chomping electrician, had worked for decades at a psychiatric hospital in Buffalo, and he knew from crazy. He'd be sympathetic, Louey felt. Or maybe she should talk to both of them to lay out her suspicion that Lupo had gone nuts in some kind of serious, clinical way, and that a a psychiatrist, maybe, or some other kind of expert, should examine him and put him on medication before he killed someone. But then she thought that if she said anything like that, that she would seem like the classic "disgruntled employee" complaining about her boss because she knew he was going to give her a bad evaluation. And besides, she wasn't really disgruntled with her job at all. In fact, she was perfectly gruntled. She liked her job—except for him! So she never said anything.

But now she said something. She said it to Joe Arnier.

She said yes.

She knew what she would do: She'd get an apartment in downtown Albany, so she could walk to work each day. She didn't like Albany—she'd lived there during her unhappy high-school years—but she'd be out of Lupo's clutches and working with people who, as Joe said, appreciated her. She'd also be near her dad and Ree, who had not long ago moved to their "empty nest" in the outskirts of Albany. Good. She could see her dad more. Maybe she could get him to make up some new Three Kid Detective stories, as he had when she was a little kid.

She gave a month's notice to her landlord and got her deposit back.

There. Done.

Judy's husband, Dave, and his son, also named Dave, helped Louey move. They managed to cram all her stuff, including her bed, dresser, pillows, couch and kitchen table, into their pickup truck. She preceded them in Fury with her two chairs, her clothes, several boxes of books, her towels and bedding, and the few things she hadn't packed because she needed them that morning: her shower curtain, a bottle of shampoo, a slightly damp towel and her goldfish, Murray. Murray was between her legs in a little round bowl with a piece of aluminum foil crimped over the top of it, all the way to Albany. He seemed to mind neither the ride nor the sloshing around, though she did avoid quick accelerations and slowdowns, and was careful to take all the corners in Albany very carefully. When they arrived just a few minutes after Louey, the Daves carried everything up to her second-floor apartment. They declined to stay and have lunch with her, though she invited them to a nice Lebanese restaurant a few blocks away. They also refused any money, so she sneaked two 50-dollar bills, paper-clipped together, into the cup-holder of the truck just before they took off.

Louey's new gig went well. She loved it that she could walk to work. She found her "bullpen" colleagues pleasant, though not particularly funny or creative. But then they all had boyfriends or spouses to go home to right after work, so she never really got to talk with them about books, or sports, or politics, or anything at all that wasn't work-related. She often walked home for lunch, and she could eat and read her mail and get back to the office in plenty of time.

People liked her writing. The legal department, especially, became her fan club. The attorneys sought her to write about their victories in arbitrations, and about the contracts they helped negotiate that achieved some kind of precedent or were unusual in any way. They especially liked it that Louey always got quotes from the local shop stewards and officers, praising the lawyers' hard work. When she put in boiler-plate quotes from the lawyers praising the CSEU members and officers in return, and ran the stories past the lawyers themselves, the stories usually came back with not a single suggestion for any changes.

Not very long after Louey had finished setting up her files and mug and mug-holding "tree" and her "In" and "Out" boxes and placing the two planters of painted-leaf begonias and prayer plants on her desk just so, she got a call in the middle of the morning. It was Judy, in Fishkill. Five minutes later, Louey knocked on the frame around Joe's open door.

"May I come in?" she said shakily. But by then she had already come in and closed the door behind her.

He'd been typing, but he looked up and said, "Sure," pointing to the chair that faced his desk.

She sat down and said mechanically, "Joe, Tom Lupo just walked into the Hall of Fame of the Trotter, in Goshen, and slashed his throat from ear to ear."

Even before Joe had started back in his chair as if he'd been slapped, Louey started asking herself the obvious questions.

Why hadn't she said, "He's crazy! He needs help! He's gonna do something bad—something dangerous!" Why hadn't she told anyone about his hallucinations while driving Judy to Fort Montgomery? At the time, she recalled, she'd told herself, *Well, I'd only sound like a 'disgruntled employee,'* the phrase the Record wretchedly, unfailingly, used when describing someone who opened fire at work. It would sound like she was disparaging Lupo only because he'd given her that lousy performance review. Besides, she had already nailed an even better job working for a boss she loved, here in Albany: Why bother regaling folks with tales of Tom Lupo's weirdness? She'd just forget him. Water under the bridge. Forget about her little stint in Fishkill altogether, in fact. Start fresh.

That had been her attitude. And it had served her well, until now.

In answer to Joe's question, Louey replied that the only people who as yet knew about Lupo's suicide attempt were Lupo's wife; Judy and Alice; and now Louey and Joe.

A woman named Janice White, who was the Hall of Fame of the Trotter's new "education director," was starting to lead a tour at the very moment Lupo had pulled up in his Lincoln. This was unusual in that the Hall of Fame of the Trotter saw only two or three tour groups a month except during Hambletonian Week each year, and it was nowhere near Hambletonian Week. But when she slid open the barn door to admit her guests—a family of five from Canada—they were all greeted by Mother's Little Helper, a brown 2-year-old trotter from Schenevus, munching the hay that lay beside Lupo's supine and blood-soaked body. Ms. White told the police that at first she thought Lupo was some kind of jockey-mannequin that had fallen off a shelf, but then she saw the angle of his head, and his neck, and his shirt, and the black, black blood.

Lupo survived, thanks to Ms. White running back to her office and calling an ambulance. Meanwhile, the Canadians stood transfixed for a few minutes and then silently made their way back to their car. Before they drove off, they wrote a note on an envelope and left it on the ground just outside the barn door, with a souvenir horseshoe from the gift shop holding it so it wouldn't blow away. On it were their names and their address and phone number in Moose Jaw, Saskatchewan. They would be glad to talk to the police, but for now they thought their two pre-schoolers had seen enough.

The most senior field rep in CSEU Region 3—an incompetent named John Day—was appointed to fill in for Lupo while CSEU searched for a permanent replacement. The Goshen General Hospital emergency-room surgeon on call stitched Lupo up fast and transfered him to the

Middletown Psychiatric Unit. There he was put on massive doses of Lithium. And apparently he was OK after that, but neither Louey nor anyone else at CSEU ever heard from him again.

Before the end of the year, the union's board of directors made a momentous decision. To support their top priority, they voted to allocate thousands of dollars for an ad campaign in newspapers, TV and radio stations, subway cars and billboards, to prevent the state legislature from closing its mental hospitals.

Joe called the PR staff to tell them about the plan. It would be PR's job to come up with an overall theme for the campaign, and the union's very expensive ad agency would then produce and place the ads.

"So, what's our overall theme?" Joe asked the bullpen. He had blocked out all day for this. Lunch would be brought over from Club 21, the fancy restaurant next door, where many state legislators could be found drinking lunch each day. Joe removed the cap from a thick black marker and poked it menacingly toward them as he turned over a big, floppy page of the flip-chart on the easel in his office. "Short and punchy! Short and punchy! Yell out stuff! No criticisms; just ideas!" he said.

At first, the ideas from Colleen, Adele and Ralph were lame, though they all went up on the flipchart.

"Short and punchy! Come on! Think of something!" Joe said around mid-morning.

Louey thought of something.

"They call it deinstitutionalization. We call it dumping,"

Louey said. "There's an extreme closeup of a poor, old, scared-looking woman. The words are in two lines across the top, with 'deinstitutionalization' by itself on the lower line. The rest goes in two lines right next to her face, with 'dumping' in big, bold letters by itself on the lower line. And across the bottom, we say, 'Tell your legislators: Don't close our mental hospitals.'"

There. Done.

They spent the rest of the morning coming up with a proposed timeline for *Public Sector* stories; press, radio and TV interviews; and other ways to strengthen the campaign. Tweaking was performed, but by the next day Joe had a theme and timeline to present to Terwilliger. They had a week's work done in a day. And the union had a PR campaign that successfully stopped the state's mental hospitals from closing—for a while.

Louey became dissatisfied with her apartment. It was too dark and quiet and filled with unsmiling old people; there were no laundry facilities; the hot water was unreliable; she had a lot of little complaints like that. As she approached the end of her lease, she found a new apartment just a few blocks away, even closer to CSEU headquarters in downtown. She got CSEU's janitor, a friendly Irishman with a pickup truck, to help her move. The new apartment was an airy one on the second floor of an old brownstone in downtown Albany's Center Square area. It wasn't too expensive, and there was a washer and dryer in the basement. The long, narrow hallway led from the large living room past the bathroom to the kitchen. Off the kitchen was a surprisingly large bedroom, with two big windows looking over the building's backyard to the walls and windows of other brownstones. All her furniture fit fine in that apartment. She used her "extra" room, which was reached through an archway off the living room, as her "den," and for the den she bought a bright orange sofa-bed for company.

Like, in case Clare wants to visit! she told herself. *Or Annie! Or Charlie and Frank! Or Sandy and Tim! Or anybody!*

She also bought herself a beautiful rolltop desk at a second-hand store, and because it provided such a fine place to write, she started writing more.

Still, something was missing in her life. Her work friends were nice, but they were all married. She couldn't call them up and say, "Want to go for a hike? Want to go to a concert?" Much less, "Want to go Washington Park and throw a ball around?" Everybody was married except a couple of her friends from college and the Record, and they were now scattered around the country or living with their boyfriends. Danny and Sue, of course, had been married forever, and were totally grownups, with kids and everything; even her little sister was married. There were no adult women's sports teams that she knew of; where else could she make friends? It wasn't a boyfriend she was looking for—it really wasn't, though she'd love it if there were a guy she could be friends with and do things with. Louey was resigned to never getting married; she wasn't pretty enough to attract anyone, and she wouldn't want to marry anyone to whom looks were important anyway. So that wasn't it; she just wanted to have a smart, cool friend or two to hang out with, and something to do, other than work and write. She jogged around and around Washington Park, which was just a block from her building. She could work up a good sweat jogging—a new fad among health-conscious young people—but she felt both conspicuous and lonely doing that, and it bored her, too.

Dear Diary,

There's nobody to play with. It's awful when your friends get married. And my friends from the Record are not just married; they all live far away now. Charlie and that guy Frank she married, whom I hardly know, are both in law school in Buffalo. How can Charlie have married someone I don't know? Sandy is down south working for Planned Parenthood and singing in the choir and volunteering in a million other ways at her church, and who goes with her to volunteer at all these food banks and fundraisers and all that? Her husband Tim! She found a boyfriend in, like, two minutes after she left the Record, and in, like, an hour later, they were married! I sure as hell won't be seeing much of them anymore. And Annie's reporting at the Bergen County News, covering the entire middle of New Jersey! I'll never get to see any of them again. I'm going to start volunteering somewhere.

Louey's stories for the *Sector*, like those of her colleagues, covered anything Joe assigned to her, but it wasn't long before she developed two related specialties. One was stories about contracts signed after tough negotiations by the union's field reps and the various locals' bargaining teams. The other was the many stories suggested to her by the union's Legal Department. Her stories about contracts signed with municipalities, even those where the raises won were quite small, were spun so that they focused on the other improved benefits. Local shop stewards loved it when she quoted CSEU lawyers praising their negotiating committees and rank and file members for showing solidarity in the face of management intransigence and unreasonableness and cheapness. Usually, after getting the basics of the situation that brought on the grievances in the first place, Louey got rather standard quotes from the CSEU lawyers in the case, expressing admiration for the honesty and courage shown by the members involved. Sometimes they would just say, "Just make up some bullshit quote from me and send it over; when do you need it by?" She would tell them her deadline, and they would initial the story, OK'ing it, and send it back via interoffice mail. The members also enjoyed being quoted in the *Public Sector* saying how delighted they were with the victory won by their union's top-notch lawyers.

Steve, a lawyer from the Law Department, one slow day called her to tell her about a case he'd resolved. It wasn't your everyday story, he said; he was very excited about it.

"This should definitely be Page One in the *Sector*. Honest. Stop the presses. Are you ready?" he said.

Phone squeezed between shoulder and ear, notebook open, pen in hand, Louey was ready.

An arbitrator had awarded six members reinstatement to their jobs, with full back pay and a written apology, after they'd been suspended for over a year!

"Wow, what were they suspended for?" Louey asked.

"Well, they *said* the members were sleeping on the job. But they weren't! They all worked the overnight shift at Letchworth Village State School. They were all very diligent employees! And management said they'd been found—get this—sleeping on the pool tables in the day room!"

"The pool tables? Aren't they awfully hard? That's a crazy thing to make up! Who would believe that? Pool tables are made of slate, aren't they?"

"Yeah! Put that in the story! The managers there were so stupid, to think they could get away with a frame-up like that. It's a violation of labor law to fire people for union activity, so they had to reinstate them all, with full back pay."

"They were CSEU activists?"

"Get this: They were the local president, vice-president, and four shop stewards! The case dragged on for a year because management fought us every step of the way. They wouldn't let it drop, even though they knew they were dead wrong. But in the end, we won!"

Louey got quotes from Steve about the details—about how the "Letchworth Six" stuck together and didn't cave even when management offered them money if they'd all resign, and how they went to all the hearings together, wearing their CSEU T-shirts, which Steve got photos of. He gave Louey many quotes about how Righteousness Triumphs in the End.

When she asked him what management presented as their so-called "evidence," he said, "They showed all these phony photos of people sleeping on the pool tables, with the hands on the wall clock showing 3 o'clock. Overnight staff is supposed to work midnight to 8 a.m. You couldn't make out their faces, though, and that was the point—it could have been some residents, taking a nap! And then, and this was just as bad, it turned out that the clock in there was broken!

It had been stuck at 3 o'clock for years. The residents didn't care; if they want to know what time it is, they ask an aide. And they didn't have a single witness; all the other aides backed up our guys a hundred percent. All they had was the photos, and the statements of these two management guys from Albany who drove down there in the middle of the night to take the photos. They claimed to be 'eye-witnesses,' but they couldn't tell the patients from the aides! And that's the whole thing: Residents can do anything they want in the day room. They can take a nap if they want, and if the couches are unavailable, there's nothing that says they can't use the pool tables. It's not against the law."

"You mean, they sent these two guys to Letchworth to photograph 'CSEU members' sleeping on the job, when they knew it wasn't even our members? Just so they could fire union activists?" Louey was now really warming to this story. The injustice! And yet, justice triumphed in the end, thanks to our CSEU law firm!

"Yeah, that's what got me. They never consulted with the union at all. They didn't even have the decency to talk to us. If they had, we could have explained it to them and this whole thing could have been avoided. But the arrogant bastards, they were so sure they'd win after they sneaked these two guys in at 2 a.m. and framed our members."

"Wait. Two a.m.?"

"Yeah! They came in the night like the Gestapo!"

Well, there was her lead. And not only her lead, but set off in quotes, the 36-point headline in that week's *Public Sector*. Wow. This was a prize-winner, for sure. "They Came in the Night Like the Gestapo," the *Sector* banner head proclaimed, and Louey and the "Letchworth Village Six" and the CSEU Legal Department were getting all kinds of praise. Especially Steve, a photo of whom, as the lead union lawyer in the case, graced Page One. And then everything fell apart.

Louey waltzed into the office at 8:25 a.m. the following Monday as usual, only to find Joe's door shut. Oh-oh: Joe's door was never shut.

She could hear that a conversation was going on in there, but she couldn't make out what was being said. It sounded like multiple visitors. Over the next few minutes, as the rest of the bullpen filed in, each one came to an abrupt halt and mouthed silently to Louey, "What's happening?" as they took their seats. And she shook her head and raised her shoulders and her hands, palms up, and whispered back to each of them, "I don't know. He was in there with the door closed already when I came in." No one spoke.

It was about 10 when Joe's door opened and two old men, maybe in their 60s, walked through the bullpen, out the door of the PR suite and down the hall to the elevators. They were wearing white shirts and ties, but they were carrying their jackets while rolling down and buttoning a shirt sleeve.

"Louey, come in here, please," Joe said from his doorway.

Oh God. She grabbed her pad and pen and went in.

"Shut the door, please," he said as she entered.

Oh no.

As soon as they were both seated he shoved the *Sector* across his desk towards her and said, "Where did you get the information for this story?"

"Steve gave me all the info, and then I called the local president, who said how pleased he was to be vindicated, and how our members' dues are so very well spent, you know, and those were the only two people I talked to. I attributed it properly, didn't I? Did I miss something?" she asked anxiously.

"You didn't verify the facts with anyone else?"

No. No, she hadn't. Why would she do that? That wasn't the point of their little PR organ. Its whole purpose was to present the union's point of view. But had she written something that wasn't true? That would be awful.

As it turned out, everything she had written was true. The problem lay in what she *hadn't* written.

Louey hadn't written—because Steve the Lawyer hadn't told her—that actually there were 22 aides who'd been charged with sleeping on the job, and that the other 16 were all found guilty and fired, and that their firings had been upheld. No one had told her that the CSEU "victory" was really a settlement. The six would be reinstated, and the other 16, none of whom were CSEU office-holders or shop stewards—would be let go. That was the settlement. The two men in Joe's office had brought with them a copy of the arbitrator's decision, which ratified their version of the story.

"You never asked Steve for a copy of the decision?" Joe said without looking at Louey.

"No."

She had never asked for a copy of any decision in all the time she'd been working for the union. Neither had Colleen, or Roger, or Adele asked for copies of the decisions they wrote about. Why would they do that? The whole purpose of the *Sector* was to present the union's point of view. She got all the information for her stories from the union's lawyers and officers. Joe knew that very well.

"Well, from now on, you will."

"OK," she said quickly, nodding.

New policy. I can handle that; it's just that it'll take more time to write each story, that's all, is what she told herself.

She was looking down at her pad and scribbling on it as if taking notes, but really she was just trying not to cry.

"Do you know who those two men were, who were in here with me for over an hour?"

She had a sick feeling that she did, but she shook her head, still looking down.

"Do you want to take a guess?"

She shook her head, looking up but away from Joe's face.

The two men in Joe's office were the Department of Mental Hygiene employees who'd traveled to Rockland County to take the photos and document the malfeasance at Letchworth Village.

They were an interesting pair.

Born into Jewish families in Germany, they both had been interned in the Auschwitz concentration camp. They both had been sent from there to Dachau, where they were mere hours from death by starvation when Ike's Allied troops burst in. After learning that their families had been killed, each of them, unbeknownst to the other, immigrated a few years later to the United States, landing in New York. It was many years later when they met for the first time, working for the Department of Mental Hygiene in Albany. Something in their identical European accents and formal manners made them begin asking each other about their pasts. They'd been best friends, as well as colleagues, from that moment on. They'd each married and had families, one in East Greenbush across the river, and one in Ballston Spa, up north. One was a writer, the other a photographer, for the DMH.

Oddly, the omissions in Louey's story, which made it almost comically incorrect, weren't what grieved the two men, Joe said. It was only the headline.

"After telling me what really happened in this so-called 'victory' of ours," Joe said, "as if I weren't sick enough already, they stood up and took off their jackets and rolled up their sleeves and showed me the numbers the Nazis had tattooed onto their arms. I nearly puked. I never want to see that again in my life. And here we are comparing them to the Gestapo! What were you thinking, to put that into the story?"

He didn't say it in a mean way, but he was frowning at her and slowly shaking his head. He truly wanted to know the answer.

"I was quoting Steve," Louey said miserably.

"Well, the Gestapo took their parents and siblings and one of their grandparents out of their houses and shot them. Steve didn't tell you *that*, did he. And Louey, of *course* they had to 'come in the night!' That's when the employees were sleeping on the job! They wouldn't have *caught* them if they'd come during the day, would they!"

Now it was Louey's turn to feel nauseated. Nauseated and faint, and she was starting to feel as if she really, really had to go to the bathroom.

"Should I write the correction? Or the 'apology,' should we call it?" she managed to ask.

"No," Joe went said, "they don't want a correction."

"They don't? Are they gonna sue us for libel?"

"No, and I don't think they'd win, because we never mentioned their names. As far as our readers are concerned, they're just these two anonymous Nazis."

Louey winced.

"And here's the other thing you should know: They're both CSEU members themselves. I see we omitted *that* from the story, too. Louey, we try to never make any CSEU members look bad in any publication. These men read that story in the *Sector*, for God's sake! They just wanted us to know the truth, and to be sure that what we're saying is true before we print it. So I promised them that. That's the least we can do. That's what we're *supposed* to do."

"I'm so sorry," Louey said. She should have asked. CSEU was at that time in a unique, and ultimately untenable, position among labor unions in that it represented many people in state government who were actually supervisors of other CSEU members. It had happened more than once that some CSEU members had filed grievances against other CSEU members. Louey was aware of that; Joe had told her that during her job interview.

She didn't know what to do. Her head dropped and she held her face in her hands and finally, she cried.

"I'm so, so sorry," she wailed. What would her grampa say, who had escaped the tsar's army? What would her bubbe say, who'd lost her cousins in the Holocaust? What would her father say, who'd served in World War II? She had called these two old Jews Nazis and now, on top of everything else, she was pretty sure she was gonna poop in her pants.

"Well, it wasn't really your fault," Joe said quickly, shoving a box of tissues across his desk to her. "But I wanted you to know about it, so you can see how things can go wrong if you don't really dig. And don't worry: The next person in this office is gonna be Steve. You can go." He was one of those men who couldn't stand to see a woman cry. But he quickly added, "When you feel better, I mean." He sat back in his chair and smiled. "Want some coffee? Or tea, I mean?" He knew she didn't like coffee. How was your weekend?"

Louey managed a sad smile, and said, "No, thanks; I'm OK," without looking at Joe, and headed for the bathroom.

But she wasn't OK.

January 26, 1977
Dear Diary,

Why is nothing ever simple? The longer you live, the more complicated everything gets. All I want is a simple life.

She noted wryly in her journal that here she was, feeling sorry for herself when she was probably the seventh- or at worst, eighth-luckiest person in the world. She was born in the post-World War II U.S. to two college-educated European-Americans in the wealthiest democracy on the planet, and she had a wonderful family and great friends (though none nearby that she could hang out with), a good job and good health, a paid-off car, a nice apartment, a great stereo with lots of records, money for books, and time to write poems and stories. She really shouldn't be complaining.

She needed to stop paying so much attention to herself, that's what she needed. She was getting too self-involved. She needed to get out more. She decided to do exactly what her father had begun doing in his old age: She took up serious birdwatching. She would see if there was a club she could join. And even if there weren't, she would buy a good pair of binoculars and stumble around the park in her off-hours, looking at birds.

God, I'm becoming an eccentric already, and I'm not even 30! Oh, well: Somebody's got to be eccentric. So, let's give 'em something to talk about. That's what Dad would say. But I do find the birds fascinating. We walk through a hail of birds every day, and never notice them and don't know their names. What kind are they? I hear them at night. Why are they flying at night? What do they have, night-vision? When do they sleep? Why are they singing? How do they hear, without ears? Where are they going? Do they have friends? What are they doing? What are they looking for? How long do they live? How come you never see a dead bird?

That spring, she bought herself a good pair of binoculars and borrowed a field guide from her father, who was delighted to lend it to her. And she did indeed start stumbling around Washington Park, a block from her apartment, in the evenings and early mornings, looking at birds.

Mostly she saw robins and house sparrows, but one morning she noticed a very striking bird that was hopping across an expanse of lawn. She got a good, close look at it through her binoculars.

The bird fascinated her. She had never noticed one like that before. She figured it must be exceedingly rare. She'd look it up later, but right now she was writing quickly in her notebook. *Hilarious, clown-like costume! A big black handlebar mustache! Dozens of black spots all over its white front, like measles! A red yarmulke! Bold, black, crescent-shaped bib! Big long, black bill. Black-and-white striped back, like a zebra! Plus, underneath, its wings are yellow all the way to its armpits! When it finally flew away, I could see a big white patch on its rump. Well, this will be easy to look up in the field guide: Nothing in the world looks like this. I wonder if anyone has ever seen anything like this!*

Just a bit later that same day, she also saw a gorgeous little bird singing in a tangly shrub near the park's long, narrow pond. She had never seen such a bird before.

A bright lemony-gold body with a silly black Lone Ranger mask! What is this: a goldfinch at Halloween? There's even a thin white ribbon bordering the mask's top edge, so it really stands out. And yet back, wings and tail are drab! It sings over and over, "Witchety-witchey-witchety-witchety." It's a Witch-Bird! I'm going to call this in to Ripley's Believe It or Not!

She sat down, cross-legged, on the grass right then and there, hoping to find her two special birds. But what if they were so rare they weren't even included in the book? Her dad's field guide was a very thin, basic one, written in the 1950s. She might have to call the Cornell Lab of Ornithology and describe these rarities over the phone. They might even name them after her, once they'd confirmed the sightings and come and taken photos of them and everything. *Birdus levitatus; Birdum loueyanum.* As she rapidly started flipping through the pages, she thought she would surely be famous.

The first bird, she found, was listed in her little guide in the "most common species of New York State" section: a Northern Flicker. To add spit to the insult, the book specifically noted that it was also "of least concern" to environmentalists.

The second bird was literally called a Common Yellowthroat. Also "of least concern."

Dear Diary,

This is like when I lived in Fishkill and I took to walking around the roadsides looking up the names of all the flowers I came across. Everything I thought was the most gorgeous and exciting thing I'd ever found, when I looked it up, turned out to have names like, "Common Ticksore," or "Prickly Pigweed," or "Stinking Rue." Well, I wasn't sorry then, and I'm not sorry now. At least I've learned something. These two birds are my new friends, and I know what happens next: Next, I'll see them everywhere. There's a lot of people who don't know the names of the common things that greet us every day. I really want to know their names.

I'm going to start trying to draw my weeds and flowers and birds. That will help me see the world as it really is, instead of as I think it should be. When I try to draw birds, they always come out looking like cartoons. That's because I don't really draw what I see; I draw what I think I should be seeing.

Early one Sunday, Louey was stuffing way too many clothes into one of the two dryers in the basement of her building. She slammed the door before any clothes could fall out and started putting quarters into the two quarter-sized slots in the metal slide on top.

"Oh, are you putting money in there?" The very pleasant voice behind her came from a woman taking clothes out of the other dryer.

"Yeah; aren't we supposed to put two quarters in? There's two quarter-sized slots here in the slidey thing, right? So I thought we're supposed to put two quarters in! That's the way I've been doing it, and it seems to work fine."

"Well—I'm Nancy from the first floor, by the way—you actually don't have to put *any* money into it. We all found that out long ago. You just push the slidey thing in and it starts up perfectly well without any money in it!"

"You're kidding."

"No! Needless to say, no one mentions this to the landlord, though you'd think he'd figure it out from the fact that there are zero coins inside it week after week."

Louey followed Nancy's instructions, removing her quarters and then pushing the slidey thing in all the way even though it was empty. The machine started fine.

"Holy crap!"

They laughed. There was nowhere to sit in the little laundry room, so Louey invited Nancy up to her apartment for "coffee and gossip." Nancy accepted, but she said she had to fold and put away her laundry, and could she come up around 4 p.m.?

She could. And when she came, she didn't come empty-handed.

Dear Diary,

There's this startlingly beautiful woman who lives right be-low me. She looks like the classic Irish lass, with platinum, curly blonde hair and the bluest eyes you ever saw. I almost can't take my eyes off her. She looks like a model; she really does. She has white-porcelain skin and long, long polished nails. We met in the laundry room last week, and I invited her to come up and shoot the breeze after our clothes were all done. She arrives at my door with a bottle of wine and two beautiful, stemmed glasses and a china platter of cheese and crackers with little cornichons and mustard!

She is by far the classiest human I've ever met. She makes me feel like she's a tuxedo, and I'm a brown shoe. But we hit it right off. She's really smart and funny, and we've been having the best damn time together!

She's a graduate of Clark, and she got her master's in poetry at Oxford, in England; her thesis was on T.S. Eliot. She's work-ing for a travel agency called Top Flight Tours, which is in the basement (!) of a building on State Street. They specialize in tours of Ireland, and the pay stinks but she gets to lead tours all over that country several times a year. She takes groups—mostly old people—on walks or rides to farms, castles, universities, pubs— east coast or west, north or south.

I said to her, "Oh, cool! So, you get to go back and see the Auld Sod, huh?"

"It's not <u>my</u> Auld Sod," she says. "I'm Jewish!"

It turns out her name is Nancy Gottfried, and she was in the same Sunday School class at Temple Beth Emeth as my sis-ter Clare. So, she's three years younger than I, that means. (Well, who's <u>not</u> younger than I am, anymore?) She grew up across the *river, in East Greenbush. She has two brothers, both younger than she is, and all three of them went to East Greenbush schools, so I never bumped into any of them when I was at Albany High.*

But here we are.

Nancy loves baseball and football and is deeply knowledgeable about them—college and pro level both, she can tell you names, numbers, records—everything. She played on her highschool softball team. Now, though, being a grownup and all, she's reduced mostly to watching sports on TV. (Sound familiar?) When I told her how I resent so much that there are no opportunities in this crappy town for women to play sports, she said she heard there's a women's softball "beer league" starting up in the summer where the teams practice one evening a week and play for real late on Sunday afternoons. After each game, the teams go back Horney's Grill, the bar that sponsors the league, and they give your table two free pitchers of beer, as long as you're wearing your team T-shirt. They have good burgers there, too, apparently.

She's going to look into it and we'll both join, if they're still accepting members. That would be so fun! I'd do it if Nancy would do it, for sure!

Nancy Gottfried was also a terrific flutist. She could have played with the Albany Symphony Orchestra, and in fact had auditioned her way into a chair with that group, but had only then discovered a terrible thing: She had clinical stage fright, and could not produce a note when an audience was watching. She tried talk therapy, medication, hypnotism, acupuncture and marijuana; nothing worked.

One night Louey noticed a flute case and music stand in a corner of Nancy's living room.

"Wait. That's you I hear playing every night? I thought it was a recording!"

Nancy assembled the instrument's pieces and improvised a few amazing, ethereal tunes when Louey demanded to hear her play.

The following Saturday, Nancy went with Louey to buy a flute. She ended up getting not the Gemeinhardt "student model" that Louey thought would be good enough, but the silver-plated "intermediate model," which cost more than $300, but what the hell.

Studying flute will be a way to learn to read music, she told herself. *And God knows, I have nothing else to spend my money on.* Louey loved music of all kinds, most notably her beloved rock 'n' roll, and wanted to know how it worked its magic. How certain chords made her cry when they rhymed—when they "went" with each other; how people knew where to put their fingers on the keys or the strings at the right time, just by reading; how people could "play by ear," and what that even meant.

Her lessons with Nancy consisted of a half-hour lesson followed by an hour of watching a local Public Broadcasting System TV program together—a show featuring two movie critics whose commentaries they found highly amusing, even though they almost never had seen any of the movies being reviewed.

To Louey's satisfaction, she found that after a while, she could produce a clear sound on her flute, rather than a raspy rush of wind. And then, not too many weeks after that, she actually could read five or six elementary tunes in the book Nancy made her buy, and she could play some of them "correctly" in two different keys, too. She figured she played about as well as the average middle-school flutist, though she practiced less and less as she began writing poems and journal entries more and more.

The awkward part is paying, she wrote in her diary. *I feel funny giving Nancy her ten dollars at the end of the lesson, as though she's not my best friend. I try to hand her the dough with a very clipped, cheerful, "Here you go, bud!" Likewise, it must be hard for her to criticize my lousy playing, though she does it in such a nice, helpful way.*

I tell myself I'm going to go right back upstairs and practice for an hour after each lesson, and sometimes I make it to 15 minutes or so before my brain wanders off, and then that's it until about a half-hour before my next lesson, when I try to "cram." What a lousy student I am!

It turned out that the women's bar league *was* still accepting members. Teams were formed and each assigned different colored T-shirts. The women asked to be on certain teams depending on their favorite colors, and the bar tried to accommodate them. Purple, red, orange and blue T-shirts were highly favored. Unfortunately, it was sort of a "first-come, first-served" deal, and Louey and Nancy were among the last-come. They were assigned to the wretched White team.

The schedule suited them perfectly. They were to practice on Thursday evenings—a free night for both Nancy and Louey—and play their "real" games on Sundays at 4 p.m. On Sundays she and Nancy threw their gloves in her car and drove together to the games.

At the first practice the coach—a short, fat Italian guy named Richie—saw how easily Louey caught line drives and fly balls, and how fast she was getting to them. He quickly assigned her to a position called "short fielder," which she guessed was his idea of a joke, because she was only 5-foot-2. She liked it, though. Her job was to play a few yards directly behind second base, and several yards in front of the outfielders. From there she roamed like a center fielder with a weak arm, backing up the infielders who let balls bounce past them or roll between their legs, and backpedaling to snag flies the outfielders could not run fast enough to get to.

Nancy was assigned to third base, chiefly because she knew where third base was. Also, she knew what to do when a ball was hit her way. But most amazingly, despite her perfectly lacquered, inch-and-a-half-long nails, she turned out to have a bullet-like, accurate throw across the field. You could hear it sizzling through the air like an arrow. She would have made many, many assists if the first-base player ever deigned to extend her glove to catch the ball instead of ducking as it whizzed toward her.

"Sharon, you're supposed to use your glove to catch the ball! That's why it's got that big leather part in the middle of it!" Louey called once, trying unsuccessfully to make the first-base player laugh.

"Oh yeah? No way! I tried that once, and it hurt!" the White Team's very own Marv Throneberry shot back angrily.

The White Team came close to victory in three or four games as autumn approached, and even won a couple. The season then ended mercifully, with free barbecue, music and beer for the coaches (all male) and players and their boyfriends in the backyard of their sponsor, Horney's Grill.

One of the things Louey noticed during the season was that all the other players on her team were younger than she. They were even younger than Nancy. During practices and games, they talked about really stupid-sounding movies and TV shows she didn't care about or had never even heard of, and how drunk they had gotten last weekend and how many times they had passed out or puked. Louey had no interest in these things at all.

Wow, I'm getting old, Louey thought. *I'm, like, the oldest person here. Well, of course I'm the oldest! Who plays softball in her 30s? Everybody else is married and has babies by the time they're 30. I guess it's good to be old, though. I mean, you're always getting old, from the moment you're born. Getting old is the surest sign that you're still living, right?*

A nurse practitioner at Upper Hudson Planned Parenthood, around the corner from Louey and Nancy's building, performed abortions on Tuesday evenings from 6 to 8 p.m. and Saturdays from 1 to 3.

A coven of busybodies had started protesting outside the building at those times on those days, waving signs at passersby and yelling at the women entering the premises that they were killing babies and should be ashamed and were going to go to hell for "murdering your own children." The busybodies parked their cars in the Planned Parenthood lot, so that patients and staff couldn't get in. Then UHPP installed signs on both sides of the driveway saying: "Parking for clients' vehicles only. Others will be towed at owners' expense." The busybodies parked their cars there anyway, moving them only when the tow trucks arrived, but they soon tired of this. UHPP also installed security cameras and was able to have some of the busybodies arrested for trespassing. Then the busybodies started taking photos of the staff and patients as they entered, and putting up "Wanted" posters of them on nearby trees and light posts. "Wanted for Murder," they said.

This was all covered in a Knickerbocker News story saying that UHPP was looking for volunteer "Patient Escorts" on "abortion days" to walk women from their cars into the building. Louey decided, putting the paper down, that she would be a good Patient Escort. She could do it on Saturdays.

One, it pisses me off that these people want to force women to have babies against their will. They're trying to prevent women from aborting unwanted pregnancies because, why? Because to them, babies are the punishment you get for having fun, and they're mad that you might avoid that punishment, because they sure didn't! "If I had to suffer, you do too!" That's their motivation!

And two, it would give me a chance to kick somebody's ass who richly deserves it.

She walked in one day, filled out an application to be a Patient Escort, and within a week was the proud owner of a neon-yellow vest and Non-Violence Training Manual. She signed up for Saturday afternoons, and that was one very satisfactory item she could check off her To-Do list: *Volunteer somewhere. Make yourself useful. Help somebody.*

She was good at it. She never did have to kick anyone's ass, but she succeeded each week in helping women go comfortably into the building. Not a single pregnant person turned around and went back to her car, and that made Louey proud. Her style mostly involved smiling warmly and linking arms with the patients and talking calmly to them about the weather, their families, how simple the procedure was, and other little topics, and occasionally waving dismissively in the general direction of the protesters.

Sometimes there were nuns. Six of them, the "Flying Nun" kind with the long black habits and the white wingy things on their heads, would show up together, emerging from a van like a team of ecclesiastical bank robbers. They knelt, three on each side of the driveway in an attitude of prayer, hands pressed together, fingers pointing toward heaven. But they had rubber gardening mats to kneel on. *Cheaters!* Louey thought. Also, their eyes weren't always closed; they noticed, and called out, as the patients came in.

"You're murderers!" one of them shouted to two women who were going into UHPP together, one on each side of Louey.

"No they're not; they're people whose birth-control failed! What do *you* use for birth control?" Louey called back to her. That nun shut up then and spun around, as if Louey would be insulted by her silence and the back of her habit.

"It's not too late to repent!" another one called.

"It's not too late to mind your own business, either!" Louey called back. She knew she wasn't supposed to "engage" with the protesters: That was the first rule in the Training Manual. But she couldn't help herself, sometimes, because she so enjoyed annoying the nuns.

"Hi, girls!" she called merrily to them as they arrived with their signs. That seemed to rile them more than anything.

No one had ever called them anything but "Sister" before, probably.

"Sisterhood is powerful!" Louey often shouted with a big smile as she strode past them, big smile, fist raised, as if she were at an Equal Rights Amendment rally.

She hadn't written to Danny in a while. She composed a long letter telling him about her "Escortions to the Abortions," as she called her volunteer work for UHPP. She sealed it with lavender-colored sealing wax using a heavy seal imprinted with a swallow. Her sister had given her that sealing-wax set for her birthday.

She got a return letter a week later.

"Those nuns better watch out," Danny wrote, "or Louey Levy will send them Flying! But don't worry. Someday there'll be an abortion pill you can get in private, from your doctor. Then nobody will know who's having an abortion, or when or where they're having it. Then you'll be out of a job."

If only that science-fiction scenario could ever come true, Louey thought. She had to admit, a lot of crazy stuff Danny had predicted over the years did come to pass. Still, an "abortion pill" was not going to happen. What a nut.

What about a cancer pill, Danny? When is that going to happen? she thought, eyes in full-roll mode.

Louey was proud of her volunteer work with Planned Parenthood. She ordered herself some business cards that said, "Louey Levy, Patient Escort, Upper Hudson Planned Parenthood." Her phone number was printed in small letters off to the right side, near the bottom. She had it printed in a typeface designed by Frederic Goudy, who lived just north of

Newburgh at the turn of the century. A box of five hundred was the smallest she could buy, but she ordered them anyway, from a local printer. The union bug on the cards had more words than the card itself, but she thought they looked very cool. She went straight to Nancy's apartment as soon as she got them home.

Nancy got a laugh out of them but after admiring one for a bit, gently asked, "Louey, what is the purpose of these cards? I mean, who are you going to give them to? The reason I'm asking is, the patients you're escorting are already there, right? They're there for their appointment, and they're already in the parking lot, aren't they? And they know to just wait for the woman with the Day-Glo vest when they get there; isn't that what happens? So, who would you hand these cards to? And why is your home phone number on them? I mean, are the patients ever going to call you?"

Louey spoke not a word for several seconds. She just stood there, catatonic, as it slowly dawned on her that the words on those cards might be perfect in the "volunteer work" section of some future résumé, but made no sense on a business card. There was no one to whom she would ever have occasion to hand such a thing.

Louey then performed such a good impression of Emmett Kelly's "Weary Willie," the sad clown—head down, bottom lip out, shuffling slowly across Nancy's living room toward the door—that her hostess ran to her and rubbed her back, laughing and irrationally looking on the bright side.

"It's OK; they're really beautiful cards, and you can use them for a lot of things. You can put a few in your ... in your Treasures Box, and take them out and enjoy looking at them when you're in your 70s!"

They both laughed, as the idea of Louey living that long and still remembering anything at all was hilarious.

"Or, you can use them right now, to jimmy locks! You can make shopping lists or write haikus on the back of them! You can ..." Nancy had run out of ideas.

"... Yeah! Flip them for heads or tails, to see who bats first, or who receives the kickoff!" Louey suggested. "Or smack a fly on a window with the whole box! Or use them as fire-starters on a hike, instead of having to gather kindling!"

"Why not? Or tape some together to put under the leg of an unbalanced table! Or stand on them, to reach a very slightly higher shelf!" Nancy added.

"See? See? I knew they'd be useful," Louey said. They parted laughing.

Less than a week later, Nancy presented her pal with a classy, green-and blue paisley silk "business-card envelope" that softly clicked shut with hidden slender magnets. Only Nancy would be that thoughtful. She was afraid she'd hurt Louey's feelings with her remarks about how useless her "business cards" would be. Louey was delighted by this *objet d'art*. She put five or six of her "Patient Escort" cards into the new case and slipped it into one of the many pockets of her shoulder bag. As Nancy predicted, however, she never used them at all, and immediately forgot about them.

After the wretched "Gestapo" incident at CSEU, Louey couldn't stop thinking about the people housed ("ware-housed," as she bitterly thought of it) at Letchworth Village, and the staff sleeping on the job there, and how not long ago there had also been a terrible scandal that had given CSEU a black eye, involving the way the staff at another place, Willowbrook State School in Staten Island, had treated people with disabilities.

She thought back to her summer jobs as Recreation Director at an overnight camp in the Catskills when she was in college; how she'd loved the residents from the big State Schools who arrived there each Monday. She cried every Friday afternoon as the campers climbed onto the buses to go back to Wassaic, or Letchworth, or Willowbrook. They hugged Louey with big smiles, without seeming sad about what they were going back to. They just enjoyed the hug. *That's something I would do well to emulate, right there*, she thought each time. *I am way too sentimental.* The two dozen or so camp staff members, except for Louey, the cooks and the nurses, were all college students majoring in social work, and to Louey's astonishment, all of them—every single one—had younger siblings with Down Syndrome. Also, many of those siblings, she learned from her colleagues, had not just Down Syndrome, but other conditions, as well: Heart problems and diabetes were common. That same rotten luck applied to the campers. Louey had to watch carefully that no one was "overdoing it" during recreation period. Despite her vigilance, she had several campers faint on her.

The campers had various types of retardation, but those with Down Syndrome were Louey's favorites. They touched her heart. They had kind of an odd look—many of them had tongues that frequently protruded, and they had sort of flat, moon-y faces—but they were unfailingly cheerful and kind, and they had the most beatific smiles. Plus, they were always looking her right in the eye and saying, "I like you," and giving her a hug, and they vied to hold her hand while they walked from one activity to the next. She had to be careful not to play favorites—she made sure to hold hands with many different campers each day.

Roxie, from Wassaic, was, at 42, one of the oldest campers that summer. In addition to Down, she also had epilepsy, and at Wassaic they made her wear a football helmet so she wouldn't hurt her head when she fell and shook against the floor.

This is God's idea of a fun experiment, Louey thought one morning as she knelt next to a nurse over Roxie's shaking body. *He's up there going, "Let's see how much misery we can put on one person."*

Each evening after supper and activities like movies or Wildlife Walks in the Woods, campers and counselors gathered around the flagpole for the lowering of the flag. Before pressing the "play" button, the camp director always asked if there were any campers who knew the words and would like to be "our guest star" and sing along with the tape-recorded music of Taps. One night, Roxie got up the courage to raise her hand. The director selected her to go to the middle of the circle, near the flagpole, and sing.

She did a very sweet job. "All is well," she sang from inside her helmet; "safely rest"; and then came the big, loud finish: "God is nice!" She ended with a flourish, bowing deeply.

The counselors looked at one another, failing to suppress chuckles. Some of the women, trying not to laugh, lowered their faces and wiped tears from their eyes.

Roxie ran to Louey, who was applauding and nodding vigorously.

"Good job, Roxie!" she said. "Excellent! I didn't know you could sing so well! Wow!" But it didn't work. Roxie was upset.

"Why are they laughing?" she asked anxiously, looking around the circle. 'Did I do something wrong?"

"No, no!" Louey quickly replied. "Not at all. You were perfect! It's just that it's not 'God is *nice*,' that's all. At the end there, you don't say, 'God is *nice*.'"

Roxie fixed her with a horrified gaze.

"God's not *nice*?" She grabbed Louey's arm, truly panicked.

Louey wrapped an arm around Roxie and walked her back to the activity center. There she stole two ice-cream sandwiches from the freezer and sat down with Roxie on the back porch, where no one could see them. She explained about the silly, old-fashioned word "nigh," and how it meant "near," and how nobody uses that word anymore anyway, and how Taps was much better the way Roxie sang it.

I'm probably putting her into diabetic shock with this ice cream, Louey thought. *The nurses would kill me if they saw this. But, screw 'em. This is more important.*

July 22, 1968
Dear Diary,

I guess I don't care very much about stealing. I think the only real sin is wasting your time, and that's not even mentioned in the Tanach. Our time is all that G-d guarantees us, and we never know 'til we're taking our last breath—and sometimes not even then—how much time we were given, and exactly how precious it is. And we've taken thousands—maybe millions of breaths, if we live to be old! But how many are we grateful for? And how many do we use to do good in the world? In the end, the thing I'll really regret is all the time I've wasted. Not the lies I've told, or the stuff I used to steal when I was a kid—just the time! All those minutes that add up to hours and then days, and then weeks, months, years ... each one is unique because it happens at a time we'll never get back.

While Louey was still being a Patient Escort at Planned Parenthood, the Albany Times-Union ran a story about the upcoming national Special Olympics competition, which that year was being held at a college campus in upstate New York. The story focused on the fact that the event would be attended by famous actors and professional athletes. It listed the roster of celebrities who had already committed to attending the event and serving as judges and referees. At the end, the story named some of the events, including track and field, that the special athletes trained for year-round. Reading it, Louey had a feeling that Special Olympics was for her. It would be outdoor work, it would involve physical exercise, it would be working with people with developmental disabilities again ... and how she missed that! It was perfect. Not even knowing whether or not there were any openings available for volunteers, she sent a letter and résumé to Hank Marwell, the executive director of Region 10 (Albany area) Special Olympics. She was surprised at how fast she got a call back, asking her to come and see him.

The interview took place at his home office ("Hank Marwell, Financial Advisor," was the sign on his lawn on the west end of Albany).

Hank had thick white hair clipped into a brush-cut, which, along with his square jaw and erect posture gave him a sort of military look. He seemed not exactly unfriendly, but more than a bit distracted. She noticed a photo on his desk of a boy with Down Syndrome and, to be polite, asked if he had a Special Olympian in the family. Yes he said, that was him, his son Lance. Lance seemed to be about 13 or 14.

"What event does he do?"

"Swimming."

"Love that smile," she said, gazing at the photo with genuine warmth. Hank took way too long before saying, "Yeah," looking neither at Louey nor at the photo. He was fumbling in a drawer for something.

He asked her if she could coach track and field, and she said yes, panicking that he would then quiz her on specifics: what events are in the decathlon, how many laps in a mile, how many lanes in a track, or how to perform the hop, skip and jump. She suddenly realized miserably that she really knew nothing of either track or field.

She needn't have worried. Hank's follow-up questions numbered just one: what size shirt she wore. Upon delivering herself of the word, "Medium," she realized that the interview was over. There were no papers to sign, no congratulatory handshake, no nothin'.

"Do you like red?" he asked.

"Yes! Love red!" she said brightly.

He handed her a medium-sized red T-shirt with the words HEAD COACH imprinted over the left breast and the Special Olympics logo and "Track and Field" over the right. He told her he'd need her on Wednesday evenings from 6 to 7 p.m. and Saturday mornings from 9 to 11. Just those three hours a week. Was that OK?

Yes. Yes, it was. She had nothing to do on Wednesday nights, and on Saturdays she'd have plenty of time to get back downtown in time for her 1 p.m. shift at Planned Parenthood.

He then asked her when she could start. Next week, she said. He rose and handed her a clipboard with some lined sheets listing the names, addresses and phone numbers of the athletes she'd be training. He also gave her the key to the equipment shed, next to the field house at SUNY Albany.

"All the equipment is in there," he said. "The mats and high-jump bars and stuff. You'll have three helpers there, and they have lots of experience, so don't worry about anything. Don't give that key to anyone else." And he escorted her to the door.

"OK? So long. Call me if you need anything."

That was it: World's Shortest Job Interview.

A man of few words was the expression that came to her mind.

She had entered Hank's office as a job applicant and left as Head Track and Field coach for Special Olympics Region 10, Capital District.

Cool!

All 14 athletes named on the clipboard were there her first Saturday. Some of their parents—not all—sat on the bleachers and chatted for the whole two hours the athletes practiced. Louey poured energy and hours into her new position. She drove to SUNY Albany twice a week where, with her three helpers, she set up the high-jump poles and pads and got out the batons, the starting blocks, the timers, the softballs for the throwing event, the write-on, wipe-off board for recording athletes' times, and the first-aid equipment that, thank the good Lord, she never needed. The Olympians met on the athletic field if it was nice out, and otherwise in a smallish gym in the field house, which seemed to be always unlocked and ready for them. She understood quickly why she was chosen as Head Coach—her three assistants were teenaged SUNY Albany students, more interested in gabbing with each other than in the progress of the athletes. They were all the same height, and slender. They wore sweatshirts bearing the letters of the same sorority. They had the same length and shade of blonde hair, pulled back into ponytails. Also, they all wore the same shade of beige makeup, including a kind of beige lipstick that was then in fashion. Louey found them indistinguishable, as well as inseparable, and could never remember their names. Speaking of them with Nancy, she always referred to them as the Beige Girls.

The assistants were a bit casual about showing up on time, or even showing up regularly at all. Also, they already knew each other well, which put Louey in the "outsider" role that she'd often reluctantly had to play. This feeling dated back to her days in high school, when she often felt as if she were the only serious student, and certainly the only one who wasn't part of some entrenched clique. To make matters worse, the difference between Louey's age and theirs made her feel old—out of place on the athletic field of a college campus.

In truth, the assistants weren't much needed. One would

have been enough, or more than enough. They contributed nothing to the coaching and little to the encouragement to the athletes. She figured their main role—and her own—was to be a smiling, back-patting fan club, running and jumping beside the athletes in practices and applauding their every effort. Louey instituted a new procedure: She whistled everyone into a circle at the end of each session and complemented every single athlete by name for something, especially noting those who had improved their performance over the previous week, or who had tried hardest, or who had helped another athlete who was having a hard time, and starting a volley of applause for each one and then another at the end, which everyone joined in enthusiastically before coming to her for hugs and then being escorted off by their parents or aides.

Louey tried to engage the Beige Girls; she really did. She asked their year in school (all sophomores) and what they were majoring in (social work, all three). But they never asked her any questions in return, and after their monosyllabic responses, they would resume their sophomoric gossip as soon as possible. It took Louey a while to notice that each assistant gave special attention to one athlete apiece, and to learn that those athletes were their very own younger siblings. On only one occasion did the Beige Girls have anything resembling a conversation with Louey. They were hauling the mats and high-jump bars back to the shed when one of them turned to her and asked, "Does one of your children have retardation?"

When she said No, she had no kids, "In fact, I'm not even married," and no one in her family had any developmental disabilities, it literally brought them up short. They stopped, brows furrowed, mouths open, unmoving, unblinking. Now they were all looking at her. They dropped their mats and tilted their heads. Louey decided to stare right back; she was just as puzzled as they were and she wanted to know what was so weird about her answers. Finally, the shortest of the Beige Girls wrinkled up her face, shook her head and said, almost belligerently, "Well, why are you here, then?"

They looked not only confused but even a bit offended, as though without someone with retardation in her family, Louey had no right to be there. As though she were taking the rightful place of someone who had a child or sibling with retardation, who should be the Head Track and Field Coach of Region 10 Special Olympics.

Instinctively she wanted to shoot back, "For the same reasons you are," but she edited that part out and started with the rest of the sentence: "To help people with retardation to feel good about themselves. To help them get more physically fit; to get them outside and help them enjoy being active and building their strength and agility and confidence, and to help them make new friends." She said it rapidly and loudly and confidently. She really had no idea why that would perplex them. And finally she couldn't help herself, so she added, "You know—for the same reasons you are."

"Oh, are you divorced, then?" one of them ventured hopefully.

Because maybe one of my ex's kids has retardation, they must think. And when he married me, he must have had a kid with some kind of developmental disability, and so I must be that kid's stepmother, they figure. Because no one else would volunteer, except a sibling, or a parent, or a step-parent. That's it: I must be a step-parent. Because nobody in the world my age could be never-married. Wow. College kids think I'm old.

"But our little brothers—and sister—have Down Syndrome! We're here because we live with them! We know what it's like! We know how sweet they are, and how people make fun of them!" another Beige Girl said.

"Yeah! People don't know what their problems are and how good they are until they live with them!" the third one added.

All very fine, but it sounded to Louey as if they were objecting to something. They looked as though they might stamp their little beige feet.

"And I admire you so much for doing this!" Louey said. "I'm on your team! I'm completely with you, and I'm just volunteering my time and energy to prove it. I'm here to back you up. See what I mean?"

Louey thought she heard one or two of them mutter, "Oh, OK. No problem. Good." And with wan, beige smiles, they picked up the mats and silently walked the rest of the way to the shed. But that confirmed Louey's suspicion—which was never contradicted—that she was unique. She was the only person involved with Region 10 who wasn't a first-degree relative of one of the athletes.

Dear Diary,

I don't blame them for thinking I have kids. G-d knows I'm old enough, in my 30s, to have several. They probably never met anyone as old as I am who isn't a parent. Still, saying that some-one with __no__ developmental disabilities shouldn't try to help people with them is like saying that a healthy person shouldn't want to be a doctor. Or that white legislators shouldn't fight for civil rights for Blacks, or that well-fed people shouldn't share food with hungry people. What in the world are those girls thinking? Is Special Olympics some exclusive little club that no one can volunteer for unless you have people with retardation in your family? What a stupid, close-minded attitude! It's like a fraternity where you can't get through "Pledge Week" unless you're a first-degree relative of one of the athletes.

Eventually Louey found the Beige Girls to be adequate, albeit sullen assistants. She started to wonder if maybe she'd beaten out one of them for the Head Coach position. At her interview, Hank sure acted as if he hadn't had any other volunteers, though.

She did love the athletes, and she did love wearing her "Head Coach" polo shirt with the Special Olympics logo and the lanyard with the shrill steel whistle.

The Olympians themselves, of course, were wonderful. Louey learned their names right away, "cheating" by writing them in a notebook both during and immediately after practices (*Marty: short, heavy, diabetic, wants to hold my hand the whole time; mom keeps flask of OJ underneath bleachers. Vicki: excitable, runs head-down. Mel: hugs himself, rocks, smiles and nods constantly; doesn't talk; doesn't seem to know what's going on*).

Many of the athletes were multiply handicapped, and Special Olympics had a whole separate wheelchair division they could compete in, as well as a process whereby a helper could run alongside a blind athlete, with both of them holding onto the same baton. At home, Louey added to her notebook brief descriptions of her athletes' events, their strengths and weaknesses, what they were improving in and what they needed the most help with. She ran along with the runners and jumped along with the jumpers, always cheering and applauding their efforts. She demonstrated proper high-jump technique, describing a capital "J" in her path to the bar, which was barely higher than the foot-thick landing mat. She showed them how to throw. She walked over to the bleachers afterwards and introduced herself to their parents or siblings or aides—whoever was taking them home. And she got to be special friends with some of them.

Dear Diary,

Yes! They really are getting better. Everybody's getting better, if only a little. You can see the progress, and it's so cool! Every week, their times are getting lower, their jumps longer or higher. I think part of it may be just because they want to please me and earn my praise. Of course, I praise every single one of them for trying, every single time. Everybody's getting to be friends, too, as they compliment one another and pat one another on the back just like I do. It is so damn nice to see them being so happy and proud of themselves!

One night, Hank showed up at a practice for the first time since Louey interviewed with him. The Beige Girls had told her that Hank didn't do any coaching himself; Jimmy, the swimming coach, drove his own son and Lance Marwell to and from practices. Why didn't Hank himself ferry his son to practices? Other kids, other commitments? Another part-time job? Louey never asked and never found out. Didn't matter. But this one time, he showed up at the athletic field while she coached her athletes. He watched from a few rows up on the metal bleachers and, at the end of practice, came down to the field, stepping sideways over the lower rows. He asked his Head Coach if she'd like to go to a three-day convention for Special Olympics coaches that was being held in Syracuse this coming weekend, just a few days away.

"Your hotel room and meals would be paid for," he said. "It's kind of fun. I go every year. I can only take two coaches. Jimmy, our swim coach, always goes with me, but you can come with us, if you want. I think you'd get a lot out of it. You meet other coaches from around the state, and learn from their experiences, and see how they do what they do. We leave on Friday afternoon and get there in time for dinner. There's a couple of seminars and workshops on Friday night, and the keynote this year is by Christopher Reeve—you know, the guy who plays Superman in the new Superman movie?"

She would have gone anyway. But: *Christopher Reeve? The World's Handsomest Man? Who lives across the river in Columbia County, and is involved with all kinds of environmental advocacy? Her idol, her hero?* Why, yes. Yes, she would go and hear Christopher Reeve speak. And maybe get to talk with him later. In the bar.

"There are workshops and seminars all day Saturday, and again Sunday morning; you sign up for whatever ones interest you. Saturday night there's a party, and we leave right after lunch on Sunday. It's fun! I'll pick you up at home and drive us all out and back, and drop you off at your house again on Sunday afternoon. What do you say?"

She said yes. She had not spoken with Hank since her interview, and she thought it might be interesting to get to know him on the boring, flat, two-and-a-half-hour drive to Syracuse. She had ridden that stretch of the Thruway many times during her years in college. Jimmy the swim coach she didn't know at all, and in fact she had never seen him. She figured he must spend all his coaching-time in the big swimming center the college had pompously named the Natatorium. But maybe on this trip she would get to know him.

She took a half-day off from work on Friday to get ready for the journey. When Hank rolled up in front of her building in his big, black Lincoln, she was already on the stoop waiting for him. Wearing jeans and holding onto her shoulder bag strap and lugging a backpack too, she looked a bit like a kid waiting for the school bus.

"This all you got?" Hank said, throwing her pack into his trunk. She had crammed a simple dress into the pack, in case Saturday night was supposed to be kind of "formal." She also had a bra, two pairs of undies and a pair of pantyhose stuffed into a pair of high heels. Plus, she had two rolled-up T-shirts and a pair of sweatpants in her pack, because after all, these were Gym People she was going to be meeting with. Her kind of people. And she knew the hotels now provided each room with shampoo, so yes. That was all. That and her book. She never went anywhere without a book.

"Boy, you sure don't pack like my wife!" Hank said, and Jimmy, who'd not even got out of the car but who'd remained sitting there in the passenger seat with his window rolled down, chimed in, "Mine, neither!"

"Wow, this is like a limo! I feel like a VIP, back here!" Louey said, figuring this would please her driver.

"Yeah, it's a nice car," Hank replied.

Louey looked at her watch: They were leaving at precisely 3 p.m. *Points for punctuality*, she thought.

The men began chatting, more or less inaudibly to Louey. At the first pause in their conversation, she tried to offer a few questions, just to be polite, and maybe learn something. Scooting over to the center of that plush back seat, she leaned forward to ask delicately if Jimmy had a Special Olympian in his family. He did. His son was a swimmer.

She knew it! Nobody in the history of the world had ever got involved with Special Olympics unless someone in their own, personal, nuclear family had retardation of some kind. It was like a rule.

Louey had never met him. She didn't even know where exactly the Natatorium was. She knew it was in one of the buildings surrounding the athletic field, but she had only heard about it.

"And how do you two know each other?" she asked, turning her head toward one, then the other of her companions. "Did you meet through Special Olympics?"

"We worked in the State Police for what, 20 years, Hank?" Jimmy said, and Hank just nodded.

"Oh, so you're old friends, then," she said, uselessly. "You were Troopers?"

"Yep," Hank said.

That was the end of any conversation involving Louey for the next 45 minutes. The two men seemed to be jabbering away with each other up there, but the steady hum of the tires and the air conditioner was loud and lulling. They asked her not a question and directed not a comment toward her. Sitting behind them, she could make out almost nothing they said. At first, by leaning forward, she tried to hear their conversation. She put her head nearly between theirs and looked from one man to the other as they spoke, trying to seem interested. But they were talking about things she couldn't understand and about people she didn't know and things that had nothing to do with Special Olympics.

She sat back. She knew exactly how long this ride would be—knew everything about it, in fact. They could take either the Thruway or Route 20. Route 20 was her favorite way to go, with its funny little one-stoplight villages and the World's Biggest Gum Wrapper and Dig Your Own Gemstones and the New York State Cheese Museum and the State Champion Pumpkin Patch and the Christmas Surprise Caverns and Giftshop and so much more. Plus, it was free. The downside was, on Route 20 it would take them a half hour longer to get to Syracuse. If they really wanted to be at the Hotel Syracuse by dinnertime, she figured they'd take the flat, boring Thruway.

They took the Thruway.

They jumped on at Exit 23, close to downtown.

God, I would never do that. But I guess when you're a grownup, you don't care about the extra 20 cents you'd save by getting on at Exit 24. Why do I still think of myself as Not-a-Grownup? I have my own apartment! I have a job! I do my own laundry! I'm a grownup! Wow. How did that happen so fast? I was a college kid about a minute ago, wasn't I?

You do save 10 minutes this way, though, by not going through all the Albany traffic.

Louey scanned the roadside and spotted her favorite bird: a big adult red-tailed hawk. He was just sitting there on a high, bare oak branch, still, posing, lording it over the whole road.

He's looking for mice and snakes, for sure. Meanwhile, here we are with hundreds of other cars and trucks, rattling and roaring, polluting his air with our exhaust, poisoning and cutting down his habitat a little more every year. There's too many humans, that's for sure. And what value are we adding to the universe? God must be spinning in Her grave.

She gave up on trying to be sociable and scooted over directly behind Jimmy, so she could lean against the door and think up a poem and fall asleep.

About 45 minutes later, she was awakened by a dramatic reduction in the car's noise and speed. Hank was pulling over, and not just into the slow lane, but all the way onto the right shoulder. He quickly and smoothly came to a stop and rolled down his automatic window. No one said anything.

A New York State trooper walked up to Hank's window and said, "Good afternoon."

"Good afternoon, officer," Hank said, handing him something that Louey assumed was his driver's license.

The trooper looked at it for about two seconds and handed it back to him.

"Have a nice day," he said.

"You too," Hank replied. The cop walked back to his car.

Hank waited for the trooper to continue westbound for a few moments. Then he turned on his left blinker and pulled back onto the roadway himself.

From the start of their quick slowdown to the resumption of their trip, Hank and Jimmy had spoken not a word. Now they continued conversing as though nothing had happened. They didn't mention being pulled over at all. It was as if it had never happened. Had she dreamed it?

Louey was astonished. She wanted to say, "What the hell was that?" but something told her to let it go. She figured it out pretty quickly: Troopers must have I.D. cards showing their occupation, and the unwritten code must be, "Never ticket a fellow trooper." That must apply to former troopers, as well. Hank probably flashed such a card, or something like it.

Eeny, meeny, miney, mo: Catch a trooper, let him go, she said to herself. *That must be what they teach them at Trooper Training School.* Hank and Jimmy were talking to each other now exactly as before. They never mentioned having been pulled over any more than you would mention having seen a license plate from New Jersey. It was nothing to them.

Louey began to wonder if they'd forgotten she was even there. She feared they'd reach the Hotel Syracuse, get out of the car and be startled to find someone in the back seat. Maybe they'd pull their ex-trooper guns on her and kill her! Shoot first and ask questions later!

She looked around to see if she could figure out where on the Thruway they were. Her watch said 3:45; they would have passed Amsterdam and should be somewhere around Fonda, she thought. Even with their little adventure with the trooper. (Heck, that didn't add thirty seconds to their trip!) Then she saw a road sign: "Utica, 15 miles."

Utica, 15 miles. Did I see that right? She held her watch to her ear; it was working fine. She'd wound it just that morning. And yet she saw it; the sign clearly said, 15 miles to Utica. If they were really just 15 miles east of Utica, which was 95 miles west of Albany, that means they'd gone 80 miles in ... *45 minutes? No. Because that would be ... Here's where some math skills would come in handy ... Wasn't this on a math test once? Let's see ... No, that can't be right. That would be, like, 120 miles an hour, wouldn't it? No. That's gotta be wrong.*

A hundred? That can't be right, either. Do it again. This time on paper.

Let's see: 80 is to 45 as X is to 60. Would that be how to set it up? Yes! That would tell you how many miles per hour you're going. Wouldn't it? Yes!

Eighty miles, 80 on top, is to 45 minutes, 45 is on the bottom, put in the colon, as how many miles, X, that's the top, is to 60 minutes, on the bottom. So, divide 4800 by 45 ... Before she got the answer, she saw another sign: Utica, 5 miles. Utica was 95 miles from Albany. She didn't know much, but she knew that. She had driven, and been driven, back and forth across the Thruway from Albany to Syracuse more times than she could count. It was 95 to Utica, and that was always a welcome landmark, because then you had just one more hour to go, to get back to college. In the days when cars went 60 miles an hour.

Holy crap: Were we going 106 miles an hour? No; that can't be right. Can cars even go 100 miles an hour? I always thought that "100" on a speedometer was just a decoration. Well, obviously, you can *go that fast ... if you're an ex-trooper. Holy crap.*

In another half hour, they were at their hotel.

I've gotta write to Peg about this, Louey thought. Her old roomie, born and raised in Binghamton, would get a kick out of this. *Albany to Syracuse in 90 minutes!* No, wait: *To hell with Peg; I've gotta write to NASCAR! Hank's gotta have the land speed record. And he seems like he drives like that every day.* "Nothin' to it; we ex-troopers can drive as fast as we want! We can drive like there's nobody else on the road, and we'll never get a ticket!" *I can just hear him saying that.*

Jimmy and Louey brought their stuff into the hotel while Hank pulled around to park in the garage. Jimmy stood by the revolving door at the front entrance to wait for his friend while Louey got her name badge from the Special Olympics Welcome Table, near the registration desk.

A pudgy little boy with Down Syndrome was sitting at the desk. Louey guessed he was about eight or ten, though she was bad at guessing the age of Down Syndrome kids. Beside him sat a young woman who was dressed quite elegantly, in a suit with a short skirt, earrings, and makeup including mascara and bright red lipstick. Louey guessed that this woman was the boy's older sister.

The woman checked off her name and gave her the program for the weekend along with a large, colorful plastic bag with a self-handle. Inside the bag were a lanyard with a plastic whistle (not as cool as her own) clipped to it; a white, foam ball with red, baseball-type stitching on it to exercise your hands with; a roll of disc-shaped, green-and-white-striped peppermint candies; a pen and a small, spiral-bound notebook; an Event Evaluation Form and, oddly, a tiny and rather cheesy measuring tape on the plastic housing of which was written, "NYS Special Olympics Really Measures Up!"

The boy gave her the most glorious smile and nodded a bit, not quite looking her in the eye as he slowly pronounced, "Welcome to our Convention! What size are you?"

"Medium, I think," Louey replied.

"Medium!" he said, spinning around in his chair. He bent over and a minute later came up with a T-shirt with the Special Olympics logo on it.

"Here! This is for you!" he said, presenting it to her gingerly, with two arms underneath it as if it were a newborn baby. It was still sort of folded. He smiled a big, happy smile, chin up, lips closed.

"Well, thank you!" she said in return. She shook it out so she could see it in all its glory. "Oh, it's beautiful! I'm Louey, and what's your name?"

At this he pushed his chair back, rose and took her hand, closed his eyes and, still smiling broadly, bowed low, like a Frenchman, and slowly said, "Seth. Pleased to meet you." And instead of letting go of her hand, he kissed it.

"Oh, you are so nice! Are you an athlete, too?" she said.

"Yes." He leaned across the table and hugged her, and she hugged him back.

"What event do you do?"

"Powerlifting."

"Powerlifting! That is so hard! You have to practice a lot for that."

"Yeah. I practice every day. I'm very good. I won second place last year, in Region 10."

"Region 10! You're from Region 10? So am I!"

"Yeah. I'm going for the gold!"

"Seth, sit down, please. There are other people waiting to

register," the woman said. "You can talk later."

Seth sat and Louey said, "OK, well, I hope I'll see you at dinner, Seth; thanks for talking to me!" She waved at him. He slowly said, "Thanks for talking to me, too. See you later!" and waved back, all smiles.

She didn't even know powerlifting was a Special Olympics event, but Region 10's powerlifters would be practicing in the SUNY gym, not on the athletic field, so it was no surprise that she'd never met Seth. Oh, well: This would give her something to talk to Hank and Jimmy about on their way home.

Louey was glad for having a big single room. She had plenty of time to write to Peg on Hotel Syracuse stationery with her new pen before dinner, which was more than an hour away. There was supposed to be a "cocktail ice-breaker" going on until then in the banquet room. Louey wasn't interested in cocktails, and it didn't seem mandatory, so she had no intention of going unless Hank called and asked her to come down. When she finished writing to Peg, she still had a few minutes, so she pulled out of her backpack the book she was right in the middle of: *Fear and Loathing in Las Vegas*, by Hunter Thompson. She was finding it delicious.

Am I the only remaining human who still hasn't read this book? She asked herself. *It came out, like, six years ago! This is so great! God, if only Hunter Thompson was still at the Record when I got there! I would love to have met him.*

Finally, she couldn't put it off any longer: She had to go down to the banquet room for dinner. She stood for a while trying to decide if she should wear her jeans with her brand-new T-shirt, and maybe even her lanyard and whistle, along with her nametag. It would be a look, for sure. Maybe Christopher Reeve would take notice of her! But then she thought, No, maybe you were supposed to get dressed up for this dinner. She sighed, pulled on her pantyhose and little dress, which emerged from her backpack not too wrinkled at all, and her shoes with the little heels, and went downstairs, locking the door behind her.

In the banquet hall, she couldn't find Hank or Jimmy. Well, she didn't really want to find them, but she supposed she should sit with them, especially since she didn't know anyone else. Maybe you were supposed to sit with your Region. There were more than a hundred grownups milling around in twos or threes or fours, and no one was seated yet. She felt panic rising in her chest as she realized for the first time that she wasn't sure what Jimmy looked like. During that whole, amazing 90-minute car ride from Albany to Syracuse, she saw only the back of his head. In Albany, he never came to the athletic field; he had no reason to. Louey figured he probably just made sure everyone was dried off and dressed and out of the locker room when swim practice was over, and then he locked up and drove Lance home.

The wait staff, men and women alike, were dressed in black suits with white shirts and black bowties. They were circulating with trays and offering people little free things from them. Teensy hotdogs, wrapped in bacon and skewered with teensy toothpicks; tiny sandwiches with no crusts; and small, colorful square napkins. Louey wasn't hungry, but she considered taking something, since it would give her something to do with her hands. She felt very self-conscious and her dress had no pockets.

Hey, maybe Lance will be here! I wonder what Hank's kid is like. Oh, no. Wait a minute: Of course he's not here. He would have come with us if he were coming! Anyway, this is just for the coaches. What about my little friend Seth? Hmm. Maybe I can sit with him.

Finally Louey spotted Seth, sitting by himself at one of the big, round tables. He was eating canned fruit from a little bowl. Relieved, she strode over, pulled out the chair next to his and said, "Hi, Seth! May I sit next to you?" Finally she had someone to talk to.

He looked up, nodded and smiled wanly, looking straight ahead instead of at her. "Yes."

"Remember me? Louey!"

"Yes." He nodded, but he didn't look at her.

"Are you having a good time?"

"No."

"Me neither."

"I thought there would be sports." He had returned to his salad.

"There's no sports tonight?"

"No," he said, stabbing a wet slice of banana. "Tomorrow, I'm gonna show how to lift. But nothing tonight."

"Oh, maybe there will be more athletes tomorrow and then there'll be, like, competitions and everything. But I guess we just have to wait 'til then."

"My mom said I had to come today," he mumbled, frowning and staring at his bowl. He thrust out his lower lip.

"Well, yeah! You had to help with registration, right? You were sitting at that table and making sure everybody got their stuff! You were the most important person there! I don't know how we all would have gotten our bags and those nice T-shirts and all our stuff, without you!"

"Thank you," he said. He smiled his huge, proud, closed-lips smile and put his head on her shoulder. "You're my special friend."

"Aw, you're my special friend, too."

Louey hugged him with her left arm and let her head rest on top of his while she patted his left shoulder. She felt stupid for not looking at tomorrow's events in the program. That would have told if indeed there were going to be any demonstrations by athletes tomorrow. She hoped for Seth's sake that he was right, but she was doubtful, because she didn't think the hotel had a gym, so where would demonstrations take place? Here in the banquet hall, with all the chairs and tables moved aside, maybe?

"Seth, do you know if there are any programs around here anywhere?"

He straightened up and said, "There's more out there," without pointing or indicating in any way where "out there" was. She knew where he meant—the reception area—but she didn't want to leave him all alone, because he looked so lonely by himself. Where was his mom? Anyway, she figured she'd stay with him for now and go back to the registration table and get a program later. She asked Seth about himself. He had no brothers or sisters. He didn't go to school: His mom taught him. His favorite show to watch on TV was "Sesame Street."

"'Sesame Street!' I love Sesame Street! I love Cookie Monster!" Louey said.

"Yeah," he said. "I love cookies, too."

"Which do you like better, chocolate chip cookies or oatmeal raisin cookies?"

"I don't know."

"How old are you, Seth?"

"Ten."

It was quite a while before anyone else sat down at their table, which had already been set for eight places. The first person who did so, drink in hand, was the lady from the convention registration table. She seemed exceedingly chipper.

"Hi, I'm Rosie Cartright." She smiled brightly. "I'm Seth's mom. I see he's found a friend."

Oh wow, so she is his mother. So, she must have had him when she was what, twenty? Because she doesn't look any older than me. That's absurd. That's an absurd age to have a kid. Your life hasn't started yet! Well, I guess hers did. Yikes.

Rosie pulled out the chair on the other side of Seth's, put her drink down there and slung her shoulder bag over her chair back. Before she sat down, she removed a few stapled pages from her bag and set them beside her drink. She then placed a business card on the table in front of Louey's big, empty dinner plate. Louey picked it up and examined it as though it interested her.

"ALL Children are Precious," it said. "Rosie Cartright," it said underneath that. "President, Capital District Right to Life." And her phone number and address were below that.

Rosie walked around the table, setting business cards beside the plates at each of the five empty places.

After she'd made her rounds, she finally sat, and immediately leaned far forward so she could see past Seth.

"Do you have a card?" she asked Louey.

"A what?"

"A business card."

"Actually, I do, but they're in my purse in my room." Louey wasn't quite sure that was true. She never used the cards that CSEU had printed for her when she was hired. The union had given her a box of 500, as they did for all new hires, but there hadn't been a single time, under any circumstances, that anyone had ever asked her for one, and she would never think to offer one to anybody unbidden. "Here's my card": It sounded so pretentious! Besides, it seemed as if she only talked face-to-face with people who fell into one of three categories: those who already knew who the hell she was; those who asked for her name, title, address or phone number and for whom she then jotted all that down, forgetting about her cards, since she always had a pen and paper on her; and, the most populous category by far, those who didn't care a fig about her name or contact information.

"I always keep mine with me," Rosie said. "They're so important. You never know when you're going to meet someone who can help you later."

"You know, you're right. I'm going to have to start doing that. I'm Louey. Louey Levy. Seth's such a great kid!"

"He sure is. He's the joy of my life. Well, guess what: I have big news. It turns out I'm going to be the keynote speaker tonight! Christopher Reeve has contracted measles!" Rosie didn't seem terribly upset by this downturn in Superman's life. In fact, she seemed a little giddy about it. Louey, however, was more than disappointed enough for both of them.

"You're kidding. I mean, when did you hear the news?"

"His wife called the statewide president, Morris Hall, earlier today, and Morris asked me to step in. He was just diagnosed this morning! The Reeves couldn't believe it either! Isn't that crazy?"

"But, measles? Are you sure? I thought only kids get measles! And by the way, wasn't the measles was wiped out, like, fifty years ago?"

"That's what I thought, too. What a disaster! We scheduled this event with his people six months ago. But anyway, I volunteered to step in. I had to rush like hell to get my speech ready, but I'm all set now!" Rosie waved a few typed pages with one hand while lifting her stemmed, V-shaped glass for a quick drink with the other.

"Oh, wow!" Louey said, sitting back in her chair. "In other words, you really had to leap tall buildings in a single bound to get that presentation finished, huh?"

Rosie's face grew serious. She put her drink back down, quickly took a pencil from her purse and made some notes on one of her pages.

"I'm going to use that," she said quietly. "That's good."

Louey imagined that the statewide Special Olympics organization had public relations people who had spent hours trying to get the Post Standard and the local TV and radio stations to cover this event. Surely they would have used as bait the fact that Christopher Reeve, the movies' new "Superman," was going to be the main speaker. Now, would they come? Did anyone tell the press about Superman's measles? If not, they'd be awfully mad if they showed up expecting to interview or photograph him, and he wasn't there! Before Louey had a chance to ask her about that, Rosie was up and walking around among the other tables, handing out her business cards and getting the cards of others.

Louey never saw Hank or Jimmy the whole evening. A married couple and a group of three sat at Louey, Rosie and Seth's table; she never caught their names. Dinner wasn't bad: chicken with mashed potatoes and overcooked vegetables. As dessert—a dish of ice cream with a cookie pressed into it at a rakish angle—was being served, Rosie pushed her chair back, saying to Louey, "Here, you can have mine." She took her notes with her, but she left two extra pages, stapled together, face down between her plate and Louey's, with a pen on top of them. As she rose, she patted them and whispered to Louey, "Don't let them take this. Guard it with your life. I'm going to use it later." And with that she grabbed Seth by the hand and led him away. His dish of ice cream sat at his place, already starting to melt.

A few minutes later, Rosie and Seth, still holding hands, appeared at the podium that had been set up in the front of the room. With them was a tall man who had to bend downward quite a bit to get his mouth close enough to the mic. He smiled broadly and said, "Good evening, ladies and gentlemen, I hope you're all enjoying the dinner that was sponsored by our friends here in Region 12. I'm your host, Morris Hall, president of New York State Special Olympics. As you may have heard, Christopher Reeve could not be with us tonight, as he's been diagnosed with—of all things—measles!"

He waited, nodding grimly, while several attendees gasped, "Oh, no!" and "That's awful!" and turned to their neighbors, mouths agape, making surprised-crowd noises. But many of them, apparently, had already heard the news.

"Luckily," he continued, "we have with us tonight a little lady who's more powerful than a locomotive." The people smiled.

Cheesy, Louey thought.

"When I told her what had happened, she flew out here, faster than a speeding bullet ..." the people laughed.

"And, leaping tall buildings ..." Louey mouthed, nodding.

" ... and, leaping tall buildings in a single bound, arrived here from her home in Schenectady with her own Special Olympian, Seth, to fill in for Superman. You know her as the president of the Department of Mental Hygiene's Advocacy Committee, or as the youngest-ever president of the Capital District Right to Life ..."

Louey did not change her expression as she surveyed the room's high, chandelier-larded ceiling and silently asked the good Lord, *How did I not see this coming? How stupid am I?* And, *Can I go home now?* But the good Lord wasn't finished with her.

Rosie did a solid job at first, garnering applause several times during her 15-minute presentation. She talked about how rewarding Special Olympics is for the athletes and volunteers, about the new events that would be added this year (table-tennis and bocce), and announcing where the next state and national events would be held. But then Superman's stand-in veered far from the flight plan.

"Ladies and gentlemen, hard as it is to believe," she said, "there are people out there, including a majority of the Supreme Court, who think that promiscuous, selfish young women desiring nothing but glamorous careers and a fun time, should be allowed, for their own convenience, to end the lives of children like my own Seth, here—the light of my life and a joy to all who know him. Wave to the people, Seth." Seth waved, and smiled his big, beautiful smile.

Louey thought of some of the women she knew who'd had to have abortions. *What if you're neither promiscuous nor selfish, Rosie? What if you already have six kids and a low-paying job? What if you're finding it hard to take care of the kids you already have? What if you were raped by your own goddamned father? What if you're fatally ill right now, or a heroin addict? What if you know that you wouldn't be a good mother—that you'd eternally resent his existence, and that you'd abuse him like your own parents abused you? What if your doctor told you another pregnancy might kill you? Why don't you mind your own business?*

"I'd like to ask you all now, by a show of hands: Who here is glad I didn't choose to abort Seth?" Of course, all hands shot up, including Louey's, but Louey saw what was wrong with the question.

Nobody's sorry you have Seth; the point is that anyone who doesn't want kids shouldn't be forced to have them! That's all there is to it. You don't know what problems these women are having; why don't you just trust them to do the right thing and mind your own business?

"Now they can tell who has Trisomy 21 and who doesn't when the child is still in utero," Rosie continued. "Soon, they'll be mandating abortions for those who do. And then, millions of beautiful Olympians like the ones we all know, with their big smiles and even bigger hearts, will be murdered, just so that these so-called feminists can exercise their so-called 'choices,' any time they want, for nothing but their own convenience!"

Right, lady. Women just whimsically say to themselves, "What should I do this weekend? Visit Grandma? Take the kids for a hike? See a movie? Oh, I know: I'll have an abortion!"

"Where in the Constitution does it give women the right to an abortion? You can search and search, and never find it! What amendment is that?" Rosie continued.

Ninth and Tenth, Louey replied silently. "The naming of certain rights in the Constitution shall not be construed to deny others retained by the people." Also: "Powers not delegated to the U.S. nor prohibited to the states are reserved to the states, or to the people." Not to mention the Fourteenth, the Due Process clause.

"We can't let this happen to our precious children! I'm asking you tonight to sign the 'Petition to Prevent the Murder of Millions.' We started it in Schenectady just last month, and I'm proud to say it's already gotten thousands of signers. Louey, will you get that petition going around, please? It's right there on the table. It's for the New York State Legislature, demanding that they repeal the immoral 1970 law that set the precedent for Roe v. Wade."

Louey turned over the stapled pages Rosie had left her. Only Rosie's name and address were scrawled on it, so far. Louey rose slowly and circumnavigated her table, offering the pen and paper to the people while whispering, "Don't feel like you have to sign this," to each one.

They had to move their ice-cream dish away to sign the thing, and many of them had to find and put on their reading glasses, and sometimes the petition got a little wet, and sometimes people had to push so hard with the pen that it poked through to the tablecloth, but four of the five at her table signed it. She moved silently and even more slowly to the next table, looking downward, trying to be as inconspicuous as possible. Some attendees declined to sign, shaking their heads or waving her off with tiny gestures as she approached. To them she nodded vigorously a few times and moved on to the next person. When she was just about halfway through the room, the lights were lowered, and someone began showing a film of last year's statewide finals. Now it was really too dark to sign anything. And then, the first three people at one table said, "What's this?" as she placed the petition in front of them; they had forgotten all about it.

Here was her chance.

"Would you please pass this to the next table when you guys are done with it? I have to go to the ladies' room," she whispered to a woman seated near the middle of the room. The woman nodded dubiously and laid the petition down on the table next to her coffee cup.

Louey, of course, hoped the petition would somehow get lost, as so often happens when such things are passed around and no one knows who is to get it next. Then Louey really did go to the bathroom, where she spent an inordinately long time in order to avoid seeing Rosie again. From there she went straight back to her room and finished reading her book. Then she wrote in her diary:

It's so offensive when people assume that, because I trust pregnant women, that means I don't love Seth, or any other handicapped kid! I want every Seth, and every other Down Syndrome kid and every other kind of kid in this whole world to be loved by their families and given a good life. A lot of people can do it perfectly well—they can raise a kid who has developmental disabilities and requires all your attention, all day, every day. I mean, I couldn't, but I respect those who do. But to say that every woman who doesn't want to carry a pregnancy to term must give birth anyway, must neglect the family she already has, and her education and career and friends and her own soul, to take care of that one kid, when she's too scared, too young, too old, too not-ready to have that kid at all—to force her to give birth to a kid she doesn't want—that's just cruel.

Why can't they trust women to make the right decision for ourselves? A lot of women with unwanted pregnancies are going to have an abortion even if it's illegal, like they used to do when they had to have them done by quacks in dirty rooms and alleys. If they made it illegal again, that would just bring back criminals with no medical knowledge, performing abortions at exorbitant rates and killing or maiming the desperate women who sought them out.

The next day, Louey attended seminars on coaching track and field; on the "co-morbidities" that most frequently go along with Down Syndrome; on the latest Marine Corps stretching and strength-building exercises, which was fun because the attendees got to do the exercises; and on new surgical techniques to treat heart defects and new drugs to treat the gastrointestinal problems most common in people with Down Syndrome. Back in the banquet hall, there was indeed a demonstration by Seth of the proper techniques for powerlifting, after which Louey was the loudest applauder and cheerer and the first to hug him when he was finished. She did not see Rosie Cartright all day, except at Seth's demonstration. Rosie didn't attend any of the seminars that Louey went to. That night there was a movie about President

Kennedy's family, and then on Sunday they had breakfast, during which Louey, deliberately avoiding Rosie, sat with a group of chatty people from the host city of Syracuse. Next on the schedule was a "free-wheelin'" (as the program described it) question-and-answer session with Morris Hall right there in the banquet room, about "Anything That's On Your Minds." It was just as that session was beginning that Hank found Louey for the first time since they'd arrived. He stood beside her and leaned over and quietly suggested that, instead of staying for lunch, they leave when the Q&A was finished. They could eat somewhere on the Thruway, he said, "if we're hungry." Louey was happy to do that.

"OK. Should we meet in the lobby when this session's over?"

"Yeah."

Hank then left to sit with Jimmy on the other side of the room.

Louey filled out her Event Evaluation as soon as she'd finished breakfast, even as Morris Hall answered questions in a most un-freewheelin' way. At the end of the Q&A she folded her Event Evaluation form in half, slipped it into the slot in the big box at the back of the hall and went up to her room. There she brushed her teeth, checked around to make sure she wasn't leaving anything, put two single-dollar bills on the bureau for the maid, put on her jeans, sneaks and new Special Olympics T-shirt, donned her backpack and slung her purse over one shoulder as well. Then she went back downstairs to wait for her traveling companions near the front desk.

That's where Rosie Cartright found her.

"Oh, there you are!" she called. "I'm glad I ran into you! I wanted to get your business card! Don't forget! You promised!" She was dragging two large, rolling suitcases, while Seth hung onto her left arm.

Louey smiled and said, "Oh, that's right! Hi! Hi, Seth! Hey, I'm glad to see you again, because you didn't get to have any ice cream last night, and there's ice-cream sandwiches in that case right over there next to the desk, and I wanted to buy you one! Can he have an ice-cream sandwich, Rosie?"

"No," she said. "He has diabetes."

Well, she wasn't expecting that.

"But don't forget, you promised to get me your business card, and I'm not letting you escape 'til I get it."

"Oh yeah. Let's see; I know it's in here somewhere," Louey said, rummaging through her shoulder bag.

"Is that all you brought? Just a purse and a backpack?" Rosie asked, alarmed at Louey's lack of luggage.

"Yeah, I travel light."

Son of a gun, there it was—that fancy business-card holder Nancy had given her! She was glad to be able at last to take it out and actually give a card to someone, even if it was Rosie Cartright. She removed the silk envelope and whipped a card out of it. Rosie studied it for a long time, like an Asian tourist. As she put it into her own purse she frowned and said, "You know, it's a funny thing: Our petition got lost last night, or someone made off with it."

"Oh no!" Louey said, delighted and deeply gratified. "I started it going around, and I was nearly done but then I asked someone to take over for me because I had to use the ladies' room, and when I got back, the event was all over! I

was sure he'd returned it to you, but you mean, he didn't?"
She hoped the "he" would help throw Rosie off the scent.

"No. No, he didn't. It just disappeared, apparently. Or
someone 'disappeared' it."

Louey tried to look upset. "Did you ask at the front desk?
Is there a lost-and-found?" she said.

"They said nothing had been turned in, and it was probably left on a table, and the custodial staff probably threw
it out with the trash. But, oh well: I'm not letting it get me
down. We'll get this bill passed anyway. We're gaining mo-
mentum every day. Failure is impossible!"

*Wait, is Rosie using Susan B. Anthony's famous remark about
the inevitability of women's suffrage, to say hooray, men are going
to take away our right to abort unwanted pregnancies? The right
that we fought so hard for, and whose absence killed so many people? Oh my God, Susan B. Anthony is spinning in her grave. All
right, let it go and let's get outta here.*

"Yeah!" Louey said, nodding once.

Rosie's heels clicked loudly on the floor as she wheeled
her large suitcase toward the front door.

"Bye, Seth!" Louey called, waving.

He stopped, turned and smiled broadly, holding one
hand with fingers spread like a flagman signaling, "stop."

Hank didn't stop for lunch on the road.

"Is that OK with you?" he asked Louey, glancing into his
rear-view mirror once they were all in the car. "I figure we'll
be home before lunchtime."

It was fine with her. And of course, they were home well
before lunch; this time, however, they avoided that annoying
two-second delay that happens when you get pulled over by

someone who works for your former employer.

She tried her best to make pleasant conversation.

"Man, that Rosie Cartright sure is youthful-looking! Seth told me he's 10, but to me Rosie doesn't look like she's more than 20!"

"Oh, don't you know her story?" Hank replied. "She had him ten years ago, when she was 16. She talks about that all the time."

"Yeah, don't get her started, whatever you do," Jimmy added.

"But you mean ... she's only 26? That can't be true."

Impossible. That's crazy! I thought she was at least my age, but even then, to have a 10-year-old, when you're only 26? Yikes!

"It's true. It was in all the papers in December, when she was the youngest person ever elected chairperson of the Capital District Right to Life. She doesn't let anyone ever forget it, either. Believe me, she'll be glad to tell you all about it sometime. Sometime when you've got, like, an hour and a half, I mean."

Hank added details. "Yeah, we're getting a little tired of hearing it, but she dropped out of high school and gave up all her plans for going to college, and having a career, and everything, to take care of her kid, God bless her. But now she's involved with the Right to Life thing, so that keeps her busy."

"Is she married?"

There was a brief silence.

"*Now* she is, yeah," Hank said. "Her husband's a nice guy. He's a firefighter in Schenectady, way older than her. Second marriage for him. He's got three kids of his own, who live with his ex-wife up in Fulton County. Real nice guy. Doesn't come to any of these things with her, though."

Her weekend in Syracuse inspired Louey to write a letter to the editor of the Knickerbocker News about the importance of women being able to have safe abortions. She took out her new, Special Olympics pen and notebook from her shoulder bag and made a few notes. But when she got home she wrote not a diatribe about abortion, but a poem about traveling. That's how poems can jerk you in the direction they want to go.

The Lord of Exit 23

As grey and gnarly sticks, your jagged throne,
thrust against the morning mist and tear it,
you pierce the frosty air with gaze unguessed,
and trust that we commuter-fools can bear it.

We don't look up: We're blind and blank below.
And through a thousand sighs, with wizened eyes
and withered souls we fumble for our tolls
and go about the day not well nor wise.

We lurch in lurid traffic toward our rackets,
but you don't mind that slugs can't hear you sing.
All unadored, you work your wheeling sunward,
there to seek the worthy of your wing.

Big bird, brown bird, beam a blessing downward;
sail in silent spiral for your soul's nobility.

Fly your holy arc above the featherless and feeble
and commute this working-day, and set me free.

Your grace, the soar and swoop of you, the might,
the awesome flight, your sacred scope and see
proclaim that you alone will reign forever,
O redtailed Lord of Exit Twenty-Three.

A whole year went by fast, and then Christmas time rolled around again. Louey bought two boxes of nice cards with a dove or a snow-covered stand of pines or just the word, "peace" on the front and nothing inside. She then bought two rolls of "Seasons Greetings" stamps. All of this could be used for either Christmas or Chanukah—the former, in fact, fell right in the middle of Chanukah that year. Then she got out her "Addresses" folder and started writing.

She wrote slowly and clearly and artistically, in a script big enough to be read by her older relatives who had known her grandparents and small enough when writing to recipients her own age so that she could include a few fun details about what she'd been doing lately, while asking about them and their families and offering good wishes for the new year (in the case of the goyim) as well. She kept a cup of water on her roll-top desk so that she could "wet her whistle" often as she licked the 40 or so stamps on the cards she was sending out. On the backs of some of them she whimsically affixed Christmas Seals or other fun stickers she had been sent as part of various organizations' fundraising campaigns.

Whom should she send a card to back in Fishkill? Judy,

for sure. And then Alice, too, and … who else? There was actually nobody else down there she had become friends with or even cared about, except Luke Qualesworth, good old "Q." Luke was different. Luke was pure. Luke she loved. Luke was married. She sighed.

Now, what was his wife's name, again? She knew it at one point, but she couldn't come up with it now that she needed it. She didn't have to address the card to both of them, but she also didn't want to write, "Merry Christmas to you and your wife"; she wanted to use her name. She'd call Judy from work the next day. Judy would know.

About a week after the new year began, Louey got a letter—a letter, not a card—from Q.

"Dear Louey," it began. "Thanks for the card. Sorry I'm so late replying. I guess you didn't know that Cathy and I are divorced." It went on for just a couple more sentences, wishing her a good new year, etc., but then there was one other thing, a real shocker: He was coming to Albany in a couple of weeks to interview for the union's Director of Education position, which had just been made available due to the death of the fellow who'd held it for about three decades.

She wrote back immediately, offering her apartment as a place where he could stay if he wanted to stay over. "I've got plenty of room, including a brand-new sofa-bed," she added after pacing around the block thinking about whether to include that last phrase or not.

He came to her apartment, where she made spaghetti with butter and olive oil and thinly sliced carrots, olives and onions and fresh-ground parmesan cheese on top—no tomato sauce at all—and a green salad, and she also served coffee and large scoops of the brand-new Ben and Jerry's ice cream that everyone was talking about. She had chosen a flavor called Ridiculous Raspberry. The whole meal was a hit.

Louey had made a list of some of the recent classified ads in both the Knick News and the morning paper, the Times Union. She asked Luke his price range and requirements for an apartment, and was happy to learn that he had modest tastes (no air conditioning required); a laundry room in the building would be ideal, but he could always take his clothes to a laundromat—he and Cathy had always done that. As a single man, though, he had no desire to own a washer and dryer. Louey did not fail to point out that, if he took an apartment somewhere in Center Square—where her building was—he could bring his laundry to her building and do it in the basement for free. That information tickled him.

He could use either two bedrooms or one, if the place was, like Louey's, big enough for a sofa-bed. He didn't have much furniture, and for the most part he'd always borrowed books from the library, rather than buying them.

Then they walked around Center Square for an hour, talking about where he might find an apartment if he got the job, and enjoying quiet Albany. Albany was always quiet in the evenings, after all the state employees left the Empire State Plaza empty. He caught her up on all the Region 3 gossip. When Lupo got out of the nuthouse, he had moved to Michigan, where the Postal Workers Union, bizarrely, had hired him as their executive director.

"I wonder what he put in his résumé," Louey said. "I mean, he couldn't say, 'At my last job, I tried to commit suicide. But now I'm good!'"

"Well, I guess you don't have to take a psychological exam to get a job with a union," Luke noted.

Or a newspaper! Nobody ever gave me one, thank God! she thought. Some words from Bob Dylan's song, "It's Alright, Ma (I'm Only Bleeding)" came to her: *If my thoughts and dreams / could be seen / they'd probably put my head / in a guillotine ...*"

They walked through a few nearby streets, looking at the nice brownstones that were being renovated there. Too bad there were no vacancies in her own building. Then Luke asked her if she liked to go hiking, and she said yes even though she hadn't been on any real hikes in any real mountains to speak of. He told about his family in Maine and how he grew up hiking in the state parks and mountains and sailing in the ocean on his family's boat.

Finally they returned to Chestnut Street.

The sofa-bed went unused. They didn't say a thing. Their clothes came off as fast and quietly as underpants falling on a carpet.

They made love. And then, instead of sleeping, Louey thought about some things.

She thanked God that she had a prescription for birth-control pills. They weren't perfect, of course, but they worked better than anything else to prevent you from getting pregnant. Plus, they made your periods so light that you didn't even have cramps! Baruch haShem! Plus, no side effects at all—at least not for her. A real miracle of modern medicine. She knew now that the world was changing for the better, and she thought about how she could help make that happen. Maybe by volunteering with some good-guy organizations? Maybe by writing, somehow? Her life was full of possibilities. God, these were good times, and the best time ever to be young.

Then she thought about language. This is what Louey Levy did instead of sleeping.

Why do they say the sperm fertilizes the egg? Actually, it's the other way around: The egg fertilizes the sperm and makes it into a new organism whose cells divide and divide so it becomes more and more like a person until, nine months later, out pops Jennifer! Or whoever. The woman is the gatekeeper for all this—quite literally. Her *body decides which little spermie is good enough to enter and be fertilized. All the others die. Men wrote the books, so they always say the penis "penetrates" you, like you're a fort; like you're a military campaign! They even call women they've slept with their "conquests." But really, it's the woman who gives the best little sperm the honor of joining with one of her eggs to create a new person.*

People she respected believed and often said that the expression "making love" was a euphemism, and that if you were honest you would say, they "fucked," or they "had sex," or "had intercourse." But "fucked" was just vulgar, and "intercourse" sounded to her like something you might have on the concourse of the Empire State Plaza: Someone you recognized came clicking toward you in her high heels on that long, marble floor crowded with state workers, and you waved and said hello and she waved back and said hello, and then right there—you'd had an intercourse. It was like saying you "had lunch," only not as interesting.

To Louey, "making love" now seemed a perfect

expression—one that God would approve of. *You make love increase in the world, with your own unique actions. You create a whole new batch of it, where there wasn't any before, just lust, or curiosity, or even adventure, none of which is bad, but when you open your whole self to someone "else"—if there even is an "else"— you really are making love. You're creating love together, and you become part of that love. You dissolve into it. It's like making bread. You should make it every day, really. It's a staple. It's the staple. But when you're trusting your whole self to someone with all your flaws and eccentricities and sorrows, and they're giving theirs to you, with all their anger and trust, you are actually building up the supply of love in the world, and I'm sure God is smiling because you've added your own unique batch of love to the universe, and that makes it more calm and happy.*

She smiled in the darkness, calm and happy and proud of herself for having pleased Luke and God so well that night.

Luke was lying on his side facing her, and Louey peered down at his restless penis. It wasn't hard and red anymore; it was just a wrinkled snake dreaming in a patch of black brambles. What was it dreaming of down there, though?

Well, sex. That's the only thing a dick dreams about, probably.

Every so often, endearingly, it grew a tiny bit bigger all by itself, as if it had taken a deep breath and was holding it. It would raise a little off of Luke's thigh as if sniffing around for something.

Oh, that's adorable! It's like it's saying to itself, "Nope, no other males around here, don't worry; go back to sleep," and then millimeter by millimeter, it exhales and lowers itself back down. My guardian! Protector of my virtue! This happens, like, every few minutes, and yet it doesn't wake Luke up at all. God, I would be laughing all night if my body were doing that! God, men are so funny!

Was she a bit surprised that Luke got the job in Albany? She was not. Was she a bit disappointed that he decided to go ahead with his plan to get his own apartment, instead of moving in with her? She was. But in full Good Sport mode, she helped him find a place in Center Square, not far from either her or CSEU headquarters. And when they'd finished moving his few pieces of furniture into his new place, they celebrated by having a sleepover at her apartment, because they couldn't find the box with his sheets in it.

In Albany, he could have all the lovers he wanted in his newfound freedom. He told her that at age 19, still an undergrad, he had wed this Cathy person mostly to confound his father. His father did not like the idea of him marrying so young, and so he did it. He and Cathy stayed married for more than nine years, childless, until of all things, she had an affair with a guy at the place where she worked.

At work! How awful, to have an affair with someone at the office! Louey thought. And yet, wasn't that what she was kind of doing? Well, Luke wasn't at "her office" yet. He would be in two weeks, though.

In late spring, Luke asked Louey to dinner at his place. During the meal, after a few glasses of chianti, he asked if she liked camping.

"Yeah!" she said. "I love to go camping! But I haven't had a chance to, recently." Fortunately, Luke didn't ask how long "recently" was. She could as well have substituted, "ever," except for the fact that she and Charlie Farley had driven to Nova Scotia one fall with a borrowed, four-person canvas Boy Scout tent that took them from 4 in the afternoon to 7:30 at night to set up. By the time they got it to stand up by itself, it was too dark and they were too tired to cook dinner, so they didn't eat anything. Then it rained torrents all night, and the rain weighed so heavily on the tent's top that it drooped lower and lower till it was almost touching their faces, and they had to kick at the roof all night long to keep it from collapsing on them, but Charlie's legs were much longer than Louey's, so really it was Charlie who did all the kicking and Louey might as well have been a turtle lying on its shell next to her. They laughed 'til they cried. It was one of Louey's best vacations ever.

What she meant when she told Luke she loved "camping" was, she loved "hiking." She had bought herself a pair of sturdy, heavy hiking boots when she moved to Albany, but she had no one to hike with. Nancy was not a hiker because she couldn't stand mosquitoes.

Luke asked if she'd ever hiked Mount Marcy.

The highest peak in New York State? No, but she'd love to! She'd love to! She'd love to see Lake Tear-of-the-Clouds, famous in the Levy family for being mentioned in her mother's great poem, "The Rhyme of Rip van Winkle." Lake Tear-of-the-Clouds could be found somewhere on Mount Marcy—she knew that much.

They set the date not for the next weekend, but the weekend after that, when it would be at least a little more likely that the snow would have melted up there.

"I've never done it either," he said. "They say it's the

hardest hike in, not just New York, but the whole Northeast. There's a few different ways to do it. There's the shorter but harder one, and others are longer but easier. The shorter way is way, way shorter, though—like, four miles shorter. That's a lot when you're that high and going up that steeply. I'm thinking we should go that way. Here, check this out and see if you agree."

He showed her a topographical map of the Adirondacks, one of many he kept perfectly folded in a wooden box in his bedroom. She sat on his bed with him as he traced the contour lines with a fingernail. They were extremely hard to see, because they were so close together, but he had an excellent, large magnifying glass in the same box and, using it, she got the awful point: Mount Marcy was 5,344 feet high. They figured they'd have to hike for five hours to get to the top via the "short" way, and just a bit less coming down, even though the summit was only eight miles from where they'd be camping.

Eight miles up?

She agreed that they should go the "short" way. They would camp somewhere around Lake Placid—not at the Adirondack Loj, which charged you, but at a free spot nearby, off of South Meadow Road.

They would lay out all their stuff on Friday morning and spend Friday afternoon driving to Lake Placid. They'd camp out there, and then get up at the crack of dawn Saturday and start their hike, and be at the summit, Luke figured, if all went well, by noon, and then be back at 6 p.m. and camp out once more and then on Sunday, strike their tent and have a leisurely drive home.

"Oh, cool! Let's do it!" she said.

They did it. Luke had every kind of hiking equipment and all the camping supplies Louey could ever imagine, including a huge, heavy backpack whose internal frame extended above his head when it was loaded onto his shoulders. Hers was a much smaller, lightweight one that couldn't hold much more than some gorp (the raisins, chocolate chips and chopped walnuts that Louey so enjoyed mixing together), two water bottles and a raincoat, even when fully stuffed. Luke's pack had flaps and straps and clips hanging off it so he could bungee-cord their tent, camp stove and both their sleeping bags to it. He also packed two canteens of water; a Swiss Army knife; a compass; topographical maps of the entire Adirondack region they'd be in; matches in a plastic medicine bottle, so they couldn't get wet; two metal measuring cups that could double as mugs; water purification tablets; two cans of Sterno; paper napkins; little pots that fit into bigger pots; little pans that fit into bigger pans; two potholders; two things that served as both forks and spoons; a big roll of toilet paper; two big zip-closure bags for garbage; several tea bags; a zip-closure bag of coffee grounds he had pre-measured to make six cups of coffee; little containers of non-dairy creamer that Louey had liberated from a coffee shop a week earlier; a film canister filled with liquid hand soap and another filled with dish detergent; and a pair of extra-powerful binoculars. Louey would wear her own, regular birding binoculars around her neck, even in the car. You never knew when you would need them. She took her camera, too, to lay at the foot of the passenger seat.

Into the back of the car they threw Luke's raincoat, their

loaded backpacks and a canvas "food bag" holding several extra bags of gorp; a zip-closure bag of oranges that Louey had sliced up; four bags of instant oatmeal; two packages of all-beef hot dogs and the fancy, two-person tent that Luke had bought at the LL Bean store in Maine when he was still married. They also packed four extra canteens for water they could get from streams along the way in case they needed them, plus two half-gallon-size water bottles pre-filled with water and two empty ones; their sleeping bags which, Louey was happy to discover, zipped together nicely; and of course Luke's camping dishes and pans and forks and spoons. They each brought two changes of clothes and, Louey found out, Luke had a bunch of condoms with him, despite her reminding him that she was on The Pill.

"Jesus—Hannibal crossed the Alps with less crap than we're taking on this trip," Louey said, looking at it all. It was so exciting, though. They just laughed.

Thus, adequately provisioned, they drove in Luke's eight-year-old stick-shift Saab to the Adirondacks, and they hiked Mount Marcy.

It was cold and the trails were muddy, which made for treacherous footing, but there was no one else there, and at the top they could see not only all the rest of New York's High Peaks, the Green Mountains of Vermont and the White Mountains of New Hampshire, but also Mont-Royal in Canada, if Luke was reading his maps correctly. And surely he was. Louey trusted him.

On the way down, tromping on the twigs and rocks, he said out of the blue, "What was it like to lose your mother?"

LOUEY LEVY'S HEADING HOME

She was startled and excited by the question. He really
wanted to get to know her! She told him how her mom had
died when she was nine, and about how her father had tried
to raise his three kids with the help of a wonderful nurse he'd
met at Saint Luke's while her mother was ill, and about how
Abe's parents had come to Newburgh from New York City
to help raise them, and how they had then all had to move
to Albany, with its terrible school system, which was why she
had skipped a grade and ended up going to college when she
was only 16, and finally about her time on the Record.

Luke, in his turn on the mountain, talked about his father.
He felt that he had disappointed his father in many ways, including by getting divorced, even though it was Cathy who
had cheated on him. His father felt Luke should have done
more to keep the marriage together. There had never been
a divorce in the upright, WASP-y Qualesworth family, and
Luke had somehow disgraced the family name by breaking that tradition. Qualesworths do not get divorced! But
Luke did not feel particularly attached to their traditions,
one of which was sending their sons off to boarding school.
His parents sent him to an all-male, extremely strict boarding school in Exeter, New Hampshire and rarely saw him
the whole four years he was there. He spent summers with
his maternal grandmother in Maine. The Qualesworths had
moved to Liberia when Luke's father got a job as the head of
the Peace Corps there. But then, Luke had infrequently seen
his father even before that, as Cal Qualesworth was running
about the U.S. working for Democratic candidates. When
Cal himself was at Harvard, in fact, one of his roommates
was John F. Kennedy, and they shared a noblesse-oblige-y

way of looking at social problems, as well as a career in the Navy. But Luke had never had a warm, loving dad like Abe Levy, and for that, Louey felt sorry for him. For that, Luke smoked, drank and did pot when he could, and vowed to be a different kind of man from the kind his father was.

Louey decided to trust Luke with her sorrow, and he decided to trust her with his anger.

They talked about a lot of things on their camping trip. He was concerned because he had read that the birth-control pill had been found to cause some awful side effects in women who'd been taking it for more than a few years—"thrombosis in their legs and stuff." She had heard that, too. She said she'd go ahead and try using a diaphragm, which had no side effects at all but seemed like a comedy act to insert. From the descriptions she had read, it sounded like folding a trampoline and trying to slide it into a straw. There was gel you could use, though, and apparently, you got used to it. Luke was relieved that she was OK with trying a diaphragm, and she was deeply glad that her continued good health was a priority for him. She made a mental note to get fitted for a diaphragm at Planned Parenthood as soon as she got back to Albany.

She told him she was concerned about how much he smoked. He said he didn't smoke "all that much"—mostly just when he was out at a bar with the guys from CSEU—and Camels went so well with beer, or a bourbon.

"They just seem to go together, you know what I mean?"

She did not know. But she decided not to nag him about it. She wanted very much not to be a nag or a drag or a hag.

Luke also said that he was getting involved with what he

called "the New Spirituality." He regretted having had no religion growing up and was deeply curious about them all. He was going to join a "shamanistic drumming group" that he had learned was starting in Albany. He had already bought a drum for it. He asked her what she thought of him spending time drumming in his off-hours, in a Drumming Circle.

Well, it amused her, that "shamanistic drumming group," and it was all she could do not to laugh, but she felt sorry for Luke's lack of religious practice growing up, and she admired his exploring the "New Spirituality" and "Altered States of Consciousness," as he called his forays into dope-smoking and this apparently trance-like drumming. She told him about the admiration part, but not about the amusement part, as she didn't want to hurt his feelings. What an interesting character he was!

Morning came soon.

Dear Diary,

You never really know someone until you've hiked up a mountain and camped out with them. Because then you see them when they're not trying to impress you, they're just trying to make it over the next goddamned boulder, or find the next blaze. You know if they whine when it rains or gets cold, or if they blame someone else for not bringing matches when really no one brought the matches, and you know every time he farts and he knows every time you fart and you know his reaction to farting, like if he goes, "Eww!" or "Excuse me," or if he just laughs it off. You find out if he remains cheerful when he's exhausted or is getting blisters. You find out if he's physically fit. You find out if he stops and looks back often to make sure you're OK when he's real far ahead of you. You find out if he eats the stuff you brought even though it's not his favorite, and if he's calm and cheerful even when that noise might be a bear, and also you find out if you have things to talk about and can make each other laugh for hours and also if you like being quiet together, keeping a companionable silence in the midst of G-d's awesome creation.

I feel as if I really am getting to know Luke now. In fact, I may know him better than anyone else knows him. And I like him even better than I did before.

It wasn't really very long before they bought a brownstone near Center Square. They asked Nancy Gottfried if she would like to rent the bottom unit when her current lease was up, and after taking one look at the beautiful apartment where Louey and Luke would be her only neighbors, she gave her landlord one month's notice—that's all he needed, according to the lease—and started packing. Now Louey and Luke could use the rent they'd collect from Nancy to help them pay their mortgage each month. And it was in the following spring that:

Reader, she married him.

No one had ever been surer than Louey Levy that she would never marry, nor have cared less than she about it. She wasn't pretty enough to attract men, and even if she were, they would be awful. They wouldn't share her values. They wouldn't be honest, ethical, kind, physically fit, industrious, gentle. They wouldn't be committed to justice and equality for all people, nor to repairing the world, nor to appreciating its beauty and the goodness of it. They wouldn't be intellectually curious. Most of all, they wouldn't be funny, and they wouldn't appreciate her sense of humor. So, she figured, she would go it alone, content to play the role of the cherished friend and the homely but funny sidekick to gorgeous women like Nancy, or Charlie and Annie from the Record.

And yet here came Luke Qualesworth. And on top of everything else, he had a beautiful, deep, strong speaking voice, and was so handsome that she was secretly proud and continually a bit surprised to be seen with him. She was sure that she detected in people, learning that they were an "item," a barely suppressed smile of amusement at this mismatched pair—this striking, tall, smart man with this short, funny "tomboy."

They rarely bumped into each other at work because he was usually off leading seminars on workers' rights, or helping to negotiate reimbursement and paid time off for workers to attend job-related courses, while she was in the office, writing. Luke still failed to see the value of publicizing his own work, so he never came running to the Bullpen with a list of his achievements. But they enjoyed hearing about each other's little work-related adventures. In addition, Luke sometimes was able to break free to accompany Louey when she went to lunch with her dad downtown, or to dinner with him and Ree in Slingerlands.

When they told her father and stepmother of their plans, they immediately offered to host the event in their backyard. They would rent and set up folding chairs in front of the chuppah—the wedding canopy under which the ceremony would take place, as in Jewish custom—so everyone would have a good view of the ceremony, and they'd rent a big tent and tables for the luncheon afterwards, and they'd pay for the caterer, too.

Luke and Louey decided to marry in late spring, so that they could hold the ceremony outside and it could be kind of informal and inexpensive, and then they could go somewhere great for their honeymoon.

"Dress as you would for a picnic," their invitations said.

She got back a reply from Sandy Miller that brought her up short. Two years earlier, during a vacation from the Record, she had gone to visit her parents in Traverse City and had run into an old friend, Lew Wood, from college. They had rekindled a flame that neither of them had realized had ignited during their days at the University of Michigan—they'd both always described themselves as "just good friends." This Louey already knew, from a long letter she'd received over a year ago and read aloud to Luke, interrupting herself occasionally to regale him with highlights of her hijinks with Sandy. Sandy and Lew had eloped, to avoid Sandy's dad insisting on paying for a wedding. They moved to Atlanta when Lew got a really good job there. Louey had their address and phone number safely in her beaten-up, fake-leather address book. But now Sandy wrote that, apparently making up for lost time, she was more than eight months pregnant with twins, and ordered by her doctor not to travel.

Luke bought eight light bulbs so he could practice smashing a "glass" at the end of the ceremony—another Jewish custom that Louey requested. Despite having been brought up in no religion at all, he admired and wanted to learn more about hers. He had no intention of converting, but he was intellectually curious about it and occasionally went to temple with her.

"Luke, in three thousand years, no one has ever failed to smash the glass," Louey sighed as she stood on an asphalt path in Washington Park, handing him light bulb after light bulb.

"Well, I don't want to be the first," he said, stomping hard.

The third Jewish custom Louey wanted to honor was an exchange of rings. The man had to bestow upon the woman a ring worth at least two pennies, Bubbe told her, though Louey couldn't seem to find that anywhere in the Bible.

Louey's grandparents knew from Jewish weddings. They had been married for 67 years. Luke and Louey often went to their house in Albany for Shabbos dinner, bringing wine to go with the brisket and the carrots with honey and raisins that Bubbe always made. Louey didn't get how her grandfather could be so skinny—he felt more like a coat hanger than a person, when she hugged him—and yet eat so much of his wife's good cooking.

Growing up, the Levy kids enjoyed seeing the ancient folks' love and respect for each other, and hearing Grampa's stories about playing the violin in a traveling band in the Old Country, and about his many narrow escapes from the Cossacks and the Tsar's men and then his career at the pocketbook factory and the cheese store in the Lower East Side of New York. Louey solicited information from both Bubbe and Grampa on how they'd managed to stick together for so long, when divorce was becoming more and more common.

Forgiveness seemed to have a lot to do with it.

Kindness also.

Forgetting some things, too.

As you get older, you get more and more like yourself, Louey thought. In recent years, Grampa had started getting even more filled with desire to spread God's love throughout his neighborhood. He would walk around with his cane, nodding and smiling and saying hello to everyone he saw, until he found a bench in a playground over a mile away where he could sit and smoke his cigar and read the *Jewish Daily Forward.*

Louey walked with him now and then, when she had time.

He studiously watched the children playing, and he would rise as fast as he could to help any of the little ones who fell down.

"Here! Here!" he cried as he dabbed one little guy's bleeding elbow with his white hanky. "You see? You're getting better already, and soon you won't even remember this!" Maybe the child would remember and maybe he wouldn't, but someone would remember. Louey would.

Would her memories change with time, though? Would they get re-shuffled, or maybe drop out of the pack altogether? Time was something that Louey often felt short of. She and Luke got only two weeks' vacation a year, and they had to use it carefully, combining it, for example, with a holiday or a weekend, or even taking a few personal days on either side of it, to make it last as long as possible.

Once when she was young and accompanying her grandfather on one of his walks, she asked if he sometimes thought that time seemed to be passing faster as the years went by, and if he knew what happens to the time we spend.

"Time? When you've accumulated your whole allotment, it goes back to the good Lord who gave it to you," he said. "It's all there is, is time. It's the *only* thing there is. In reality, we've got nothing but time. And in the end it becomes nothing, as well as everything. You see? It becomes both! As long as you live, you keep accruing more and more time; you drag it around in an ever-lengthening tail behind you, until finally when you pass into *ha-Olam haba*—the next world—time disappears. You leave your tail behind! There is no past or future—only right now, forever. For then you have become time itself."

Grampa Levy didn't live to see Louey and Luke's wedding. Just a few months earlier, as peacefully and quietly as he had lived, he became time itself.

Louey didn't know what happens to your soul when you die, but her Grampa surely had become molecules of pure love. She didn't "think" that; she knew it, because she felt a few of those molecules very strongly at times when she needed them most. She was comforted and inspired by them, and determined to do things from now on that would make him proud, instead of being lazy and wasting her time. And she would start just as soon as she knew what it was that she was supposed to be doing.

Louey's grandmother was comforted by all the relatives who came from New York for the funeral, and by the big "party" they had afterwards at Abe and Ree's house, where Bubbe got to talk to many relatives whom she hadn't seen in years. It felt a little wrong to Louey that her Bubbe kept calling it a "party," but that's how Bubbe referred to it. Louey enjoyed hearing her family reminiscing about Grampa and meeting her Dad's political friends and eating the challah and jam during the days they sat shiva after that. Bubbe laughed a lot during all that time, and that in itself was a comfort to Louey.

Laughing during Shiva says, 'Life goes on; we all go through this sad part, and this is my time to be sad, but later I'll have a time to be happy again, and you can get a glimpse of that time even now,' she thought. But wow, to be able to laugh after your husband of 60-some years dies—that's really strong. Or wise. Or both. Or something.

As for Louey, she hoped her own grief was the kind that made her a stronger and better person. She determined to be as much like her Grampa as ever she could. She liked it that people at the "party" referred to him as having "passed." She disdained euphemisms, and had spent a good deal of her time at the Record deleting them from the stories that came across the copy desk, but this one—"he passed"—she liked a lot. It wasn't even a euphemism, she thought—it was the truth.

He did pass. He certainly did, and he went on to a higher place. It's like in school, if you do well enough in your grade, at the end of the year you "pass" and go on to the next grade. If you don't, you "fail" and have to stay behind. But real life is a test that God lets us all pass, as long as She knows we tried. And at the end, if you've tried hard enough to make the world better and if we were kind to God's creation and treated it gently, like Grampa did, then don't worry: You'll pass. You'll go on to a new grade of existence. We should always remember that.

In the Jewish traditions Louey was reading about, the bride doesn't have to give the groom anything, but that was unacceptable to her, so as their wedding neared she and Luke went to a jewelry store and bought a plain, flat, wide ring she could give to him during the ceremony.

And then, with about a week to go, Bubbe asked Louey if she was all set for the big event.

"Yeah, we've got everything except the ring," Louey said. "Luke still has to get me a ring. I mean, we bought one for him, but I want kind of a special one. I don't want a regular one. I want it be different. I haven't seen one yet that I like very much. I may have to settle for an ordinary one, I guess. I like the kind that don't have any jewels stuck into them, or pointy things sticking out of them, or anything."

"Here," Bubbe said. "You can have this one." And with that, she slid off the fourth finger of her left hand the thin gold ring that Grampa had given her in February of 1913. The year was inscribed on the underside of it, along with "14k."

"Oh wow, it's beautiful, Bubbe!" Louey whispered. "Are you sure? Are you sure you want to give it to me?"

"Yeah. You can have it. I don't need it anymore," Bubbe said.

Louey was surprised to find it fit on her finger perfectly.

"Oh, thank you so much!" she said, and hugged her grandmother, who was now even shorter than Louey, and who was getting, Louey noticed for the first time, as thin as a ribbon. That was odd; she had always been as chubby as she was cheerful.

That ring, and the little silver Jewish star on a thin silver chain that Bubbe had given her for her 16th birthday, were the only pieces of jewelry that Louey ever wore. Neither of them did she ever take off.

Clare Levy began asking Louey, via weekly long-distance calls, about her wedding dress. Louey didn't have one, and had no intention of spending money to buy something she'd wear only once. She thought she'd wear that nice suit she had, the red miniskirt and jacket, with a white blouse. She'd buy a pair of new, white shoes with two-inch heels that wouldn't be too uncomfortable and that wouldn't sink into her dad's lawn, and that she could wear again if another fancy occasion ever came up.

Clare would have none of it. She mailed Louey a long, floral-printed bridesmaid's gown she'd worn at a friend's wedding, and in the accompanying letter inside the large manila envelope, begged her to have it tailored to fit her. Only a fancy dress would do, Clare insisted. The whole family would be scandalized otherwise. They would be ashamed of her. Luke was going to wear his nice tan summer suit and a tie—he wasn't going to buy anything new. But the bride-to-be knew her sister: Clare was afraid Louey would wear a pair of jeans. And if that happened, the Levy with the famous vocal cords would probably never use them to speak to Louey again.

The only person who loved Luke as much as Louey did was her father. He, like Louey, seemed a bit amazed at the pairing, but then he was probably ashamed of being amazed, as well. It was clear, though, that he was profoundly glad that someone could see and know and love his daughter and want to live with her and protect and honor her for the rest of her life. He took Luke out to lunch whenever their mutual schedules allowed, and they talked, according to Luke's reports, about manly things like government and unions and politics. Abe was technically what he called a "Rocky Republican," but stood firmly with Luke on all the important issues of the day. They also probably talked about Louey, Louey knew, but she never asked about that, because she didn't want to look like she was fishing for compliments.

"Boy! What a smart guy you've nailed down!" Abe would say to her on the phone in the evenings after some of these tête-à-têtes with her intended. He would report with future father-in-law pride on Luke's encyclopedic knowledge of labor history.

"He is a really nice, sharp guy, and he's a great story-teller," Luke would say about her dad, nodding vigorously. When Louey asked what stories her dad had told, it turned out they were always about some senator, and how he'd gotten some controversial bill passed, or how it had failed due to some humorous personal failing or chicanery on the part of his opponents.

Louey often asked Luke what they had for lunch, just to see if he'd noticed. He never could remember either Abe's lunch or his own.

Only a few times did Abe get to meet Luke's parents, Cal and Verna. When they drove from Maine to visit, Abe would take everyone out to dinner and they would chat amiably for hours, once or twice shutting the place down. Abe told Louey that the tall, distinguished-looking Cal, with his shock of white hair, reminded him of a college president, and he was practically in love with Luke's quiet, witty mom.

"What classy people!" Abe said. "And with two houses in Maine! It's like a compound, up there!"

The Qualesworths had a large, main house on the coast of Maine, and also a small, auxiliary house in the woods nearby.

"They're like the Kennedys, for Chrissake!" Abe said.

The day was a blistering hot one, though it was only late May. The wedding was set for 11:30, and then there would be a lunch for everyone afterwards. Luke went to help set up the chairs in Abe and Ree's backyard while Louey went to pick up Bubbe and drive her out to Slingerlands. She arrived in plenty of time; there was no assigned seating, but she wanted Bubbe to nail a chair right in front of the chuppah.

When Louey got to Bubbe's house, the grandma seemed ready to go. Her hair had been done the day before, and she was wearing a nice dress and her best clip-on earrings. But she was distraught.

"I can't find my teeth!" she cried. Her face did look hollowed-out, as though there were nothing between her rouged cheeks.

"Really? Where did you put them?" Louey asked, and realizing what a stupid question that was, she laughed; unlike her grandmother, she found the situation quite funny. She started lifting up the magazines on the coffee table, as though a set of false teeth might be under them.

"I don't know; I had them in last night!" Bubbe said.

"Well, don't worry; I'll find them!" Louey was a good finder. She quickly surveyed the small space that Bubbe lived in. It was a two-story house, but the second story was really just a finished attic that once served as a bedroom for Louey's stepbrother Marc and was now used as a storage area. Bubbe never went up there. Louey knew it wouldn't take long to search every square inch where those teeth could possibly be.

"Where do you put your teeth when you go to bed?" Louey asked.

"I put them in a little shissel with water on the lamp-table, and then I put the tablet in it! But the shissel isn't there!"

"Shissel," in Yiddish, means "container."

"What kind of shissel?"

"I don't know; whatever I have. A water glass, usually."

There was nothing but a small table-lamp and an alarm clock on the narrow nightstand between the two single beds. The nightstand had no shelves; nothing had fallen down behind it.

The two windows in Bubbe's bedroom faced north, so there was never very good light in there.

Louey went to the kitchen to get Bubbe's flashlight to look under both of the beds.

Nothing there.

"Did you put the garbage out last night?"

"No. They don't pick up the garbage on Sunday."

Phew. Good. That sealed it. That meant that even if Bubbe had accidentally tossed her false teeth into the garbage can, they were somewhere in this house. Louey knew she would find them. She looked in the two big, deep pockets of Bubbe's apron and in all the pockets of every coat, dress and sweater in her closets and hamper. She had taken everything down from the shelf above the pole in the coat closet, and then put everything back. She inspected every drawer in Bubbe's dresser. She looked in both the main compartment and the zippered pocket of the black leather handbag Bubbe almost never had put down during any waking moment over the past 50 years. She looked through every shelf of the medicine cabinet and she pulled back the shower curtain and looked in the tub and among the things on the tank behind the toilet and in all the little jars and cups and bowls and saucers and plates that decorated her kitchen table. She pulled out the four chairs around the table and looked on their seats. She looked under the kitchen table and on top of and under the coffee table in the living room. She looked on and under all the cushions of the couch in the living room, and then she looked under the couch, as well.

Then she took a deep breath and determined to go through the garbage can. She had a plan: She would take the can out to the backyard, lift the plastic bag out of it and if there were a lot of crap in it she would lay it on the grass, take a pair of scissors, slice it open lengthwise and pick through the contents like an archaeologist. But through good luck, there was almost nothing in the garbage can at all—just a few tuna fish cans, an empty can of sliced peaches, an empty ExLax box and some napkins. Louey could easily see that there were no false teeth in there.

Then she thought of something.

"Did you have your teeth in when you ate dinner last night?" she asked.

"Of course! I couldn't eat without them."

"What did you have?"

"Fish! And cottage cheese with peaches. I had just a little cottage cheese left, so I wanted to finish it, that little bit."

What a stupid question. What did it matter, what she ate? Sometimes Louey amazed herself with her own stupidity. Still, undaunted, she continued the search. She was down now to the cabinet under the sink, where the scrub brush and dish detergent and rags were; and the refrigerator. Yes, both were crazy ideas, but Louey reasoned that Bubbe absolutely could have put her teeth in either of those places. She was in her late 80s now; she had other, more important things to think of than where her teeth were.

She's probably planning what she'll say to Grampa when they meet up in Heaven, Louey thought. *She might be making a list of all the things she needs to tell him, like what the family's been doing and how this world has been going. She could easily put her teeth somewhere weird, when she's remembering all the things she's done and the friends she's had and the parties she's thrown and how the leaves look in the fall and how the city sidewalks smell in the summer ... and Dad, and us! She's got important things to remember. I'm sure I'd do that, if I ever lived to be her age. I'd spend my time remembering, and forget where my teeth are, too.*

Bubbe had lately been walked home more than once by the assistant pharmacist at the drugstore a block and a half away. He knew Rachel Levy from the many prescriptions she had filled there, and he knew her address. He knew to charge all her prescriptions to Abe Levy, and he even had Abe's phone number, at work and at home. He had permission—in fact, he had instructions—to walk Bubbe home whenever he noticed her standing outside the pharmacy for 10 or 15 minutes at a time, holding her new bottle of pills in one hand, her black pocketbook with its round handle over her other forearm. There was no bus stop there. She always claimed to be waiting for no one, yet she admitted that she didn't know where she was supposed to be next.

Louey opened the door to Bubbe's refrigerator. On the shelves were half a head of celery; three and a half onions; a half-empty jar of mayonnaise; two separate bowls of leftover tuna fish, covered with plastic wrap; a bowl of leftover stewed prunes, covered with plastic wrap; a small, brown plastic jar of instant coffee; an open box of raisins; a carton of milk; an apple; four dinner rolls and four pats of butter, liberated from the Jewish Community Center's "Senior Lunch Bunch" a week ago and squirreled away in a paper bag from the pharmacy; two oranges; three quarter-pound sticks of margarine, which Bubbe insisted on calling "oleo"; a half-empty can of sliced peaches, covered with plastic wrap; and a lidded 8-ounce carton of cottage cheese.

For some reason that she never could explain, even to herself, Louey picked up the carton of cottage cheese and shook it.

It rattled.

"Bubbe, c'mere! Check this out!" Louey called, setting the carton on the kitchen table. She knew she had it.

"What's that?" Bubbe said.

"Listen!" Louey said, shaking the container once more.

They both listened.

"Bubbe, cottage cheese don't rattle!"

Triumphantly, she revealed its contents.

"What? How did my teeth get in the refrigerator!" Bubbe burst out laughing as she asked, then quickly answered her own question. "I must have put them there!"

They both smiled with satisfaction at Bubbe's excellent

powers of deduction and their successful search. With her teeth returned to their proper place in her mouth, Bubbe needed only to remember to grab the aluminum-foil-covered dish that sat on the little table just inside to the front door. It was Bubbe's Famous Apple Crappe, Louey's favorite dessert. Her grandmother always pronounced it "Apple Crap," only because, for some reason, she could never remember the word, "crisp." Out of respect for the dish, though, Louey believed it should be spelled in an elegant, French way. The day before, Bubbe had asked what she could give Louey as a wedding present, and Louey had replied that the wedding ring was the gift of a lifetime. But then Bubbe also asked if she'd like a pan of Apple Crap for the reception.

Why, yes. Yes, she would. Could Bubbe also give her the recipe?

"Sure!" Louey wrote it down then and there, exactly as Bubbe said it.

Bubbe's Famous Apple Crappe

Peel, core and slice six nice apples. Cut each slice in half.

You need 2 separate tablespoons of cinnamon, 2 tablespoons of white sugar, 2 teaspoons of fresh lemon juice, 1 cup of brown sugar, ¾ of a cup of oats, ¾ of a cup of flour, a pinch of Kosher salt and a stick of oleo. Cut the oleo into 8 pats that you then cut each pat in half.

Turn the oven to 350 and rub a little piece of oleo—not one of the 8 pats you cut up, another little piece —over the bottom and sides of a nice 9x9 glass baking dish, or you can use 9x13, doesn't matter.

In one big bowl, mish together the apples, the white sugar, 1 tablespoon of cinnamon and the lemon juice. Then spread the whole mess evenly into the baking dish.

In another bowl, put all the topping things. That's the other tablespoon of cinnamon (or you can put 2 tablespoons, no one will complain), the salt, the brown sugar, the oats and flour and the 8 pats of oleo. Mish everything around in the bowl with your fingers or you can use 2 forks. Stop mishing when it turns into nice pea-sized lumps. Spread the topping so it's nice and even over the apples, and then don't smush it down! That's the most important part. Don't smush it! Leave it alone, and it will spread out by itself. Bake 50 minutes or so. When the top is gold and bubbly it's ready to eat, or just taste it to see. Top with vanilla ice cream.

The truth is, years earlier, when she was still living in Newburgh, Louey had received from Bubbe that oral recipe and had transcribed it word-for-word onto a sheet of notebook paper. She had even taken that piece of paper, decorated with spots of oil and smudges of cinnamon, to college with her, but she had no chance to cook in college and had promptly lost it. Now, reading the recipe the day before her wedding, Louey had a vague feeling that something was missing.

Oh! She asked how many people the recipe served. That information always was included right at the top of the recipes in every cookbook. Her grandmother looked at her incredulously and said, "What do you mean, how many. Did we ever not have enough? Did anyone ever say we have too much?"

The wedding was quick and delightful. The glass broke, with one dramatic stomp by the manly Luke Qualesworth, into eighteen little pieces. Holding the chuppah were Peg, who was asked to do so just moments before the ceremony began; Louey's sister Clare; Jake, who'd driven all the way from Washington for the event; and a young Catholic priest ("Call me Richard") who was a friend of Luke's whom Louey had never met until that very day. The priest was known in the Albany Catholic community as a terrific musician and singer. He was also a member of Luke's Shamanistic Drumming group. To Louey, he looked like a particularly sexy college kid. He didn't wear any clerical collar or priestly vestments of any kind—just khaki pants and a nice jacket with a big green pin in the lapel that read, "Justice for the Palestinian People." Louey hoped her father wouldn't be able to read it without his glasses on or that, if he could, that he wouldn't say anything about it.

The ceremony in the backyard was accompanied by the singing of a bright red bird at Abe's bird feeder.

"Look!" her dad said as everyone was being seated. "We have a rabbi, a priest and a cardinal!"

Rabbi Bloom spoke a few words, proclaiming to the assembled that unions are wonderful things, but that the best union of all is holy matrimony, "the union of two hearts and two minds, committed to creating something better and more holy than themselves."

During the reception, Clare led the attendees in singing the International Ladies Garment Workers Union theme song, "Look For the Union Label" ("it says we're able / to make it in the USA!").

Louey was truly happy that day because she finally got to introduce Nancy to Annie, who had to leave right after the ceremony to get back to New Jersey, where she had been promoted to city editor of the Bergen County News; and to the newly minted lawyer Charlie Farley, who'd come in from Buffalo with her now-husband, Frank. Frank, like Charlie, specialized in "poverty law," and had met his future bride while they both were working for Buffalo Legal Aid. Nancy, with her brilliance and her MBA, had already risen a few rungs up the ladder in the International Finance Department of the Ford Motor Company in Michigan, and had driven to Slingerlands in her brand-new, company-provided black Crown Victoria. She got a new car every year for free, she said, as a benefit of having a management-level job in her department. When Louey saw it she said, "Jeez, I like your hearse ... or did you steal a cop car?" and Nancy said, "I don't care what it looks like; I feel very safe in it."

Mike from Sports, now working in the marketing department of ESPN in Connecticut "but hoping to get an on-air gig soon," was there, baseball cap set backwards on his head, which you could anyway tell was balding. He'd brought a Frisbee, and the friends tossed it around before and after the ceremony, trying very hard not to trip over the tent's guy-wires, talking and catching up and getting to know one another as they played.

No one, including Abe Levy, mentioned the priest's political button, and he left without eating, shortly after his chuppah-holding duties ended. He came over to Louey and Luke's table and whispered to Luke that he had to run to console a Black man whose wife had recently died in childbirth.

The newlyweds rose.

"Oh God, Richard, did the baby make it?" Louey asked quietly. She momentarily felt kind of sick, just thinking of that. What could be sadder than the death of the child a woman had died giving birth to?

"Yeah, but she weighs barely four pounds. They think she's gonna live, but the mother was only about eight months along when something went wrong," Richard said. "The baby needs our prayers as much as the father does."

Louey closed her eyes and did offer a silent, intercessory prayer as Luke gave Richard a big hug and walked him to his car. She then dashed to her parents' kitchen, found a small paper bag under the sink, ran back out and hurriedly stuffed a fried chicken leg, a brownie, a bunch of grapes, a can of soda and a napkin from the buffet table into the bag, so Richard would have something to eat on his way to the bereaved new father. Then she ran back through the house, out the front door and across the yard, and was able to hand the bag to Richard through his car window just before he pulled away.

On her way back, she figured that that would be as good a time as any to change into the jeans and pretty blouse and sneaks she'd stowed in the guest room, so she'd be comfy and dressed like her friends now were. It took her only a minute to do that; then she returned to the tent.

The bride and groom hung out with their friends and played their favorite songs, amplified by Luke's hideously expensive, huge, flat speakers that looked very much like a pair of doors. Booming out were the songs from Paul Simon's "Graceland" album, Joni Mitchell's "Blue" album, many Bob

Dylan and Eagles and Ritchie Havens albums, and of course, Beatles albums. They also played a Brook Benton album with his great song, "Don't It Make You Want to Go Home?" It sounded to Louey like a church song. She didn't know why, but it always pierced her heart and made her cry. Maybe it just reminded her that time was passing, and that she already had had people come and go through her life whom she loved and missed. She wandered inside while that song played and stood by herself beside the back door, where no one could see her, and where she could listen to it by herself, mouthing the words and dabbing her eyes.

The music played and played all afternoon 'til most everyone had gone home.

Louey hung out for a long time afterwards with Peg and Peg's new girlfriend. Charlie and Frank had their first child, Mary, in tow. Louey was happy to introduce Luke to Jake and Mike from Sports, and to catch up and reminisce with them both. Luke knew that ESPN was a new, sports-only TV network, and so was able to make pleasant conversation with Mike. Jake was still very aware of what was happening in Newburgh; he'd kept in touch with the remaining bureau staff. There were only two reporters there now because the paper had laid people off to save money. Which didn't make any sense, because who would buy a paper that didn't cover their community well? That was crazy, they all agreed.

Couldn't the union do something, Louey asked?

The union could do nothing. The union was so weak, it was all but useless. They were thinking of decertifying the union, and joining the Teamsters. Or maybe even starting their own, independent union. Jake was still keeping up with the labor news.

Wow, things have changed so fast at the paper in just these few years, Louey thought.

Darkness had started to fall before everyone left.

"Well, that's a stone off my heart," Abe Levy said to his wife as he drained a plastic flute of champagne and carried his paper plate to the trash can.

Because he thought I'd never get married, Louey knew. *Like the Fathers of Old, Dad believes that a grown woman can't be happy unless she's married. He could never understand that I was already* happy! *I've always* been happy! *I think that's one reason why Luke loves me: Opposites attract. He's a very thoughtful, serious person, with a tendency to be angry. I'm cheerful, and without me he's … what's the opposite of light-hearted? Heavy-hearted?*

But, let it go. Dad's happier right now than all the rest of us gathered here combined. So, this is very good.

They honeymooned in Guadeloupe. Louey had chosen it as a destination because there she could practice her rusty French and they could swim in the absurdly blue Caribbean and run on the beach. As soon as they'd checked in to their room, Louey walked out onto the balcony and sailed her diaphragm into the ocean like a Frisbee. She'd brought it just so that she could make that dramatic, humorous gesture, but she wouldn't be needing birth control anymore. If she got pregnant, good. If not, they could always adopt. Either way, she and Luke would be good parents; she was sure of it. They would raise good kids. They'd be kind and funny and athletic, and because of Luke, they'd be smart. A whole team of them. Four, maybe. Four would be a good number. But Louey was already solidly into her 30s. They'd better hop right on it.

Luke and Louey did hop right on it, but nothing happened for a long time. Was she was too old to have kids? Was she all out of eggs? Month after month went by, and then another year, with no pregnancy. Should they forget about it, and just adopt some kids? Or should they find out if something correctible was wrong? They decided to take the medical road. Louey started with her general practitioner, who found no reason for her to be infertile but gave her a referral to an OB/GYN. That guy did an internal exam and also a complete blood count. It took a couple of weeks to get the results, which uncovered no problems. The OB/GYN literally scratched his head, as people do in cartoons. He then recommended she go to the brand-new fertility clinic that had just opened at Albany Medical Center. There they started all over again with the examinations, the blood drawings, and the family history. Only then did Louey recall her father's recent comment, over lunch at Club 21, that her mother, too, had had trouble getting pregnant. Indeed, Louey's parents were both quite a bit older than her friends'—she had always noticed that. She asked him how long Ruth Abrams had tried to get pregnant before she had finally succeeded not once but three times. Abe claimed not to know much about "girl problems" and said he couldn't remember the details.

"And anyway, after we had Danny, and you were born 14 months later, we kind of figured we could forget about that infertility crap. We thought it must have been psychological. The whole idea of infertility just sort of flew away like a ... like a stork, you know?"

The infertility clinic's staff had not been chosen yet, but the Acting Director told Louey that she needed to have a "cone biopsy." The Big Day came and Louey arrived via gurney at the operating room, her lower half covered by a five-foot Handi-Wipe.

Albany Med was at that time a "teaching hospital." The doctor asked if she'd mind if his class of students watched the procedure, since they'd never witnessed a cone biopsy before. Five silent young men were already lined up in the room, masked and gowned.

Louey's thighs, from her butt to the backs of her knees, had been placed at a ninety-degree angle with respect to the gurney and a sixty-degree angle with respect to each other, exposing the nadir of the resulting "V" for all the world to see. Her lower legs dangled irrelevantly from a pair of brutally spread-apart stirrups.

"Sure; have a ball! Anything for science. Hi! Hi, boys!" She waved maniacally to her audience. The students silently crowded in so that their faces loomed over the doctor's hands and Louey's no-longer-private parts.

The cone biopsy, like all her other interactions with doctors in this matter, did not reveal any problem with Louey.

Undaunted, the infertility guy gave her a supply of needles, along with several vials of medicine that had to be injected into her hip once a week by Luke. Luke did not like this. Louey did not like this. But they did it to mollify the Fertility Goddess.

Though impressively painful, those shots, too, failed to work.

Louey wrote a long, comical letter to Sandy about her Troubles, and from the dark swamps of Georgia, Sandy wrote back: "Has Luke been tested?" A few weeks later, in the early fall, Modern Medicine determined that their problem could be easily solved, requiring only that Luke have an amusing operation on each of his testicles.

In mid-December, Louey packed her tampons as they left for Maine to visit Luke's parents for Christmas. No doubt her period would come, as it had last year, during their Maine trip. The Qualesworths spent the two weeks before and after every Christmas at the family's small log cabin that Verna's grandfather had built in the hilly woods a quarter-mile above their huge year-round house, which sat right on the harbor of the Pemaquid peninsula. Luke's sister, Lucy, always joined the gathering, driving the two hours down from her home in Bangor. The old, fireplace-heated cabin was charming, but it had a very delicate septic system. This had prompted Verna—probably decades ago—to thumbtack a handwritten note on the wall over the toilet: "PLACE NOTHING IN THE TOILET EXCEPT BODILY WASTE AND SCOTT TOILET PAPER." So, Louey had to wrap her used tampons in toilet paper and stuff them into a zip-closing plastic bag, which she had to keep in her backpack until they were on their way home, when she could drop them into the first garbage can they spotted.

But this year her period didn't come at all, the whole two weeks they were there. Neither Louey nor Luke mentioned it; maybe they were both afraid they'd jinx it.

Then January came and went, and still no period. On the first of February, Louey went to a drugstore on her lunch hour and bought one of the new, over-the-counter, instant-results pregnancy tests. It came up positive. But that couldn't be right, could it? She went back and bought another one:

Same result. What was the accuracy rate of these things, any-way? But yet, she had never missed one single period in her whole life, goddamn it, since she began having periods way, way too young, just after her mother died.

Finally, she told Luke.

"Holy crap," he said. She thought he sounded more stunned than happy.

A week later, she scheduled an appointment with a nurse practitioner at Upper Hudson Planned Parenthood, who confirmed the good news. And six weeks after that, she scheduled a rather novel procedure, amniocentesis with ul-trasound, to be performed by a doctor at Albany Med. It would reveal if the baby had any genetic abnormalities, like Down Syndrome. After all, she was getting so old, she was more likely than most first-time moms to be carrying a kid with Down. If this baby made it to term, Louey would be 35! There was no way she would carry a baby for nine months only to have it born with an incurable condition. Not know-ingly, anyway.

When the doctor had the equipment all set up, he asked Louey if she wanted to know the baby's sex.

"No!" she said, alarmed and angry. "Who would want to know that? Why would I want to know that?"

"Lots of people want to know. Don't you want to know what color to paint the baby's room?"

"I'm painting it red, yellow, green, blue and white, and if you tell me the sex of this baby I'll kill you. I'm serious. I do not want to know. I just want one surprise in my life. I just want to hear that, 'It's a boy!' or, 'It's a girl!' Just one, stinkin', little surprise. OK? Is that asking too much? Don't tell me, and don't let anyone else tell me," she said, glaring about the room at the aides and assistants.

"OK. We'll hold this sheet up so you can't see the screen." Everyone but the doctor chipped in to hold the sheet so she couldn't see the ultrasound screen, which had been wheeled into position near her knees.

The doctor then drew an "X" with a black felt-tipped marker on her just slightly rounded belly, right near her belly button.

"What are you doing?" she asked.

"Learning my letters," the doctor said. "No, I'm marking the spot where we'll go in."

"You've got all these high-tech monitors, and you're using a Magic Marker?"

"Why not?"

Offhand, she couldn't think of a reason why not. Wouldn't the needle's tip poke some black ink into her uterus? She did actually think of that, but she thought it might sound ridiculous, so she didn't mention it. She decided to ask another one:

"How big is this needle?"

Grinning, he held it point upward, right in front of his face. She asked, quite calmly, how could he be sure he wasn't going to prick the baby with it. But she never heard the answer, because she fainted. When she awoke, a nurse was patting her hand.

"You did great, Mrs. Levy," she said. "The baby's fine. The needle got nowhere near the baby. See? I told you it would only take a minute."

Louey didn't remember even seeing this nurse before,

much less any such prediction. But, fine. Whatever. That same day, they had the results: With God's help, they were going to have a healthy baby! Louey was leaning a bit toward hoping it was a boy, because she thought Luke, despite his protestations of neutrality, would like a boy better. He followed her lead in referring to their future family member as "Shmendrick," Yiddish for "goofball." Now all they had to do was wait another 25 weeks. The baby would come in mid-to-late September.

With the happy results of the amniocentesis in hand, Louey and Luke went to her parents' house for dinner. They brought a bottle of champagne with them in a brown paper bag, and when they finished dinner, Louey told them the news.

"Hey, mazal tov!" Abe shouted. "When's the big day?"

"Right around my own birthday! Cool, right?"

That was cool. The expectant parents went home and made love, another activity neither of them was sure they could continue to engage in for much longer. But for now it was better than ever. She let herself hope: Would she really have Luke Qualesworth's baby? What would they name it if it were a boy? Surely he would be tall and strong, like his father, and smart like him, and grow to be a kind, sensitive man who would devote himself to repairing the world.

And what if it were a girl? She would be funny and fun, and athletic, too. Louey would have to teach the kid baseball; Luke had never played. He didn't know one end of a baseball from the other. But Louey would love doing it, for sure. This kid would celebrate and exclaim boldly and fiercely about all the beauty in the world—its music, its mountains. She would be a good friend and a good writer.

Louey would tell Nancy and Peg right away to let them know about the pregnancy, but when would she tell the gang at work? Would she have the guts to do the natural-childbirth thing? How long would she take off after the delivery? What fun things to think about! This was going to be fun.

At her next OB/GYN visit, after checking her pulse and looking at her weight and blood pressure readings, the doc asked her a series of questions, ending with, "Do you drink?" Yes. "How much?"

"Once a week, on the Sabbath, my husband and I kill most of a bottle of wine—sometimes the whole bottle—with dinner. Also, I always have a beer with the team after the game whenever I get to play softball."

He looked at her and then at her chart and then at her again and said, "Keep doing that."

When Louey's midsection had grown to the point where she had to wear "pregnancy clothes," she happily told her boss at Planned Parenthood the news. The boss congratulated her heartily, smiled and, with tears in her eyes, asked if Louey would mind if she shared the news with the whole staff.

Why, no. No, she wouldn't.

And would she want to continue serving as a Patient Escort? Please? Please?

Well, of course! She would be more valuable than ever with her tummy big as a beachball, waddling along beside people who were about to have their abortions. That would confuse the hell out of the morons who stood outside on Saturdays yelling about how the workers "hated babies."

The year wore on, and toward the middle of August UHPP held a surprise shower for her at the end of her shift. The medical staff and educators gave her boxes and bags of cloth and disposable diapers, baby oil, nipple cream, crib sheets and blankets in bright colors because she didn't know which sex the baby would be, throw-up rags, breast pumps, baby bottles, rattles and crib mobiles and a sweet, huge card that everyone had signed. To top it all—and so that she could wheel everything home—they had all chipped in for a beautiful, navy-blue stroller—the kind you could easily fold up and put in the car.

Meanwhile, somebody in CSEU's Human Resources Department had decided that a co-ed adult softball game would be just the thing to organize as a "team-building" exercise. They'd scheduled the game for a Thursday evening right after work.

Good! That meant she could play. Their opponent would be the Albany County District Attorney's Office, which was able to field a team only because some of them brought their girlfriends or spouses. CSEU would have Louey and Luke; Luke's best friend, Bruce; and Bruce's wife, Leslie. Leslie, a nurses-union official, had been Louey's pal back in their college days at Syracuse U., and it had been a total shock to Louey a few years earlier when Bruce announced to Luke and Louey that he had met and fallen in love with Leslie at a labor convention in New York City. CSEU also had fielded other amiable teammates: Colleen and Adele from PR's bullpen and their boyfriends; Arnier's assistant, Roger; and Ralph the cartoonist. They needed every one of them, since they would be going by the women's-softball rule of ten players on a team. No one else at CSEU had volunteered for this, although a few others said they'd come to cheer.

It was early September, and it was getting dark earlier now. The field was in the municipal park near the Governor's mansion. As they began, the tall buildings of the Empire State Plaza were already casting long shadows across the field. The CSEU team, shooting the breeze as they tossed a ball around among themselves, realized that they had no pitcher. Laughing, Leslie said she'd give it a try. She had played slow-pitch in high-school, and volunteered that, underhand, she probably could still throw strikes, "now and then." Very slow strikes, but strikes nonetheless.

There was a "real" umpire, a fat guy with the black shirt and the chest pad and the mask, who was paid equally by CSEU and the lawyers and who had already set up the bases by the time the teams arrived. He gathered all the players around him and told them they'd be playing seven innings.

The umpire tossed a quarter, and CSEU's captain, Bruce, called heads and won. Then Bruce, who had never played any organized sport of any kind, decided to do something tricky.

"We'll bat first," he announced. Louey, in the ensuing silence, shook her head, turned her palms skyward and made the "What-the-hell-kind-of-decision-is that" face. Bruce said brightly, "I figure, we'll score so many runs in the first inning that they'll be disheartened!"

The players on the lawyers' team ran to their positions in the field, happy to be the beneficiaries of the "disheartening strategy." The ump, before donning his face mask, walked over to Louey.

"Are you sure you want to play?" he whispered, frowning

as he looked a couple of times from her face to her eight-months-pregnant midsection. Rubbing Shmendrick's temporary home, she yawned and said casually, "Yeah, we need the exercise. And the extra weight lets me hit farther." The ump said nothing and continued to look seriously at Louey's face as he walked, very, very slowly to his spot behind home plate. She was momentarily afraid he was going to call off the whole game. Finally he sighed and said, much too softly, "Play ball."

Louey's first two times up resulted in an easy grounder to the shortstop and a lazy fly straight to the left fielder, who was playing way in for her. Now it was Louey who was disheartened. For the first time in her life, she felt like an easy out.

"Come on, baby; let's go," she said as she took off in a futile attempt to reach first base in each of her at-bats.

She felt comically slow, as though she were trying to run through the deep end of a swimming pool.

Then came the seventh inning, with the score tied at nine-all. There'd been a lot of running and booting the ball around and yelling, and it was getting dark, and even though this was supposed to be just a "fun game," everyone on both sides was getting more and more serious. They'd put too much into it. They all really wanted to win it now.

Leading off, Louey hit a fly ball over the first baseman's head. That arrogant attorney called for it and backpedaled, but not fast enough—he should have turned and run several steps before relocating the ball. Meanwhile, because the first baseman had stupidly called for it, the right fielder got a late start toward the ball and could corral it only after it had bounced fair and then rolled quite a ways out of bounds, so that Louey, for the first time all game, was safe. Then it was Bruce's turn. He hit a mighty shot that would have been called an inside-the-park homerun, if there were only a wall marking the far edge of the park. But there were no walls in the park, so he ran fast around the bases as a young assistant prosecutor chugged the equivalent of a city block 'til he was able to pick up the ball and shoot it back in. He had a cannon for an arm, and accurate, too, but the ball bounced once and was not quite in time. Bruce reached home plate a nanosecond after Louey did. Safe! And safe! Eleven to nine! Wild cheers and applause greeted Louey and Bruce. Then Adele, Colleen and Ralph all distinguished themselves by striking out in the space of about one minute, each one complaining to the ump, "You can't even see the ball! How can you even see the ball? How could you tell that was a strike?"

They were strikes, but the PR Department had a point: It was quite dark already, and as for artificial lights, downtown Albany after 5 p.m. might as well be the Gobi Desert.

The first pitch to the leadoff hitter for the lawyers was called a ball, and Louey loudly gave the umpire the benefit of her opinion: "Oh, come on! Put your night-vision glasses on, will ya?" He did not seem amused.

The first two hitters ended up striking out, missing wildly at Leslie's 20-miles-an-hour offerings. But then the tables turned, and a two-out rally began. The infielders couldn't see the grounders that came at them, and the base players couldn't see the balls that were being thrown to them, and before anyone knew it, CSEU was leading just 11 to 10, with the bases loaded. A young woman came to bat as her team cheered, "Come on, Sally! You can do it! Do it again, Sally! Do it like you did before!" (She had earlier hit a long double that, if she hadn't been so slow a runner, might have been a homerun.)

"No batter, no batter, no batter!" Louey yelled.

Crack.

Louey could tell from the sound that it wasn't hit hard, and she could just make out a pale streak going up in the direction of second base. She started running in from her position in short left field, arms pumping wildly. If only she could see the ball again.

Then she saw it! It looked oddly big and white against the charcoal-grey sky.

"I got it!" she called out.

Adele, somewhere near second, was looking frantically on the grass all around her and yelling, "Where is it? Where is it?" She thought it must be a grounder, like the other lawyers' hits that inning. Of course, the runner on third had taken off and was heading home.

But Reader, not everyone who's heading home actually reaches home, do they? Still gaining speed, Louey did a perfectly timed dive and, fully outstretched, skidding on her nearly-nine-months-pregnant midsection, snagged the ball a few inches above the ground. It made the lovely clean-catch sound as it fell into the leather webbing of her glove. She did a forward roll and popped up like a gymnast in a floor routine, all the while holding her glove over her head, the big white ball lodged in it for all the world to see. Then she transferred the ball to her right hand and continued trotting home to present it to the lawyers as Exhibit A. To heighten the impression of nonchalance, she pantomimed extra-slow gum-chewing. If only she had a piece of gum in her mouth right then, she would blow a bubble with it, and that would have been the coolest thing ever.

Louey had saved the game! She tossed the ball to the ump. Now would come the lawyers' moaning and her own team's wild cheering and applause and the back-pounding and the "Oh my God! Did you see that?" and the "How the hell did you do that?" and the "I can't believe you caught that ball!" and the …

Silence. The world had stopped spinning, and the scene in the park had turned into a painting. No one moved; no birds sang. A distant tune that had been playing on a boombox ended. Everyone was looking at her, but not in a good way. The other team's members, among whom she was now standing, near home plate, had all taken on the same expression. Their mouths were open, but no sound was coming out. Her own team, except Ralph, their catcher, was still out in the field. She found Luke's form and saw that he, too, was immobile, his lips pursed as though he were in pain and trying to say, "Ooh." The umpire's jaw, too, was agape, but he was the first to regain signs of life. He stared at her disdainfully as he yanked home plate out of the dirt.

"Are you sure that was a smart thing to do?" he said. He shifted his gaze between her face and her stomach a couple of times as he walked away. He continued glaring at her and shaking his head as he lifted the bases and silently put them in his big sack.

Then someone, somewhere must have shouted, "Green light!" because the other humans in the scene finally, one by one, stopped staring at Louey and began looking at Luke and walking toward him.

The lawyers wandered off, shaking their heads, offering no congratulations to the CSEU players and saying nothing, even to one another. Leslie ventured, "Louey! Are you OK? Do you want to go to Albany Med, just to get checked out?" Luke, having now reached home plate, wrapped an arm around her and said, "You OK? You want to sit down?"

She got it; they thought the baby might have been hurt. But the baby was fine. The baby loved it. Shmendrick was proud of his mom.

"Yeah!" he was in there saying. "Nice catch, mom!" Louey was sure she could hear him.

"I'm fine," she said dismissively to her scandalized, horrified, traumatized teammates. "The kid's fine. The baby doesn't feel a thing; he doesn't know if I'm upside down or right-side up; it's all the same to him. He's like a fish inside a rubber ball. A rubber ball filled with water, I mean."

Now they all had something to talk about for the rest of their lives, but Louey didn't care. She had been doing a lot of reading about fetal development, and she knew she was right. She looked to Leslie to back her up. Leslie was a nurse.

"Well, it was a very fluid motion you made, and if you never felt any pain, then the baby probably didn't either," Leslie said.

At Horney's Grill, Louey could barely wedge herself between the seat and the table at the booth that she and Luke, Bruce and Leslie had chosen. She was dying for a good blue-cheese burger and a beer, but the waitress brought Louey a glass of milk instead of the Labatt's she'd ordered. She laughed as she pointed out the error, but the waitress insisted she had heard correctly, and that Louey had indeed ordered milk. Luke, Bruce and Leslie all claimed not to remember.

It turned out that Louey was right about the pregnancy—well, about most of it. In late September, Rebecca Ruth Qualesworth was born at Albany Med, healthy as a shortstop.

Striding breezily into the hospital at 7 a.m., holding an overnight bag in one hand and Luke's hand in the other, Louey insisted that she not be given any pain-killers and later, after ten hours on the delivery table, regretted it. She learned a new phrase: "occiput posterior presentation." Luke was bent over in his facemask and paper gown, uselessly holding her hand and sweating profusely, when he offered tremulously: "Do you think it would help if you changed positions?"

"Yeah!" she growled, raising her head as far as she could. She jabbed a finger into his chest and added: "With you!"

The good news was: They got to keep the kid.

Dear Diary,

It's so strange. You drive to the hospital as two, and you come home as three. Three separate but conjoined humans. Forever. All for one, and one for all. Boom. Just like that. Where before, you were just two (and before that, one). Now, here we go with Rebecca Ruth Qualesworth. Oh, boy. Life!

At first, they did things together, all three of them. Right away, they drove to the Catskill Mountains so that Rebecca could be blessed by the guru—that is, the leader—of the whole, worldwide Siddha Yoga movement. The tall, robed woman with the white line down her nose and the red dot in the middle of her forehead touched Rebecca with a long ostrich plume (or some kind of feather—Louey didn't recognize what kind of bird it had come off of). The guru only left India once or twice a year, but she happened to be residing at the Catskills ashram for a month or so right around the time of Rebecca's birth.

As time passed, Luke went to the ashram more and more often on weekends. He always invited Louey, and she could have gone with him if she'd wanted to, but she never went. It didn't have any profound effect on her the way it did Luke, and then she never knew when the baby would start crying or need to be changed, or when she'd start squealing for reasons Louey couldn't fathom, and you were supposed to be silent in the Ashram, both inside and while on its expansive, wooded grounds. So she stayed home with Rebecca.

Things are working out perfectly for me, Louey wrote in her diary. *This is amazing! Everything is perfect right now. I don't need anything in the world to change. So please, G-d, let me never forget what Grampa always used to say to me: This, too, shall pass.*

Before she was two, Rebecca was taking her meals with her parents in a yellow plastic toddler's chair with seat belts, cleverly designed to hook over the edge of a table using the baby's weight to hold it steady, so that the kid could sit high and be part of the conversation. It came with its own little tray.

One morning, Louey found that Rebecca had climbed out of her crib and was sitting on the floor of her room "reading" to her Cabbage Patch doll Tamika, who was propped up against the dresser. Huge milestone! This meant that Rebecca could now toddle to the bathroom by herself if she had to go in the middle of the night. Previously, she would call to her mom to help her remove her diaper and deposit her on the cute yellow plastic "Toddler Pot" beside the real toilet. In a flash after adopting this new routine, Rebecca and Louey agreed that they needed to go out and buy "big girl" underpants in whatever pretty purple and pink designs Rebecca chose.

The Qualesworth baby was very motherly to the other tots in her daycare center, playing "teacher" to any and all who could stand it. Her vocabulary was astounding. Of course, Louey and Luke both read to her, but she often came out with things she couldn't possibly have heard around the house or daycare center.

Or could she?

Louey instituted a rule that, since Rebecca now was sleeping on that mattress on the floor, she had to "make her bed" by smoothing the top sheet and blanky and propping her stuffed animals nicely around her hard little pillow before toddling into the kitchen for breakfast.

One morning she toddled in unusually early. Luke, who'd been pouring himself a cup of coffee, stopped to lift her up and then lower her and strap her into her fancy toddler-seat. Louey sowed a field of Cheerios on its white tray. Rebecca sucked apple juice from her Sippy-cup and said, "Is today a daycare day?" Before answering, Louey looked at her suspiciously and said, "Wait a minute. Rebecca. Is your bed made? Did you make your bed before coming in here?"

Rebecca Qualesworth grew pensive. She tilted her face

to the ceiling and frowned a bit, as though trying to come up with a satisfactory response to this complex question. She pursed her lips, studied a Cheerio and tugged at her chin like a rabbi at his beard.

"Not *per se*," she finally replied.

Luke and Louey figured out ways to share hikes with Rebecca. When she was brand new, they tucked her into a special backpack made to hold kids, and she obligingly napped for most of their adventures. Later, she enjoyed lacing up her own little hiking boots and exploring the trails with them. They held her hands over rocky terrain and lifted her over streams, and of course they needed to go more slowly because of her tiny steps. But she quickly became a game hiker. Before she entered first grade, she often pointed out spiders, toads, skinks and red efts that they'd not noticed. She was endlessly fascinated by all the little creatures.

Luke began spending most weekends at the ashram in the Catskills, to meditate and attend special programs. There he met two or three fellow "seekers," as he called them, from the Albany area, and soon they began carpooling to and from the ashram together. Louey knew them all, as they also occasionally met at one another's apartments in Albany for meditation sessions. At Luke and Louey's place, they went up to the carpeted attic and sat at his puja table for an hour or so. Louey could smell their burning sage and hear Luke's drumming while she read to Rebecca and put her to bed. Then the group repaired to the kitchen for the fruit salad or pita and hummus that Louey prepared for them, and she often joined them for amiable chitchat before they all took their leave.

One of the group was a woman named Aileen, who had been chosen by the Indian guru to be a sort of deputy guru for their local group. Luke went to Aileen's apartment one evening a week to meditate.

Sometimes Aileen would drive Luke to the Catskill ashram, and sometimes he would drive her. Sometimes it was just the two of them, and sometimes they went with one or two of the others. He said. Louey gave her total blessing to this; she enjoyed reading or playing with Rebecca at home or at the playground in their neighborhood, or walking with her the few blocks to the free New York State Museum and looking at all the fun exhibits, when Luke was away.

Abe Levy, however, was from another generation. He just didn't get that a man who went away for the weekend could still be very devoted to his wife and child. Louey tried explaining to her father that nothing to speak of happened at the ashram at all. As Luke conveyed it to her, all the seekers did was chant and meditate and drum and listen to lectures, led on special occasions by the head of the entire, worldwide Siddha Yoga movement and at other times by his own local guru, Aileen from Cardinal Street.

Abe frowned and shook his head when Louey tried to explain it to him. He didn't understand that a married man could be friends with a woman he wasn't married to, and spend time on weekends with her, instead of with his wife, if everything was OK with their marriage.

"Aren't you worried that he's running off with this Holy Bimbo every weekend? I mean, a married man goes off every weekend to ... to do what with her?" Abe asked Louey one Saturday when he'd taken her and Rebecca out to lunch.

Louey laughed and laughed. Oh, how she laughed.

"Dad, they're meditating! She's his *guru*, for God's sake! They sit cross-legged for two hours; they wouldn't be able to do anything after that even if they wanted to! Besides, the women sit on one side of the room—it's like a huge tent—during these things, and the men on the other. I've seen it. We took Rebecca there once. They have men's quarters and women's quarters, and even married couples have to split up while they're there. And it's not every weekend, anyway. But it makes him happy. So, let him be happy, I say!"

"You're amazing," Abe said, shaking his head. And let it go at that.

Rachel Levy, meanwhile, was starting to wander. She was wandering not just around her house, now, but also around the streets of her neighborhood, and asking strangers, whom she mistook for relatives, "Excuse me, do you know what I'm doing here?" One time, the Albany cops called Abe at the Capitol to say, Come and get her. Then it happened a second time. That's when Abe moved her into the same Jewish nursing home where her husband had lived for the last few months of his own life. Ironically, she was put into the very same room in the Dementia Unit where Sam had been.

She was at the Daughters of Sarah just a few months when, one early spring day, Abe called Louey to say that Bubbe had died in her sleep.

"Oh, I'm so sorry, Dad," Louey said. Because that was what you were supposed to say, when you were a grownup.

"Yeah, me too. She was in no pain, though. She never felt any pain. She just died in her sleep, they said."

When she hung up, she sat down and wept and thought of all the things she should have said to her grandma, and some of the sweet, sweet things her grandma had done for her. Then she stood up and paced around the living room. Then she sat down and wept again. Then she stood up and paced and thought some more. Then she sat down again. Then she called her father back and asked if there were some people she could call: Did Danny and Marc and Clare know? Did Aunt Shirley? Should she call the rabbi? A funeral home? The JCC? Abe told her to call her brothers and sister, if she wanted to, but he'd make all the other calls. He wouldn't have the funeral information until the next day, probably.

So she did that, and then she continued her comforting routine of sitting and weeping and pacing. She did the thing that Jews had always done; she covered all her mirrors with towels.

There was some relief in it. Abe no longer had to worry about Bubbe getting lost in Albany or giving all her money to some stranger, or getting hit by a car or forgetting where she was and saying what he called crazy things, like, "Why am I here?"

Louey, however, had always found it enchanting when her grandma would walk into a room and say, "Now, why am I here?" or, "Now, what was I supposed to be doing here?" and burst out laughing.

That's a good question, Louey thought. *That's the best question of all. It's what we all should be saying, with every breath we take: Why am I here, and what am I doing? I think God gives you those questions Herself, to keep you focused on the important things and remind you not to waste your time, especially as you come to the part where you have very little time left. Those questions are to make you wonder why you ever blew off your tree and started floating down the river with the other leaves in the first place. Am I doing what I'm supposed to be doing? Have I accomplished anything, have I been kind to anyone today, have I made their lives easier to bear? It made Dad so sad to hear Bubbe say, "Why am I here? What was I supposed to be doing in this room?" but I hope that's what I keep asking myself when I'm old. In fact, we should all be asking that question of ourselves every day!*

"Is this really what I'm supposed to be doing?" That should be tattooed on my ass.

When her grandmother died, Louey promised herself, *I'm not ever going to fail to ask myself that question. I'm going to ask myself that question every day.*

At the funeral, Rabbi Bloom said it was written that truly righteous people were given the blessing of choosing the day on which they would die. Ray Levy had chosen that day, he said, because it was the day before Passover, and we are commanded not to be sad during the eight days of Passover. By then, Bubbe's shiva period would be over. What a blessing this righteous one had given us, by choosing that day! Ray Levy had wanted, above all, for her family to be happy and to enjoy one another's company. When anyone was sad, she'd try to cheer them up. And when anyone was happy, Bubbe was happy.

Well, that's great; now I'm really sad! Louey thought, wincing and smiling at the same time.

Abe and Ree Levy came to Luke, Rebecca and Louey's house on the second night of Passover that year, instead of the first night like they usually did. They had the traditional brisket with noodle kugel, carrot tsimmis and green salad, and then for dessert Louey served everyone Bubbe's Famous Apple Crappe. Everyone ate it slowly, in silence, and tears fell into Louey's bowl.

Rebecca started first grade with a great sense of humor and a sunny personality. Her school was just a few blocks away in downtown Albany, and most of her classmates were from poor Black families or from Mexico or overseas. Rebecca's favorite activities were playing teacher and writing and illustrating poems and stories, as well as swinging on the swings and pushing other kids on the swings in the park nearby. When her dad was away on weekends—which was more and more often—she and Louey would go to the State Museum, where she could run around its carpeted halls and exhibit rooms for as long as she wanted. As a 5-year-old, she knew the museum and its staff as well as her own house. She usually strode directly to the replica New York City subway car. Climbing aboard, she swung from the car's triangular straps and, like a gymnast, let go and landed on the row of inward-facing seats. She then spun around and jumped back up again and swung a few times before releasing and landing on the seats opposite. She would intersperse these antics by shinnying up the metal poles and sliding down them, spinning around and around as she went. She knew where the dioramas were of the Lenape Indians and the Iroquois Indians. More than once, she confidently directed lost-looking tourists to the exhibits they were seeking as if she were a staff member. Louey let Rebecca wander among the exhibits, chatting with staff and visitors alike, while she—Louey—would remain on the subway car, reading or writing and sipping her coffee like any good rider on the IRT.

Man, this is a good life, she wrote in her diary. *Thank you, G-d.*

Reader, he left her.

Abe Levy was right. Luke had been having an affair with Aileen.

Dear Diary,

My Husband has Run Off with his Guru. That's the title of an article in a woman's magazine, if I ever heard one! And yet it actually happened. And now I've written it out, so it must be true. I mean, how funny is that?! There's got to be a limerick in here somewhere. He said he was going to meditate, / but really he went off to fornicate. / (What kind of guru / does a married man screw, / the Seventh Commandment to violate?)

It was on New Year's Eve that he told her, when they had dropped Rebecca off with Nancy, who'd sworn a few days earlier that she'd be happy to play and read and watch TV with Rebecca and put her to bed on her pullout sofa, and to eat breakfast together with her the next morning, and play teacher or go out and make snowmen if there were snow. Louey and Luke's plans, which they'd agreed on earlier in the month, were to go to an outdoor New Year's Eve "First Night" event in downtown Albany, walking among various free entertainment venues or hopping free shuttle-buses among them, while partaking of the fancy meals and drinks that would be offered at several designated spots. But an hour after they dropped Rebecca downstairs at Nancy's, they were back.

"What happened?" Nancy asked. She seemed not so much alarmed as curious, as though they'd forgotten to drop off some medicine for Rebecca or something.

"Sorry; we decided to just stay home. It's too cold out for all that outdoors crap," Louey said. Nancy said OK and quietly gathered up Rebecca's clothes and toothbrush and dolls, which they had just finished unpacking, and stuffed them back into her little suitcase.

She knows something's wrong, Louey thought. *But she's not saying anything.* And she felt certain that not only Nancy, but also Rebecca probably knew something was wrong. Both the baby-sitter and her little friend seemed confused and disappointed: They had already decided to stay up 'til midnight and watch the ball drop over Times Square, and they had already unpacked Rebecca's things and were starting to heat up the milk for the mugs of hot chocolate to go with the cookies they were going to make.

This is what had happened: After they left Rebecca with Nancy and went back upstairs to prepare for—Louey thought—their big night out, Luke said, "Louey, sit down. I have something to tell you." He said it as soon as they'd shut the door behind them. He walked to their living room couch.

"Sit down?" He'd never said that to her before. That's something someone says when he's about to fire you. And, "I have something to tell you?" Had someone died? She went with him to sit on their living-room sofa, her upper body twisted toward him and her arm on the back of the couch.

She faced him with great curiosity, but her stomach was churning.

He said he'd been unhappy. Well, he'd never been the sort you'd describe as "happy." He'd always been a serious person, and more quiet than usual lately—but unhappy?

Why?

This is what he said:

She wasn't spiritual enough, he said. She had no respect for spirituality.

Pardon?

She was always looking for things to do for "fun," he said, and fun wasn't the point: The point was to be joyful. And he wasn't feeling joy when he was with her. Only when he was with Aileen. Because Aileen was spiritual.

What did I do wrong? Just tell me what you want me to do! I can change!

This is what he said: There was nothing she could do. In fact, see? That was the problem: She always wanted to be "doing" things, while what he really needed was someone who wasn't always looking to "do," but just to "be" … like Aileen. Nothing Louey could "do" could change what she really "was."

"What do you mean? What am I?" she cried. She came apart from herself. She really didn't know what she was. Or who she was. Or where she was.

"Well, you're sarcastic about my spiritual practice."

OK, now, that was really, really untrue. For a moment she came together again, and began to defend herself.

"No, I'm not: I respect and admire your spiritual practice! I don't mind when you guys meet upstairs to meditate! I'm down here making the fruit salad for afterwards, when you do that! Give me an example of what you mean!"

"I've heard you tell your friends and family that I 'sit around and hum to myself.' Chanting my mantra and performing sacred chants in a Siddha Yoga pose is not 'humming to myself.' It's being at one with the universe. And I need to live somewhere where I can take off my shoes when I come inside, like I do at Aileen's house. We leave the vibrations of the world outside so that we can make our home a sacred space. I've decided to move in with Aileen."

Decided? He's decided? Shoes? He was leaving her over shoes? Now, that was really crazy. Crazy, but easily fixed.

"What? I don't need to keep my shoes on!" She ran across the room and flung open the door to their little balcony.

"Here!" she cried, yanking off her left sneaker. "Here! I don't need them!" She chucked the shoe hard and far over the railing. It landed on the tree lawn across the street. Voice wavering, she yanked off her right sneak. "Are you kidding? I don't even care about shoes! We can leave them all outside: I don't mind!" She winged her other sneaker. It hit the front passenger's-side window of a parked car and fell to the mushy, icy street.

Luke hadn't risen from the couch.

"That's not the point," he said. "You can't change who you are by doing things. I'm going to move out. I'm going to move in with Aileen."

"Wait. Aileen—isn't she a Lesbian?"

Louey had assumed Aileen was a Lesbian because she was in her 40s and was living—or had been living, the last Louey knew—with a friend of theirs, a woman who worked in the state's Department of Labor Relations.

"Well, I guess she was in a Lesbian relationship at one time, but now she's not, anymore."

Wow, Louey thought. *You must be such a stud that you changed a nice, normal Lesbian into a slavering heterosexual adulteress. What a man! Wow; that must be the ultimate sexual compliment for a man. Oh, no: He's right. I guess I am sarcastic.*

What was he saying? What did this mean?

"Are we getting divorced?" she asked, dazed.

"Yes ... I guess so ... eventually."

Oh my God; I'm getting divorced! What'll I tell Dad? This will kill him!

"Take Rebecca with you," she said, nodding vigorously. "Whatever you do, take Rebecca. A girl has to grow up with her father." She had grown up with only her dad, and what would she have done without him?

Clearly, he wasn't expecting that response. He sat in silence for a long time before saying, "I think she should stay with you. Aileen only has one bedroom. This way it'll be less disruptive for Rebecca, because she'll be here with you like always."

"OK," she said, meekly, but she didn't know who was saying that, nor who had said the other thing she'd said. She vaguely thought, as though in a haze, that what Luke had said sounded like something that, in another, parallel universe, might actually make sense. It also sounded as though he had already thought it all out. As though he'd made a plan.

"OK, but you have to tell Rebecca. What are you going to tell her?" she asked.

"I'll tell her the truth. I'll tell her that I was unhappy

here. And I'll tell her that I'll always love her."

And that's what he did. The very next day, New Year's Day, Louey announced to them both that she was going shopping for a few things at the grocery store nearby, and walked out of their apartment, because she knew she couldn't stand to be there, and when she came back, carrying nothing at all, he had done it; he had told Rebecca, and their daughter was sitting on his lap crying.

"Oh, did Daddy tell you our sad news?" she said softly. She said it in the slightly sorrowful way you'd say, "Oh, did Daddy tell you that the art teacher you love so much is moving to Plattsburgh?"

"It's OK, honey; it'll be all right," she added. And then, to not interrupt their little tête-à-tête, she added, "Oh jeez; I forgot the ... biscuits." And she turned around and left again.

She had never bought biscuits and had never made biscuits and wasn't even sure what biscuits were. She just had to say something to get out of the house, because she couldn't stand to be there.

She became a kind of automaton then, not touching Luke all through the silent nights in their bed together, keeping a hard, tight little smile on her face in Rebecca's presence, rising each day from her and Luke's bed, often watching him in bewilderment and waiting for him to suddenly whip around and say, "Wow, I'm sorry! I must have been crazy! Take me back!" Or, alternatively, to pack his things and leave—which took him only a few days to do. He left her the Saab, which had been paid for long ago. It turned out he had bought himself a new red sportscar. And then he was gone, telling Rebecca he'd come back next weekend to pick her up and take her out for lunch and a walk.

The next morning, Louey got dressed, fed her daughter, saw her off to school and went to work as if nothing had happened. *Is Luke going to work today? Does everybody know? Did he tell them, already? How awkward is this going to be?*

So weird. It's as if nothing has changed, and yet everything has changed.

That first weekend after Luke moved out, after he'd come back as he promised and had taken Rebecca out for the afternoon, Louey went downstairs with a bottle of wine and told Nancy. She couldn't stand lying to her friend any longer.

"I *thought* something was wrong when you came back and got Rebecca on New Year's Eve. That son of a bitch! That lying sneak! That hypocrite! How does Krishna, or Vishnu, or Rama-Lama-Dingdong, or whoever the fuck he prays to, feel about adultery, I wonder?" Nancy said. "Did you have any clue this was going on?"

Louey found that her voice couldn't make a voice-noise, so she said in a whisper, "I don't know." Nancy leaned in to hear her better. "Now that I look back on it, he was getting gradually more and more quiet and distant over the last few months. But he never said he was unhappy—until—you know—that night."

"Unhappy my ass! He's just that kind of a person who's not happy unless he's unhappy! What a hypocrite! What a lying sneak! What a son of a bitch! What are you going to do? How is Rebecca taking it?"

It was that last question that crumpled Louey. Nancy hugged her as she shook and cried.

"She'll get over this," Nancy said. "She's really strong and smart, and she probably has a million friends whose parents are divorced—those who know who their fathers are at all."

It was true that, in Rebecca's inner-city elementary school, there was no lack of broken homes. Fathers were not around in abundance among Rebecca's friends. Louey made a mental note to call Rebecca's teacher and principal and tell them what had happened, so they'd be careful to keep an eye on her for a while and see if she seemed especially sad, or distracted, or anything.

For now, it was soothing for Louey to have something to talk about other than her misery. The societal, economic and historical causes of the deterioration of the nuclear Black family and the meteoric rise in incarceration of Black men were wonderfully restorative topics for her, and plucked her up a little. Nancy provided cheese and crackers, and she and Louey talked and ate and cried and drank all afternoon. And not just on that one day, either.

As time passed and Joe or Louey's pals in the bullpen casually asked how Luke was, or what she and Luke had done over the weekend, or whatever, she would tell them the truth, and shake her head and gossip with them a little bit—no more than she could stand—about how shocked she was, and let them choose sides the way people always do when they're friends with both members of a couple that's getting divorced, but she was trying to act as normal as possible, and the crisis didn't seem to affect her work at all. In fact, if anything, she threw herself into it more than usual. People didn't talk to her as much as they used to, because they didn't know what to say, but she was secretly gratified to see that they all seemed to be on her "side," and that no one was talking to Luke anymore.

Louey knew, despite Luke's neat plans, that she wouldn't be staying in their house. She would get an apartment for herself and Rebecca as far away as she could, as soon as she could. Her lawyer—all the CSEU lawyers offered to represent her, but she got an "outside" one—informed her that, if she was going to live with Rebecca while giving Luke free access to her—which is what they both agreed to put into the separation agreement—she would have to stay in Albany County. That was an unpleasant surprise; she had been thinking that maybe this would be the right time to move back to Newburgh, and start over there. Her head would be clear in Newburgh. She would have friends there. Rebecca would love it there, as she had, growing up. But the information from the lawyers led her to land not in Newburgh, but instead, as far south in Albany County as she could get. That place turned out to be a funky apartment complex in an odd little hamlet called Grevenna. An ad in the Knick News said the rent there included heat and hot water, and the laundry room for the whole complex was in the very building that had the vacancy. When she scouted it out, she put down her deposit right away. She knew she could sell it to Rebecca, because it had an outdoor pool and also a sweet little pond over which humped a small wooden bridge from which you could look down and see frogs, fish and ducks. Rebecca loved fish and ducks and adored frogs.

Louey went to Nancy's as soon as she could, to tell her she'd be moving.

"Well, guess what?" Nancy said. "I have a surprise for you, too!"

She had been accepted into a master's of business administration program at Cornell, and she'd be starting in the fall.

"I actually applied in November, but I didn't want to tell you because, first, I didn't think I'd be accepted, and then when I was, you had enough on your mind, and I thought losing the rent from my apartment would be the last thing you needed. You do get half of it, don't you? Even though I make the checks out to Luke?"

"Are you kidding? Luke keeps all the rent money in his own account. I get this thing called 'spousal support' and child support for Rebecca. Spousal support ends in three years; child support ends when she turns 18."

"Well, good, then! I hope you'll be happy to know I'm not staying around here and paying rent to that son of a bitch. I'm moving to Ithaca in August!"

Louey and Rebecca would beat her out of town. They would move in June, as soon as Rebecca finished first grade. In the fall she'd be attending the Grevenna-Reservoir Elementary school, to which kids were bussed from all the surrounding hilltowns. It was really far south. In Grevenna they'd be closer to Catskill, really, than to Albany.

"Oh, Rebecca will be a superstar in that school," Nancy said. "Those weird-ass hillbillies have never seen anyone as bright as she is."

Nancy insisted on coming upstairs with a bottle of champagne to share with Louey after Rebecca went to bed.

"I was reading in *Psychology Today* that a new study found that people need three things to be happy," Nancy said: "Someone to love, who loves you in return; a problem to be working on; and something to look forward to."

"That sounds about right," Louey said. "And I would add, for Jews: Something to read."

For the first time in a long, long time, Louey went to bed happy.

The move to Grevenna, as Nancy predicted, worked out well. The most painful part was saying goodbye to Nancy. Louey was never good at goodbyes. She was OK until after they had hugged and exchanged their new addresses and, all big smiles, said a jaunty "See ya later" to each other. Louey began to walk around to the driver's side of the Saab (Rebecca was already in the passenger's seat). For some reason she stopped as she passed in front of the left headlight, as though she'd walked into a wall. She turned and looked back at her friend, who was also as still as Lot's wife. Their faces crumbled and they came together and cried as they hugged once more. Rebecca saw the whole mess through the windshield. Then they pulled apart, laughing and crying, and Louey and Rebecca pulled away.

Shortly thereafter, knowing she would never play her flute again—she had taken lessons only so she could spend time with her friend—Louey sold that silver instrument for $10 to a secretary at CSEU whose granddaughter wanted to learn how to play.

Louey and Rebecca had time to swim or hike on weekends and during Louey's vacation that summer. Rebecca made friends not only with the other kids but also with Myra, the lifeguard at the pool. Myra was a brilliant graduate of Barnard College who had put her plans for med school on hold so she could return home to Grevenna to care for her younger brother, who had leukemia. Myra taught Rebecca to swim, and the two had many happy, animated conversations in and around the pool all summer.

In the fall, Louey walked Rebecca 50 yards or so to the school bus each day; it came right into the driveway of their apartment complex. The now-second-grader returned home on the same bus at about 3, let herself in, did her homework, made herself a snack and watched TV, called her mom and went over to play with the girl in the next apartment. It was amazing or scandalous how independent she was, depending on which of the single moms in the complex was gossiping about it.

Luke and Louey wouldn't be divorced for a year. They had found out, each from their own lawyer, that if they were legally separated for 365 days, they would automatically be divorced, and that would save them both a lot of money compared to any other way of doing it—they would spend even less than if they used one of those "do-it-yourself" divorce kits that had recently become so popular. Luke's moving out had started the clock on that one-year period.

Louey existed in a grey fog. The great Charles Schulz cartoon character Pigpen was covered in a cloud of dirt everywhere he went; in that same way, she felt she carried a grey cloud sticking to her that dulled her entire world. She had no energy and no motivation to do anything. Previously bouncy, light and agile in her movements, she now spoke and plodded slowly. She got up every day and saw Rebecca off on the school bus, drove the 15 miles or so to Albany, became mildly distracted by her work, did whatever shopping was needed on her way home, made dinner and talked or read with her daughter. Sometimes, she managed to force the ends of her lips upwards into a "smile" and jump around the living room with Rebecca to one of the new "cardio" exercise videos that had become so popular. And sometimes, when she remembered, she tried to act cheerful, but Rebecca saw right through it. It affected her; she lost her ability to sleep, and Louey could hear her sobbing late at night and into the early morning hours. Sometimes, with her soul mangled, Louey stumbled into Rebecca's bedroom; sometimes the girl padded miserably into hers. This could be at 11 p.m., midnight, 2 a.m. or later, on school nights as well as weekends.

"Why did Daddy leave us?"

"Yeah; that's what I'd like to know, too! He said he loved another woman more than me, and I could understand that, but it's just so mean, it doesn't seem like him. It seems like something somebody else would say. And he said I'm not spiritual enough for him, but I can't believe that either. I think he'd tell you the truth before he'd tell me. Here; here's the phone. Go ahead and ask him!"

Rebecca did make such calls, several times over the ensuing weeks and months, sobbing the whole time, sitting on their living-room floor in her pajamas in the middle of the night, using their black table phone with the long, long cord, holding some tissues in her right hand and continually dabbing at her face with them. Louey, sitting next to her, kept her supplied. At the end of each call, Louey would ask, "What did he say?" and Rebecca always had the same reply: "He said that's between you and him. He said he'll always love me."

The year of the separation floated past with one truly

comedic moment. In the center of Page One of the second section ("Arts and Leisure") of a Sunday edition of the Albany Times-Union, there was a huge photo of Luke and the Holy Bimbo! They were seated cross-legged on pillows on the floor of her apartment, with their full names printed in the caption! The previous day was a Hindu holiday that apparently required a lot of drumming and meditation, and wow, drumming and meditating were right up their alley. There were other Hindus sitting around with them, but the two lovers were at the center of the frame. Louey bought an extra copy of the paper and cut the photo out of both copies. One, she sent to her lawyer with a note she felt was quite witty; the other, she saved to put in her Treasures Box.

That was the end of the humor, though. The one-year separation period ended, the divorce came through, and Abe Levy had a heart attack at the Capitol and died.

Dear Diary,

Let's see. Counting from when I first sailed out of the chute, I've lost: my mother; my friends from Newburgh; my friends from college; my friends from the Record; Nancy; Grampa and Bubbe; my husband; and now Dad. Is that a lot? It feels like a lot. I mean, they didn't all <u>die</u>, but they all sort of faded away, or moved away, or just ... left. I mean, some of them got married, but still, it's the same thing, in a way ... They moved on, and left me here. Well, I guess that's not many losses, for a middle-aged woman. A lot of people have a lot more than that. And <u>everybody</u> loses their parents! Your parents are <u>older</u> than you! You're <u>supposed</u> to lose your parents. If you die before they do, man, something's wrong. Still, to me, it feels like everybody's going away.

When I was born I was the Aleph, the infinitesimally tiny center of the Big Bang, and the whole world has been expanding away from me in every direction ever since. Everybody's leaving me here alone, with no one and nothing to look forward to but loss and death and grief. And it's so lonely out here! I have no idea why, but I feel like I need to go back to Newburgh. I've got to go home. But until Rebecca graduates, I'm not leaving Grevenna. I'm not going to make her change school districts, after everything she's been through.

Her father had died of a broken heart, and Louey knew it. *He literally died of a broken heart. He was heartsick over me getting divorced. His heart was sick, and that's all there is to it. When I got married, he said, "That's a stone off my heart." I'll never forget that. Well, the stone fell back on him, and this time, it crushed him. Oh Daddy, I'm so sorry!*

Abe's best friend, Bob Herman, was his opposite number in the Assembly. What Abe was to the Senate—that's what Bob was to the Assembly. Bob, a Jew, was funny and smart, and his wife, Bea, was Ree's best friend. Just like Luke and Louey, and Bruce and Leslie! The Hermans lived a block from the Levys in Slingerlands. Louey remembered Bob once asking Abe what he had done in the War (meaning, World War II).

"I ordered comic books for the General," Abe said.

Without missing a beat, Bob replied, "Who read them to him?"

The early-December morning of the funeral was cold, bright and clear. That was good, because everyone was wearing sunglasses except Louey and Rebecca. Even Luke was wearing them, and he'd never cried, as far as Louey knew. As they said Kaddish over the open grave, it grew cold and dark, and a wind rose up. After the rabbi handed Ree the U.S. flag that had draped the casket, it started to rain. Bob and Bea and the Levys took turns shoveling dirt into the grave, Bob leaned over to Louey and pointed to the sky.

"That's God's tears," he said. "God's tears."

It rained for the rest of the year. Sometimes it rained hard, like a winter thunderstorm, and at other times it just drizzled, but it never stopped. People became used to wearing raincoats over their parkas, and stomping over and through ice and slush. They kept umbrellas in their cars and offices. Their moods grew as dark as the sky.

Louey didn't get out of bed for a long time. CSEU granted her a three-day bereavement leave as per the contract, but then she called in sick every day for a week after that.

One Sunday afternoon Rebecca found her still in bed, staring. Just staring at nothing.

"Oh, Mom, come on, it's time to get up," the little girl said tremulously, sitting on her mother's bed. She gently rubbed her mom's arm when she got no response.

And then she said, "Come on, Mom. Grampa would want you to." And she said, "All that love you had for Grampa— you can dump it on me now!"

Her little voice wavered in exactly the way Louey's did when she was trying to talk while crying. But they both giggled a little when she finished. "Dumping love" was an inherently funny idea.

Louey sat up. It was the bravest thing she had heard yet, and it was also the truest. It was the thing that woke her up. She had to go on, and be cheerful again, and stop acting crazy. She had to take care of her daughter. Abe Levy would want her to. *There's a poem in here somewhere.*

She wrote that night:

I've heard it said, and this I know: / Grief is just love with nowhere to go.

Yes. Let's go on. No more acting crazy! That's over. That's done. I have someone to love: Rebecca! Dad would want me to take care of his granddaughter, whom he loved so much, and dump all my love on her, and be strong for her so she'll have a good example to live up to, instead of a nut. Wow: I was making my daughter nervous with that bullshit! It's totally unacceptable. Of course, you're allowed to grieve; that's normal; that's what Dad would say. I can hear him saying it, with that little laugh. But you're not allowed to hurt yourself grieving, he would say; that's an offense against G-d. "C'mon," he'd say. "Get up and show that kid of yours how to enjoy life. She's a great kid."

She went back to work the next day.

The next year passed, and the next, and it got so that Louey could do her job in her sleep. But that "sleepwalking" feeling was not good for her, and she knew it. She wanted to be excited by something again. Joe Arnier suggested a weird thing to her one day, and she giggled thinking about it. She almost thought she might try it.

"Why don't you run for president of Headquarters Staff Union?" he said. "Their president just abandoned ship, and you'd be great in that spot."

HSU's membership was mostly women, but not all. There were a few men in it, who worked in the Library and Archives Department, and Fred Morris was one of them. Fred had not precisely abandoned ship; he had been offered a job by a state assembly member from Troy, and he accepted it. He'd begin working at the Assembly—which, after all, was just across the street from CSEU—in a couple of weeks. Fred grew up in Troy and had been best friends with the assemblyman's son from childhood. The pay over at the Assembly would be better, but the gig depended on the assemblyman's getting re-elected every two years.

Here is a fact about the New York State Legislature: Once elected to it, you have a better chance of dying in office than of being beaten by a challenger.

So Fred was taking a very small risk, and nobody belittled his decision to switch jobs after more than 15 years at CSEU. It had always bothered Louey that in a union with eighty-four members, their president was one of the only two men it represented.

"Who else is running, do you know?" Louey asked Joe.

"Well, of course they don't tell me, since I'm Management," Joe chuckled. "But I'm sure it will come up at their next meeting. Why don't you throw your hat in the ring? You're smart, you're reasonable, you're respected ... "

She was easily flattered. It was a longtime personality flaw that she knew she had but had never been motivated to correct. When the vacancy was discussed at the next HSU meeting, the Acting President—who was the vice-president—said she didn't want the job, as she had three kids and didn't have the time to deal with "union stuff." She asked if anyone wanted to run for it, and looked around the room.

There was one man present, and she'd be damned if they gave the position to him. Louey raised her hand and said,

"Well, I would do it, but I have a question: Do any of the other officers want to run?" The secretary and the treasurer both said no, one quietly smiling and the other ducking and shaking her head and crossing her arms over her face as though dodging a thrown brick and yelling, "No! No!" to the amusement of the workers.

Negotiations were coming up. No one wanted to be in charge of negotiations, and the president had to head up the bargaining team. That was the president's main job.

Louey remembered what that was like from her days on the Record. But this was different; this was the "union's union!" Additionally, this wasn't the union of the field reps—who were all men—it was the union of the PR department writers, the administrative assistants, and the dozens of "member services" people who answered the phones when members had questions about their pensions, continuing education credits and other benefits. Surely CSEU wouldn't give these folks—almost all of whom were women—a hard time in negotiations.

Louey threw her hat into the ring. People cheered and applauded, voted to throw Fred Morris an "appreciation party" for his many years of service, voted to hold the secret-ballot vote for president at their next meeting, and patted Louey on the back on their way out. Fred gave her his phone number and told her to call him with any questions she might have. He also told her he'd put his hinged, grey metal box of HSU-related folders on her desk in the morning, along with the tiny key to it.

HSU already had a lawyer they used as their main spokesman at the bargaining table, and they already had a negotiating team in place, most of whom had been involved in negotiations for previous contracts. No one seemed particularly worried about the outcome. They knew they were well-paid, though not as well-paid as the field reps, and since they worked 8:30 to 4:30 at headquarters and never had to go to any meetings outside the building or buy anyone lunch, they had no expense accounts. They always let the field reps bargain first, and then negotiated a quick, "me-too" contract with improvements mostly related to things like the suggestion box or the supplies in the ladies' rooms.

Louey herself was feeling quite wealthy. She realized with gratitude that she had every material thing she could ever want, and she was socking away money like crazy. At her father's suggestion, she had begun a few years earlier to invest in the stock market, finding American companies that used union labor. Abe had given her the number of the "stockbroker lady" he used, and Louey would ask her to buy a few hundred shares of a stock at ten dollars or so per share, and then look at its price a week or so later. If it was up a tick, she'd call back and ask the lady to sell her shares, and then happily pocket the two or three hundred dollars she'd made. Often she'd make that call even before her check to pay for the stocks had cleared. The lady didn't seem to mind a bit; she only warned Louey each time that those "earnings" were taxable.

"Earnings," she calls them! They're not "earnings"; they're "winnings!" And I don't care if I have to pay taxes out of my winnings. Who would mind that? Making money without working for it! It should be a crime!

She did get a big kick out of having money to spend on

nonessentials, for the first time in her life. As fall approached, she decided to buy herself a good, warm winter coat. Not the fluffy, quilted jacket she used to wear hiking with Luke—no, she wanted a "grownup coat." Because she was feeling like a grownup. It was unlike her to want something classy like that, but she developed a craving for it, like a pregnant person's craving for pickles.

She went to a local place called "The Coat Factory" that she had heard about through ads on the radio. It was, indeed, a whole department store offering nothing but expensive coats, jackets, raincoats, and leather pocketbooks. It had been so long since she'd shopped for clothing that she didn't even know what size she wore. But finally she found a coat that sang to her.

It was a coat that looked like it was made of an actual sheep, turned inside out. It was a soft sand color ("stone," its tag said) with big, easy buttons, and the lining was thick, off-white, popcorn-looking wool. She felt warmer just looking at it. It was car-coat length, hanging just to the middle of her thighs. Trimming its hem, cuffs, and the tops of its pockets, was that same lovely wool. You could turn the collar up so that that nice lining was against your cheeks, and you could practically bury yourself in it. Louey couldn't wait for cold weather, so she could wear it and never take it off.

Fall came, and negotiations had turned ugly. CSEU hadn't been able to get even a one percent raise for the state workers it represented, so management had a handy excuse not to offer any raises to its own employees. The awful thing that no one had explained to Louey was that, though HSU's current contract had been a "me-too" of the field staff union's

(FSU) pact, it was now HSU's turn to go first in negotiating a raise. If they won a five percent hike, the field staff would get the same. If they got zero, the field staff, too, would get zero. That's the way it had always been. So now all two hundred of CSEU's employees were counting on her to get a good contract—the men of the FSU, and the women of the HSU.

Management was in no mood to even talk about a raise. The quarter-million members statewide would be up in arms, they said. How could CSEU justify using their dues to give its own workers a raise, when the CSEU members got nothing? The Times-Union was full of angry letters to the editor, saying that their union was ineffective, and maybe they should look to another union for help. Maybe they should file for a representation election and get a "real" union—one with "teeth."

Louey suggested at the September HSU meeting that her colleagues should conduct informational picketing outside of headquarters during lunch hour, and before and after work. They were all for it. Walking up and down Elm Street, across from the State Capitol, with signs saying the union was being unfair to its own employees, would draw the attention of the news media, that was for sure!

So from 8:30 to 4:30 for a month, Louey wrote stories saying how great CSEU was, and before and after work and at lunch, she paced up and down the street with a handmade sign saying CSEU was not negotiating in good faith.

It got worse. It got worse and worse and worse. HSU's contract expired, and no deal was reached to replace it. Management said there were no circumstances under which they would offer a raise of any amount, in a year when state workers got nothing. And then at one session, the entire management team—Bill Terwilliger and the union's accountant and the director of the Member Services Department and their labor lawyer for internal negotiations—rose and stood in a line like chorus girls and said they wouldn't come back until HSU gave up on the idea of raises altogether. They could talk about an extra "personal day," they could talk about higher reimbursement for continuing education or any of the other "little" things the union was asking for, but raises were out of the question, and they wouldn't be back until the union agreed to that condition. Goodbye.

Inflation was high that year, and no end to it was in sight. People were worried; they needed to keep pace with it. But they also were starting to get tired of picketing. At the same time, Louey had to delicately answer questions from the press and face TV cameras and imply, without saying outright, that CSEU management was a bunch of hypocrites, and she had to answer members' angry questions at specially-called meetings about why they were making no progress under her regime. She was not a happy union president.

At the October meeting, she brought the HSU lawyer to address the group and answer questions. It was then that, despairing of ever getting a contract signed, Louey proposed they choose what the lawyer called the "nuclear option"—a strike. The vote was not unanimous. You don't get paid when you're on strike. This member had a mortgage to pay every month; this one had daycare and incredibly high nursing-home bills for her parents; this one needed to buy four new tires for her car; and on and on. People said, basically, that they couldn't afford to go out on strike. Who knew how long a strike would last? At best, they could hold out only a couple of weeks.

"Nobody ever knows," Louey said, "but the power of public shame might be enough to get management back to the bargaining table. I'm in PR. I know some of these reporters, and I know we can get our side of the story out there. I know how awful it looks and what a black eye it would give CSEU to have it broadcast all over the state that they're having labor troubles with their own employees. The Field Staff Union guys will refuse to cross our picket lines, and they may even go out on strike to support us, and that will really put the screws to management. Look, I know we can't afford to stay out very long; no one can. But I think we can get them back to the table and get at least some kind of a raise, if we all stick together in what I think will be a brief but effective strike."

The vote had to carry by three-fourths, and it did so. Just barely. If there was no contract by next week, HSU would go out on strike.

Louey went to Terwilliger's office early the next day and warned him. He said he sympathized, but it was out of his hands. The accountant said they'd be crazy to give out raises to HSU and then to FSU "on top of" an extra personal day and higher continuing education reimbursement, "both of which have costs, you know." He offered her one of his big fat cigars, but she was in no mood for his humor.

"HYPOCRITES!" was the only word on Louey's taxi-cab-yellow placard, stapled to the top of a 3-foot-long wooden slat. Other HSU members had made their own pointed, amusing or heartfelt signs, but none was as eye-catching as Louey's. It was boldly lettered with a thick black marker, carefully measured to fill out the entire poster, side to side. She wished she could have done it in Goudy Old Style, but that elegant font, while eminently readable, was not as legible from a distance as this block-style lettering.

The field staff had not gone out on strike—they had taken no position on it—but a lot of the men were developing flu-like symptoms and, therefore, not coming in to work, for fear of, you know, contagion.

As Louey had hoped, the workers' dilemma was an easy sell to the news media, and perfect headline bait. "Union's Union Has to Strike for Better Pay"; "Employees Turn Tables on CSEU"; "Union Doesn't Like It When Shoe's on Other Foot"; there were so many stories, and Louey was happy to talk to reporters from anywhere at any time of the day or night. She gave them her home number. They weren't shy about calling her, and she wasn't shy about being quoted.

The photos weren't as dramatic. The first two days of the strike, Monday and Tuesday, there were 40 people on the picket line, in two four-hour shifts of twenty people each, walking in a long, narrow oval all day long. It looked great, and that's when the most news representatives showed up. Of course, they went inside to talk to Terwilliger, too, but that was all right; the HSU members parted to make a pathway for them to reach the door, and then parted again for them, cheering as they left. Reporters weren't used to being cheered. As for CSEU's management staff—they had to come and go by the back door, off a nameless street by the loading dock, to avoid crossing the picket line.

But the next two days, attendance on the line dropped off. Several HSU members were too cold to walk for long on Wednesday, and apologetically left after an hour or so; on Thursday it was sleeting. Louey knew she had to do something to keep up the spirits of those few who were still physically with her, to relieve the tedium of walking and holding signs for hours in front of headquarters.

There was a sort of ground-level "tunnel" running right through the first floor of the building, leading from Elk Street to the parking area in back. Late in the morning, a semi pulled up, and the driver signaled that he was going to turn to go through the tunnel. Louey had a crazy idea. Impulsively, she threw herself—in her beautiful, warm, new coat—supine onto the middle of the wet driveway just before the tunnel, effectively blocking (she hoped) any delivery vehicles from entering. Her thick coat kept her surprisingly warm. She lifted her head and, chin touching her neck, and waved her sign as high as she could, praying the driver would see her down there. Ralph Ward and her "bullpen" mate Colleen shouted to him from the picket line and pointed to Louey. Louey closed her eyes and prepared to meet God in a sheepskin coat.

Louey Levy, Martyr to the Labor Movement, she said to herself. *That will be the head on my obit in the* Sector. *"Louey Levy, a most brilliant writer," the story will say, "joined Joe Hill in Heaven last week ..."* Oh wait; no, it won't! They'll have to take CSEU's side! They'll say, "Louey Levy, Idiot, died last week after a short career in the union's PR Department. To apply for her job, send résumé to ..."

He's just sitting there with the motor running. He looks like he's getting ready to gun it and squash me. I wonder if this is the part where I scream, "I'm too young to die!" And then God slaps Her thigh and goes, "Oh, yeah? That's what they all say!" And laughs Herself to death—to my death, I mean. That would be hilarious. But who would know that that's what happened, if I weren't around to write about it? I wonder what my real obit would say? I've never really accomplished a goddammed thing in my life. I've only published that one long poem. "She left a lot of unpublished stories and a whole bunch of notebooks" doesn't sound great. "But she loved her grandma and grampa, and her father and her brothers and sister, and her music and a lot of friends." It could say that. If I get out of this driveway alive, I'll have to work on my obit, and more importantly, I'd better work on it by doing something worthwhile or being somebody worthwhile, so there'll be something to put in it.

It turned out that the driver was a union guy himself—a Teamster. He got out and asked what was going on. He squatted down next to Louey and said he was carrying a one-ton roll of paper for the production of the *Sector*. He came every month, he said. This was news to Louey.

Live and learn. But how else could we print the Sector? Of course we need that paper!

Louey told him they were on strike for better pay.

"You're on strike against the union?" he asked, confused.

"Yeah. Pretty good, right? But they're an employer, too."

"Yeah. Yeah, I get that."

She said she wasn't getting up, but she pointed out that if he could go up to the corner and turn left onto South Swan and come down Washington Street, he could then turn left again onto Eagle, which would swing him right up to the loading dock at the back of the building. He said he knew that way, too, and had started taking the tunnel only because it was a shortcut. As they talked, Louey became aware of the scent of Bill Terwilliger's distinctive tobacco. He had yanked open the window of his first-floor office. There was a sarcastic smile in one corner of his mouth and a lit cigar in the other.

"Hey, Levy!" he called. "If I could afford a coat like that, I wouldn't need to go on strike!"

Still supine, she raised her head. "What's the matter; don't you believe in unions?" she shot back. This wounded him into total inarticulateness, and he was never terribly articulate to begin with.

"I sure as hell do! I've always been for the working man! A tiger doesn't change his spots in the middle of a stream, y'know!" he yelled. And with that he slammed his window shut against the sleet and his employees.

Louey spent no time contemplating Terwilliger's odd ideas of coloration in various members of the cat family, nor his faulty knowledge of proverbs, as a dark mood settled upon her.

What the hell am I doing? she said to herself. *Now I have to lie here all day in the mud like a nut, or I'll look like I've given up! And oh, my coat! My coat!* She thought she might start to cry.

But as God Herself loves working people—for there was no other discernable reason for this development—a reporter and photographer from the Times-Union arrived while the truck driver was still there. The picketers quickly surrounded them, pointing out the martyr Louey Levy, literally laying down her life in defense of justice. As Louey, on her back, explained the issues to the photographer, the driver climbed into his truck and radioed someone, and then came back and told her he wasn't crossing any picket lines. He couldn't, by his own union's rules, deliver the paper to the loading dock, he said, even if he wanted to—which he didn't. The reporters captured the whole exchange.

"Good luck, ladies," he said, and waved before driving off. After getting additional quotes from various wet HSU members, the reporters left, too.

That evening Louey started the telephone-tree they'd organized a week earlier, calling five members and telling them not to bother to picket, as the next day—a Friday— was Columbus Day, a holiday according to the now-expired HSU contract, so no one would be working anyway. Those five members each called five more members, and so on. And on Columbus Day, always a slow news day in Albany, the Times-Union led Page Three with the story of the employees of the state's biggest labor union still being on strike.

Public shame is an underused tool. The power of public shame should never be underestimated, Louey said to herself, smiling as she read the paper with great satisfaction.

The next day, Saturday, Terwilliger called Louey at home to ask if her members would accept a three-year contract with a one-and-a-half-percent raise the first year and two-percent in both the second and third, with a "re-opener" if inflation jumped by more than two percent in any of those years.

Why, yes. Yes, they would.

She started the telephone-tree all over again, telling everyone to meet for a strike-ending vote on Monday. The vote was unanimous: Yes. Take the tiny raises and run. End the strike. End it.

Dear Diary,

You can't lose 'em all, I guess: We went back in "victorious," if 20 cents an hour is a victory. "It's the principle of the thing!" we all shouted, partly because we believed it, and partly to keep our own spirits up. Anyway, hurrah for us! Reporters are calling me for comments so often I might as well be glued to my phone, and I'm thinking kind of wistfully that this moment may be as "victorious" as I'll ever get. Now all I can think of is, as Grampa always reminded me: This, too, shall pass.

The end of the strike wasn't the end of Louey's coat. The dry cleaners, as she feared, could not get mud stains out of the sheepskin. The worst of them were only on the back of it, and since Louey could only see the front when she was wearing it, that was OK with her, and she intended to keep wearing it forever. But one day, she went to the dentist.

This particular dentist accepted the state workers' dental insurance, which was the same insurance CSEU offered to its own employees. Looking at Louey's amazingly healthy teeth, he suggested she get all four of her wisdom teeth pulled.

What? I don't need my wisdom teeth pulled. He must say that to everybody, to make more money.

"They're not giving me any trouble," she said. She wasn't sure he could understand her, what with his tiny vacuum tube sucking up all the spit in her mouth. But he did understand her, and he whipped out his very best reason for performing the operation.

"Not yet, they're not, but eventually they will, and then

it'll be tougher to get them out, and you'll need more an-esthesia and it'll be a more dangerous procedure," he said. The operation might have to be done in the hospital, at that point."

"All four of them have to come out?"

"Yes, you might as well have all four done at once, and get it over with."

"How much will it cost?"

"Your insurance will cover it. It'll only take, like, twenty minutes, after the anesthesia kicks in."

What the hell. Sure. Go ahead.

It took half an hour, but he yanked all four of them. On her way out of the office, he seemed a bit apologetic.

"One of them was impacted. That's why it took so long," he said.

She didn't think it had taken long at all. He had injected her with Novocaine, and those four shots hurt like hell, but after that, she didn't feel a thing. In fact, she'd almost fallen asleep. Why did people always say getting your teeth pulled was painful? It was nothing! He gave her a prescription.

"Get this filled on your way home," he said.

"What's it for?"

"It's a pain-killer."

"I don't need it. Really. I'm not hurting at all," she said.

"You will be, though, tomorrow," he said.

She pulled up the thick, white-wool collar of her famous sheepskin coat as she opened the door to his parking lot.

There was a drugstore less than a mile away, in down-town Albany. Louey walked down a long aisle of Halloween-themed items toward the back wall, where the pharmacy area was. Several people in that aisle seemed to be staring at her and then fleeing. The ones who remained were staring at her, too.

What are you looking at, lady? Why are you pulling your little girl over to the side like that, like I'm a monster? Why the hell are those boys staring at me?

Louey looked back over her shoulder as she arrived at the pharmacy counter. Now it was clear to her that the customers—adults and kids alike—were indeed looking at her.

Jeez, these people are making me paranoid! What the heck's going on?

It took a while for anyone to wait on her. Finally a young woman with a white badge—"Pharmacy Assistant"—came over but didn't even look at Louey as she said, "Can I help you?"

"Yes, can you fill this prescription for me, please?" Louey was amused by the sound of her own voice; she wasn't forming her words correctly. It was the Novocaine, no doubt. She was still numb from it. Well, they'd figure it out when they saw the prescription for pain-killer. They'd figure out that she'd just come from the dentist.

"Um … here … you have …" the pharmacist's helper said gingerly, touching the corner of her own mouth. She handed Louey a few tissues and then placed a large, round, footed mirror on the counter.

Louey looked at her face. She was bleeding profusely out of both sides of her mouth. The blood was gushing in torrents down both sides of her chin and neck and into the thick wool of her coat collar, spilling over the collar and down onto the front of the coat, the two rivulets running together somehow and starting to form one large chest-high puddle, like a red bib. From there the blood continued to run in a thin ribbon over the buttons and on toward the beautiful white wool that decorated the coat's hem. It was starting to look more brown than red now, Louey noted.

"Oh, thank you! Oh, God!" she said, and continued dabbing at herself, using tissue after tissue from the box while they quickly filled her prescription.

They don't want me passing out in their store, she figured. *They're getting me out of here as fast as they can. Well, good.*

The dry cleaner, a Korean fellow, didn't even touch the coat when she showed it to him a few days later. He just took a step backward and slowly shook his head. She drove straight to the collection bin at the homeless shelter on North Pearl Street. From that day on, Louey just wore her old quilted, puffy-nylon hiking jackets in the cold weather. They worked fine.

Part 3:
HEADING HOME

And then Joe Arnier retired.

He gave two months' notice, like a grownup.

The gang had time to plan a nice party for him at the restaurant next door to the office, during which Louey went to the women's room more than once to stand inside a stall and lean her head against the cool, grey metal door. There would be no more Joe to edit and critique her writing, joke with, brainstorm ideas with, go to lunch with, or defend her.

Arnier took the gag gifts—the boxes of prunes, the support stockings—with good humor, and then was asked to give a little speech. He was going to do some traveling and sailing with his family, he said, and do some writing on the history of the labor movement, and maybe even write his memoirs.

"So you guys who ticked me off better watch out," he said, "or you may end up in my memoirs!"

In the quiet of the restaurant's women's room, Louey had time to think.

People say you dwindle *into old age. They say you lose your abilities and creativity as you get older. But really, you don't lose your* abilities; *you just lose your* possibilities. *That's it: You're switching your possibilities out for your memories. As you attain great age, the list of your possibilities gets much shorter, but the list of your memories gets much longer. And you can always go back and review the memories you like best, while with possibilities, you don't know what the hell is gonna happen, so half the time, they just make you anxious. I've loved getting old, so far, and I hope I get even older.*

CSEU's statewide officers had already interviewed and hired Joe's successor, a local TV "news" personality who couldn't write his way out of a bubble of spit but who knew lots of TV "news" executives statewide. Weirdly, Joe hadn't been involved in the interviews for his successor at all. He wasn't even consulted, he said.

They'd invited the new guy to Joe's retirement party so he could meet the staff and feel more like "one of the gang." He was going to start, after all, the very next week.

It's not that Louey decided not to like him; he seemed like a perfectly amiable fellow. But it was at Joe's farewell party that she decided to quit. It had become too awkward for everyone, trying to be friends with both Luke and her. Most of the folks at CSEU liked both of them, and now they felt as if they had to take sides. Well, they didn't say that, but she knew it. It was especially awful for Bruce and Leslie, whom they previously had gone hiking with and had dinner with and watched TV and movies with when they could, and who both loved Rebecca and were close with her. But Louey really couldn't stand being in the same workplace with Luke anymore, sure that everyone was looking at her and feeling sorry for her and everything.

Leave CSEU, after all these years?

Well, yes. Yes, she would. It wasn't just Luke: She was getting stale in her job. She'd lately felt as if she could write her stories without even interviewing any staff members. It was all a formula:

Local [insert local's number] has won X percent across-the-board raises and Y additional days off, thanks to the hard work of CSEU Field Rep [insert field rep's full name] and the solidarity of the members.

"This great victory is due to the hard work of the officers and the bargaining team, who refused to give in," said [field rep's last name].

Or: *'This grievance victory is precedent-setting and will have positive repercussions statewide,' said [union lawyer's name].* She would always call the local president, or shop steward and member(s) whom the "victory" most affected, but that was the only real legwork she did. It got so that she often just obtained the main points of the grievance or arbitration decision or contract from the lawyers or field staff and made up comments from them. Then she would send her stories off to the members and to the staff she'd "quoted" along with a note humbly asking them to "fix" any errors she'd made or change the quotes in any way they wanted. Nine times out of ten, she got a call back from the CSEU staff and lawyers saying it was perfect, they loved it, put it on Page One. And, of course, the CSEU members and local officers who were quoted and so richly praised loved it, too. But there wasn't much of a challenge to it. It was all a formula.

It had happened that, the Sunday immediately preceding Joe Arnier's retirement, Louey saw an ad in the Knick News for a PR job with the New York Nurses Union. That's what really got her thinking.

NYNU! she thought. *I've heard of them: They're a great union!* It was amazing how much it sounded like the exact same job she had at CSEU, except she'd be working for nurses instead of public employees. The ad sounded as if it were written for her. And the pay and benefits—was that possible?—were even better than CSEU's.

She applied, and she got it.

Yay! A new job. Maybe my life is turning around.

NYNU was headquartered just outside Albany, several miles from the Capitol. It was an easy switch from the CSEU job she'd been growing stale in. Her nurses-union colleagues were sober, sweet women, idealistic and not a bit less successful or dedicated to helping their members than the gang at CSEU, but not at all as cynical and quite a bit less raucous. Louey's duties at NYNU were practically identical to those she had at CSEU. She wrote stories for their fifty-thousand circulation monthly, broadsheet-format newsletter, *Report*. Her stories were mostly about heroic union-member nurses or about excellent benefits or raises the union had negotiated. One big difference with this job was that Louey had no interaction with reporters anymore; her colleagues in the adjoining writing cubicles ("Communications Associates," they were both called) were assigned to write and follow up on news releases for papers and radio and TV stations around the state. One, Dino DiCenzo, specialized in handling labor-relations stories and hit the road often to walk picket lines with NYNU members. He was friends with a lot of the local presidents. The other, Sue Lawrence, edited the peer-reviewed journal that NYNU published, and handled the *Report*'s calendar and listings of upcoming events and continuing-education opportunities, as well.

NYNU's PR director was a slender, elegant, older woman—a widow named Sarah Wise. It was she who interviewed Louey first, and Louey had a good feeling about her right from the start. Calm and sophisticated, with a dry sense of humor, Sarah was a good writer, a good reader and a good editor. She'd had the final say in Louey's being hired, even though the union's executive director, Helga Sturm, had also had a chat with her. That talk was more a "welcome aboard" than an interview.

Sarah's few suggested changes to Louey's stories were well-reasoned, and she presented them to her as just that—suggestions, rather than diatribes. The whole department got together monthly in serious yet relaxed and collegial meetings to sketch out the stories that should be in the next issue of *The Report*, and also each Monday to fine-tune the plans for that week's work. Soon, Louey was contributing as many solid story ideas as anyone else.

Louey's work at NYNU drew praise from the nurses and strong reviews from her boss, and her colleagues on the Communications team were easygoing and friendly. She began to hang out during breaks, lunch hours, and even on weekends sometimes with one of them, an exceptionally smart and funny young woman who'd immigrated from southeastern England. Ali Werkman had a delightful accent, thanks to having grown up in the slightly down-in-the-heels, former holiday town of Margate-upon-the-Sea. She never failed to imitate how Louey pronounced the word "water" as WAW-der, and Louey could be relied upon to mock Ali's WHOA-teh as a thigh-slapper.

On days when Ali couldn't join her for lunch, Louey sometimes sat with a book at one of the long tables in the cafeteria, or, in nice weather, at one of the picnic tables in the courtyard. Occasionally Sue or Dino joined her there, and Louey chatted pleasantly with them about their union projects or music, politics or their families. If her Communications Department colleagues weren't there, sometimes a woman named Eileen, the assistant manager of the Member Services Department, and two others from that department, an excessively nosy woman named Pauline Something and an older Joanie Something, arrived together—always together—and shared Louey's table.

One day, Pauline noticed the little Jewish star hanging around Louey's neck.

"Oh, you're Jewish?" she chirped, busily pushing a salad around in the plastic bowl she'd brought to work. "You would love our pastor!"

This, of course, made no sense. Why would Louey, a Jew, love a Protestant minister? She was curious.

"I would? Why would I love him?"

"Oh, my God; he preaches about the Old Testament more than the New one! We call him 'the Rabbi!" Eileen said. Louey waved a finger from one to the other of them a couple of times.

"You mean you go to the same church?"

The ladies smiled and giggled and nodded vigorously.

"Oh wow, all three of you? What church?"

"Catskill United Methodist."

"You go to church way down there?"

"We *live* down there. It's not very far, really," Joanie said. "It's only half an hour from here, if traffic's good."

"Twenty-five minutes, for me," Pauline piped up. "I'm in Coxsackie."

Wow, they lived farther south of here than I do, Louey thought.

"Anyway, you should hear our pastor preach. He's always talking about how you can't understand the Bible unless you've read it in Hebrew," Eileen continued. "He can read ancient Hebrew, modern Hebrew, ancient Greek, modern Greek, Latin, French, Spanish ... you name it, he ..."

"And he preaches about how everybody translates the Bible wrong!" Joanie said, and they all nodded and laughed.

"Tell her about the songs he's got us singing!" Pauline said.

"Oh my God!" Eileen said. "You would love this guy! He's trying to teach us this song in Hebrew! Nobody can sing a word of it! It's got a pretty tune, but the words are in Hebrew! It's a riot; nobody can sing it!"

"What's the title, do you know?" Louey asked. Maybe she would know it.

The three looked back and forth among themselves, wincing and clicking their fingers and saying little words like, "Oh, uh, something about ... it's about ... spring or something, isn't it?"

"No, I think it's about, let's all be friends, or something like that. Do you know it?"

No. No, she didn't.

"Gee no; I don't think so," Louey confessed. "Can you remember the tune?"

They couldn't.

"I could if you got me started," Eileen said. "I just can't think of how it starts, though. It's so hard!"

"You should come to church with us sometime; you really should," Pauline said. "You'd love this pastor. He's so smart!"

Why would Louey love a smart guy again? Luke Qualesworth was smart. Smart guys were no better than regular guys. Anyway, she was glad to have an excuse at the ready that was actually the truth.

"Ah, Jeez; I'm all tied up on Sundays. I take my kid to Temple B'nai Shalom in Albany, and I teach ethics and Hebrew there myself, while she's in Sunday school. But thanks for the invite."

"Too bad. I'm tellin' ya; you'd love this guy!" Joanie said.

In the new apartment in Grevenna, despite receiving child and spousal support, Louey had a sickening fear of not being able to get by. From reading about the new occupation of "desktop publishing," she got the idea to set up her own little business at home. She already had a computer, and she thought she could produce fliers and newsletters for non-profits in her spare time, and make some extra money. She would need a laser printer, though. She checked out the price of one in the computer store in Albany. It cost more than her first car.

Maybe it'll take me farther than Fury did, though, she thought. She bought it on a Saturday when Rebecca was visiting Luke. She wrestled the 30-pound thing out of the trunk of her car (the salesman had put it there for her) and lugged it into her mercifully ground-floor apartment. She set it down atop the metal file cabinet next to her desk and cut the box away from it like a nurse cutting a cast off a patient's leg. It overhung the cabinet by an inch or so on each side, and its thick cord would have to be pushed aside every time you wanted to open one of the drawers. When Rebecca got home, she studied it for a few minutes and sighed, "Let's call it good."

Louey carefully followed the instructions and plugged it into her computer. She was proud and thrilled and grateful to God as she watched it spit out a crisp, clear test-page. A new career was born.

One reason for her optimism was the fact that she had a good idea who her first clients would be: the statewide CSEU officers who, she knew, were running for re-election. They all knew her and liked her writing. She had, after all, written dozens of glowing stories about the achievements of every one of them. She could produce fliers for mailings and stories to plant in the news media almost in her sleep. She called and wrote to each of them, asking to be their PR representative for the election season. And just like that, she was off and running. She did not hesitate to send out stories about all of the union's good grievance and arbitration results statewide, and to make up quotes from them that tended to imply that they themselves had something to do with those results, or at least were the first to "applaud" them.

Nearly as expensive as the laser printer and its toner cartridge was the page-layout software that made "desktop publishing" feasible. It meant you could be a kind of artist, with neither T-square nor eraser nor glue, nor even much creativity to speak of. You could center any headline, make it bigger or smaller, or change its font, with the click of a button, and then switch back just as easily. You could make it look as though your flier were painted with a paintbrush, or inked with a marker. You could switch entire paragraphs to other parts of a page, or put a nice rectangular outline around the whole thing, with the click of a button. You could change the whole flier—or any parts of it—to blue, or red, or any other color.

The software, called PageMaker, was new and very hard for her to learn. There was the constant switching out of "floppy disks," which weren't floppy at all, but hard, square, flat, plastic things like beer coasters. That switching was needed to accomplish even the simplest operation: Changing the font, saving something under a different name or switching the orientation of the pages all entailed new disks and lots of anxiety. But the instructions seemed to have been written by native English-speakers—a blessing that was becoming more and more rare—and by taking one step at a time and thanking God whenever anything seemed to go the way it was supposed to go, Louey learned the damned thing.

She could insert any number of "spot colors" in her fliers, but she never did learn how to produce, or reproduce, four-color photos in her work. No matter: No one asked for them. Ninety percent of CSEU's officers wanted only a good slogan on a letter-sized piece of paper that could be folded into thirds and mailed. Sometimes they wanted Louey to do folding, inserting and mailing for them; sometimes to save a few bucks, they had volunteers do that. Most often, though, Louey's clients didn't want their fliers folded at all—they just wanted to pin them to the bulletin boards at the public employees' offices.

The hardest part of all for Louey was creating address labels, which involved creating spreadsheets, something she'd never done before, and then somehow lining up the information on all those pages with the labels she had to buy, and making them print out on the labels, with no part of anyone's name or address overshooting the label. When that happened, then all the succeeding labels also printed off-kilter, and the whole expensive page of labels had to be re-done.

CSEU's statewide secretary, Irene, was the first person to contract with Louey. She wanted her to produce four issues of a four-page "newsletter" about how great the union was doing, and the statewide Women's Equity Division that she had just organized. Louey wrote the articles and, just as in her Checkout Princess days at the Record, lined up Page One and Page 4 side-by-side with Page One on the right, flip them over and cellophane-tape them together edge-to-edge. Then she'd do the same with Pages 2 and 3 (Page 3 on the right) and step outside their apartment to spray a light coat of clear fixative on the pages and waved them around slowly to help them dry. She had read that that fixative was highly toxic and shouldn't be breathed.

Then she would put a stiff piece of cardboard under them and bring them to a print shop. What happened after that depended on how much her client wanted to pay. Irene wanted Louey to deliver the newsletters to her folded in thirds and already stuffed into envelopes; she and her husband would stamp, seal and mail them.

It went well, and this side-gig of Louey's meant that she had enough money for rent, utilities, food, clothing, laundry and occasional treats for both herself and Rebecca.

Dear Diary,

Well, I am now batting a thousand, and what an advertisement for myself that is! All my clients won! Would they have won without my help? Well, of course! I saw a recent study that showed that a sitting member of the New York State Assembly has a greater chance of dying in office than of being voted out. I'm pretty sure it's the same with union officers. Incumbents have an almost insurmountable advantage: Every time something good happens, they either take credit for it or put out a news release saying they "applaud" it. Sales of Ben-Gay must explode in election years, with all the "applauding" that's done! But let us not dwell on that minor point. Let us celebrate!

After election season, in the spring, Louey sent out a mailing to all the statewide associations in the Albany County phonebook. That initiative generated a grand total of one client—a group called Biz Pros, headquartered in Albany, that represented small-business owners. They'd just recently organized so that they could get health insurance for themselves and their few employees at a reasonable rate. Louey produced an eight-page monthly newsletter for them for $1,000 a month. She wrote all the stories ("Spotlight on Joe's Fix-It," etc.), laid it out and delivered it to them to get it printed and mailed themselves. Biz Pros members liked Louey's writing and told the association that they looked forward to getting each issue. The staff invited her to their Christmas party at the end of the year and gave her an enormous wicker basket of fruit that also had nuts and foil-wrapped candies and tiny chocolate bars tucked around inside it.

Louey left the party earlier than almost everyone else, thanking everyone and wishing them happy holidays and noting that she had to get back to Grevenna to "beat the weather," as it was already starting to snow. The executive director insisted on walking her to her car and carrying her gift basket for her. Somewhere in their slippery driveway, he told Louey that his longtime secretary had had a baby and left, and this new woman, Pat, he'd hired happened to be an expert in PageMaker, so he was going to use Pat to produce their newsletters from now on.

In other words, Louey was fired. A bit bemused, Louey told him she'd enjoyed working with him and wished him the best of luck and said she'd always be available if the new person needed any help with anything.

Rebecca Qualesworth became a Daughter of the Commandments not as soon as possible after she turned 12, as most Jewish girls do, but almost a full year later, when the weekly Torah portion—the part Rebecca would have to chant in Hebrew—would be Numbers 12:1-14. It's the passage wherein Miriam and Aaron criticize Moses' wife because she was a black African. As a punishment, God turned Miriam "snow white." Rebecca wanted to talk about the delicious irony there. She also wanted to note that God did nothing to Aaron except yell at him, and she wanted to point out the unfairness of that. So it was June when Louey invited her brother, Danny, her stepbrother, Marc; their wives; her sister, Clare, and Clare's family; and all of Rebecca's friends to come to Temple B'Nai Sholom in Albany to hear Rebecca chant that Torah story and to hear her interpretation of it and her commentary on it, and then to enjoy a luncheon together afterward.

One of the people she invited to the Bat Mitzvah ceremony and luncheon was Rebecca's middle-school music teacher, a huge, lumbering bear of a man beloved by students and parents alike. Jimmy Britenstine, whom the kids all called Mr B, was not only a creative teacher and a fine choral conductor and accompanist, but also a prolific composer and performer of pop tunes and a serious fan of jazz, the Beatles and rock 'n' roll in general. Louey and he were constantly exchanging their favorite CDs with each other. She had met him through the school concerts she'd attended, where he'd installed Rebecca as leader of the alto section. Louey always went backstage to thank and congratulate Jimmy after the concerts. He and his wife, Judy, had two girls about Rebecca's age, one older and one younger. Rebecca had gone to their house in Catskill for sleepovers a few times, and Louey had hosted the Britenstine girls in her little apartment—sleeping bags on the living-room rug—as well. Jimmy and his family became great friends with Louey and Rebecca.

Dear Diary,

Jimmy's just like me. G-d should give people like us "frequent crier" points. We are pierced by the beauty of the world, as well as the sadness of it, and our joys and sorrows come spurting out of us because they overflow us as if we'd been stabbed in the heart with an ice pick. We can't help it. G-d forgives us. I hope. But I just find it so endearing in this burly goofball that he cries when he's thanked or recognized in any special way, as well as when he's sad.

With her share of the money from Abe Levy's life insurance, Louey bought Rebecca a portable electronic piano, five octaves long. She asked Mr. B who in their neck of the woods could teach Rebecca how to play it. He recommended a woman named Annette who lived just a few blocks from them in Grevenna. She played the organ in his church in Catskill and made extra money by giving private piano lessons. Louey called her immediately, and from then on, Rebecca had a "piano teacher on staff," as the student herself put it, and Louey had a new friend.

Never having been to a Bat Mitzvah ceremony before Rebecca Qualesworth's, Jimmy B was very moved by it all, and said so. He brought a white hanky, and used it to dab his eyes when the rabbi said that Rebecca's grandfather would have been so proud of her. But everybody was crying along with him, because they had known Abe Levy and how deeply he had loved his granddaughter.

Mr. B and Judy chatted with Louey over lunch in the synagogue's social hall afterwards as Rebecca ate and played with her pals. Over dessert, Jimmy mentioned that his church was putting on a farewell concert for their pastor the next day, and that as the church's music director, he was going to be MC-ing the event. Louey and Rebecca should come, he said. It was free, and there would be a chicken dinner afterward.

Sure, why not? What church was it? Where was it?

"Catskill United Methodist. CUMC! Right off 9W in

Catskill! Not fifteen minutes south of Grevenna. I'm so sorry you never got to meet our pastor. He's so Jewish! He's like, the most Jewish guy I've ever met. You would love him."

"Oh you have got to be kidding," Louey said. "Three women I work with at the nurses' union talk about him all the time!"

"Oh, Joanie Brown and Eileen Matuszak! That's right: They work for the nurses union!" Judy said, snapping her fingers in recognition. "They've been members of our church forever. And who's the other one?"

"Pauline something. I can't think of her last name. All three of them work in a different department from me, and I only see them at lunch."

"Pauline. Huh. I don't think I know a Pauline from church. Do you know a Pauline, who works for the Nurses Union, Jimmy?"

He did not.

"Anyway, they can't stop talking to me about your pastor," Louey said. "That's all they talk about: how smart he is, and what a character he is, and how 'Jewish' he is, and blah, blah, blah. And now he's leaving?"

"Yeah, he's being transfered to Long Island."

"Ow. Yikes. That's awful. What's his name, again?"

"Alfred Reece. Alfie, we call him," Jimmy said. "He's so smart it's unbelievable. You would totally love him. He preaches about the Old Testament so much, we think he's one of those secret Jews. What do they call them? Marranos! We call him 'the Rabbi!' And his wife is a sweetheart. They've been our best friends for, like, eight years." He lowered his head, and Louey was afraid he was going to cry as she pondered the coincidence.

Does everybody in the whole world go to that church? Did Christians make some kind of pact to prank me by saying they go to Catskill United Methodist when there's really no such place? Or is it real, and all human beings go there, except me and Rebecca? Do bishops sneak out of their cathedrals to hear this guy after they're done handing out the wine and crackers? Does Rabbi Karsten drive down there on Sundays, when B'Nai Shalom's Sunday School is over?

Louey agreed to go to the concert at Catskill because, why not? All her responsibilities from the Bat Mitzvah ceremony and party were over; she could relax and enjoy a little concert.

A free concert, and Jimmy B's directing it! In a church, no less! Cool.

Louey and Rebecca arrived at CUMC ten minutes early, only to find the pews already nearly filled up. There must have been two hundred people there, at least.

Why can't B'Nai Shalom ever have this many people in attendance? It looks like Yom Kippur in here! We should put on concerts. Our sanctuary is as big as this one, when they pull back the folding doors. What a good fundraiser that would be! Why don't we hold concerts?

They hesitated at the door to the sanctuary, and the greeter looked around dubiously for a pew that wasn't jam-packed. A lot of people were still standing around and talking with one another, which made it even harder to figure out where any empty spots might be.

"Come on; we'll find you a place!" the greeter said to Louey. "Are you two together?"

"Yes."

She handed Louey, but not Rebecca, a single program; they must have been running low. As they started slowly down the middle aisle, following the greeter, Eileen from NYNU happened to wrench around and see them. She was seated pretty close to the middle of the room.

"Louey! Hi! Come on! Sit here!" she mouthed, waving rapidly toward herself and pointing to the space next to her.

Rebecca and Louey squeezed in next to Eileen, glad to get seats. People were now standing in the back, and more folks were still streaming in.

"Thanks! This is my daughter, Rebecca."

"Hi, Rebecca; I'm Eileen."

"Man, if the fire marshal sees this, we're all under arrest," Louey said.

"I know; isn't this great?"

"Where's the pastor?" Rebecca asked, scanning the room.

"I don't know; he's around here somewhere," Eileen said. "I can't even find Joanie! Jimmy wanted to make sure he was seated in a pew like everybody else, but I think he's in the front row somewhere. He's not to speak, or stand up, or anything, Jimmy said. Just enjoy the concert. Poor Janet, Alf's wife, is downstairs helping get ready for the dinner we're having afterwards. Their kids were fighting, so they left them home with a sitter. Are you staying for the dinner?"

Louey had no desire to do that in this crowd; she could imagine how long the buffet line would be, or how long it would take to get served if it was a sit-down thing, and besides, she had a ton of great leftovers from the Bat Mitzvah party. She said she had planned dinner with her relatives, who were coming from out-of-town that night. And that would have been very close to true, in a world in which time didn't run in the constrained way it does in this one.

"I've got a brisket in the oven right now," she added for good measure.

"Are Joanie and Pauline here?" she asked.

"Yeah, somewhere. Good luck finding them, though, in this crowd!"

Louey couldn't see the front row from her vantage point, and didn't know what the pastor looked like anyway, so she gave up looking for him and settled back to review the program.

At that moment Jimmy B stepped up to the mic in the middle of the pulpit.

"Ladies and Gentlemen, thank you all for coming to this very special event! For anyone here who may not know, this is a concert that we've been planning for several weeks, to say farewell to Pastor Alfie and his family. Alfie has been here for eight years, and during that time, he has become my best friend, as well as my pastor and my spiritual adviser. But then, I'm sure everyone in this room feels the same way!"

Vigorous nodding and applause.

"Today, this concert is just for him. You're going to hear from all the musical groups we've put together over the years, thanks to Pastor Alf. And Alfie, aren't you glad? You don't have to give a sermon; you don't have to give a speech; you don't have to do anything, for once in your life, except sit back, relax and enjoy the show."

Louey looked over at the general direction in which Jimmy had aimed these remarks, but still couldn't figure out where the pastor was. She asked Eileen, but she didn't know exactly, either.

"Over there somewhere," she said, nodding toward the other side of the aisle and several rows ahead of them.

Jimmy said, "You're going to hear our men's choir; the women's choir; the mixed choir; the handbell chorus; the children's chorus; a special song I've written just for you, Pastor Alfie; and, let's see: If anyone wants to stand up and tell a few jokes, they're welcome to do that, too."

He continued: "But I want you all to know something. Last night I went to the first Bat Mitzvah ceremony I ever went to in my life, and I only hope our concert here today is half as moving as that ceremony was. A lot of us have put our hearts and souls into today's music, because it's for a man who means so much to all of us.

"So without further ado, let's get started!"

Jimmy sat down at the piano and accompanied many of the songs the people sang, while somehow directing the singers with hand signals at the same time. At the end of each song, when the applause had subsided, he turned to introduce the next group of performers. For several hymns, Annette played the organ, and she also accompanied the mixed chorus.

And then when they were all finished, he said, "All right, Alfie, if you're still awake, stand up and go to the middle of the aisle, there, because we've got something to say to you!"

This obviously was the grand finale that Jimmy had planned. Rebecca and Louey rose along with the entire congregation faced him as Jimmy played and they sang the Hebrew song, "Shalom, Chaverim," meaning, "Goodbye,

Friends." The entire song consists of just those five syllables, repeated over and over again. Well, there is one other word involved: "L'hitraot," which means, "Till we meet again." This was the song that Eileen, Pauline and Joanie found nearly impossible to learn. After the second verse (same as the first), the congregation repeated it one more time as a round, and Louey found it touching to hear these sweet, good-hearted Methodists goofing up the two words of their sincere farewell to their beloved pastor. Jimmy played the piano and sang with tears streaming down his cheeks into his beard, and Louey felt like crying, too.

Sentimentality will be my downfall, she thought.

Then she and Rebecca headed for the door, except they couldn't. Pastor Alf had made his way to the big sanctuary door and was standing at one side of it, while the people had formed a receiving line that Louey estimated to be approximately fourteen miles long.

This is gonna take 'til the Messiah comes, as Grampa used to say. Louey had no idea where Eileen had gone, but way over there was Annette, Rebecca's piano teacher! Louey caught her eye from pretty far away, but in the crush they could only smile and wave at each other.

Over the course of twenty minutes or more, Louey and Rebecca inched nearer to the door, and to the pastor they had never met. People were falling upon him and crying.

"We'll miss you!" they said. "I'll never forget how you did my mother's funeral!" "You baptized all our children!" "What will we do without you?"

Louey looked at her watch, stifled a yawn, and performed a big, slow eye-roll for Rebecca's benefit.

"Mom! Stop! We're almost there!" the kid scolded.

And then they were there, and Louey had to do her best imitation of a grownup. She and Alfred Reece shook hands, and as they did so, Louey smiled and said, "Pastor, I'm Louey Levy, and this is my daughter, Rebecca. We're friends of Jimmy B's. You know how he said he went to a Bat Mitzvah ceremony yesterday? Well, Rebecca's the Bat Mitzvah!"

He seemed genuinely delighted. "Oh, mazel tov!" he said, dusting off his conversational Hebrew. "*Mah shlomay-ach?*"

"*Tov me-od, todah,*" Rebecca replied, and they were off, jabbering away in elementary Hebrew way too fast for Louey to understand. Finally, she interjected, "I heard you're being sent to Long Island. I'm sure you'll love it down there! It's beautiful down there!"

This was one of the bigger lies she had ever told in her life. Who would love Long Island? She'd been there for union rallies. Horrendous traffic; inescapable crowds of pushy, snobbish people with obnoxious, nasal voices; waves of broken glass, used condoms and dead jellyfish on their vaunted beaches.

"But your congregants obviously love you so much: They put on a beautiful concert for you, and we're just so glad Jimmy invited us!"

There, that wasn't bad.

"I'm glad you were able to come."

"So are we! Well, take care, and enjoy your new home!"

"Well, that was lame," she said to Rebecca on their way home. "Not the concert, I mean—what I said to the pastor."

"Mom. You did fine," Rebecca said. "Don't worry about it."

Three months later, the phone rang at Louey's desk at the office. It was around lunchtime. It was Jimmy B, calling from school.

You could tell from his voice that he was crying.

"Louey, Janet's dead!"

"Oh no! Janet's dead?!"

Two seconds elapsed, as Jimmy sobbed.

"Oh my God; that's awful!"

Two more seconds elapsed before Louey added in a whisper:

"Who's Janet?"

"The pastor's wife!" Jimmy said. "You met her at the concert, remember? The farewell concert that we had for Pastor Alfie! Didn't you meet his wife there?"

She hadn't. Janet had been in the kitchen the whole time, helping prepare the chicken supper. She never met Janet.

"No. What happened? How old was Janet?"

"Forty."

"How old are their kids?"

"Twelve and ten."

"Oh my God. What happened?"

Reader, this is how God treats His friends:

Janet Reece was from a tiny, isolated farming village in the Catskill Mountains, where Alf, as a young pastor, had been assigned to his first church. It was at church, in fact, that Janet and Alf met and fell in love. She started worshiping in a town five miles away, as it would have been considered a scandal for a pastor to court one of his own parishioners. Janet never wanted to move to the little city of Catskill, much less Long Island, Jimmy said.

The thing she dreaded most about Long Island was the traffic. She had learned to drive on a tractor, and went to nursing school in an upstate county where, if you saw a car coming in the opposite direction, or if a car passed you, you smiled and waved, as chances were pretty good that you knew the driver.

Her father had died during her first year in college, but that had only made her closer with her mother and her brother and sister, who were all still living on the farm. She, Alf and the boys visited her family often.

And now, she was to move to the most crowded, traffic-riddled, speed-obsessed, fast-paced place in the state, more than two hundred miles from her home. And you had to drive through New York City and over its bridges to get there? But she knew what she was getting into by marrying a Methodist pastor, and as a good Methodist pastor's wife, she told their two sons, as well as herself, that moving every few years was all part of the fun. So when the Bishop had said to go, off to Long Island the Reeces went.

Shortly after they'd settled into their new parsonage, Janet was disturbed to find that Alf's Long Island church had no programs for kids. No youth group, no special events—nothing that would spark their love of God or offer them a chance to help their neighbors. She produced and handed out fliers, and rose during "announcements time" each Sunday to speak about that sad situation, to see if there was any interest in starting such a group.

There was. Janet arranged for an organizational meeting on a weeknight. Alf and the other parents met in one room for coffee and discussion while she met downstairs with the kids for brainstorming on what kinds of things they'd like to do together: Trips? Community cleanups? Bike rides? Helping Habitat for Humanity paint houses? Olympics-type field days? Visits to old folks' homes or pediatrics wards to perform magic tricks, or sing, or dance or tell jokes? Oh, she had a million ideas and wanted to hear theirs.

She had called a nearby pizza place and ordered several pizzas and bottles of soda that she would pick up at a certain time, near the end of the evening. She asked her son Sam, then 10, to come with her to help her carry the food while another lady stayed with the kids. The pizza parlor was less than five minutes away. It was already dark, and she turned the car's lights on. And then she started to turn left out of the church's driveway, and a drunken motorcyclist was speeding along the street, and that was the end of her. Sam, miraculously, was OK.

"Jimmy, do you and Judy want to go down to Long Island to take care of Alf? The girls can stay at our place. We have a sofa-bed and sleeping bags."

"Thanks, we might do that. I can't believe this happened. I just can't believe it."

"I can't believe it either."

When Rebecca got home from school, Louey told her the news. Like her mother, Rebecca had never met Janet Reece, but the thought of the two boys, both about her own age, having to go on without a mother, jolted and sickened her. She went into her room to do her homework as always, but emerged a few minutes later.

"Mom, why don't we plant two trees in Israel in memory of Janet?" she said.

They did that. The Jewish National Fund had been set up for just that reason. It was happy to take their check for two "memorial trees"—one nominally from Louey, one from Rebecca. A month or so later, Pastor Reece received a form letter saying that two trees had been planted in memory of Janet Reece by a Louey Levy and a Rebecca Qualesworth, giving their address in Grevenna.

Those names did not ring a bell with Alfred Reece. He later confessed that he'd said to himself, "Levy and Qualesworth; Levy and Qualesworth. I thought it was a Lesbian law firm." He had been receiving hundreds of sympathy cards, some with money inside. He was trying to respond to each one, a few at a time, but this card from the JNF intrigued him. Clearly, these were people who knew how much Israel and the Jewish people meant to him. He had a friend up in Grevenna—the CUMC organist, Annette.

A little while later, Louey was sitting at her computer when a message popped up on her screen via her AOL Messenger service.

"Hello, I'm Pastor Alf Reece and I want to thank you and your daughter for having two trees planted in Israel in memory of Janet. The reforestation of (here he had somehow switched to the Hebrew alphabet and had typed out words meaning "the land of Israel") is a (here he had typed the Hebrew word for "blessing") that means a lot to me. Thanks again, Alf Reece."

Louey was very impressed by this guy's ability to switch to Hebrew in the midst of an electronic message. In a million years, she wouldn't be able to figure out how to do that. She wrote back and hit "send."

"Pastor Alf, how are you and your sons doing?" she wrote. "My heart goes out to you. My own mother died when I was nine, and I know it sounds hollow, but I mean it when I say that if either of your boys ever wants to talk to someone about what happened, PLEASE tell them they can call me any time at … ," and she added her phone number. This is exactly what happened next: He wrote back to Louey; Louey wrote back to him; he wrote back to her; she wrote back to him. This went on and on and on and he seemed to find her notes cheering, which in turn cheered her. They corresponded using these computer messages nearly every day, and often several times a day, and then more and more often. His notes were funny and smart and touching and filled with Hebrew that she sometimes needed Rebecca to translate. He gave her his cellphone number and they enjoyed long phone calls, as well. When Passover rolled around the following spring, she invited him and his boys to celebrate with her and Rebecca and some of their other friends in Grevenna. He leapt at the chance, and everyone enjoyed the food, the singing and the silliness. From that moment forth, the Levys and Reeces never failed to celebrate Passover together.

Over the next couple of years, Alfie Reece made the hundred and seventy-mile trip each way from Smithtown to Grevenna more and more often—every time he could break away from his congregation, and every time he could find someone to watch his sons.

They started doing stuff together. The good pastor had never done any hiking; his only footwear was nice, lace-up dress shoes—one pair black, and one brown—and a pair of rundown loafers. Louey, however, knew she could work with that. She told him he needed a pair of hiking boots, and he bought a pair. She told him he needed to buy hiking poles, and he did so. Then he told her he had a bad knee.

This was a real test. She told him he needed to get it fixed. He did that too, undergoing surgery and enduring a prolonged, painful rehabilitation. He did it in winter, so that it would be rehabilitated by the following spring.

Meanwhile, every talent Louey discovered in Alf—and there were many—delighted her, but the best of them all was his music. Alf Reece was a good musician. He could improvise on Rebecca's little electric piano sweet tunes of all kinds, and he had a soulful, big voice that belied his small stature. He could play and sing dozens of hymns by heart, but he also could read music as easily as Louey could read words on a page. This gave her the idea to ask him to play some of the classic rock songs that she loved so well. He knew none of them.

She asked him to play some of the great "American Song Book" songs by Sinatra, Ella Fitzgerald and Cole Porter that she loved so well. He knew none of them.

Alfie was the child of a pastor and a church musician; his mother was a Julliard graduate who, all her adult life, had played the organ in her husband's churches and others, and she had taught Alf to play the piano like Mozart, when he was just a tot. But he had never learned a thing about popular music.

Louey decided that she could work with this. She attacked her new project enthusiastically. She made sure that he heard plenty of pop and rock songs at her place, and it was clear from his comments and questions that he appreciated and respected both the writing and the playing on a lot of them. She bought him folk and blues songbooks and songbooks of the tunes of the 1960s, and he played them all well on Rebecca's little piano, as well as on his own upright piano in Long Island. She also made sure to bring along her "oldies" and her Dylan CDs when they were driving together. In this way, Alfie Reece's musical education progressed rapidly.

At some point they both realized that they were going to get married. They didn't know how or when or where, but they knew it was going to happen.

Reader, I hope that this little tale hasn't bored you and that, if it has, at least it has made up in brevity what it lacked in excitement. But Louey and Alfie's real love story was to continue forever, and they both knew it.

They would move in together—somewhere—only after Rebecca graduated, of course. Alf's older son, Jon, would start college two years after Rebecca, at which point the younger son, Sam, would be entering his junior year at Smithtown High. So, Alf and Louey were planning on having a "commuter marriage" for a while. Louey didn't mind the thought of it at all. There was no way she'd make Alf's sons move to a different school district: Her own family had moved once when she was supposed to be going into ninth grade, and it hadn't worked out well.

Meanwhile, they began the delightful task of thinking about where they could rent—or buy—a place together. It would be a place where Louey could live after Rebecca's graduation, and where Alf would join her after his own kids left home. It would be somewhere between Grevenna and Smithtown—some place that wouldn't be too hard for Louey to commute to work from. Louey was sure she could get a job doing public relations or fundraising for some nonprofit just about anywhere, but she adamantly ruled out moving to Long Island. Besides, she loved her job at NYNU, and wanted to keep working there. Alf couldn't leave Long Island until the Bishop transfered him again—but, the Methodist system being what it was, he wouldn't have to wait long. Alfie was very familiar with the needs, the history and the politics of the Methodist church, and he knew that wherever his next assignment was, it would be upstate, much closer to Louey. So, the only question now was: Where could they find a little love-nest—an apartment, or maybe even a condominium— that was something like halfway between Grevenna and Smithtown, so they wouldn't have so far to travel to see each other? Hmmm … Louey was thinking, somewhere in Ulster County, maybe, or across the river in Dutchess? She knew nothing about Putnam, but she could investigate. She didn't like Westchester, because of the stereotypes she held about the snooty rich people there. Also, that would be too long a commute for her. She hated driving in Westchester.

She removed all her maps of New York State from her car and pored over each one. Some places would be too far for him to drive; some, too far for her. Every stupid county between Albany and Suffolk had problems. Some were too expensive; some were too conservative. When she checked the local papers, she found that several charming little villages had no affordable apartments for rent that were big enough for them, for Louey needed a room to write in. The maps became a huge, wrinkled mass, like the fitted sheets she could never fold. She and Rebecca had to lift their knees high to step over them. And then:

"What about your old hometown of Newburgh?" Alfie said.

They bought a hundred-and-ten-year-old clapboard house on Bayview Terrace. It stood at the top of a cliff in Newburgh, at the bottom of which flowed the mighty Hudson. The minute she saw it, Louey felt that it had been waiting for her all the years since the Levys had moved away. It was, in classic real-estate jargon, "a real fixer-upper." But they had two years before Rebecca would graduate. That would give them plenty of time to "fix it up," starting with ripping off three courses of shingles from the old roof and installing a new one. They would rent it out for a couple of years, and after Rebecca graduated, they'd move in. Or at least Louey would: She wouldn't mind commuting the ninety miles each way to her job. Her father had made that commute every working day for years, and she would now be following in his tire tracks. She actually liked the idea.

But Alfie would have to stay with his congregation in Long Island until the Bishop sent him elsewhere.

Newburgh was not the same city she had grown up in—it had suffered from decades of unrelenting bad management, leading to serial plagues of abandoned buildings, drugs and violence.

Nothing that can't be fixed, she told herself. The city had some great new strengths, as well. Half the people were speaking Spanish now, instead of English! Bodegas, gas stations, check-cashing businesses, pawnshops, grocery stores, laundromats and restaurants flew the flags of Honduras, El

Salvador, Puerto Rico, Peru, Guatemala and, most frequent-ly, Mexico. Bonus: Louey was taller than all the Spanish-speaking women, and most of the men! The people she was not taller than were Black. Most of the white people had fled starting in the harrowing 1970s and 80s, including her own brother and his family, who had absconded to Florida. Oh, well: Now she could learn Spanish!

And she would figure out what the hell had happened to her poor dear city, and she would fix it.

From the little curved promontory on which Bayview Terrace stood, you could look eastward over one of the broadest expanses of the Hudson, and take in the scene that adorns the New York State seal: Mount Beacon, South Beacon Mountain and the Hudson Highlands. You could also look due south, at Bannerman's Island with its ruined castle in the middle of the river, and beyond to the long grey walls of West Point. Just there the river takes a sharp east-ward bend, and West Point's acreage juts so far out that from Newburgh it looks as if that vaunted military academy forms merely the southern shore of a huge lake. You couldn't see north at all from their little house; the buildings on the next block got in the way. But there was nothing worth seeing north of them anyway—just the Newburgh-Beacon Bridge and, beyond that, Poughkeepsie.

Their "Little House on the Promontory," despite its age and its quirks, was special to them to begin with, and grew dearer to them every day. It was "a real fixer-upper," but it was theirs.

Louey began spending a lot of her weekends driving between Grevenna and Newburgh, repairing, painting, mowing, meeting the neighbors, hauling ladders, paint cans, brushes, rollers and turpentine to the basement and dealing with banks, tax collectors, plumbers and electricians. It was an exciting, fun time for her, filled with imaginings and possibilities. It also brought a regret: She had to quit her volunteer work with Upper Hudson Planned Parenthood, because her Saturdays were now fully booked. They threw her a nice party on her last day, with cake and ice cream and balloons and lots of gag gifts alluding to the long commute to work she'd have every day, when she moved to Newburgh. They gave her dozens of old rock 'n' roll cassette tapes to keep her awake while driving. What great, dedicated people they were! She would miss them.

Rebecca sometimes accompanied Louey on her jaunts to Newburgh, though sometimes she preferred to spend her weekends in Grevenna at a friend's house.

Alfie still needed to be in Long Island with his congregation from Saturday through Thursday each week; he got only Fridays off. But sometimes he could escape to Newburgh early, especially since his congregation had bought him a cellphone for work, so that they could always be in touch with him. On his commutes to Newburgh, he laid it on the passenger seat, put it on "speaker phone," and talked to a parishioner or his district superintendent or his bishop as he drove. Each time he left Long Island, he had to get a babysitter for his sons, even though they were now teenagers. And when he did come to Newburgh, he usually had to leave right after lunch each Saturday, so he'd have time to prepare his sermon.

The good pastor insisted on cooking Sabbath dinners for Louey, and she was delighted to discover in him another great talent: Alf was a top-notch, adventurous and enthusiastic chef. The refrigerator and gas stove were working now, and Louey had brought a few pots, pans, plates, mugs and utensils from Grevenna. He would tell her to just sit—on the kitchen floor, as they had no chairs or table yet—and talk to him while he whipped up and served three-course meals that they would eat on a picnic blanket spread out on their front porch. Alf seriously believed that no meal was adequate without at least three courses and a good wine.

She offered to cook, but he insisted.

"What flavors are you interested in for dinner tonight?" he asked at his first foray into the kitchen.

The question confused her. No one had ever asked her that before.

"What do you mean?"

"Well, I mean, are you in the mood for Indian? Thai? French? Russian? German? Italian?"

Stop right there.

"Italian!" she said.

"And do you prefer northern Italian, or southern Italian?"

Note to self: Marry this guy.

Louey and Alfie actually had known for a long time that they would marry, but neither of them could ever recall when they first knew it. Maybe forever.

This is a good man, she knew. *This is one who'll stick with me, in sickness and in health, in craziness and in sanity,* she knew.

Alfie had already stuck with her in the only bit of sickness that hit her. One day she had a minor outpatient procedure at Albany Med. It involved anesthesia. Anesthesia—she didn't know it at the time—made her sick to her stomach, and it also had the amusing side effect of making her lose her short-term memory. The procedure was scheduled well in advance, for a Friday when Rebecca's dad was to bring her to his house for the weekend. Here Louey Levy was, well into her 40s, still having her periods. (... *as I will for my entire life,* she wrote bitterly in her diary. *This is G-d's way of getting back at me for not liking to be a girlie-girl. I'll have these horrendous freaking periods 'til I'm 80. I might as well call the Guinness Book of World Records now, to reserve my place in it.*)

Anyway, her menstrual flow lately had been coming out kind of weird; instead of a fluid, it looked like little chunks of liver. When she consulted her gynecologist about it he said she should have, that very week, a new thing called a uterine ablation, which he jocularly described as "having your uterus poached." It would take only a half hour, 20 minutes of which would be the filling-out-of-forms part and the kicking-in-of-the anesthesia part. But she would not be released from Albany Med, he said, unless someone was there to drive her home, because the anesthesia made even normal people "loopy." When she told Alf about this upcoming adventure, he instantly said, "I'll come and get you," and then spent the next two days arranging for his sons to stay at other people's houses that weekend, lining up a guest preacher at his church and rescheduling meetings with three congregants; one committee of his lay people; a Long Island interfaith group; his Bible-study group (which it would be his turn to lead); his District Superintendent; a commission of the Northeastern

Jurisdiction of his denomination; and his bishop.

And he did come and get her.

On their way home from the hospital, Louey was starting to feel sick to her stomach. Just as they were approaching the turnoff to the Thruway, she said, "Honey, could you please do me a favor? Could you take 9W instead of the Thruway to Grevenna? And go, like, real slow?" She knew he didn't like stupid two-lane roads, and she knew he didn't like to go, like, real slow.

"Sure," he said, swerving sharply back onto the road and turning his blinker off.

She lowered her window and turned her face to the fresh air.

"And could you stop at that gas station that's right there, and get me a Coke? I'm feeling a little sick."

"Sure," he said, swerving into the gas station's parking area. "I need to get gas, anyway."

He was back in a jiffy with a can of Coke, and a Dr. Pepper for himself. Then he pulled up to a pump and filled up the car, while Louey slowly sipped her soda. When they got home she couldn't remember how they had gotten there, or what day it was or why Rebecca wasn't there, and that made her panicky, thinking she was going crazy (crazier than usual). The anesthesia must have had a weird effect on her brain. Alf calmly coaxed her to try to remember by giving her hints, and slowly she started to remember everything, and then he put her to bed and sat beside her, reading her a book of Hebrew poetry by Yehuda Amichai until she fell asleep.

The next day he went on a hike with her, even though he had a bad knee. That's love.

Also love was when he went through an actual operation on that knee, knowing how important hiking was to her. It turned out to be a more difficult surgery than advertised, but with physical therapy he healed well, if not terribly quickly. As they picked their way over rocks and roots and sloshed through streams in the Catskills, Alf often bounced sermon ideas off Louey, and they saw that their spirituality was deeply the same—that is, the ways in which they knew and experienced God, if not the buildings in which they worshiped. Alfie had a whole casserole of languages that he read, wrote and spoke, and he explained at length and frequently how Christians had mistranslated the Tanach in sometimes fundamental ways. Alf was the most Jewish man she'd ever met, which was one reason why she loved him.

As they sat on a log by a waterfall near Indian Head Mountain one day, waving at mosquitoes and noshing on nuts, raisins and chocolate bits, she asked why he continued to study languages, so long after college. He was currently learning Korean.

"Being able to communicate with as many people as possible is a way to honor haShem, don't you think?" he replied. "God created all these different people and cultures and languages; the least we can do is get to know them a little."

They resumed climbing and reached a junction where Louey consulted her map. "Whoa, this unmarked trail isn't even on the map! It looks a lot straighter than the trail we're on," she said, "but I doubt it's easier. I doubt it." As she concentrated, using her compass and trail directions from the New York-New Jersey Trail Conference, Alf launched into a discourse on the letter "b."

"Do you know where the 'b' comes from, in 'doubt?'" he asked.

"No," she said curtly. She bent her face so close to the map, to discern its contour lines, that her nose almost touched it. Alfie decided to make good use of the silence.

"Well, there's no 'b' in the French word for 'doubt'; it's just, 'douter,'" he said. "But French is descended from Latin, and Latin has 'doubt' as 'dubitare,' which gives us, for example, our word 'dubious.' So if we got our 'doubt' from the French, and therefore don't pronounce that 'b,' then who put the 'b' back into the spelling of it, and when? And why? I suspect it's because European classical scholars at some point wanted to go back to the Latin origins of words. What do you think?"

Louey nodded and made the mm-hm sound, but would not have cared if 'doubt' were spelled with an "l" or a "z." She wanted only to find the right path, and she found it.

Newburgh was where Louey discovered that her beau had distinct ideas about menus. Every dinner, according to him, had to have a "theme." Alf's Italian-themed dinners always featured homemade pasta as a first course, and a green salad for dessert. Louey's idea of a good dessert was a brownie sundae, but she could adjust.

During their "Year of Fixing the Place Up," Alf and Louey had sweet Sabbath dinners in Newburgh with wine in their mugs and candles stuck into the tops of old wine bottles, as one might find in a college dorm. Yet here they were, middle-aged. In fact, more than middle-aged: Is your 50s still your middle age?

Alf always said the blessings along with her, which gave him a chance to show off his perfect Hebrew. He joined her in the kiddush before clinking their mugs, and he also never failed to say the Hebrew prayer over the freshly baked loaf of bread that they then ripped apart like a wishbone. He never asked that they say a Christian "grace" at all, though she would have been happy to do that.

Later, they found in the basement at Bayview an odd, wheeled contraption that the previous owners had left in the house, and they shlepped it upstairs and set places for meals on that. She was sure it was made of medium-density fiberboard, because of how enormously heavy it was. Neither of them could figure out what it could possibly have been used for. They couldn't even decide if their "table" was solid or hollow. Because of its weight, Alf thought it was one solid piece. Louey guessed hollow and proposed that a heavy treasure of some kind must be secreted inside it. But there were no hinges, and the thing didn't rattle. In shape it resembled a coffin much more than a table. It was a white-painted wooden box on casters. Louey by then had brought two folding chairs from Grevenna, but there was no room for their legs under the white monstrosity, so they had to sit oddly far apart across the "table" from each other in the candlelight. Luckily their "table" was on four casters, so that they could shove it around the bare floor. That meant they could stand on it as they painted and plastered and patched the walls, until Louey liberated a stepladder she found in the basement of her building in Grevenna.

In his old age, Louey's father had often remarked that he'd lived his entire adult life in cities on the Hudson, and yet had never had a view of the river. Louey felt that by buying the place on Bayview Terrace, she had somehow rectified that for him, and that as she and Alf fixed the place up, he was smiling and nodding his approval.

Alf himself smiled and nodded his own approval most enthusiastically when Louey proposed that they should have, as a joint goal, to make love in every single room of the house on Bayview, including the musty, cold basement and the brutally hot attic.

"We'll have to get started on that project immediately" he responded. "Because in this mansion there are many rooms."

"Yes, and life is very short," Louey added.

Though their usual rendezvous locale was Newburgh, Louey occasionally visited Alf and his boys in Long Island. On the weekends when Rebecca was visiting her father, Louey sometimes drove down to Newburgh only to park her car in front of the house on Bayview, walk across the bridge to Beacon and take the Metro-North train to New York. From there she would walk across town from Grand Central to Penn Station and get a Long Island Railroad train to Smithtown, transferring at Huntington. It was a long, varied trip, filled with different people and sights and events each time. Into her backpack she stuffed a nice outfit and shoes, pantyhose and earrings for these journeys each time, so that she would look nice at church, where Alf soon began introducing her to his congregants as his "fiancée." That startled and amused her a bit: She had never been referred to as anyone's "fiancée" before. Luke had just called her his "friend," which is what she had called him, too.

Alf's sermons often emphasized Jesus's Jewish faith or

pointed out how the English translations did not convey the humor or the poetry of the Old Testament Hebrew. Louey was gratified to learn, not just from his current parishioners but also from the reports of his congregants back in Catskill and her own conversations with him, that those sermons were not delivered just because she was there; they were central to his theology.

Especially, she loved the music. Those Methodists can sing. She was startled and delighted by the song, "Just a Closer Walk with Thee," which sounded to her exactly like "Release Me," by Eddie Miller, James Pebworth and Robert Yount. "I am weak, but Thou art strong," the hymn started; "Jesus, keep me from all wrong." Often after church, Louey would improvise, using the same tune but the country song's words: "To waste a life would be a sin; / Release me, and let me love again." On her way back to Beacon on the Hudson River Line after one particular visit, as she gazed through the window at the sunset over the Hudson, it dawned on her that that's what she was doing—she was loving again. Alf knew better than she had let herself know how much Newburgh was missing from her life. He was the one who'd brought her home. He knew her and he loved her anyway, and he accommodated her eccentric need to return to the dear little city of her youth. Plus, despite the poor reputation it had earned over the decades since the Levys had moved away, he would accompany her there. That was real love.

She kept humming her made-up country hymn, with those mashed-up words, over and over in her head on the train, all the way home. She knew now that the ties were broken that had bound her fate to Luke Q's, and that she had done the right thing by joining her life to Alf's. She felt healed. She felt calm. She felt happy.

On the weekends when Rebecca wasn't with Luke, Louey hung out in Grevenna so she could do fun stuff with her daughter. Packing for the move to Newburgh did not count as fun stuff. Instead, they did birdwatching or roll-erblading, or went hiking in the Catskills. They pedaled up and down Albany's new bike path or took off for bike-riding adventures in weird, rural areas around the state. Their bikes lay awkwardly on top of each other, pedals tangled in spokes, rubbing grease into the back seat, but they didn't care. Their helmets, backpacks, lunches, snacks and water bottles rolled around in the trunk. Wherever they went, Louey always brought her camera, and they took photos of the scenery and of each other. Rebecca especially liked examining the frogs and toads they came across in and around any streams and lakes they might pass. She would squat down in any kind of muck to get a closer look at them.

Louey always tried to find routes that, for at least part of the way, bordered lakes or streams, or the Hudson itself. As they pedaled near a vernal pond one early spring day, Louey, in the lead, heard what she thought was a large group of ducks quacking, but didn't see any. She called back over her shoulder, "Do you hear those ducks? Where the hell are those ducks?"

It wasn't ducks.

The teenager had already pulled over, dismounted and tip-toed up to the pond's soggy edges, getting her sneaks and the bottoms of her socks thoroughly wet.

"Oh, hello, little one!" she said pleasantly to a small, warty something. "What are you up to today, hmm?"

As Louey came closer, Rebecca whispered excitedly, "Look! A little wood frog! Aren't they cute? They sound just like ducks, this time of year!"

"Where?" Louey said. She didn't see any damned frog.

Rebecca pointed a stick at it. It was mottled brown and tan, with a black part around its eyes. It had dived partly under some leaves and was quite hard to see. But finally Louey saw it.

"Oh, cool! Wood frogs? Never heard of those. You sure it's not a bullfrog?"

"Mom." Rebecca gave her an exasperated look. "Bullfrogs are much bigger! Bullfrogs are huge! And they don't sound like little bitty ducks. You know what bullfrogs sound like: They go, "Glunk, glunk! You know—like the song!"

"Glunk, glunk, said the little green frog one day ..." Louey sang in her off-key voice.

"Shush!" her daughter commanded. They spent a few more minutes engrossed in their amphibian. The leaf moved as if it were a blanket and the frog, under it, a squirmy kid. Louey tried to grab it right through the leaf, but it shot away into the pond.

"Oh, don't! Don't touch them," Rebecca said, *post facto*. "Why would you do that? They've got all kinds of bacteria and parasites on them, and then you'd get it all over your hands! And anyway, it stresses them out, to be picked up! How would you like it if a big giant reached down from the sky and lifted you up a hundred times your height?"

"Oh for Chrissake, Jane Goodall, give it a rest, would ya? How do you know so much about wood frogs, anyway?"

They got back on their bikes and Rebecca said, "We froze one in Science."

Dear Diary,

Rebecca, with no help at all, is growing into a strong, beautiful woman. She's a really talented singer, but she's even a better writer than singer. Sometimes for school and sometimes just to amuse her friends, she writes funny skits and stories. She loves languages and does spot-on imitations of accents from around the country and around the world. Most of all, she loves the natural world and all its creatures and features. Everything from the stars to the starfish, from the seas to the seahorses, from the deserts to the forests and from the oceans to the puddles, fascinates Rebecca Qualesworth. She knows her gneiss from her schist. If she's a bit of a "science nerd," she's a particularly funny and friendly one. Energetic and kind, a loyal friend and terribly tuned in to the feelings of others, she's far too sensitive to the beauty, brevity and injustices of life. And now, guess what: She got accepted by her first-choice college, in New York City! That's just a little over an hour south of Newburgh, by car or train. So, she'll be a totally reasonable distance from me, and yet a world away. OK, well, this is going to be good. This will be fantastic. Every night, I look through the course catalogue Barnard sent Rebecca. I want to take every course they offer! "Race, Science and Reproductive Justice!" "Imagination's Role in Memory and Vice-Versa!" G-d, I want to take every one of them! But, how cool it's gonna be for Rebecca to be a strong, beautiful woman in New York City! And I'll be good with it. I really will. I won't be lonely, or worried about my little roommate, or anything. I won't miss her at all. I'll just be happy for her, and cheering for her.

I do, however, feel a poem coming on.

Turn and Go: To a Daughter Headed for College

For just a few seasons—it didn't seem long—
I had a girl who could sing a song.
Now just some cold, then one summer more,
and off she'll go to write the score
of a life original, bold and free
(a life to be lived without me. Can it be?)

A season of petals, a season of sun,
a season together, and then we're done.
The crisp, red leaves and then the snow:
Just one more year, and off she'll go.
The leavings that our lives are made of
leave us stronger, so they say.
Child, there are only two great stories,
and one is the story of going away.

She learned to sing, she learned to write,
but an empty swing was her favorite sight.
Up in the air, 'til she thought she could fly,
up in the air so high:
And then after seeing what she could see,
she'd always come back down to me.
And now she's grown. I should have known;
my dancer with the days has flown.

There are times we glide right over,
and moments our lives emboss.
Child, of the two great stories,
one of them is the story of loss.

She made us laugh, she learned to swim;
she held the hands of me and him.
But not together, not for long:
We learned to sing a different song.

In April, we walked her past puddles.
"One, two, three: Swing the baby!" we'd all-together cry.
We held her hands in ours, he and I.
And launched her ahead of us, tugging each our own way.
He knew that soon he'd have to say
the time had come to separate us.
How cruelly, now, the seasons date us.

Child, you were just six when the thing we were building
(And we didn't know what it was—you're not supposed
to know.
You're just supposed to take care of it. You find out when
it's all done,
what it is) fell apart.
On you and your six-year-old heart.
Off your father went with another; your mother
and you stayed behind 'til she could stand it no longer.
Then we left, too. Was it you who said I'd find another?
And that you would always have a father?
Well, don't bother to remind me; you were right.

Leavings are a blessing, as well as a blight.

Comic, mimic, mediator,
blood-pressure elevator,
muse, musician, truth-teller,
Hobbit, sculptor, candy-seller,
story-writer, wreath-maker,
pianist and heart-breaker,
joker, jumper, jogger, biker,
gift-giver, mountain-hiker,
poker-player, Hebrew teacher,
tutor, poet, prophet, preacher,
Buddhist, Hindu, Christian, Jew,
I will miss all these in you.
But when the ice becomes the water,
turn and see: You're still my daughter.

So goodbye, my Someone. If parting can be
between two such as you and me,
then I wish I may and I wish I might
have the strength to do it right.

Too many years too soon have passed!
What now to say, what wisdom fast
for you to weave into your song
and take away and hold for long?

The simple song is still the truest;
the angels sing it from above:
Child, there are only two great stories,

and the greater of these is the story of love.

Here's all I've learned and all I know:
When it's your turn, just turn and go.

Rebecca's graduation fell on a Friday. As a special gift, Jimmy B let her conduct the school chorus in their "Graduation Concert" of four songs. Facing the choristers in her blue cap and gown and her bright red, high-top sneakers, she climbed atop a little box and blew into a pitchpipe and said something to them before the National Anthem and the other songs that made them all laugh, but that no one in the audience could hear. Louey made a mental note to ask what it was she'd said to them that was so funny, but forgot to ask until much later, and by then Rebecca had forgotten.

The day after that, Louey and Rebecca moved to Newburgh. They arrived just a few minutes ahead of the moving van, and spent the rest of the day unpacking their few pieces of furniture, stowing their dishware, towels, and personal items, and re-shelving books, records and CDs.

Alf was working in Long Island, as on all Saturdays, so they were on their own in deciding where to put everything. Rebecca insisted that she would have no use for her little piano in New York City, and that Louey should keep it in Newburgh.

They sent out for a pizza and worked long into the evening before falling onto their newly reassembled beds in their respective unfamiliar bedrooms. Alfie arrived just before midnight, and late the next morning, he and Louey got married at Washington's Headquarters, a few blocks from Bayview.

The wedding was just a brief ceremony at that funky historic site. The site's director had told Louey that yes, they could set up the caterer's big tent on the lawn and have the ceremony, as well as the luncheon, under that cover, and stay until dusk. The only two rules were that there could be no alcohol and—oddly—no amplified music. And yes, the use of the site's great lawn, with its gorgeous, commanding view of the Hudson River, was free. No one had ever asked to get married there before, at least not during his tenure, he said, so he had no price sheet. Just don't bring alcohol onto the property, and don't use any amplifiers.

A rabbi and a Lesbian Methodist pastor officiated. Alf broke the glass with neither practice nor problems, and then everyone took pictures of the newlyweds, and of one another, and of the river behind them. Children ran around the lawn playing tag, launching oily bubbles from wands, and flying kites.

With her Aunt Clare, Rebecca had written a parody of the Dixie Cups song, "Chapel of Love." They performed it together under the tent to great laughter and applause. All in attendance demanded they do it again.

After Louey waved goodbye to the last guests, she looked around the now-empty grounds of the historic site and wiped her hands upon each other and then upon the flowy silk wedding-pants that Rebecca had picked out for her. She smiled with pride and relief at her achievement. She'd got through three major life-events all in one weekend: her daughter's graduation, her move back to her old hometown and her wedding.

Over the years during which Louey worked at NYNU, the union had grown in membership, achievements and reputation, and the Communications Department was credited with much of its success. Things ran smoothly, and there were few surprises. But then one day soon after Louey's move to Newburgh, there was a surprise: At a regular Monday-morning meeting, Sarah suggested to the team that Louey be allowed to work one day a week from home—Fridays, to be specific—"as an experiment."

Sarah said she'd been concerned about Louey's hundred-mile commute, especially in the winter, with the ice and snow sometimes making the Thruway treacherous. But she'd been thinking about it, and there was no reason Louey couldn't make her calls and write her stories from home, and email them in. She wondered aloud if anyone else would object to her implementing this change to Louey's schedule. "Because," she added flatly, "I have no intention of extending the offer to anyone else, so don't even think about it. It's just because of the distance Louey has to travel every day. But please, go ahead; I'd like to hear everyone's reactions." She sat back in her chair and looked around at her staff.

Several seconds of silence ensued. Louey had the accurate feeling that everyone was looking at her, and only feared that they could see her trembling with excitement. Finally she said in a near-whisper, "Gosh, I would be so relieved and … and grateful if I could do that. But of course … the truth is … I think Sue and Dino could rightfully say, you know, 'How come I can't do that, too?' Because that's *such* a gift!"

Dino piped up immediately. "Well, I don't have a hundred-mile drive each way. I can *walk* from home to here! So,

I don't mind at all!

"I want Louey to be safe, too," he added with a smile. "I mean, if she ever spun out on an overpass, that would mean more work for me, right?"

Sue was just as gracious, and what Louey thought would be a long list of very understandable objections never materialized. In this way, a decision that turned out to be a massive change in her life took almost no time or trouble at all. She was to start her new schedule that very week.

"Consider this change to be the Communications Department's little wedding gift to you," Sarah smiled.

One day a week to work at home! And of all days: Fridays! She couldn't wait to tell Alfie and Rebecca. She would work harder than ever. She could make all her calls from home, do all her interviews from home, write all her stories from home and email them to Sarah; this was going to work just fine. She would make sure it did.

And it did. The "experiment" was given no time limit, and never got one. Louey worked just as hard on Fridays as on every other day. Surprising even herself, she didn't goof off at all. She called in very near 5 o'clock on most Fridays, to make sure that Sarah had received this or that email and to ask if there were any changes she should make to her stories—and also to be sure Sarah knew she was still on the job at that hour.

And on those Fridays when Alf could leave Long Island a bit early, they could get to Temple Beth Jacob in time for services.

Dear Diary,

This is really not just the best job I've ever had, but also the best job that could exist anywhere on the planet for anyone who both likes to write and wants to help working people. I know I've been a nomad in my so-called career, but this I could do forever.

Alf and Louey's next-door neighbor on Bayview Terrace was a conservative Republican state assemblyman who quickly became great pals with Louey. He used some contacts to get Rebecca a summer job she could walk to in the city's recreation department. When they weren't shopping for college supplies, Louey and Rebecca spent their weekends hiking. Sometimes they'd go with Alf on Saturday mornings, and sometimes they'd go on Sundays, when he was already back in Long Island. But most of the summer Rebecca spent planning and packing for her biggest adventure yet: her college years in New York City.

When the time came, Louey dropped her off with heroic restraint. She didn't want either Alf or Luke to accompany them; she wanted it to be just her and Rebecca. She shed no tears that Rebecca could see; she saved them for the drive home. Back on Bayview, she went straight upstairs to the quiet little room that had been her daughter's for only a few months and fell onto the empty little bed and sobbed while Alfie silently patted her back. Then she thanked God for email and cellphones and trains. Then she got up and told Alfie all about how strong and beautiful the women in Rebecca's dorm were, and how clear it was that Rebecca would love going to college in New York. And then they went downstairs and tucked into the three-course dinner that Alfie had made them and drank the wine.

It was a dark and miserable day for Louey Levy and the nurses of New York State when Sarah Wise retired. She had put twenty years in, though, and had plenty of plans for reading and writing and volunteering and visiting with grandchildren, so the Communications Department, and all of NYNU, wished her well and accepted their fate. Louey and Ali were keeping their fingers crossed that Sarah's replacement would be Sue, who had been with the department longer than anyone else, always had good story ideas, and knew the players, both staff and key members. But it wasn't to be.

How the new redheaded, obese Communications boss, Martha L. Hind, got hired was a mystery much discussed at NYNU and never solved. She was quite useless as a team member; she seemed to just sit in her office and criticize their stories via nasty emailed notes. Unlike Sarah, she never proposed any ideas or projects during the team's monthly or Monday meetings, and seemed not even to have read past issues of *Report*, and yet she was shocked and offended when the staff didn't come to the meetings with several different ideas apiece. What were they thinking when they hired her? She was almost aggressively unfriendly. No one liked her. Plus, she had two unfortunate characteristics, in addition to her weight and her badly colored hair: She was almost totally deaf, and as she walked along, every time she put her left foot down, she farted. Ali and Louey, whose cubicles were the nearest to Martha's office, would spin their chairs around after she lumbered past, and cross their eyes at each other and hold their noses and wave their hands rapidly before their faces to try to disperse Martha's posterior effluvia, and wipe their eyes and try not to giggle out loud.

One day when they were alone in the lunchroom, Ali smiled mysteriously and said, "Levy, I've got a theory."

"You do? Well, don't worry about it. I had one once, but I got over it."

"No; seriously. I think Martha is opposed to labor unions."

Louey squinted and looked off into the distance as she stirred her coffee for a few seconds.

"That would be the perfect explanation, if it weren't for the fact that it doesn't make any sense at all," she said.

"Think about it, though! She might have thought the word "Union" in "Nurses Union" was just meant to convey, 'Group,' as in 'the American Civil Liberties Union!'"

"You mean you think she applied for Sarah's job and got through all her interviews—who interviewed her, though?—and did all her research about NYNU, without ever realizing that we're a labor union?"

"Could happen, Levy. Could happen. Maybe the ads just said, 'professional association,' not 'labor union.' Nobody in our office proofread them, did they?"

The humor of Ali's idea appealed to Louey, if not its plausibility. She hadn't seen any of the ads in the papers and nursing magazines that NYNU had taken out announcing the opening, but surely they had said that NYNU was a labor union. She shook her head and laughed.

"You're a riot, Ali."

For reasons she told no one, Martha L. Hind decided early in her tenure that she didn't like Louey's work. Well, she also wasn't particularly fond of anyone else's work in the

GENIE ABRAMS

Communications Department, either. But the ominous thing was, she also didn't like Louey's schedule. She called Louey into her office one day and said she was thinking of making Louey "go back to working five days a week like everybody else." She said she'd let Louey know, but she was giving it a lot of thought, as it seemed very unfair to her colleagues.

"Sue and Dino actually approved of it," Louey pointed out. "That was the condition on which Sarah offered it to me—only if it was acceptable to them. And it's only because I have to drive a hundred miles each way."

"I know, but that's your own choice. No one else is responsible for your bad choices," she replied.

"Well, Sarah Wise thought it was a good choice. I mean, she suggested it, and that's why I'm doing it," Louey said.

"We'll see, but it doesn't seem to me like it's working out," the boss said.

"OK, well, thanks for the warning," Louey said. She couldn't think of anything else to say.

In desperation, Ali and Louey drove on one lunch hour to Ali's apartment and called Sarah, with whom they'd kept in touch. They told her everything they could about their new boss's behavior and asked if she had any explanation for it. Sarah said she'd already heard the same complaints from field reps and staffers in other departments. And not only had she not taken part in the interviews of Hind, but they'd never even spoken.

Unreal! That was the same thing that happened with Joe Arnier and his replacement at CSEU. They don't let the "old guy" interview the "new guy?" Who would be better than the "old guy" to evaluate the people skills, writing skills and editorial chops the

— 400 —

candidates bring? Yet apparently hiring wasn't done that way anymore. Management was so stupid—even management of a union.

Louey thought that maybe they just weren't giving Martha a chance—that she was overwhelmed, terrified and clueless about what she was supposed to be doing, and lonely because she talked to no one at work. So, trying to be friendly one morning at the coffee machine, she asked Martha what her middle initial stood for. Martha always used it when signing letters, memos and emails.

"That's an inappropriate question to ask anyone in a work environment, much less your supervisor," was Martha's quick reply.

She was serious.

"Oh! I'm sorry."

As soon as she got home that evening, Louey emailed Rebecca about the run-in.

Together, they wondered what the "L" might stand for. Rebecca asked her to wait a few minutes: She said she'd discuss the matter with her roommates and get back to her.

Loser, Loathesome, and Lazypants were their initial offerings, which Louey thought were brilliant. A few minutes later Rebecca sent another email asking, "What's her last name, again?"

"Hind."

"How about, LickMyB? Because then she'd be, Martha, LickMyB Hind!"

Pastor Alf was in Long Island that evening, but Louey emailed him the story of her latest interaction with her new boss and put the question to him as well.

Just fifteen minutes later, he emailed back the name that stuck.

"Lammergeier," he wrote. It was a mythological beast that showed, according to his Oxford English Dictionary, "unabashed cowardice, taking advantage of any animal in distress. Its only food is the bones of other creatures, which its extremely acidic stomach can quickly dissolve. It gets its nourishment from the marrow of its prey."

The next day, Louey told Ali that Alf had discovered Hind's middle name; Ali told Dino and Sue; they told *Report*'s graphic designer, and no one in the office from that time forth, ever referred to their boss as anything other than "the Lammergeier."

Louey also found the word in one of her birding books, as another name for the bearded vulture, which was an actual, not mythological, creature. There was a photo. Man, that was one ugly bird. Previously, Louey hadn't believed she would ever call any bird ugly. She scanned and emailed the photo to Rebecca, and got confirmation of her opinion in the form of an immediate "Ewww!" And not many photos revolted Rebecca Qualesworth, who had decided to major in natural science.

Living in Newburgh, Louey had developed an ever-growing desire to climb Breakneck Mountain. Across the river and six miles south of Beacon, looming over Route 9D, the mountain was clearly visible from Bayview Terrace. By reputation, the loop hike she yearned to do was the most difficult non-technical climb in the east, and also the most rewarding, because of the views. The most spectacular ones were actually not at the wooded peak, but along the way up. Hiking guides listed it as a "must-do-before-you-die" adventure. Thousands of young people from New York City jumped off the Metro North trains at a special "Breakneck stop" every spring and summer to attempt it.

Finally, one fall morning, Louey could stand it no longer. She grabbed Alf and off they drove with their backpacks and water bottles. After considering the pros and cons of it, Alf brought along his hiking poles, too.

It was rocky and steep; in places, almost sheer. You needed to find handholds and footholds at the same time, and some of them were only an inch or so wide. Also, you needed to be sure you didn't step into a crevice that your boot could get stuck in. Louey, heart banging, sweaty cheek flat against the rock, not looking down, spread-eagled and clutching a half-inch-wide ledge, spent way too much energy cursing her pathetic sixty-two inches of height while her biological brother and sister, neither of whom had ever climbed a mountain or wanted to, were down safe on the ground somewhere at that moment, just loping through life with their long limbs. Just loping blithely along, not caring that their sister was about to die.

The only reason Louey didn't cry was that she couldn't. If her lungs expanded as necessary for sobbing, she would tip over backwards and plunge several hundred feet onto Route 9D, and traffic would be backed up for hours, and how would Alfie get down? From where they were, you couldn't go back down the way you came up. Her legs were too short to reach the only tiny crack, above her and off to the right, that looked like it might work as a foothold. She couldn't see him, but she knew her husband was there.

"Alf, I'm scared!" she whimpered.

He was directly below her, feet together on a tiny mat of grass the size of the top of a barstool. He steadied her by saying calmly, in his deep, pastoral voice, "If you don't want to go any farther, I can help you get down to where I am, and then we can take the easier route. Look: It starts right over there!" He pointed to a painted sign off to his left that, cartoonishly, said, "EASIER ROUTE," and had an arrow pointing to the woods skirting the sheer boulder she'd partly ascended.

She'd seen that sign just a few moments ago, and scorned it. She'd disdained it. She hadn't come this far only to take the wimpy way up. She figured they were three-quarters of the way to the top! She also knew she couldn't go any farther up the rockface she was clinging to. There was no ledge to pull herself up by and no reachable crack for either foot.

"I'll be happy to go whatever way you choose," he added. "You decide."

Those words gave her confidence and new energy. Knowing that Alfie was right there and would somehow catch her if she fell, knowing that he'd somehow help her get down to the "EASIER ROUTE" sign if she needed to, changed everything.

He could reach her from where he was, and she asked him to give her a shove. With Alfie pushing her up, one hand on each butt-cheek, she giggled as she reached up and off to her right, stepped on a ledge so slim it might have been imaginary, and immediately launched herself up another few feet, then another few, and there saw that the trail—white paint on the rock—led in a more lateral than vertical path from here on. She felt a surge of optimism and adrenaline as if she were on cocaine. She knew she'd make it; she knew the hardest part was over. It was her turn to be coach and cheerleader.

"Did you see how I did it?" she called back to Alf. "It's really not that hard! It won't be hard for you, at all!" Hiking poles still being held tight by the bungee cords of his backpack, Alf climbed using the same hand- and foot-holds she'd used, and:

Reader, they made it.

An older hiker—that is, a hiker of their own age group—approached them when they finally found a place to rest, on a small rock in a wooded area a foot or so off the trail near the top. He smiled and asked Alf ironically, "How are those hiking poles working out for ya?" Because of course, they'd been all but useless on the ascent of Breakneck.

They could laugh along with the old dude, because it was clear that the worst was over, and now it would be all rolling terrain and photography and an easy downhill through lovely woods.

If I died right now, I wouldn't mind, Louey told God as they began to hear the traffic on Route 9D again. She was healthy, she had a good job, her daughter was enjoying the best women's college in New York, and this guy loved her. *This* guy! This guy, who was so calm, and good, and whom she loved so much, and who loved her in return. And now they had done Breakneck! Ten feet behind Alf, she stopped and turned her face toward the sky. She closed her eyes, and tears rolled backwards into her ears. *I know how blessed I am,* she whispered. *I really do. Thank you for this good life you've given me. I love it, and I appreciate it.*

One otherwise unremarkable Tuesday in spring, Louey arrived at work after her long drive, tossed her coat over the back of her chair, turned on her computer and noticed on her desk a small envelope—the size you'd use to send someone a party invitation—with one word hand-written on it: "Confidential." Inside was a single sentence the Lammergeier had typed saying that since Louey's work was "unacceptable in every way," she should consider herself, "henceforth," to be "on probation."

Wow! Henceforth! Not just "starting now," but "henceforth!" She obviously gave this a lot of thought. And, unacceptable "in every way!" Not just in some ways; in every way! That's exactly what Tom Lupo said, which is how I ended up in Albany in the first place! Nothing but glowing reviews for nine straight years from Sarah Wise, and now with absolutely no evidence whatsoever, this lady comes along and says I'm unacceptable. OK, well, that does it. I'm done.

As soon as she got home, Louey called Alf to ask how he'd feel if she quit NYNU. "I'm pretty sure I'll get some kind of severance pay, and maybe I'll be eligible for unemployment. I can restart my old desktop publishing business, doing PR for some nonprofits around here," she said. "I bet I can make almost as much money as I'm making now." She had no evidence whatsoever for that statement.

"I'll support you in whatever you want to do. I'm for you," he said gently. "You won't be able to collect unemployment if you quit, but I'm pretty sure I'll be transfered to a church somewhere closer to Newburgh in July, with a raise in salary.

Just think: I won't have to commute so far to see you! We'll get along fine. Don't even worry about it. I only want you to be happy."

The very next day, Lammergeier found a one-sentence memo on her desk, in a little envelope marked, "Confidential."

To: Martha L. Hind
From: Louey Levy
April 6, 2005
My last day working for NYNU will be April 20; henceforth, you can look for my replacement.

She had nothing lined up. She just quit. Just like that. It made her so happy, leaving that note on Lammergeier's desk! *God, what a hot-head I am!* she told herself, giggling.

What would she do, though? What jobs were available near Newburgh? Could she even make a living doing desktop publishing here? She knew damned well that she could not. For years now, every nonprofit, government agency, restaurant, union, ambulance corps, real estate firm, bar and grill, lawyer's office, roofing company, bank, warehouse and whorehouse had someone on staff who was an expert in PageMaker, and therefore could produce flyers and newsletters, even in four colors, as if it were nothing. Any secretary, or "administrative assistant," as they were now called, could do the thing that had been her unique specialty just a few years ago. Of course, those newsletters were dull, had no style and were full of typos—but management of corporations and nonprofits alike hardly knew or cared about spelling or grammar anymore, it seemed. The world was being buried in an avalanche of computer-generated communications of all kinds—ads, news, entertainment, sports, everything—that were all awful and that made Louey's once-rare talent seem cheap and easy to come by.

I'll find something. Maybe I can do PR for the local Planned Parenthood or some Jewish agency or some other good-guy group. Who's hiring, though? I'll just check the paper every day. "Anybody would be glad to have you," I can hear Dad saying. "Buck up, old girl." Don't worry: I'll get something. I'll be fine, Daddy.

Then she fell on her bed and wept.

One of the first things Louey did after moving back to Newburgh was to join the Bayview Neighborhood Association. She hoped to revitalize the old city, starting with her own street. There was no question that Newburgh needed some love. Forty-two years of bad management had invited "White Flight" and the resulting decay and an influx of gangs, drugs and crime. The thing that irritated and puzzled her the most was the trash that littered the sidewalks. She bought herself a "reach extender" and spent nearly every spare hour picking up trash on sidewalks all over the city.

What pride she took in her new hobby! She continued it throughout the rest of her entire life in Newburgh. Day after day after day, she collected dirty needles; dog poop; empty crack baggies; cigar wrappers; glass and plastic bottles, broken or whole, completely or partly empty, that had contained booze, soda, juice or water; thousands upon thousands of cigarette butts; candy, gum and junk-food wrappers of all kinds; Styrofoam containers, cups and lids from diners or donut-and-coffee places; millions of bits of Styrofoam from when people had, from anger, despair or boredom, ripped takeout cups and containers into confetti; "roaches" dropped from marijuana joints; greasy paper bags; half-empty, ant-riddled cans of cat food, left out by well-meaning residents; cardboard boxes and small condiment containers from fast-food places; the occasional African-style weave, probably pulled from someone's hair during a street fight; heavy, soggy diapers, neatly folded into tight little packages; lids from all the bottles; wet, filthy T-shirts; and old shoes. If the 4th of July or Halloween was near, costumes, masks, sparklers and spent bottle rockets were added to her trove. She wore gardening gloves for this hobby and carried a pair of pruning shears. When she saw a tree with mulch dumped into a volcano form around its trunk, she followed Rebecca's instructions and scooped it away to make a moat so rain could reach its roots better, and harmful insects would be somewhat blocked from crawling onto it.

The city's friendly residents often came outside to offer her water or cash for her efforts, or to call out blessings on her from their stoops. They pointed and smiled and said, "Here comes the Trash Lady!" or, "Hi, Tree Lady!" The marijuana dealers on Liberty Street ducked into their bodega-headquarters and emerged to offer her blue energy drinks in big plastic bottles. She found it all very touching. And best of all, when she was done with each block, she could look back and see where she'd been.

This is what I'm here for, she wrote in her journal. *This is it. The block of Liberty Street I did today looks so peaceful now. Even people driving by lower their damn radios, as if they're in a hospital zone. People talk more respectfully to one another when*

I'm in front of their building, and everyone's friendlier. It's like they've come into a different place. Every single day, I make new friends on the streets, because people walking along stop to thank me. Either that, or they tell me I'm crazy, because tomorrow it'll be just as bad as it was today. I've got to call our Department of Public Works and ask if we need more cans on the street corners, or if we need to make landlords provide more trash cans for their tenants, or what.

But this is the life: looking back and seeing that it's better where I'd been, than where I hadn't been. If only for a minute. Every time I pick up a piece of broken glass, I go, "There! That's <u>one</u> piece of glass no kid is going to fall and cut himself on!" And I get to do that a million times a day!

Louey soon was elected secretary of the neighborhood association, and she seemed to energize the whole group. She and her eccentric neighbors organized trash-pick-up parties, holiday celebrations for the kids, block beautification projects and "marches to the mic" at City Council meetings to press for enforcement of building-code regulations. They organized walking tours of the historic sites and the new developments at the riverfront. Now that she was "gainfully unemployed," as she put it, Louey could spend even more time building coalitions among residents and city officials to bring Newburgh back from the brink of bankruptcy and despair.

One evening, Louey was sitting on the living-room couch, sipping a glass of wine and making lists of projects she could undertake to benefit Newburgh. Alfie was in the kitchen listening to NPR and deciding what to make for dinner.

"Would you prefer the flavors of northern India tonight, or southern India?" he called.

Louey couldn't tell the difference between the flavors of India and Indiana, and couldn't care less what Alfie made. She knew it would be delicious.

"You choose, honey," she said. "Surprise me!"

Just then she heard a rapping on the big window of their front door. She knew it was one of her friends: No one but a Newburgher would knock at a doorway that featured a beautiful, hardwired bell that had been installed less than a month earlier for six hundred and eighty dollars. The reason the doorbell cost that much was that the licensed electrician they found (they were not allowed, by the city's code at that time, to hire anyone but a Newburgh-licensed electrician) claimed he had to snake a wire down to the basement for the project, and it took him six hours of exploratory surgery with power tools before he found a way to do that. Louey had the six-hundred and eighty-dollar bill for that project mounted, framed, and hung in their bathroom so that she would never forget how stupid she'd been to hire that guy. From the moment she had it installed, only Jehovah's Witnesses rang the six-hundred-and-eighty-dollar doorbell. For some reason, her friends and neighbors ignored it and knocked on the door's big, centered window. At six dollars and eighty cents, the new device would have made a perfectly acceptable doorbell. It was an ivory-colored button in the middle of a three-inch-high, decorative flat stone that looked a bit like a brooch. It was set about chest-high in the right side of the doorjamb, exactly where the doorbells on every other house in the world are located. You'd have to be blind to miss it.

Be that as it may, there was a knock on the front door's big glass window.

As she approached the door, Louey saw through the window a whole chorus of neighbors on her front steps. What was this, Grownup Halloween? She would have been surprised that they weren't carrying little bags and wearing costumes, except that it was June. And they were grownups.

The group, all of them friends from the Bayview Neighborhood Association, comprised a doctor; a member of the city's executive staff; a Latino pastor; two retired women who were soon to be each other's wives; a nurse's aide from the apartment building next door and a Black guy who owned the house on the other side of Alfie and Louey's and who worked in a rock quarry across the river.

Louey had no idea what they wanted, but she knew immediately who had organized the posse: the doctor, who was standing at the pinnacle of the phalanx. The doctor was a persistent little person who was very generous to all the good causes around town and passionate about trying to get the taxes lowered on her beautiful house around the corner that she shared with her husband Rocco and her dog Bruno. (Or perhaps the dog was named Rocco, and the husband Bruno. Louey could never keep them straight.)

Extremely curious, but more amused than curious, Louey smiled and opened the door only halfway. There wasn't room for seven visitors plus herself to sit in the little enclosed porch, and if she invited them in she'd have to invite them to stay for dinner and they certainly would stay, once they smelled the onion-heavy beef-and-vegetable stock Alfie had been simmering on the stove all day. She smiled, clapped her hands rapidly and lightly and chirped, "Oh, are you gonna sing me a Christmas carol? It's kinda early."

The doctor was not to be distracted by any silliness.

"Listen," she said, pointing a finger at Louey. "You have to run for City Council." Louey let that sink in for a moment. She wasn't one to beat around the bush, the Doctor wasn't. And she was very smart. But here she was simply incorrect.

"No, I don't," Louey smiled, with as mild a tone as she could manage. "Good night, now."

The doctor literally put her foot between the door and the doorjamb, so that the door couldn't close. Louey didn't know that people really did that. She thought it was just an expression: "I couldn't get my foot in the door."

She opened it wide then, without inviting them in.

"What are you talking about?" she said, looking suspiciously at the grinning posse.

"You have to run," the Doctor said. "We have idiots on Council. They don't know what they're doing. Our taxes are ridiculous! But now the city's changed its charter so that each ward is going to have its own council member, and we want you to represent our ward. It's only a part-time job: Council only meets twice a month. You care about Newburgh, and you know how cities work. And don't worry: I'll finance your campaign. You have to do it. You can't say no." She spoke those words not as a proposal or a plea, but as a universal, eternal truth, the way a math teacher might say, "You can't divide by zero." The other neighbors were looking up from the lower steps, as silent as bobble-headed plastic dolls. The Doctor had rounded them up, apparently, only for optics.

Louey said, "Are you nuts? Why don't you get somebody *smart* to run?"

The Doctor shook her head emphatically and said, "No. We already asked all the smart people, and they all said no."

And that, dear Reader, is how Louey Levy ended up on Newburgh's City Council, and to this day there are still people in the city who can confirm this in every detail.

Oh, there was a Campaign, and a Campaign Committee, and a Campaign Treasurer (Alfie). By taking this position, he had to file monthly reports, and agree never to let The Candidate know who had contributed to her campaign nor how much, nor how much of it had been spent on what. He also agreed to be part of her Campaign Contingency Committee (Reader, don't ask; it's a real thing). There was also a humiliating pleading before the city's Democratic Committee and the county's Green and Working Families parties for their endorsements and a request for the Record's endorsement (but they don't endorse for City Council elections, a policy about which Louey had known for some forty years, but she thought they'd make an exception for her, hahahahaha). Then there were twelve or thirteen brunches and pizza-fueled Strategy Sessions she had to attend, hating each one for many diverse reasons. She invariably found them tedious after the first few minutes, even though they were all about her, and she doodled many a doodle and wrote many a ribald rhyme and several salacious slogans in her notepad during those sessions, while people volunteered for various tasks.

There were phone calls to make and flyers to write and fold and then to stuff, illegally, into people's mailboxes, and lawn signs to plant on her supporters' lawns, all paid for through the generosity of the Doctor. There were also model letters-to-the-editor that Louey herself drafted (because, who better?) for her friends to modify ever so slightly and put their own signatures on. And there were endorsements of fellow Democrats, running for other offices that year, that she had to make, as well.

"It's how you Play the Game," the Doctor intoned.

After a brief struggle for her Party's endorsement (surprise! A stranger from another part of the Ward wanted to be elected to Council as well, but he was quickly found to have forged most of the signatures on his petitions), Louey emerged victorious.

"Levy Wins Dems' Nod," she said to herself, mentally writing the headline for a story that never ran. The Record didn't cover nominations for ward elections.

After that, the general election was a cakewalk. Louey more or less pitched a shutout, since she, like ninety-five percent of the registered voters in Ward 2, and Newburgh as a whole, was a Democrat. A few wiseguys wrote in their own names; plus, there was one write-in for Jay-Z and one for Kobe Bryant. As Louey went door-to-door in Ward 2, she learned that not a soul had heard of her Republican opponent, and to this day no one can recall that person's name.

The best part of serving on Council, for Louey, was working with Karen Mendoza, a young woman who had run in another ward.

Karen, whose family had escaped civil war in El Salvador, was, like Louey, a first-time-candidate Democrat. She was smarter than all the other candidates and Council members put together. A graduate of Brown University and a new mother, she believed fervently in the U.S. Constitution and its principles and purposes ("to form a more perfect union," etc.), understood its nuances and could recite its amendments. She cared about public policy and its ability to make people's lives better, and those were her stated, and actual, reasons for running. Louey decided to follow her as a kind of disciple, and together with a couple of other new people on Council and a progressive mayor, they shoved the City forward, as one would get a Lincoln Continental up a hill in heavy snow.

Here's the funny thing, though: Through all her venture into civic activism and politics, Louey had never really stopped working for the Record. Ever since she moved back to Newburgh, she had been sending story ideas to the executive editor, who was a stranger to her. His name, she saw on the masthead, was Mark Shapiro. He wrote the paper's editorials plus an excellent column for the Sunday edition each week. Louey admired his writing. His editorials were sharp and insightful, and his columns were funny or touching, and often both at once. You could tell he knew good writing when he saw it. Louey was flattered when, after emailing her ideas to him, he thanked and praised her as well as giving her the OK. Then she would do the research, interviews and writing and provide suggestions for photos, as well.

She never included a bill with her stories; they never mentioned money at all in their emails. But Shapiro always mailed her a check for $100 within a week of their publication.

Once she sent him a story about the lack of swimming opportunities for Newburgh residents. The city had only one pool, a 40-year-old outdoor monstrosity jammed with so many kids in the hot weather that they had to whistle them in and out in two-hour shifts starting at 10 a.m. No one was allowed to swim twice on the same day; a large sign to that effect was hung on the chain-link fence surrounding the pool area, though there was absolutely no way to enforce the rule. The lifeguards in the afternoon would have to look back through hundreds of names to prove that kids had already had a swim—if those kids had even used their real names both times, which was not a sure bet.

But the real scandal was the high school. Newburgh Free Academy had a well-maintained Olympic-sized pool in its basement, and a crackerjack swim team that sent many members to the state championships each year, yet none of the city's taxpayers or their families were allowed to use the school's pool. Every other nearby school district except Newburgh's had "open swim" hours at least once a week for their taxpayers and their families, and some offered free swimming lessons, as well: Newburgh had no such thing. Louey called every school district in Orange County and spoke with the swimming coach or the athletic director, or both, and all were eager to talk about their popular community swim programs, all prominently publicized on their websites. Newburgh's school district, with the biggest population and the highest taxes of all, kept its pool a secret.

Louey suggested the headline, which the Record did, in fact, use: "Whose Pool Is It, Anyway?" This drew a lot of letters from readers, both in the paper and online, and turned out to be one of its most-read stories of the year.

And then, she couldn't help it: She sent in a funny piece about her adventures in getting elected to City Council.

The story ran, big, with a big photo of her, and her hundred-dollar check arrived, and then her phone rang. It was Mark Shapiro, asking her to work for him.

"I know you've already got a job" he said, but City Council meets only a couple nights a month, right? It's parttime, right? It's volunteer work, basically, isn't it?"

It did. It was. It was.

"Well, we can work around that. How would you like to come to work for us? I love your writing."

"Covering Newburgh, you mean?" Her voice squeaked a little at the end of that question, betraying her excitement. She hoped against hope that her luck would hold out and he'd say yes. Not that there was a Newburgh bureau anymore. But maybe she could cover the city using her ... laptop? She had one of those. And then she could just ... email her stories to the office? From home? Is that what they did, now?

It was what they did, but Newburgh was off the table as a topic for her reporting.

"No, not Newburgh, of course; that would be a conflict of interest! But you could be our Reporter-at-Large, covering everything else, writing columns! From home! About anything you wanted! Unfortunately, we don't have a budget right now for any positions on News-side, but I have a question for you: Do you like sports?"

The Record, it seemed, had an opening on the Sports copy desk, and if she would fill in as a Sports copy-editor for a while, he would slide her over to News-side as soon as funds for a position there came through. And by working in Sports, Shapiro said, Louey would have "a foot in the door" already; she'd have first dibs on any job that came open in News-side, the one caveat being that she couldn't cover Newburgh.

Sports copy-editing, of course, would require being in the building, on the sports desk, and there would be two Monday nights a month that she couldn't be there, because of City Council meetings. He understood that. He'd see that she wouldn't be scheduled to come in on those nights. She surprised him by telling him she'd actually been a reporter at the Record some—could it be 30? —years ago. No. Couldn't be. Shapiro didn't recognize any of the names she reeled off. He thought he'd heard of Al Rome, but not Ted Daley, Tim Clay, Jake Rosen, Charlie Farley or any of the others she named. Anyway, he wasn't interested in them; he was interested in her.

Two days later, she got a call from the Record's Human Relations department saying the paper was offering her a position as a Sports copy-editor at an astonishingly low salary and asking her when she could start. She started ten days later.

The door to the Record wasn't where it had been. This one was metal and had a glass window with chicken wire embedded in it. Only after Louey had "stated her business" to the receptionist inside, who could see her perfectly well, was she allowed to open it.

Here I go, through the looking-glass, she said to herself for no particular reason as she entered, and her instinct was precisely correct: She might as well have been Alice. She turned right to get to Shapiro's office, as he had instructed her over the phone. This was not the office of Al Rome that she had walked into for her interview in 1972; that office must have been nearby somewhere, but not here. Not here at all. She was disoriented.

The newsroom wasn't where it had been, either. Where was it, though? She saw no Backshop, no light-tables, no darkroom door with "KEEP CLOSED" posted on it. No phones rang. No editors chewed on stories or yelled questions to reporters. The bang, slam, ding and rip of typewriters was gone; well, she knew there'd be no typewriters. Typewriters had been antiques for many years already. But what a difference it made in the sound of a newsroom! Here were auto-corrected words forming silently on lighted screens, their creation involving nothing louder than fingernails pressing tiny squares of plastic. Where was the Niagara Falls thunder of words being pounded into eternity? Where were reporters jumping up from their chairs and yelling, "Damn it! God damn it! God damn it all anyway!" Gone were the pages being torn from the platens; gone the paste-pots with the brushes needed to keep pages together as reporters rushed them to the copy desk. Gone, even, were the reams of paper on every desk. No phones were ringing, though a couple of Quasimodos were seen squeezing cellphones between their shoulders and ears. Where was the copy desk and who was Slot now, anyway? Louey knew not to ask; it would only show her ignorance, her age. Everything was gone. Everyone had gone away.

Reporters were neither cursing nor throwing balled-up paper at trash cans or at one another. Most disorienting of all, Louey heard no laughter anywhere—anywhere at all—as Shapiro took her on this weird "Grand Tour," as he called it. There were very few humans in the whole eerie place—well, maybe it was because they were not yet approaching deadline. Maybe everyone would show up later. The few, expressionless people she passed in the poorly-lit, cavernous room were sitting far from one another in pods of three-walled, fabric-padded cubicles, staring at computer screens or repeatedly sliding an electronic "mouse," over and over again, across the same quiet inch of its thick foam pad.

The silence! It wasn't a newspaper at all; it was an insurance office, or maybe a funeral home. Only quieter. Where were the metal desks slammed side-by-side against one another and topped by the heavy black Underwood typewriters? Where were the metal drawers crammed with old notebooks and papers and clippings, and where above all were the shouted questions and jokey answers and the urgency and the tumult? Why was it so goddamned quiet in there? Where was the Record's huge web-offset press that was once the envy of the newspaper world, that ran at three thousand feet per minute and that also cut and folded, and that shook the building and rumbled so loud that you had to shout to be heard?

Where was the darkroom, the womb from which the Record's award-winning photos were born?

Gone. All gone.

Mark led her through Wonderland to meet her new boss, the sports editor.

To get to Sports, they walked past a long display, head-high on a wall that Louey instantly, silently, dubbed "the Wall of Death." She found it physically repulsive and turned her eyes from it. Why did they have those things push-pinned up there? They were the Record's Sunday Page Ones going back almost the whole year, side by side, with the readership for each issue scrawled diagonally across it in thick felt-tipped pen. That five-digit number fell almost without exception each week: 37,020; 36,690; 35,410; and on and on and downward and downward, with slight bumps only for weeks in which a natural disaster or the death of a prominent person had occurred. On those few pages, a crude "happy face" consisting of a circle with two apostrophe eyes and an upturned bowl of a semicircle mouth was drawn beneath the sad number.

Wow, reporters have to walk past this every day? For God's sake, why don't they take this down? I know this World Wide Web thing is killing readership—the car dealers aren't advertising in the papers anymore, they're doing it online—but this is just cruel, to rub it in their own reporters' faces like this, that readership is down, as well as advertising. Why would they do this?

Just past the Wall of Death, Mark handed Louey over to Don the Sports Editor.

"Don Marwell, this is Louey Levy, the terrific journalist I was telling you about. She worked here years ago. What was it, Louey, twenty years ago, or something? You told me, but I forgot."

"Yeah, something like that, hi," she said, aiming a nod and a smile at Don. Mercifully, they glided right past the exact number of years it had been, because she would have needed pen and paper, and a better memory, to figure it out.

"Journalist?" Is that what I was? When did reporters start being called "journalists?" Probably about the same time teachers started being called "educators." How pretentious can you get? "I used to be a reporter, but now I'm a journalist." "I used to be a teacher, but now I'm an educator." "What do you do for a living?" "I'm a sixth-grade educator."

The jobs are the same: Seek the truth and tell it. That's all a reporter has to do. I mean it's essential, but it's simple. And it's simple, but it's not easy. When did reporting stop being an honorable profession? Is there something wrong with being a reporter, or a teacher, for that matter, that you can't call people that in polite society anymore? People have to give themselves a fancier title, now? Well, I suppose it's a good way to pad a résumé by a few more characters.

Don was a very young-looking man. He looked half her age, but he said he'd been there for twenty years. Shapiro left them alone, and Don rose from his computer and led Louey to the paper's huge "lunchroom." No one was there; the gym-sized room was vacant but for a TV set at one end, and some tables and chairs. It was a short walk up a broad ramp leading from the Sports department.

I don't remember any ramp. Why is there a ramp here? She couldn't get her bearings.

"Don, are you related by any chance to a Hank Marwell, up near Albany?" Louey asked as she followed him to the lunchroom.

"Hank? No, there are no Hanks in our family, that I know of. No Hanks, no Henrys, nothing like that. My family's from Buffalo, and all my relatives are still out there."

"Oh, OK. I just ask because I used to know a Hank Marwell. He was the executive director of Special Olympics in the Albany area."

"Huh. No; never heard of him. He must be from the respectable Marwells."

Now Louey knew they were going to get along fine.

Whatever happened to Hank Marwell? I wonder if he's still up there, directing Region 10. Wonder how that sweet kid Seth is doing. Seth, the Powerlifter! I loved that little guy. Wonder if he's still in Special Olympics, still doing powerlifting. I hope he's OK. You can get hurt if you don't use good form. Guys get hurt all the time doing that, even regular lifters. They have to wear a special belt. Did he use a belt? I saw his demonstration, but I can't remember.

The Region 10 gang had not made a fuss about Louey's leaving. They didn't throw her a party or anything—not that she wanted one; the athletes just lined up and hugged her when she announced that the following week would be her last with them, because she had bought a house far away and needed to get down there on Saturdays to fix it up before she could move in. After leading her final practice, some of the parents thanked her and said they'd miss her, and that was it. Hank had probably put an ad in the paper the next day and hired her replacement with as little drama as he'd hired Louey. And the truth was, Louey hadn't thought about her Special Olympians, except Seth, in a long time.

Her new Marwell offered her a seat at a smallish, round table and asked if he could get her a cup of coffee. She said, "Yes, that'd be great." He went across the room to a machine and, to her embarrassment, began fumbling in his pockets for change. Was she really letting him buy, while she just sat there? She reached into the shoulder bag she'd slung over her chairback but before she could open her wallet to see if she had any quarters, Don found the coins he needed and called back, "Cream and sugar?"

"No; just black is fine," she said. She wanted not to be any trouble, and she also wanted to take up as little of his time as possible. Instead of her wallet, she pulled from her purse her reporter's notebook and a pen. She knew that, at this hour of the mid-afternoon, he'd already begun planning the next day's pages, and orienting his new copy-editor would be a huge interruption for him.

She examined the floor. It was covered in hideously ugly linoleum tiles, a dirty, reddish color streaked with black, with several long, parallel gouges here and there, as though something heavy had been dragged over it. What had this been? Was this the pressroom? Its ceiling, unlike the rest of the building, was two stories high. But where was the Record's world-famous, ear-splitting web offset press? It was so disorienting, this orientation.

Don Marwell, smart and kind, clearly had figured out from Mark's brief description of Louey that she had left newspapers a world ago. A lifetime ago.

"Let me start by describing the system we use," he said. He set two small, steaming paper cups on the table and pulled up the chair across from hers.

Louey immediately clicked her ballpoint pen and began taking notes.

"Let me explain the work-flow. We get all the pro teams' game stories from the AP, so all we have to do is edit them very lightly and put heads on them. The boxscores come in from the AP too, so we don't have to do anything with them. We just slam them on the page. The Designer tells you how many columns wide the heads have to be and what font and size to use. As for local stories, I assign them to our reporters," he said. "They go out to the high schools and cover the games and get quotes from the coaches afterwards, if they can, and take photos."

"We don't send photographers out?" Louey asked, bewildered.

"We don't have sports photographers anymore. We just ask the reporters to take photos while they're at the games. News-side does the same thing; their reporters take their own photos, too. The plan is for all reporters to take videos, by the way, when we have our own website. That'll be next year, probably. And then the reporters will be able to post their stories and photos directly to the web."

Unedited? Louey thought, in distress. *Well, he must mean News-side lets the reporters take photos* in addition to *the regular photographers. Surely the paper still has professional news photographers, and then if a reporter gets a good, lucky shot, they can use that, too. That must be what he means. Reporters took photos back in the '70s too, sometimes, though they almost never were good enough to use.*

"Frankly, the reporters' photos are usually not too great. I mean, our guys aren't professional photographers, or anything, but sometimes they get a good-enough shot that we can use. If not an action shot, then a mugshot of the hero of the game, or something. And then the Designer can fix a lot of the problems, by, you know, cropping and resizing and lightening them, and all that."

Wow. The Record, the award-winning Record, doesn't have any sports photographers? What's happening!?

Louey, clueless, nodded sagely, while scribbling in her notebook as if she were taking notes.

"They input the stories into the System right there, from wherever they are," Don said. "Like, the guys who cover Newburgh games input their stories from the press box, which is right inside the school, overlooking the field. You remember where the press box is at NFA, right? You went there for high school, I think Mark told me?"

"No, actually, my family moved to Albany just as I was about to start at NFA," she said. But her train of thought had hit a wall at the words, "the System."

"The System?" What the hell is that? Some kind of proprietary software, must be. Am I supposed to know how to use it? I'd better keep quiet.

But then, in desperation, she blurted out, "What do you use for layout—PageMaker?"

"InDesign, you mean? PageMaker was, like, a predecessor of InDesign, I think," Don said gently. "But no, they just email the stories to us using regular email, and then the Designer lays them out. I've already told him roughly how many inches each one will need."

Oh no, PageMaker's not the only page-layout program in the world, now? PageMaker's old hat? That shows how old I am. Wait, am I old? I'm old! I've never even heard of InDesign. Thank God I won't have to use it, as a copy-editor.

Don continued, "When he's done laying them out, he just yells that they're ready, and the System moves the pages over to the copy-editors, and then you just edit and headline them in InDesign."

Oh dear God, what's "the System?" What the hell is InDesign? And most of all, what's a "Designer," in a newspaper? I'm going to have to ask. There's no getting around it. Should I just confess that I have no idea what he's talking about? No, I should be able to figure this out. "Newspaper Designer" is obviously some kind of position that's arisen in the ... wait, has it been 30 years? ... since I worked on the paper. But I mean, "Designer?" A "Designer" is that fellow who flits around your house telling you what kinds of curtains and sofa fabrics would go best with the rug in your living room. An "Interior Designer," right? That's an actual job title! But why would a newspaper use a Designer? Why would reporters send their stories to a Designer?

Louey knew enough to shut up. Anything she said would just show her ignorance, and prove how much trouble it would be to train her. Don asked her a few questions about herself: What were her favorite sports? Did she play any sports in high school or college? Who were her favorite teams?

"The Brooklyn Dodgers," she said, and he smiled. She confessed that she didn't "bleed any team's colors," as people said now; she didn't gamble; she loved to see a game well played and loved watching unusual or excellent plays, in real time and then again in replays, again and again on the web or on TV, without really caring who won. Don seemed fine with this, and even reassured by it.

He told her she'd also be editing AP stories about college and pro games from around the country, and "slamming them onto the pages." Late games from the Coast came in very late, he warned her, sometimes as late as, 1:25 or 1:26

a.m., "because sometimes they start at, like, 10 p.m. out there. And our late deadline is 1:30, so that's always fun, trying to edit and put headlines and drop-heads on those stories in two minutes. I mean, the AP stories need very little editing; you just cut them from the bottom and tell the Designer when the page is done. Or sometimes I'll just yell over, 'To hell with it, go home,' because AP's too late getting the story out, so I just write, like, 'Dodgers-Giants game too late for this edition,' and you all can leave."

At any rate, she could tell that this was not an interview; it was an introduction. Mark Shapiro wanted her to be on the Sports copy desk so that she'd be first in line for a news reporting job, and Don and everyone else knew it. The fix was in. Her next, and final, stop in this building today would be the Human Relations department, to fill out the paperwork.

"Do you have any questions for me?" he said.

She had so many questions that she didn't know where to begin, so she just said pleasantly, "No, not that I can think of right now."

Don rose and told her that on Monday, they'd have a computer and desk all ready for her, right next to the Designer.

He walked her past the receptionist and down another long hallway to H.R.

"I'm sorry the guys aren't in right now, or I'd introduce you," he said, meaning the Sports copy-editors. "They don't come in till four or so. Oh, did I tell you? Regular hours are four to one, with an hour off for dinner, but every night somebody's got to stay till 1:30, so that person can come in later in the afternoon. They take turns, I think. But don't worry about it; you'll fit right in."

She wouldn't, though; she wouldn't fit in at all. Where was the newsroom? Where was Backshop? The old paper was now just a jumble of identical cubicles scattered around a huge, open space like a carpeted gymnasium. Was anybody still working here who would remember her, from Olden Tymes? She had decided not to let Don know how little she knew of newspapering in the twenty-first century. Mostly she had just nodded, and kept her mouth shut.

By the end of their twenty-minute chat, Louey realized that one of only two things were going to happen: Either she would call Mark the next day and come clean and tell him he'd made a terrible mistake—that putting out a paper now involved technology that she had no knowledge of, and that she would have to back out and let him hire someone else to do sports copy-editing and, eventually, reporting; or she would let them hire her, on the slim chance that she could find a friend in Sports who could quietly and quickly explain to her the procedures involved in operating the software, the System and the job. Could she find such a friend, though, before her awful ignorance was discovered? It would have to be a woman; only a woman would be sympathetic enough to show her the ropes like that.

Reader, there were no women in Sports. Louey did, however, find a friend; ironically, that friend turned out to be the Designer. Not much older than Rebecca, Max Lewis sat in the cubicle adjacent to Louey's. There was a stupid, fabric-covered wall between their computers, but they easily chatted face-to-face by shoving their wheeled chairs back a few inches. She asked him—she had to ask him—very basic questions that didn't seem to annoy him at all. Max himself had been on the job just three months—it was his first job out of college—and he seemed to find his ancient colleague amusing. He was always respectful to her, treating her a bit like a grandmother. In return, she kept him fed. Each night she shared leftovers from the excellent dinners Alf cooked, which Max gobbled up appreciatively —salads, chicken and rice, brisket and potatoes, or something Indian, or something Italian, plus a fancy dessert.

It was thanks to Max that she gradually found out what had happened to everything. To everyone. To newspapers themselves, as she had known them. There was no press room because there was no printing press at the Record; it had been moved to a warehouse-sized place somewhere outside the city of Middletown. The press itself was now referred to only as "Ballard Road," as in, "OK, first edition is over at Ballard Road, so everybody can take five." The huge web press that had once been not only the pride of the Record but also an attraction for journalists from countries that had not yet adopted the photo-offset method of printing, was still in operation, but now it was running 24 hours a day every day, printing the out-of-town editions of People, Newsweek, the Daily News, and other publications. Apparently, that was the only way the new owners of the Record were making any money: doing the printing for other publications.

And of course, there was no Backshop, no darkroom, no light-tables, no compositors … and hadn't been, for … Max knew not how many years. He knew only that sometime in Ancient History, all that stuff, and the people who operated it, had gone away.

But how did they get the flats over to the press, she asked.

Well, he didn't know what she meant by "flats," but there was nothing physical that intervened between their computers and Ballard Road. Don hit a button on his computer and over to Ballard Road went all the edited, digital sports pages for each edition. The night editor, likewise, hit a button and over to Ballard Road went all the News pages. The photos, all taken digitally now, were sent to the System so the Designers could choose the best ones, and they, likewise, "hit a few buttons" and sent them to Ballard Road. There was no darkroom. They had no need for one.

The Dayside editor hit a button around 2 p.m. each day, and off to Ballard Road went all the ad pages, the comics and advice pages, and any Special Sections.

Simple as that. Weird as that. Sad as that.

Louey fell into the regular rotation of being "Late Man." You'd think the other two copy-editors would have been grateful to have her aboard, to lessen the number of times each of them had to do that from every other night to once every three nights, but no one said anything to her about it. In fact, one of them, known universally as "Silent Phil," said almost nothing to her at all, ever. Sitting atop her desk, above and just a bit behind her computer, loomed an inch-thick, three-foot-high fabric-covered divider. If it weren't for that, she'd be looking right at Phil all night. But even without the wall, he would have been all but invisible. A tall, thin man, Silent Phil somehow managed to "lie back" at work as if he were in a recliner. His head lay barely above the chairback, and he stayed that way all night, never rising, that Louey ever noticed, even to use the bathroom. He was always there when she arrived, and when 1 o'clock came, if it wasn't his turn to be Late Man, he just turned off his computer and slunk out the back door. Besides his radio silence, the only other thing Phil was famous for was that he loved, in his headlines, to refer to the Miami Marlins as the "Fish."

"Fish swamp Mets," he would write. Or, "Mets gobble Fish."

The other Sports copy-editor, making the fourth in their little pod, was a specialist: Tony the Agate Guy. He assembled all the box scores from professional baseball, football and basketball games and the results of boxing matches, golf tournaments, horse races, auto races, high-school swim and track meets and all the other material that had to be set in five-point type. Tony was constantly pushing his glasses up onto his forehead and rubbing his eyes, which were permanently red and rheumy.

Early in her job in Sports, Louey tried asking Phil questions about style—should she write of the women's pro-basketball team, "Liberty top Monarchs," or "Liberty tops Monarchs?" Or, she would lob over their divider questions like which stories to edit first—did local stories always take precedence over MLB stories? He never responded, though she knew he could hear her in the weird, silent tomb they shared.

One night she rolled her chair back a foot or so and called over to her buddy.

"Psst! Max!"

He pushed his chair back and looked over at her. She leaned close to him and whispered, "Did I do something to piss Phil off, do you know?"

"No; don't let it bother you," he whispered back. "He's

like that to everybody. Something happened once, where he almost got fired for speaking up about something. That's what I heard, anyway. And ever since then he's never said a word."

Max found his graphic-arts-based position extremely easy to handle—even rather boring, Louey could tell, as his cool, creative ideas were almost always constrained by the ever-smaller format of the paper. He was quick to help his new colleague with all her questions.

"Don tells me what stories we're expecting," he explained early on, "and based on that, I design the pages. When the AP sends over the early game stories I design the pages for them and send the pages over to the System, and the copy-editors—you or Phil, it doesn't matter, whoever grabs them first— just edit them in InDesign, put a head on them—I tell you what font and size—and let them run as full as needed. You shorten them from the bottom by dragging up their little 'window shade' thingy as far as you want. Those AP stories need very little editing, though. Then during the night, as more and more games come into the System, you drag each old story's window shade higher and higher and slap each new story in below it, edit it and write a little head for it. By the end of the night—by, like, third edition—the page might have a dozen little stories on it, instead of one big, long one."

Oh, thank God. She wouldn't even have to learn to do the thing she most feared: wrapping text around photos. InDesign would do that automatically.

"Really? How does it do that?" she said.

"Magic," Max said, smiling, and turned back to his computer.

Oh, phew. I think I'm going to be able to do this.

Between editions, sometimes, Max asked Louey a bit about her life.

"Wait. You mean, your husband lives in Long Island and you live in Newburgh?" He was smiling and frowning at the same time, as he said that.

"Yeah."

"How's that working out for you?"

"It's perfect!" Louey said. "I love it! It's what I always wanted in college, and never got to have: a date, every weekend!"

Pretty soon, though, the "commuter" part of their "commuter marriage" ended. As Alf had predicted, the bishop transfered him to a church in the Hudson Valley, much closer to Newburgh—right across the river, in Poughkeepsie, in fact. His sons were both in college, so everything had, indeed, worked out perfectly. He had to get a new driver's license, stop several subscriptions and make changes to a few dozen banking, insurance and work-related papers, but Alfred Reece was, at last, ensconced in Newburgh.

"Now we're like a regular married couple," Louey marveled during his first night at his new, official address.

"Yes!" he said.

"Is that good?"

There was an extra-long silence after the question, but then they chuckled together at the lack of an answer.

After a while, Louey started to find her job tedious, rather than difficult. Or rather, she found it both tedious and difficult, but it was starting to be more tedious, now, than difficult. She began to look longingly, when she got a chance, at the News-side copy-editors across the room who came in around the same time she did but left at least an hour earlier each night. They were almost the only people from News-side she ever saw; most of the reporters now filed their stories from their laptop computers in the field. The few who came into the office grabbed any available computer in any empty cubicle, typed their stories and left before she ever arrived in Middletown. And any who were still there when she arrived could be found busily typing behind their little cubicle walls for only a half-hour or so before they, too, went home.

News copy-editors, Louey noticed with envy, often called reporters for clarifications and asked questions of one another about which county some little hamlet was in, or the spelling of some mayor's name. To her surprise, the Desk was no longer composed of tables arranged in a "U," with a "slot man" in the middle, directing everything. It was just eight people, four facing four, slaving away in adjacent cubicles like a bigger version of the Sports setup.

The news copy-editors almost always joined forces to order dinner from various local restaurants, and jocularly dickered over the bill when the food came. They had a huge plastic pretzel-jar jammed with napkins and plastic utensils and packets of fortune cookies, hot sauce, duck sauce, salt, pepper and ketchup atop one of their file cabinets. They were nearly all young women, of the age Louey was when she first worked at the Record all those years ago. The only exception was News-side's Designer, who was, of course, a young man.

Ah, that was the life: News-side. When could she be a reporter again? When would she be able to leave this crappy

Sports copy-editing job, and start doing the real journalism she loved? Mark Shapiro paused each night for a minute to shoot the breeze with her as he walked through Sports to get to his car in the back parking lot. He would squeeze her shoulder and give her a little shake as he leaned close to whisper, almost without breaking stride: "Don't worry, we'll have something for you pretty soon. Nothing yet, but something will come up soon, I'm pretty sure. Maybe even in Newburgh. So, hang in there, OK?"

Hope! He was the Voice of Hope! Oh, how she loved him.

The exciting part of Sports copy-editing, which always came at the very, very tail-end of the night, was actually too exciting. One might more accurately call it "stomach-churning," or "nerve-wracking." The guy she was replacing, she quickly found out, had died of a heart attack at his desk. But Louey tried to force herself to think of the last few minutes of the night as the "exciting" part, or the "fun" part, so that she didn't get too scared, angry or depressed.

The exciting part, a few minutes before Late Final deadline, was when Louey and Silent Phil had to pluck from the System the AP stories that finally arrived from the Coast. Mercifully, AP sports stories were written to a formula that always told the game's result and its hero within the first or second sentence. But then Phil and Louey had to slam the stories onto the InDesign page, chopping off all of the story that didn't fit. Then they had to write the headline and also a drop-head of two or three decks, all with the same number of characters in them, none ending with a preposition; and rewrite the caption for the accompanying photo, because AP captions weren't written to Record style and contained dates and codes that needed to be deleted. All this had to be done, as Don had warned her, within about a minute and a half to two minutes. Near the end of that minute or minute and a half, Don would sometimes rise, crack his knuckles and call over to the copy desk, "Half a minute to get those headlines in, guys." Then he would stand up 20 seconds later and call out, "How's it going over there?"

Despite the madness at the end of the night, the job also entailed hours of absolutely no work at all until about 7 p.m., followed by mad bursts of getting the stories on the pages in time for the deadlines for first, second and third editions. Then an hour or two more of mostly waiting, interrupted intermittently by editing of stories from the Record's own Sports reporters about local high-school track meets, swim meets, basketball games, and so forth. Those stories sometimes required calls to reporters to check on weird spellings of names, explanations of improbable scores ("Homers helped the Goldbacks top the Middies on Friday, 95-2"), or other problems. But no matter what happened, there were always a few lulls each night.

During one of them, Louey decided she would make a list of all the words that were synonyms for "beat." Ninety percent of the heads they had to write fit the formula, "X Beats Y": "Reds Beat Jays"; "Marlins Beat Yanks," "Dodgers Beat Giants." Those three words would be followed by the score, if more characters were needed to fill up the space Max had designed for it. And who would want to read a paper where every single headline, on every single Sports page, was

"X Beats Y?" She would share her list with Silent Phil, and be the hero of the Sports Department. Under deadline pressure at the tail end of the night, it was hard to think of a good synonym for "beat" that hadn't already been used on that same page.

She started with three-letter words, perfect for stories where Max needed a head just one column wide: rip, zip, top, bop, nip. She had twenty or so of those when she started a list of four-letter words: clip, trip, bash, mash, slam, sink. After about thirty of those she went on to five-letter words: slash, trash, crush, smack; and six-letter synonyms: mangle, hammer, thrash. She focused on trying to include a wide variety of verbs depending on how the game went: Since "slip past" has the same nine characters as "overwhelm," she put them both down.

She'd been on staff about two months when one night, between editions, Max rolled his chair back and began alternately touching his fingers to the carpet and reaching up toward the ceiling, hands clasped, and bending a little side to side. Then, hands still overhead, he leaned alarmingly far back, risking breaking his mildly flexible chairback and, turning his face slightly toward his colleague, idly asked through a great huge yawn, "What are you up to, Levy?"

When she told Max about her little project, he laughed and immediately began suggesting words for her.

"Clip? Do you have clip?"

"Sure! Like, 'Habs clip Wings!' I've used that one."

"Rout? Do you have rout?" he offered. "Do you have drown?"

"Drown?" she frowned.

"Yeah, like, 'Yanks drown Marlins,' or 'Jets drown Dolphins.'"Those would work, wouldn't they?"

Well, yes. Yes, they would. She added many of Max's suggestions to her ever-growing lists, and meanwhile she tried to do what Shapiro had urged: She tried to hang in there. It was so tedious, waiting and waiting and waiting for the AP stories to come in, and then it was so nerve-wracking, having to write heads, drop-heads, sub-heads, and cut stories to fit all in a minute! She really, really, really wanted to go over to News-side.

She already knew it would be a miracle if a reporting job came up, much less in Newburgh, where there was no bureau anymore. But she would take a News copy-editing job in a heartbeat. She watched with envy each night as the News copy-editors trooped off all together at midnight or even earlier, depending on what was happening that day locally or worldwide. They all seemed to be chatting breezily with one another all night, and laughing at some of the more comical errors they'd caught, and helping one another.

The day after Louey added "drown" and "rout" to her lists, not two months into her new job, Mark Shapiro died.

Don called her at home to tell her. Mark had had a heart attack at home, just a few hours after he left work.

She couldn't believe it. He'd seemed fine at the office yesterday, didn't he? She'd seen him. He was as cheerful and bouncy as ever. He had no physical problems that Don had ever heard of. He was a skinny little guy, only 52, who didn't smoke and seemed like the last guy you'd ever think would drop dead. But Don wanted to tell her because Mark, being

Jewish, was going to be buried the next day. The funeral would be in the morning, down in Monroe, where he lived. He was going to be buried in a Jewish cemetery somewhere around there; nobody was invited to the burial except family. That way, everybody could go to the funeral and still get to work on time. Leave it to Shapiro. But Don wanted to tell her so she could make plans.

Dear Diary,

Plans? The old Jewish joke is so true: You know the best way to make G-d laugh? Tell Him your plans.

Mark Shapiro had plans—plans for himself and his family, of course, but more importantly, for me!

People say of old folks that they're "running out of time." But we're all running out of it! Time only exists in our little lives, and we are all always, from the moment of our birth, "running out of it." Look at Mark. He was only 52. He was running out of time real fast, and just didn't know it. But I'm comforted to suspect that the opposite is true: We actually get more and more time every day. I mean, I get the same 24 hours a day as everyone else, but as I age I hope and pray I'm learning how to use those hours better. What really happens is that as we attain great age, we have more and more time, until at the moment we pass into eternity (again), we find we have all the time in the world. Time doesn't hold us down anymore, because it doesn't exist.

After what she hoped was a decent interval, Louey took a minute during the early part of her shift to go into the office of a perpetually frowning middle-aged woman named Bev Lonsdale. They had never been introduced. The new publisher—but how "new" was he, really? Louey hadn't been back at the Record for thirty years! Osterhout was probably dead, by now!—had given Bev the unofficial title of "Acting Executive Editor" when Mark died. Bev wasn't writing the editorials, though. Bev was a lousy writer. They'd farmed those out to a recovering alcoholic who had been the editorial-page editor ten or twenty years ago. Louey didn't even know how long Bev had been at the Record. Maybe twelve years; maybe twelve weeks.

The door was closed, but Louey heard a voice inside say, "Yes?"

She opened it and said, "Bev, hi, do you have a minute?"

She looked at her watch and said, "Yeah, just about."

"When … when Mark hired me, it was to be a reporter. I agreed to take the sports copy desk opening only until a reporting vacancy came up in News, and then I'd get the reporting job. I just wanted to make sure you were aware of that. You knew about that, right?"

"What? That's impossible. We can't have a city council member working on News-side. That would be a total conflict of interest!" She put an elbow on her desk and held her face in her hand.

"It must be in his files somewhere, that that was the condition under which I accepted this job. I mean, we didn't put it in writing, but that was the deal."

It sounded lame, even to Louey, so she added, "Of course, I wouldn't write about Newburgh politics—that would be off-limits for me."

Desperation was seeping into her soul and voice.

"I would even take a general-assignment gig."

And be stationed in Middletown, as in the Days of Yore? Well, yes. Yes, she would.

"You do see the conflict of interest, don't you?" Bev gave her a closed-lips, wide smile in a way—slight shake of the head, eyebrows raised, chin tucked, "Now I'm talking to an especially slow kindergartner"—that made Louey want to punch her in the face.

"I don't think it would be a conflict if I were on the copy desk, though. I did that for years here, back in the '70s."

"Back in the '70s!" Something a grandfather would say.

The '70s were a thing that happened in a whole other millennium, and held no interest for Bev Lonsdale.

"Well, there's no openings on the Desk right now, but I'll keep that in mind. Thanks for coming in," she said.

The calendar pages flew rapidly off Louey's cubicle wall as they did in the black-and-white movie of Jackie Robinson's life to portray the passage of time. Max Lewis, to Louey's sorrow, moved to California to take a position called Game Developer. He was replaced by another, even younger, Designer, named Marv, who was as capable and bored as Max and who almost immediately took a graphic-arts position with the same software company in California that Max was working for; in fact, Max recommended him for both the Record job and the software-company job. How Max knew Marv was never clear to Louey, because she didn't have time to ask. Marv left the Record after only six months. Marv was replaced, before his padded chair had cooled, by another young man, and he by another one, and that one by another. The sixth Designer of Louey's tenure lasted an ungodly amount of time at the paper—more than two years—before jumping ship to produce violent video games in Oregon. Designers, all technologically brilliant young men whom Louey liked very much, kept coming and going, and the calendar pages kept flying away.

One night mid-shift, the phone rang on Louey's desk. Her phone almost never rang at work, and when it did, the caller was usually trying to reach someone else.

"Sports desk! Levy!" she said cheerfully. She enjoyed riffing on her old routine answer from News-Side of long ago.

"Is this Louey Levy?" a woman's voice said hesitantly.

"Yes."

"Louey, this is Rosie Cartright."

She knew the name from somewhere but couldn't quite place it. Instinctively she rose from her seat; she could always think better when standing. She turned so her back was to her desk, so she could concentrate better. The voice didn't sound like any of her old college friends, or any of her old pals from CSEU or NYNU. Who was it, though?

Rosie let her off the hook.

"From Region 10 Special Olympics! Years ago, remember? Seth's mother."

The 'Right to Life' lady! Why is she calling me?

"Oh, yeah! Seth! How is he?"

He's such a sweet little guy. That smile! My buddy! She hoped he was doing good.

"Seth passed away three years ago. Three years ago Wednesday, in fact."

Louey spun her chair around and sat down in it hard. She felt a little sick.

Seth had never been in very good health, Rosie said. He had been hospitalized many times for problems related to his Down syndrome—his "co-morbidities," they called them. And finally, they just caught up to him.

"Oh, God, Rosie," Louey said softly. "I'm so sorry. I hadn't heard. He was such a good kid."

"Thank you. Yes. Yes, he was. He was very special to me."

"And to me, too. To everybody! He was an angel! How are you and your husband doing?"

They weren't doing well. They'd gotten divorced.

"Oh. Oh, I'm sorry," Louey said again.

Levy, you're an idiot. Why can't I think of something useful to say? Dear God. Why is she calling me?

She spun back toward her desk and grabbed a pencil. Writing on her desk pad, she tried to figure out how old Seth had been when he died. *If he was, like, 10, in, what was it, '82? He'd be ... let's see, that was ... something ... from today ... minus three ...* Oh hell, she'd do it later. Math was always the first thing to leave her brain when she was upset.

"Louey, I'm pregnant," Rosie said. "I wonder if you can help me."

Sometimes you'll be going along with your day, or your whole life, really, in the same way you always did, with nothing ever changing, and then the phone rings and everything changes. That's what happened right then. Louey knew her immediate reaction was irrelevant and rude, but she couldn't help blurting it out.

"How old are you?"

"Fifty-two. Well, I'll be fifty-two next month."

Before her heart beat twice, Louey rose and stood again and took a couple of steps with her back to her desk, hoping for a tiny sliver of privacy, even though the new Sports Designer was not three feet from her and Silent Phil was just on the other side of the flimsy divider. Every one of the following thoughts flew through her brain:

Impossible. You can't get pregnant when you're fifty-two. Doesn't she know that? That's only ... let's see ... seven years younger than me! And who got her pregnant, if she's divorced? Wait. That's not the point. The point is, why is she calling me? *Why didn't she just call UHPP in Albany? That must be, all of what, ten miles from her house? And how did she get my number? For God's sake, fifty-one; she's not pregnant—she's in menopause! And why is she calling* me?

"Do think you can you help me?" Rosie asked again.

"Yes. Absolutely. I'll be glad to. But Rosie, can you hang on for just one second?"

"Yes."

Deadline's hot breath was on her neck. She thought they'd already edited all the Page 35 stories for the Newburgh edition, but there was one more in the System. The new Designer had swiveled his chair and was repeatedly waving mock-frantically and pointing to her computer with one hand and pantomiming typing motions with his other. Silent Phil was studiously ignoring the story, or maybe he'd fallen asleep, or sneaked off to the john. Or died; she wouldn't know.

Louey wedged the phone between her ear and shoulder and, still standing, stared at a hockey-game story from the AP. It was the final story at the bottom of the NHL "round-up" page. She needed to headline it in small type, centered in two decks just one column wide. Then she had to find three inches or so to cut from the other stories that had filled up the page in the Pike edition, and slam the new story into the now-empty space.

The Pittsburgh Penguins had beaten the Buffalo Sabres. She typed:

Pens mightier
than Swords

She cut the last paragraph out of a couple of other stories on that page, rolled up the window-shade thingy to hide the bottom nine-tenths of the Penguins-Sabres story, sent the page back into the System and gave the Designer the thumbs-up and a smile. She had taken not twenty seconds away from her call. She walked a few steps from her cubicle, which was as far as the curly phone cord would let her go.

"Sorry, sorry; you still there, Rosie?"

"Yes."

"OK, I'm good now, go ahead."

"Well, it's just that I know you used to work for Planned Parenthood, and I wonder if you can help me find a place to have an abortion."

A half-minute of silence ensued, during which Louey could tell Rosie was crying.

"I can't," she sobbed. "I just can't. I can't go through this again."

By "this," Louey figured she meant: everything. Having a kid with an incurable condition; giving him all your love and time and energy for, like, thirty-something years, and then …

then he has to go and leave you. And then your husband runs away, too.

God enveloped Louey in a cloud of kindness and reasonableness. As a result, Louey never said, "Well, well, well! Mrs. Right to Life of the Capital District wants an abortion?" or anything like that. Peg would be so proud of her! And maybe haShem would, too.

Instead, she said with no hesitation, "Rosie, you have a right to your *own* life. Don't feel bad; you're doing the right thing! And everything's going to be all right."

She could not resist, however, asking: "Rosie, how the heck did you get my number? I can't believe you even remembered me!"

It was a whole story. Rosie had saved, for more than twenty-five years now, as part of her ever-growing, alphabetized, photo-album-style collection of business cards, one from a certain Louey Levy, Patient Escort, Upper Hudson Planned Parenthood. She had kept it as a kind of joke. But she never forgot it was there: She had even taken it out and showed it to people over the years, telling, as a kind of joke on herself, the story of how she had once entrusted her petitions to a Planned Parenthood volunteer.

"Wait. I gave you one of my Patient Escort cards? I never used those! I thought I gave you one of my business cards! I was working for CSEU at the time!"

"Well, but you were also volunteering with Planned Parenthood, right?"

Oh crap. Those cards that I never gave to anyone, not even once in my whole, entire life? I must have had a few in my purse. In that nice silk envelope-thingy that Nancy gave me.

"Seriously? I gave you an Upper Hudson Planned Parenthood Volunteer card?"

"I thought you did it on purpose."

"No! I thought I was giving you my CSEU business card! But how did you find me *here*?"

This is how. Earlier that day—before the puck had even dropped at the Penguins-Sabres game—Rosie called UHPP to ask for Louey, but they said they had no one there by that name. She called Hank, who was still the director of Region 10 Special Olympics, but Louey's name didn't ring a bell for him and he didn't keep records on former volunteers. So then, she said, she went to her "collections." Every year, Rosie requested and saved all the annual reports that UHPP filed with New York State, because they always told how many abortions they'd performed that year, and she could keep track of them that way. The reports always had a "Transitions" column on the last page, where they named the staff members who'd recently retired or been hired, and ran little blurbs about them. And there, in "Transitions" in an issue from the late 1990s was a photo of Louey at the shindig they'd thrown for her when she told them she was moving to Newburgh. There was a little story with it, saying she would be renovating her house down there on Saturdays now, while still working weekdays for the Communications Department of the nurses union in Albany, commuting in her trusty old car. It ended with something like, "We wish her good luck—and safe travels!"

So then, Rosie had called the union and said she was an old pal of Louey's and was trying to reach her. A very cheerful woman with an English accent told her Louey was working nights now at the Record, down in Orange County, and gave her the Record's main number because she didn't know Louey's extension. By the time Rosie had gotten up the courage to call, the receptionist had left, and she had to start spelling Louey's name to be transfered, and at first she'd dialed "L-O-U-I-E" and heard, "There is no one here by that name" so she looked again at Louey's "business card" from Planned Parenthood and this time she spelled her name right. And that's how she finally reached her.

"Oh, wow. OK. Wow. Whew. OK. Well. Well, anyway: How far along are you, would you say?"

"About six weeks, I think. My period was due last month, and it never came."

"OK, hang on, Rosie. I'm just trying to be rational now, OK? I think you may just be going into menopause, and that's why you missed your period, right? That's the most likely reason why someone of your … of our age would miss a period, you know?"

"No. I bought one of those at-home tests at a pharmacy and it said positive."

"Well, if that's true, you're just very newly pregnant, anyway. So that's good. But Rosie, why don't you just go to the Planned Parenthood in Albany? You know—my old employer! They're just a few miles from you! They'll do it for you. They'll be glad to."

"No! No way. I can't! I can't go anywhere around here! Everybody knows me. They'd leak it to the press."

Louey's tone changed to a lower, more authoritative one, and she got a bit louder, and she left a meaningful little pause after each statement. "No they wouldn't. I can guarantee that.

They never would do that. Confidentiality is sacred to them. I know them. They wouldn't."

Rosie's voice cracked as she said, "I have to go somewhere else. I can't go anywhere around here. I'm too well-known. Isn't there a place down by you, that you know of? That you volunteer at, or anything?" She was sobbing again.

Louey wasn't volunteering at the Newburgh Planned Parenthood and, in fact, knew no one there. Of course, they would do it, for sure. But she had a better idea.

"Wait, would Binghamton work? That's more than two hours from Schenectady, while Orange County's only an hour and a half from you. So Binghamton would be better, right?"

Well, yes. Yes, it would.

Because, Louey continued, she had a friend there! Her old college pal, Peg, was the director of the Southern Tier Women's Health Center. And would help her in a heartbeat.

"Now—believe me—the first thing they'll do is, they'll check your work. But then if you really are pregnant, they'll perform the abortion, no problem. They even have a sliding scale."

"Oh, thank God. I knew there was a reason I kept your card. I knew you would help me, because you were so sweet to Seth. I can feel God's hand in this, I really can."

How in the world did she even remember me, from one stupid weekend all those years ago? That's almost freaky!

"Rosie, do you have a pencil? Here, I'll give you Peg's number, and give me yours too, OK, in case I have to get back to you. I'll run interference for you; I'll call her right now. And then you call her tomorrow and remind her that you're the woman I told her about. But don't worry, Rosie; they don't care who you are. Honest. I mean, they'll ask you a lot of questions, but they're all about confidentiality! Your confidentiality and your health. They'll set up an appointment for you real quick, I promise. They'll fix you right up." She jotted down Rosie's number on a page of the reporter's notebook lying on her desk.

Peg Jansen didn't mind picking up the phone when Louey called her so late in the night; rather, she was amused and glad to hear from her old pal. Sure enough, Southern Tier would indeed help Rosie Cartright.

"But don't ask me anything about her procedure," Peg said. "It really is completely confidential."

Dear Diary,

Why do people say "G-d had a hand in" something only when it's something good? Those are the same people who say, "G-d is on our side," as in, "Yay! We killed a million of their soldiers, and they killed only a thousand of ours!" or, "Yay! The Mets beat the Yankees!" or, "Yay! Our candidate won!" From every little victory, they conclude that, therefore: "G-d was on our side!" What bullshit.

I always wonder what the losing side is saying. If you call heads six times in a row and the coin lands heads the first, third and fifth times and tails the other three times, does that mean G-d was on your side only on the odd tosses and switched sides on the even ones, just to mess with you? That is so stupid. If G-d "had a hand in" Rosie's calling me, was that the same G-d who let her fall pregnant? Did G-d have a hand in that, too? Or was that some other G-d? More likely, I'd say, it was carelessness, or forgetfulness. Or a faulty condom.

I mean, I'm sorry for Rosie; I'm sorry about her whole life. I can't imagine having a child and pouring all my time and energy and love and hopes and money into him, only to have his life turn out to be so stinking short, and then having to say goodbye and bury him, and all his possibilities with him.

When you're a newborn, no one knows who or what you're going to be. No one knows what you're going to do or think, or how you're going to talk, or whom you're going to love, or anything. The great thing about living is, it's a constant, awesome surprise to see who you're turning out to be. You're growing more and more like yourself every day. You become bigger and more interesting and more burnished every day, because of your experiences. As you attain great age, you can see who you really are. It's like how only in autumn do leaves shed their green and show their true colors that they had underneath, unseen, the whole time. And that's the tragedy of Seth's dying so young: So many of his possibilities were clipped off that no one got to know who he really, really was. No one but G-d.

When Louey got home from work that night, even before she wrote about it in her diary, she told Alf all about her call with Rosie Cartright.

"I actually said the words, 'Everything's going to be all right!' Can you believe that? Is there anything more useless to say, when you're talking to somebody who's practically suicidal and has lost her child and her husband and needs real advice? I went (here Louey imitated the inflection of the Disney cartoon character Goofy), 'Well, don't worry: Everything's going to be all right!' I actually said, 'Don't worry,' too! 'Don't worry,' I said, 'Everything's going to be all right!' and then I outdid myself and said, 'Don't feel bad,' too! I'm such a good therapist. I'm so helpful, to people."

She smacked the side of her head twice with the heel of her hand, rather hard.

"You did exactly the right thing," Alf said. "She needed to tell her story, and you listened and let her tell it, and you provided a non-anxious presence for her to unload on. That's all you can do when someone is in grief and in panic. And you also gave her the best advice possible, which was to go to Peg's clinic. So you were very helpful, and I'm very proud of you."

Louey spent the next several days irrationally hoping to get a thank-you call from Rosie, or maybe a bouquet of flowers, or more likely, a relieved message saying nope, she wasn't pregnant after all, just going into menopause, haha, false alarm. But no bouquets and no message came. After a few weeks Louey gave up thinking about Ms. Right-to-Life of the Capital District, and, Reader, she never heard from her again.

City Council was taking up more and more of Louey Levy's time. She considered the City, and not the Record, to be her real job. She found the conflicting rights and interests of Newburghers to be hard, fun puzzles, and she considered them successfully solved when Council took actions resulting in the most good for the most people within the limits of the city's budget. It was the only kind of calculus she was ever good at. She never learned so much in her life, as she did on Council.

This is my real grad school, she realized.

The main thing she was learning was that, at least in government, better decisions are more likely to be made by the whole group than by the smartest guy in the room. Mendoza, a young, multilingual polymath, hadn't had Louey's experiences, and she hadn't had Mendoza's. Mendoza didn't know the people of Ward 2, just as Louey didn't know the people of Ward 1. Every member of Council, representing various wards, had something unique to contribute. They had to figure out together the best answers, the best projects for the whole City. And they were doing it. Little by little, Louey's dear old City was coming along.

Louey and Alf were coming along, too, now that his new church position allowed him to be home every night. Because they had lived apart so long, they were still—still, still, still, after all these years—getting to know each other. And enjoying it. They delighted in discovering how similar they were in their spiritual and political outlooks, and also in discovering the places where they differed. That's why Louey was surprised one evening as they hosted a group of neighbors for dinner to find herself oddly comfortable. She realized that she could actually, accurately, describe herself as "comfortable."

"Look at us: We're just like a married couple!" she said, looking at Alf. The neighbors laughed, but she meant it quite seriously.

"How so?" Alf asked.

"I mean, admit it, we're grownups! We have these leisurely meals with nutritious food and cloth napkins, and we're drinking beer out of glasses now, instead of cans ... and ..." looking around, she added, " ... and we have all these married friends!"

"And how about the fact that our kids have all managed to be employed?" Alf chipped in.

It was true. Jon, Sam and Rebecca all had graduated from college and were working at good jobs—the boys as music teachers, Rebecca as an educator at a science museum in Massachusetts.

At work one night shortly after that dinner, between editions, Louey got a breathless call from Boston. Rebecca almost never called her at work; Louey panicked, fearing she was having some kind of emergency.

"Mom! Guess what!" Rebecca said.

"What!"

"I'm certified in lizards!"

"Pardon?"

"I can handle all our reptiles now! I can do lizards and snakes programs in the schools!"

After details and congratulations were shared, Louey walked very slowly to the Coke machine in the lunchroom, pondering. It felt like a watershed moment in her life.

Well, then, she thought. *Well, maybe that's it, then.*

Social Security age is upon me, and my daughter is Certified in Lizards. What more can anyone ask from life?

This might be God telling me it's time to quit the Record. Again.

Face it: I'm old now. I'm totally old. I mean, how many people have stayed healthy, had a few laughs, earned a few pensions, and then still went on to see their daughter Certified in Lizards? Maybe it's time for me to tell my story. Now. Now, before my skin gets all crepe-y and crappy and all my mail is from hearing-aid companies.

She broached the idea of retirement to Alf.

"We'll get along fine. Don't even worry about it. I only want you to be happy," he said. She'd heard those words from him before, and she knew he meant them.

She got out her notebook and drew a line down the middle of a page. "Pros," she wrote at the top of one side, and "Cons" at the top of the other.

Pros: Time! She'd be able to write and hike and garden, any time she wanted to. Could she afford it, though? Well, serving on City Council was paying her a little honorarium plus dental insurance, and that insurance covered Alf's crumbling teeth, too. For healthcare, she was covered by Alfie's "Methodist Pastor's Health Insurance," which was an amazing grace. Plus, she was already collecting pensions from CSEU and NYNU, and she'd get another one from the Record. Heck, she'd worked at the paper more than ten years, counting her time as a cub reporter, editor and Checkout Princess. And then Social Security—that would pay something. Not much, probably, but something.

Cons: She could think of only one: They'd be poor. Even with Alf's income, they'd be poor. And then he would retire too, someday.

But, so what? she wrote. *We've always been poor! Hiking, birding and gardening don't cost anything. Alfie can whip up great meals out of nothing, and we'll have* plenty *of nothing! And look: We're still healthy! Life has lived us well; we can still have a few more laughs.*

The next morning, the most amazing thing happened: A moving van pulled up and four huge men moved a beautiful upright Steinway piano into the house on Bayview Terrace.

It was built in 1879 in Philadelphia, according to the brass tag under its lid. It was from Luke's sister in Maine, and she had kept it in mint condition. It had been in the family for generations, but no one up there played it, her note read. It would give her pleasure to think of Rebecca playing it on her visits home.

Rebecca did retain much of her childhood piano-playing skills, and did occasionally play a few songs on her visits to Newburgh. But it was Alf who filled their lives with classical music, church music, songs of the American Song Book, rock 'n' roll, blues, and jazz – anything that Louey could find the sheet music for, or play for him on her hundreds of albums and CDs, he would play for her. No poor person could have been happier than Louey when he played and sang, and no rich person, either.

One morning Louey was out gardening when she heard the distinctive, gruff voice of her neighbor, the assemblyman.

"Hey! Levy!"

"What!"

"Get over here, will ya?"

She walked across the little lawn to the side of his porch, amused by the knowledge of how she must look with her dirt-caked knee pads and gardening gloves on and holding her trowel in her right hand like a lantern.

"What."

He was holding that day's paper.

"Tell me something. What kind of idiot would offer you a product for a dollar in one hand, and the same thing for free in the other hand?" Before she had a chance to answer, he added, "And what kind of idiot would you have to be to take the dollar one?"

She didn't know what kind of idiot, but she knew what was coming.

"I'm canceling my subscription! For the first time in my life, I'm canceling my subscription! And what idiot wouldn't! Because we can get the same stories on your own stupid website for free! That's the stupidest thing I ever heard of! Do they *want* to go out of business? Who the hell is running that paper?"

It was true that, while the Record had a website, it hadn't yet decided whether, or when, or how much to start charging for subscriptions to its online version; nor what price to then charge for the "paper-paper"; nor whether to put some stories only online, or only in the paper, and if so, which ones. The online version was chaotic, since reporters had been instructed to file their stories, unedited, directly from the field to the web. The quality of the resulting product was the one anyone might expect.

Louey Levy's own daughter—Rebecca, the Brutus of Bayview Terrace—had already delivered the cruelest blow years earlier, in a call from college.

"Mom, I'm never going to have a subscription to a newspaper," she announced.

Alarming. Alarming and infuriating and scandalous and unbelievable. "How will you know what the hell is going on in the world?"

"The Web," Rebecca had said simply.

The Web. Louey herself, no question, already was getting most of her news—and most of her information, and most of her entertainment—from the Web.

What? No newspapers wanted by this scion of the Levy family? Ink was in her blood. Newsprint was her very life. Every day Louey could remember, going back to her childhood, a newspaper had been delivered to a Levy mailbox. Her parents had laughed and argued about the latest stories each day; she and her brother had shouted together in joy or agony over the outcomes of sporting events. Her mother had once ducked under a spread-open paper at Ebbets Field to protect herself from a foul pop-up.

Ah, but that was another story. Louey Levy's newspaper story was coming to an end.

Well, Rebecca and her whole generation were "reading the papers," in a way: They were reading many newspapers' stories online. Some papers (not the Record) had already figured out a way to prevent their stories from being forwarded to non-subscribers, and some papers (not the Record) were charging people a fee to read any of their online stories at all, or any beyond the first few. Some were charging a pittance for ads on their websites, and some had already begun charging a substantial amount. Some (not the Record) had figured out how to survive and even thrive in the Digital Age.

The Record had been sold, resold and then resold again, to bigger and bigger chains, each sale resulting in layoffs of reporters and copy-editors. No one knew what anyone's title was any more. The new management was paying a Consultant a sickeningly high fee to help the paper "move to the Web."

"The Web is the future of journalism!" the Consultant exclaimed to the remaining staff, in a series of bleak seminars in the Record's lunchroom. He put bowls containing round stickers with mindless sayings on them on a table where everyone had to sign in and where a normal company's seminar room might sport bagels and coffee. His assistant, seated at that table, earnestly suggested that the staff slap the stickers on their shirts and wear them at work and while off-duty, among "civilians," as well. No one did.

On one such "seminar day," the stickers were printed with three bold, upper-case letters: TWF. The Consultant asked what the group thought the letters stood for and then, after three seconds of silence, announced proudly: "Think Web First!" He tried to get everyone chanting that.

"Come on! Think! Web! First! Think! Web! First!" he yelled, pacing a few steps in each direction and frantically waving his hands toward himself, a cheerleader on a silent psychiatric ward.

Louey placed her sticker, its paper backing still affixed, atop the notepad on her lap and wrote, diagonally upward from each initial, what she thought the acronym really stood for:

"Team, We're Fucked."

In response to a question from a reporter, the Consultant said that they should, "of course," continue to strive for accuracy, but advised them not to "let accuracy hold you back." Worry about speed, he said. Speed was paramount. "Be first! Other papers are right on your heels! Sprint across that finish line before they catch you! Go, go, go! Copy-editors can always fix the story later, at their leisure, and correct any errors in the 'errata' column." Copy-editors, of course, had no "leisure" to correct the stories that were already online, which would involve reading the stories all over again.

And then one day, the paper's "Corrections" column, at the Consultant's recommendation, disappeared forever.

That made it appear to readers as if they suddenly were making no mistakes, when the truth was, they were simply no longer correcting their mistakes.

Well, that's it, Louey thought. *I'm bailing.*

She wrote to Danny in Florida:

In other words, it's not a newspaper anymore. We're not seeking the truth and telling it; we're just trying to ... what? I can't even tell. Make money? If so, we're very, very bad at it.

He wrote back: *Give it a rest. Sue and I don't subscribe to a paper anymore, either. The Web is the future.*

Human Resources told her the years she'd worked for the paper in the 1970s wouldn't count in determining her pension, as they were "too long ago."

"What kind of non-sequitur is that? They should count *double!*" she said.

"Only your 21st-century years count," they said.

Most of my years have been 20th-Century years. I'm an artifact of another century, to be dug up with amazement one day, like the skeleton of a mastodon. I do not belong here.

Human Resources didn't see things her way, and neither did the latest new management, which, unbeknownst to Louey, had been offering no pension plan at all for anyone hired in the past two years.

She turned in her two weeks' notice, a note that was sadder but barely longer than the one she had left the Lammergeier. The Web had won.

"So, what are your plans for your retirement?" Alf asked

her in bed that night.

"I think I need to write my story."

"You've written many stories."

"Yeah, but you know … *my* story. The story of … of my life, I guess. I feel like I need to write it down, to see if it made any sense, at all."

"You have a great story to tell!"

She was discouraged, though. Louey Levy was discouraged.

"I don't know, honey. My memory is getting so … um … creative, now! There's things I remember from my childhood and college days, and my union days, and my newspaper days, that when I tell about them, people who were there look at me and go, 'What? That never happened!' Or they remember it a completely different way. But maybe that's what people do when they get to be my age: They start to fail. Maybe I'm just failing."

"You're not *failing*, Louey; you're *succeeding*! You're succeeding in growing closer to God every day!"

Dear Diary,

This online, virtual version of life isn't for me.

Dave says that people soon will have chips implanted in them, so they won't have to go to all the trouble of clicking a button or speaking into a phone when they need information. And I wouldn't be surprised if he were right. There'll be no newspapers, so everyone instantly will be able to know everything and understand nothing. Without newspapers, there'll be no context, no background, no corrections of untrue words.

And I will very happily step back from it, and finish life with Alfie in the old, analog way.

I'm looking forward to it! It's funny: As you get older, people say you're "deteriorating," because your muscles aren't as strong as they once were, or you put your teeth in the cottage-cheese container, or you have to shut your eyes and snap your fingers for a minute before you find the word you want, or you take longer to do stuff. But you're not deteriorating at all: You're changing! You're progressing! I mean, it's <u>good</u> to go slow, so you can learn the birds and bugs and plants all around you that you never noticed before. And it's <u>good</u> to ask for help carrying stuff, or opening stuff, or whatever. People <u>like</u> to help, and you're giving them that chance! Not to mention, it's funny as hell, the words you think you hear when people are saying or singing something completely different. It's like G-d is giving you some good laughs at the end, as a reward for all the years you've put in. Plus, your body is going through just as many changes, and just as rapidly, as it did in puberty. Every day, something new!

Alfie's right: We're all getting closer to G-d. And if you're lucky enough to attain great age, I mean, you're almost there! You're getting ready for your next adventure.

We old people don't bother remembering unimportant things, like where we put our teeth. Instead, we recall the times when we felt life the most deeply—the good and the bad. Good friends and good times become even more precious to us, and more appreciated, and when we recall hurting someone years and years ago, we're not too proud to apologize and ask for forgiveness. Because what's the point of being proud now, when we're all headed for paydirt? And we ask ourselves that most important question of all—"What am I doing here?"—in just about every goddamned room we enter.

So. Now that I'm good and old, what do I want to do next?

The
MX Book
of
New
Sherlock
Holmes
Stories

Part XXIX
More Christmas Adventures
(1889-1896)

THE MX BOOK OF NEW SHERLOCK HOLMES

STORIES

PART XXIX
MORE CHRISTMAS
ADVENTURES
(1889-1896)

SOUTHAMPTON STREET

359

EDITED
By
David
Marcum

OFFICES

TRADITIONAL HOLMES
ADVENTURES
COMPILED FOR THE
BENEFIT OF THE
RESTORATION OF
UNDERSHAW

ISBN Hardback 978-1-78705-930-6
ISBN Paperback 978-1-78705-931-3
AUK ePub ISBN 978-1-78705-932-0
AUK PDF ISBN 978-1-78705-933-7

Published in the UK by
MX Publishing
335 Princess Park Manor, Royal Drive,
London, N11 3GX
www.mxpublishing.co.uk

David Marcum can be reached at:
thepapersofsherlockholmes@gmail.com

Cover design by Brian Belanger
www.belangerbooks.com and *www.redbubble.com/people/zhahadun*

Internal Illustrations by Sidney Paget

What hikes do I still need to take? What projects have I left unfinished? What books should I read, and which ones can I give away? What things in my poor, dear, crazy Newburgh, still need to be fixed? And what stories should I tell, to make people see that we're all one—or at least, to give them a few laughs? I need to make a list. Because that's what I feel like I'm doing. Like Dylan said, "I feel like I'm knockin' on Heaven's door." I just hope Heaven doesn't open it too soon!

The sun had not yet set. A Carolina wren was crawling around the suet-feeder. Chickadees, titmice and cardinals were snagging seeds from the tube-feeder and carrying them into the tangle of the dogwood's branches while mourning doves processed across the ground below for leftovers.

Alfie knocked on the open door of Louey's little den overlooking the river and the hills. She was peeling clear plastic film from a big package of legal-sized yellow notepads.

"Mmmm. What smells better than brand-new notebook paper?" she smiled, holding the pads to her chest and snuggling them as though they were her own babies. "Other than a newspaper," she added.

"Did I leave my glasses up here?" Alf asked in reply.

"They're on the half-wall by the front door! Don't you remember? You put them there when the bell rang, like, ten minutes ago, and it was the Jehovah's Witnesses?"

"Oh, right!" Alfie winced. He lightly smacked his right temple with the heel of his hand and turned back. "Gosh, I'm getting so old that I can't remember anything," he said.

"That's funny," she said softly, though he was already on the stairs. "I'm getting so old that all I can do is remember." She plucked a pen from her jar and started writing.

CPSIA information can be obtained
at www.ICGtesting.com
Printed in the USA
BVHW071714021121
620543BV00001B/20